C000144445

Kith

JULIE ROWBORY

First paperback edition August 2021

ISBN 978-1-7399145-0-9

Book design by David Rowbory
Cover art by Charlotte Yoder
Maps by Melissa Nash
www.melissanashauthor.wordpress.com

Set in Baskerville 11pt
with accents from Minion Pro

For David, Rebekah, Elizabeth, Abigail and Helen

For my parents, Bobby and Ann Magill

THANKS

I am grateful to many people for the contribution they made in the completion of this novel. They ranged in age from nine to their seventies and represented nine different nationalities.

Thanks to those who read it at its various stages and gave me feedback, even if that was just to say they had enjoyed it: Anne Alford (for forgiving me when I made her cry), Abraham Garba Azi, Lionel and Susan Bidwell, Jo and Caitlyn Birks, Agnes Brough, Ryan Buttacavoli, Bridget Carroll, Richard Chiabuotu, Hedley and Bola Clemo, Emma Copeland, Asha, Conor and Jack Creighton, Donald Garvie, Merv Gunn, Jennifer Harper, Michael and Bev Harrar, Gemma Herbertson, Jen Hunt-Taylor, Samuel Kefas Idi, Rebekah Keiller, Nim Kempton, James MacDonell, Mike, Diane and Johanna Manville, Isyaku Isa Mato, Louise Miscampbell, Gareth, Katharine, Eleanor and Daniel Mort (for help ranging from reading very early chapters to Daniel's entertainment of Helen while I edited), Ali Robinson, Keith and Margaret Rowbory, Kathleen Spence (for adding glamour to the grammar), Lisa Tincher, Darryl Turner, Carrie van Dorp (who quite literally lost sleep over the book!), Janneke Verhaar, Rachelle Wenger, Paul Worth, Zach and Christy Yoder, and Mark and Sarah Yoder. Many of these also helped with proof-reading, as did Rachel Ellison, Daso Hassan, Hauwa Lafe, Katharine and Lowenna Norton and Mike Rueck.

Thanks to my wonderful book group in Glasgow for the evening we had discussing the novel. Your insights were so helpful in the final editing stage: Andy and Naomi Baxter, Sari Cabrera, Jennie Campbell, Mari Craig, Cara Ritson and Hannah Worth. And thanks so much to Edward and Catherine Lobb for their encouragement to keep writing, for saving thrushes from untimely song and for Edward's sermon on Psalm 119:81-88 that inspired the closing paragraph of 'Wordcraft'.

I am grateful to the staff and MRH, Miango for providing such a restful environment. Much of the novel was written and edited there, and the beautiful surroundings and delicious food were just what I needed to get the work done.

Thanks to Rick Creighton for his help with personality types as I developed my characters, and to Alex Thomson for answering my questions on Old English and Old Norse. I'm also more than grateful to Rachael Beale and Sam Parkinson for all their invaluable advice about the publishing process.

I am indebted to Kathy Vanderkloet for her amazing eye for detail. She weeded out the vast majority of the typographical errors in the book, and Kathie Turner and Ruth Wake found many of the rest. I am grateful to all of them.

Many thanks to Sarah, Alice and Peace Joseph and to Blessing Gideon. Their eagerness to hear the next part of the story helped to keep me motivated and they kept my life in order when I got a bit lost in the ninth century.

Anna Chiabuotu and Charlotte Yoder were the original Thurstan fan club. Their live comments on each chapter were invaluable (and sometimes hilarious). They taught me that other people could love Brinin, Oswald, Thurstan and the others as much as I did. The process was repeated with Emily Gaddis and Christina Riepe, and all their feedback had a real influence on the final version.

Matthew, Rachel, David and Anna Harley were my wonderful neighbours while I wrote my first draft. I lost count of how many cups of tea Rachel gave me. Her infectious enthusiasm helped to keep me writing on the days when I wondered if I was insane to attempt it.

Charlotte Yoder's beautiful hand-drawn seax on the cover is the result of many months of research, design and sketching. It was wonderful to have the art created by someone who had read and loved the book. I would also like to thank Mary Mayhew for her input into Charlotte's work. The fantastic maps were produced by Melissa Nash, and Dee Donaldson lent excellent graphic design advice.

Many, many thanks to my parents, Bobby and Ann Magill. They always encouraged me to write and valiantly curtailed their amusement when my early attempts at 'novels' contained such glaring problems as the dead being left unburied. Thanks for all your years of support.

Rosie Weston has been my friend for more than twenty years. Her careful reading and honest feedback were indispensable in the last stages. My final draft owed a lot to her involvement and her obvious enjoyment of the novel made the sometimes tedious rewrites feel worthwhile.

Without Alanna Creighton, this book would never have been written. She first saw its potential when it was no more than a few paragraphs and an idea. She read and commented on all my early drafts. We spent many hours discussing characters, style and plot. She gave honest and constructive criticism at each stage and told me what was working well and what wasn't. Most of all she made me feel that it was a story worth telling.

Finally, thanks must go to my family. I am grateful to my daughters: to Rebekah for suffering enough ninth-century history to last two lifetimes; to Elizabeth for our wonderful adventure to see the Anglo-Saxon village at West Stow; to Abigail, always ready with a cuddle; and to (the then four-year-old) Helen for often reminding me that the 'Ogun-Saxons' did, in fact, have socks. My husband, David, has been fantastic throughout, from the initial idea to the final formatting. I cannot begin to list all the ways in which he helped to make it happen, but without his reliable, and often humorous support, I would never have written a novel.

Thanks for your many and varied contributions. I am grateful to God for all of you.

SPEECHHOARD

	IPA	
Æ/æ	[æ]	short 'a', as in 'cat', eg. Æthelred, Rædwald
a	[ʌ]	mostly long, as in south of England 'castle'
c	[k]	hard, as 'k' in modern English, eg. Cynestan
ea	[ea]	'ey-a' (**not** 'ee'), eg. Ealmund is 'Ey-almund'
œ	[œ]	as in German 'ö'
wig	[wi]	'wee', eg. Eawig is 'Ey-a-wee'
y	[y]	mid-word as in German 'ü', like 'ee' with rounded lips, eg. fyrd

WORDHOARD

Ærist (pr. *Arist*)
    rising, resurrection

Ætheling
    close relative or heir of the king

bookskin (Old English, *bócfell*)
    vellum for manuscripts

Child (Old English, *cild*)
    a title of dignity for a youth of higher social position

Englafeld
    Englefield, Berkshire

Ealdorman
    a prestigious noble man, just under the king/royal family in rank

fyrd (pr. *fürd*)
    militia gathered from freemen

fyrdmen
    men who fight

gospeller (Old English, *godspellere*)
    evangelist, Gospel writer

jarl (pr. *yarl*)
    a Danish leader or chief

leafworm (Old English, *leáfwyrm*)
    caterpillar

kith (Old English, *cýþþu*)
knowledge, friendship, kinsfolk, native land, home

minster (Old English, *mynster*)
monastery

moot (Old English, *mot*)
a meeting, village court/council

Readingum
Reading, Berkshire

seax (pr. *sax*)
a knife carried by every free person, symbolic of freedom

spearwort (Old English, *sperewyrt*)
yellow iris

thegn (pr. *thane*)
minor aristocracy with duties to the king

threeleaf (Old English, *þrilēfe*)
wood sorrel

Waneting
Wantage, Oxfordshire

Wielea
Wells, Somerset

Wintanceaster
Winchester, Hampshire

Witan (more properly *Witenagemót*)
a national council

workreeve (Old English, *weorcgerefa*)
overseer of workers/slaves, estate manager

writing-seax (Old English, *writseax*)
stylus

MAPS

NORTHUMBRIA

MERCIA

ENGLAND in 870

EAST
ANGLIA

Readingum

Wintanceaster

Waneting

Oakdene

The Minster

Wielea

WESSEX

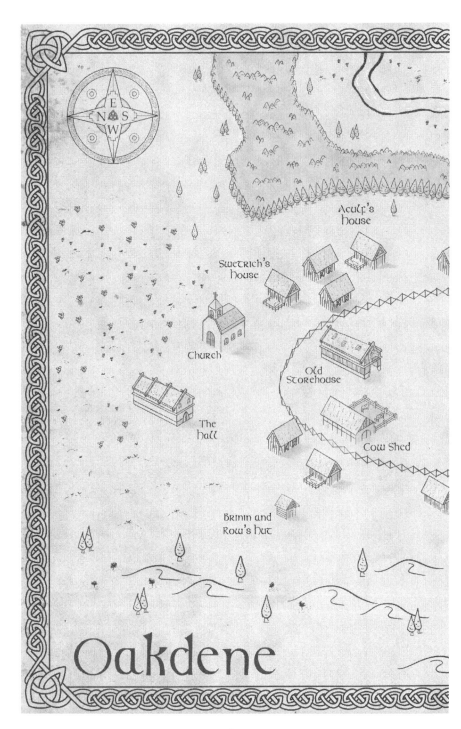

Aculf's house

Swetrich's house

Church

Old Storehouse

The hall

Cow Shed

Brimin and Row's hut

Oakdene

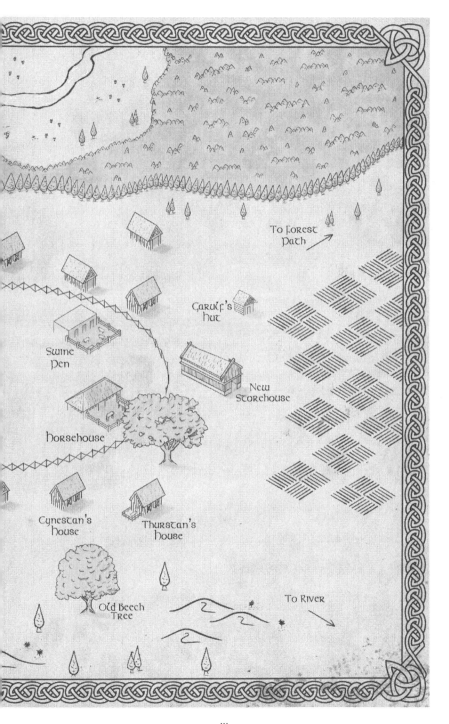

To Forest
Path

Garulf's
hut

Swine
Pen

New
Storehouse

horsehouse

Cynestan's
house

Thurstan's
house

Old Beech
Tree

To River

WESSEX, FEBRUARY 870

VALOUR

I t always began with something small—spilt milk, a frightened child, a shadow in the doorway a little too soon. All Brinin's troubles began small and they all ended the same way. Who could be smaller than Ebba, nine winters old and crying behind the storehouse? She was too small for anyone to see there, too small for Brinin to walk by. They both knew what Aculf, the workreeve, would do when he found the milk. No wonder she was scared. So Brinin chased her away and slipped into the storehouse to clean it up himself. He shouldn't have been in there at all.

The creak of a hinge and the swift darkening of the gloom inside was the only warning he had that Aculf was watching him from the threshold. What good was a warning? There was no way of running even if he had wanted to.

'What are you doing in here?'

Brinin straightened up from where he had been crouching and turned to face Aculf. Why waste answers on him? Ebba was gone now, unthought-of somewhere with her mother.

'What did you do to that milk?'

Beyond Aculf, outside in the last light of evening, Brinin could see a boy chasing a chicken. Why waste words on Aculf? The first blow was sudden, burning Brinin's cheek, but he had known it was coming. The shadow had already warned him.

'Answer me! What are you doing in here?'

Beyond Aculf, outside, two men walked together towards the hall. Aculf raised his hand again, and another blow fell stingingly on the first one.

'Speech is wasted on you, you thieving hound!' Aculf grabbed the neck of Brinin's shirt and dragged him outside and round behind the storehouse. He shoved Brinin to his knees and tightened his grip on his stick.

Beyond Aculf, the grass grew longer by the storehouse wall, brushing against the wood. There was so much beyond Aculf, though Aculf didn't know it. Why waste fear on him? Kneeling in the mud, Brinin shut his lips and waited.

When Aculf and his stick were done with him, Brinin left, angry now but still with nothing to say. He came upon Oswald waiting uneasily in the shadows of the buildings nearby.

'He beat you again? I heard it.'

Brinin nodded and kept walking.

'He's beating you more and more,' said Oswald, walking alongside him. 'I don't know what's to be done!'

Done? What else could be done but feel it, keep his mouth shut, then walk away aching to wait for the next time?

'Aculf seems to hate you. He seldom beats anyone else and, even when he does, he shows mercy when they ask for it.' Oswald stopped short of asking if Brinin might think of doing the same, but Brinin understood him nonetheless.

'When you're lord here,' said Brinin drily, 'likely you can find a better man to take his place. Until then, there is nothing to be done.'

The pale winter sun was low in the sky when Brinin reached the little hut he shared with his older brother. It sat on the western edge of the village where the land began to rise to meet the tree-lined hills. From here, as the sun sank behind the hills, they could look down over the thatch of Oakdene and to the forest bounding the land to the east and south beyond the fields.

Row had already fetched their food from the hall and was sitting on a stool outside as he ate it. Brinin pulled up another stool alongside him and sat down where the thatch sloped low. He saw Row frown slightly as he handed him his bowl, his eyes darting from his cheek, likely reddened by Aculf's hand, to the knees of his breeches still wet and dark with mud.

'Aculf again?' said Row.

'Who else?'

What good was there in talking about it? Speech couldn't undo what had been done. Row didn't press him. He never did. They understood each other well, Brinin and his brother.

'We did well to gather all the wood for the new storehouse as quickly as we did,' said Row. 'I overheard Aculf telling Baldred how slow we all were but he always says that, and there was a lot of wood.'

'If he did any of the work, he might know more about it.'

Row raised an eyebrow. 'If you didn't hate each other so much, you might have an easier time.'

There had always been fire in Brinin's hair, but it was his eyes that burned in the evening light.

'Hate? He isn't worth my hatred.'

Evening-meat had already begun when Oswald reached the hall, warm with fire and lamplight. His father, Edrich, Thegn of Oakdene, had gathered some of his men to talk over the land, the village and the kingdom. The rich smell of roasting meat hung in the air, and men and women rushed about serving food and drink. Edrich was so deep in earnest speech that he did not stop or even seem to see his son. Oswald slipped into his place as swiftly and unseen as he could, thankful for the men and the battle talk to keep his father busy. It was better not to be seen when he came late.

'We must ready ourselves for war,' Edrich was saying. 'The kingdom of East Anglia has been utterly overrun by the Danes. Edmund the King is dead, minsters destroyed, abbots and monks murdered. The Danes are ruthless, wholly unbridled, and we would be fools to think they are not looking to Wessex—Oswald, you're late! They are on our threshold, and we must be ready for them. I foresee that when I ride to the Witan before Easter, Æthelred the King will wish to talk about how we defend this kingdom. In the

3

meantime, every man of us who knows how to wield a sword must strengthen himself, mind and body, to stand against them.'

'P… please forgive me, Father,' stammered Oswald. 'I was walking and… and it took me longer to come back than I thought it would.'

'It's happening altogether too often. You must be where you are meant to be and not so far off that you cannot come back in time. This isn't the first time I have spoken to you about it. And while I think of it, Brother Wilfred tells me that you did not go to him this afternoon. What have you to say for yourself?'

'Nothing but to b… beg forgiveness, sir. I was working on my b… bowmanship and when I got back it was already too late but… but I have learned—'

'See that you beg *his* forgiveness and that by the time you do see him you know whatever he wanted you to learn. I shall ask him.' And he turned back to his men before his son could say any more.

Oswald kept his head down and busied himself with his food, so the men would not see his burning face. He sighed, only a little, not so loudly that his father would hear—he would never dare do that. Why couldn't his father have waited and chided him later when the men had gone?

'I saw you with your bow,' whispered a voice suddenly at his ear. It was Edith, his younger sister, coming up unseen to press a cup of ale into his hand. 'You are so good at it now. While I was watching you didn't miss a shot!'

Oswald smiled at her. The men had all heard his father. Edith had heard, and he could always trust her to be ready with a kind word when he needed it.

'Now to the land,' went on Edrich. 'Aculf, what of the new storehouse?'

'The wood is ready now, my lord, but the work has been slow, and we have not yet started building it as I had hoped. We might be quicker were the men not so slothful. I hope we can put it up tomorrow or the day after.' Aculf took a drink of ale and wiped his mouth with the back of his hand. 'There is something else I want to speak to you about, my lord. I found the slave Brinin in the storehouse. I don't know what he was doing in there, but he had spilled a bucket of milk. I had to beat him for it, but he was most unbiddable even then. He is overproud, my lord.'

Oswald loathed Aculf then. Whatever Brinin had been doing—and Oswald didn't know—he would never trust anything Aculf said of him. He had a way of twisting things when he spoke, of bending them into something else. Why didn't his father see it? Perhaps his mind was too full of the Danes. If only Oswald could think of something to say on Brinin's behalf. If only he dared to say it.

'Overproud? It is not for a slave to be proud,' frowned Edrich. 'Did he try to stop you from beating him?'

'No, my lord, but—'

'You said he was unbiddable. What did he do?'

'He would not speak or answer me at all and he looked at me with a boldness unfitting in a slave. As I said, my lord, he is overproud. It was not the first time he has behaved like this.'

Oswald heard Thurstan, who had no love for Aculf, mutter to himself: 'A boy who shuts his mouth and takes a beating may surely *look* without being called overproud!' His words gave Oswald courage.

'Father, surely—'

'Wait, Oswald! Aculf, there is no place for a proud slave in Oakdene, or anywhere else as far as I can see. We are not harsh here, as some are, but he must learn to tame his pride and know whom he should fear. As workreeve, you must do whatever is fitting to teach him that.' He turned back to Oswald. 'What did you wish to say?'

'Nothing, Father,' he mumbled, his courage shrivelling as quickly as it had sprouted.

Edrich frowned slightly. 'It comes to mind that I wished to ask about your warcraft. Thurstan, what can you tell me?'

Thurstan, who taught Oswald the use of the sword, spear and bow, smiled warmly.

'He wields the sword well, my lord, the spear with great skill and is a better shot than many grown men I have known.'

5

'Good. I shall come to watch you myself in the morning, Oswald.'

And Oswald's heart withered within him.

Across the village from the hall, Brinin lay staring into the darkness, too sore to sleep, too tired to stay awake. He could bear pain. His days and weeks were speckled with it: blistered hands, work-weary limbs, a throbbing back. It was harder to know that the days and weeks kept stretching out in much the same way, whatever Oswald liked to think. These were the nights he missed his mother. She would have hidden the tears she thought he never saw, and they would sit by the firelight as she told her tales of brave men and their great deeds of valour. Battles and dragons and storms. And Brinin would fall asleep and dream of the time when he would do such deeds himself. The dreams were as dead as his mother now, unless it was somehow valour to take a beating to shield a little girl.

WORKMEN

'Come on, Bruni! Time to be going,' said Row, giving Brinin a shake to wake him the next morning.

Lying on a couple of fleeces in the corner, Brinin sighed and stretched, still sore and stiff in the chill before dawn. It was bitterly cold as they left their hut, walking briskly to keep warm. East beyond the trees, bare and stark, the sky was turning a pale amber in the dwindling darkness. A low mist hung over the fields, like the thin wisps of cloud made by their breath, and all around them were the sounds of birds and beasts and men beginning to wake.

'At least there's no rain,' said Row, pulling his cloak a little tighter around him.

'Not yet. Better a cold morning than a muddy one,' said Brinin.

Aculf was nowhere to be seen—he could linger in his house if he chose to. But he would soon be there with his lengthy speeches, as though he were the only man in the village who had ever turned his hand to work. Brinin drew two large buckets of water to carry to the hall. Why wait for Aculf to tell him what he already knew? There were beasts to feed and lead out to graze. There was wood to hew, water to draw. There was endless work to do each day, and it was too cold to be still.

Brinin was still making his way to the hall with the water when Ebba came running along with an empty basket.

'Aren't you going to help your mother with the milking?' he smiled.

'We've done it already! I'm going to see if the hens have laid any eggs. There weren't many yesterday.' Ebba glanced over her shoulder fearfully, as if she half thought Aculf would be lurking there. 'Did you clean up the milk?'

'Every drop!' laughed Brinin. 'Aculf doesn't even know you were in there.'

'But when he sees that the milk is gone…'

'Then he still won't think of you. Don't be scared. I know he won't. But if he comes and sees you standing here, he'll be angry. You should go and look for the eggs.'

The thought of Aculf coming was enough to make Ebba dash away, and not too soon. Brinin had barely set down his buckets when he heard a bellow from behind.

'You! Come here!'

It was almost as if Aculf didn't know Brinin's name. When was the last time he had called him by it? Brinin couldn't remember. He was always 'you', when he wasn't something worse.

'There is too much work today for you to stand idle!' snapped Aculf as Brinin reached him.

A man who had tarried by his fire until the sun was already up likely knew about idleness. Perhaps Brinin should try it some day and learn what it was like.

'Gather all the dung and take it down to the heap. Then come back to me. Do you understand?'

It took no great wisdom to understand that. Brinin nodded unsmilingly and went to fetch a shovel and the dung-barrow. The stench would cling to him for a time, but that was a small price to pay for work where Aculf would not stand nearby to watch out for the smallest mistake or slackening. Brinin went from oxen to cows, from sheep to swine, carefully scraping up as much muck as he could. He had emptied the barrow more than once before he went to find Aculf.

'Why were you so slow? Slack as ever!' Aculf shoved Brinin towards a large pile of beams and boards. 'The wood for the new storehouse. Shift it over to the fence—all of it, mind—and be quick about it!'

'Why?' Brinin said it before he could stop himself, though he seldom said anything much to Aculf if he could help it. But at Aculf's bidding he had spent much of the day before dragging the same wood to where it now lay, not much more than twenty feet from the fence. There was no need at all to shift it again.

Aculf's answer came as a sharp blow to the side of Brinin's head. Aculf meant to begin early that day and had not had his fill the evening before. It wouldn't be the sun that made the day a short or long one.

'Do you dare to ask me why? Edrich Thegn has told me to break you of your pride and teach you whom to fear. It's time you learned to heed me. You don't need to know why! Now, go and shift the wood!'

He didn't need to know why? Even Aculf could not be such a fool as to think that he didn't already know. Without another word, Brinin walked away. That was always better than speaking aloud what was in his mind.

It was heavy, slow work with only his anger to help him with it. Before long Brinin's shoulders, arms and back were aching, and he was only half done some time later when Row came up from the fields to eat.

'Bruni! What are you doing?'

'Ask Aculf.'

'He *told* you to? But why?'

Brinin answered Row with only a look and dropped a beam onto the new woodpile with a crash.

Row sighed. 'It will be quicker if I help you, and better before Aculf comes back and sees that I am.'

When the work was done—needless work when they could have been doing something else—Brinin stopped with Row to eat, squatting down near the fence.

'Did Aculf not say why he wanted you to shift all that wood again?' asked Row.

'I know why, and he knows I do. This won't be the last trouble today.'

Row frowned. 'He's looking for fault with you, and we needn't give it to him. I was going to help Garulf look over the ploughs for mending. You do that, and I'll stay here. Then you can keep away from Aculf for a while.'

'I'm not afraid of him.'

'I didn't say you were, but why ask for trouble?'

Even if he wasn't afraid, didn't Row speak wisdom? And Garulf was everything Aculf wasn't. He was the oldest man in Oakdene, fallen into slavery during times of hunger, and he knew more about the land than anyone. Almost every plough he had ever used he had built with his own hands. He already had the ploughs out on the grass when Brinin found him.

'Row sent me to help you,' said Brinin.

'It's good to have your help! You're always quick to learn what I show you.' Garulf nodded to the plough he was working on. 'Look at this.'

For a time their speech was all coulters and ploughshares. Brinin loved to work with Garulf. He was so wise and so skilled in everything he did that even the hardest work by his side felt lighter and gave Brinin knowledge.

'My granddaughter tells me you helped her with some spilt milk yesterday,' said Garulf, after a while. 'It was kind of you, though I have scolded her for going into the storehouse in the first place.'

'It's no trouble to clean up a little milk.'

'Likely not. Then it wasn't you I heard Aculf beating yesterday evening? It sounded like someone was having a lot of trouble. I don't know who—he didn't make a sound. It may not have been you, but when I heard about the milk I did wonder if that was why Aculf was angry.'

Brinin kept his eye on the coulter, the ploughshare, the grass beneath them. He hadn't done it to talk about it afterwards. Garulf seemed to see that as answer enough.

'I thought it was you,' he said. 'You're a good lad, Brinin. Don't let Aculf dishearten you. Now, these three ploughs seem to be sound, but let me show you how to mend this one.'

FYRDMEN

'Have you got your line?' asked Thurstan.

'Yes,' Oswald whispered. 'Six inches up.'

'Wind?'

'Slight breeze to the left cheek.'

'Feel the weight?'

'Yes.'

'When you're ready.'

Swift and straight the arrow sang from the bow. Oswald watched it glide away from him and embed itself in the target with a dull thud. It was a good shot. Oswald lowered his bow and turned to Thurstan.

'Well done, Oswald!' Thurstan patted him on the back. 'You're a bowman now. There's not much more for me to teach you that you won't learn from that keen eye of yours. As long as your hand stays steady, your arrow should go where you want it to. You judged the wind well.'

'There's only a light wind today. I should come out when it's stronger. It would be harder then.'

'If by some witchcraft I could make the target grow legs and run while you shoot at it, I would do it! But you're right. We should make it harder.'

Thurstan turned to his son, Tidræd, who stood beside them, bow in hand, shifting from foot to foot in his eagerness for his own turn.

'Tidræd, pull it back another twenty feet or so.'

Oswald watched as Tidræd ran across the grass to do his father's bidding. He'd often felt like Tidræd, keen to shoot but made to watch. But he was older and the thegn's son, so he went first. And his father would be coming soon. Perhaps it might not be so bad. He'd done everything well that morning.

'Are you ready?' said Thurstan, when Tidræd was beside them again.

Oswald nodded and slipped another arrow from his quiver. Tighter and tighter he drew back his bowstring, keeping his gaze along the shaft of the arrow to the target beyond. He shifted his aim, only a little, kept it steady. The weight was good, ready now, almost ready.

'Well, Thurstan!' Oswald heard his father's voice suddenly behind him. 'Let's see if the boy can shoot as well as you say.'

Oswald started, and the arrow flew wide. Why did his father have to speak just then? It would have been such a good shot, the kind he only seemed to do when his father wasn't there. Why couldn't he have crept up unheard and seen what a good bowman he was?

'Go back to your mother, Tidræd,' said Thurstan gruffly.

'But, Father, I haven't had—'

'Are you going to heed me?'

Oswald could hear the warning in Thurstan's voice, and he wasn't his son. Likely Tidræd heard it too and knew it only too well. He opened his mouth, half warlike, then swiftly thought better of it. He sighed and sullenly walked away.

'My lord,' said Thurstan, turning to Edrich. 'Your voice startled him. He's a fine bowman, and that's the first shot he's missed all morning. Perhaps he should try it again.'

'There are plenty of startling noises on the battlefield,' said Edrich, 'but let him try again if you wish.'

It was too late now. It was always too late once his father started watching. Oswald drew another arrow and took aim, but his neck, his jaw, his mind were all drawn as tight as his bowstring and again he missed the target, this time only by a hair's breadth. He lowered his head and bit his lip. Thurstan laid a hand on his shoulder.

'The bow is more for hunting than for battle, after all,' he said.

'The spear is for battle,' said Edrich, handing Oswald a long battle-spear. 'Perhaps you will do better with that. Tell me how it is wielded on the field.'

'The spears are thrown at the foe.' Let him speak of warcraft, even if he had forgotten how to use his bow. 'Sometimes, a brave warrior may break out from behind the shield wall and run before he throws. This makes the spear faster and more deadly, but the warrior himself risks death to throw it.'

'Good,' said Edrich. 'See how far you can throw.'

Oswald took a deep breath. He could do this. He was always good with a spear, too good to forget even with his father watching. He raised his spear above his shoulder, ran and threw. The spear flew high, straight and far, the shaft quivering slightly as it passed through the air. It was the best of throws—he knew it was—worthy of a fyrdman. He turned hopefully to his father.

'Better,' said Edrich. Not overflowing praise, but it was as much as he would get. When did his father ever overflow with praise?

Edrich walked over to where some shields and wooden swords lay on the grass. He picked up a shield and sword.

'I think the best way for me to see how you wield a sword is to fight you myself,' he said.

Oswald's gut tightened. Anything but that. Give him another boy—any of them—or even one of the men, and he could fight them and might even win. Give him Thurstan. He wouldn't win then, but he'd make Thurstan work hard before losing. But he couldn't swing his sword and strike at his father. Not that, not even when bidden. His father was standing, sword in hand, ready to fight. He had to heed him. There could be none of Tidræd's warlike sighs.

At first he fought well enough. He was swift-footed and quick-eyed, dodging, blocking, leaping aside. Try as he might, though, he couldn't get near his father with his own sword. Why did he keep missing? Then came the time to strike, but he wavered and lowered his shield unknowingly. A blow from his father's sword fell heavily on his shoulder.

'Use your shield, boy!' shouted Edrich.

Biddable, he raised his shield as his father's sword came rushing towards him. He deftly leapt away and swung his sword back at his father, only to be blocked again. What was wrong with him? He was fighting like a child! Another cut, another swing, another miss.

'Strike, boy, strike! Come at me as you would a Dane!'

As a Dane? That would be well and good if he were a Dane and not his father who could quell the slightest wilfulness with a look. And he wanted Oswald to strike at him! If his father were only Leofwine or Beorn... Perhaps he could think that he *were* one of them. Oswald brought his sword down on Edrich as hard as he could, but it caught the shield boss and was flung from his hand. At the same time, a mighty stroke from Edrich's sword on his shield sent him reeling backwards, and he fell to the ground.

Edrich cast aside his shield and sword and stood looking down at his son.

'If the Danes do come,' he panted, 'they'll cut you to pieces.'

Then he turned and walked away, leaving Oswald breathless, bruised and belittled.

Oswald could still remember the time the Danes had come, not to Oakdene, but to Wintanceaster. Only five winters old then, he had heard men and women talking when they didn't know he was there. The Danes had come in great ships across the sea. Swarming from their ships, fierce and godless, they burned and killed wherever they went. All the way to Wintanceaster they had come and stormed it and set it ablaze. And Oswald, wide-eyed in the darkness, had spent many nights in fear that they were coming to Oakdene too.

He could still remember how his father had gone away to fight them. His father was strong—he had often watched him with his spear and sword—but the Danes were so fearsome that Oswald had been worried that they might be stronger. Sometimes he had seen his mother weeping, and everyone seemed to be waiting, waiting all the time. Then one morning, his father had come back with his men, fewer than he had left with. Oswald's mother had wept again and, gathering into the hall to feast, everyone had listened to his father as he told how Osrich Ealdorman and Æthelwulf Ealdorman had led them onto the field, and how side by side they had fought the Danes. Some of their swordbrothers had fallen, some even from Oakdene, but their foes had been defeated and put to flight.

'On your feet, Oswald.' Oswald, still on the grass where he had fallen, looked up at Thurstan. 'No good sitting there, is it? You'll do as well against the Danes as any of us. You've even unsworded me a few times, and few men in Oakdene can say that. You were fretting about it this morning, that's all.'

'Won't I fret when the Danes come too?' he said bitterly, as he stood up. 'If I forget everything when I fret, then I'll have no hope at all.'

Oswald trudged back to the hall, weapons hanging wearily by his side now. The Danes so feared, so dreaded, were drawing ever nearer to Wessex. There would be battle to do. But however fierce they were, that morning no Dane seemed as frightening as his own father.

PRAYERMEN

Oswald, waxboard and writing-seax in hand, made his way to the little church with heavy feet that afternoon. He was fond of the monk and liked to learn with him, but who runs eagerly to be told of his wrongdoing? And he was still bruised, mind and body, from the morning. Brother Wilfred was sitting in the light that streamed through the doorway, not angry, only waiting as he always was, and Oswald felt a little smaller.

'Ah. You have come today,' said Brother Wilfred.

'I'm sorry I didn't come yesterday, sir.' And he was sorry now and not only doing his father's bidding. 'I was working on my bowmanship and...'

'You forgot?'

Oswald, somewhat ashamed, couldn't bring himself to say he had forgotten. 'I... I don't think I... forgot, sir, but I am sorry and I beg your forgiveness.'

'I would understand an unwillingness to come if I dealt with you harshly, as my own masters dealt with me. I often wished myself almost anywhere else—sit down, my boy—but have I ever struck you, or even been angry with you when you have made a mistake or been slow to understand?'

'No, sir.' Why was this worse than a stern upbraiding? It didn't even leave him room to pity himself as he bore it. It was like soft rain, barely felt, that drenched a man nonetheless.

'You have been quick to learn, but I fear that you have been slow to understand what you have. You now have what hardly a thegn's son, hardly an ealdorman's son in all of Wessex has, what even Ælfred the Ætheling has not had for long: learning. In asking me to teach you, your father gives you what he has never even had himself. Have you forgotten that? The reading, writing and little Latin we do together are not only ways for us to while away the afternoons. They put learning into your hands at a time when there is little of it in this kingdom. Any freeman may have knowledge of the bow or the sword, and it is needful in such days as we live in. Almost no one may have the knowledge that I have been giving you. Do not slight it.'

Just as the mildness was beginning to sting, it was over. Brother Wilfred smiled and picked up a small chest from the bench beside him.

'There is nothing in Oakdene with more worth than what I have here. I've been waiting until you were ready to see it.'

Had Brother Wilfred been hiding gold in the church? Oswald watched as the chest was opened, and the monk lifted out a few sheets of bookskin and set them on the writing-board. Not a golden hoard, but if they had been he could hardly have handled them more carefully.

'You remember I once told you about Bede, that most learned of men? What we have here is from his book, the *Historia Ecclesiastica Gentis Anglorum*. The time has come for us to go beyond words on your waxboard.'

Oswald had seen gold but he had never seen a book of any kind. There was a thrill in bending over the bookskins because their meaning was not hidden from him. Everywhere he looked he could see words he knew. Was there nothing in Oakdene with more worth than this?

'Now, here we have only a little of the book. It would take too long to tell you how I came by it, so that can wait for another day. I want you to read it aloud to me and tell me the meaning in English. I think your Latin is good enough now.'

Brother Wilfred took Oswald's waxboard and wrote the words *'Historia Ecclesiastica Gentis Anglorum'*.

'Let us begin with the name of the work. Do you understand it?'

'*Historia*—history. *Ecclesiastica*—something to do with the church?'

'Perhaps we can say "A Church History".'

'A church history. *Gentis*—of the people. *Anglorum*—of the English. So, "A Church History of the English People"?'

'Good. Now for the book itself. Let's sit a little nearer the door. The light is rather dim here. That's better. This is about the time of the saintly king, Oswald of Northumbria, who happened to share your own name. Bede writes about the holy bishop, Aidan. Read to me from here.'

'*Numquam divitibus honoris sive timoris gratia, siqua delinquisset, reticebat,*' read Oswald slowly. 'I don't know *reticebat*, but I think the rest is about honour and fear.'

'The word *reticere* means "to keep silent". I will write it on your waxboard so you can learn it. Go on.'

'He never kept silent through fear or honour of the rich, if they sinned.'

Perhaps the bishop was bold as well as holy if fear did not keep him from speaking. Perhaps he was too bold and holy to feel it.

'Yes, that begins to draw it out. Can you keep going?'

Together Oswald and Brother Wilfred opened the Latin and pulled out the meaning and as they read, Oswald understood the worth of a book. It was like a tale well told by a skilful tongue. It took him to another time and place, to people he had not known before. It put another man's thoughts into his mind and made them his own. Even the most skilful tongues are stilled, but this book was still heard long after the writer was dead. Hadn't Bede died long ago and far away? Yet he sat with Oswald and spoke to him in the church.

'Here, sir,' he said suddenly. 'Here, where Aidan the Bishop frees the slaves. What does that mean?'

'It means that, when the bishop was given gifts of money, he used them to buy the freedom of those who had been unjustly sold into slavery.'

'Can that be done? A slave can be made free?'

'Yes. A man can become a slave in many ways, and there is more than one way for him to be freed. A slave's freedom can be bought, though the lord must be willing to free his slave in this way. Sometimes the lord himself may choose to free him, or perhaps have some of his slaves freed on his death, for the love of God and the good of his own soul. Slaves have often been freed when a bishop dies.'

This was a thought that Oswald had never found in Oakdene. Had he met Bede then he would have thanked him on his knees for giving it to him! If slaves could be free, if the holy bishop had freed them, could that be the way to end all Brinin's troubles?

'Do these things happen even in Wessex? Not only in Northumbria or East Anglia or… or other kingdoms?'

'Of course, though who knows what is happening in Northumbria or East Anglia now that they have been overrun by the Danes? Have you never heard of a slave being given a seax by his lord as a token of his freedom?'

'No. I have never heard of any slave being freed. All my father's slaves have been slaves for as long as I can remember.'

'Why do you want to know about this?'

But Brother Wilfred couldn't have that answer yet, not until he had thought it all out and found a way to do it.

'I've never heard of such a thing before. I thought that once a man was a slave, he would always be a slave.'

'Freedom can be given to a slave, though perhaps it is more seldom than it ought to be. Aidan the Bishop showed kindness to the poor and the slave, and we can learn from him. A dear friend of mine, Sygbald, is a prior here in Wessex and he, like Aidan, turns no one away from his minster and does not even ask them if they are slave or free. But we are wandering from our work. Let us look again at all the words that have been new to you this afternoon.'

Oswald had to keep his thoughts on his Latin then because he knew that his father would ask about him. But his mind was full of freedom. Surely if it could be got, he could find a way for Brinin to get it, and then his friend could be rid of Aculf for good.

FRIENDSHIP

The unlikely friendship between Oswald the thegn's son and Brinin the slave was a long one. They had always known who the other was, but it wasn't until after their eighth winter that Oswald had taken Brinin brotherlike to his heart. Brinin, at first, had hardly dared to think that the son of his lord might look upon him as a friend, though he had been the one who began it all.

He had been picking early blackberries from a place he knew near the river when he heard a scream. Rushing down to the river bank, he was just in time to see Oswald rise up then start to go under the water again. Brinin, barely stopping to think, snatched up a stout branch that was lying nearby and lay down, reaching the branch out as far as he could. Somehow Oswald grabbed it, and Brinin heaved him out of the water.

For some time Oswald lay gasping and spluttering on the river bank. At last, when he found his breath again, he sat up and flung his arms round Brinin.

'You saved my life!'

'I'm glad I could help you, sir.'

'Now that I owe you my life, you must call me only Oswald. Aren't we almost like brothers now?'

Oswald never told his mother and father, who had forbidden him to play near the river, saying that he was too reckless to be trusted there. He told only Edith, his sharp-eyed younger sister. He knew she would likely learn of the friendship anyway, and she too loved Brinin for her brother's sake.

Cold from long sitting in the draughty church, Oswald found Edith sewing a shirt by the hearth in the hall. He sat on a stool beside her, huddled as near the fire as he dared to melt away the chill from his body.

'Do you think Brother Wilfred will speak well of you to Father?' asked Edith, turning the cloth over in her hands and running her eye along the stitches.

'He may. He seemed to be happy with what I learned today.'

'Was he angry with you for not going to him yesterday?'

'Not like Father sometimes is, though the way he spoke to me made me wish I had gone.' But for once the need to please his father was not uppermost in Oswald's thoughts. He leaned towards his sister with an earnest whisper. 'I learned something today. Did you know that slaves can be freed?'

'I think I heard someone say something about it once. Why were you learning about that?'

'I'll tell you why another time, but it made me think of something. Did you hear what Aculf was saying last night? Anyone could see that he hates Brinin and wants Father to hate him too.'

'If what Aculf said last night was true, then surely you can see why he doesn't like Brinin.'

'True? How could it be true? Didn't you listen to him? Overproud! There's only one man in Oakdene who's overproud, and it isn't Brinin!'

'That isn't what I meant. Don't you see that if Brinin said nothing at all, even when he was beaten, Aculf would hate that? He wants to be feared and have everyone think how very great he is. If he couldn't make Brinin speak to him, think how angry he must have been.'

'It's not right! Aculf looks for fault in Brinin. He *wants* to beat him! I know he does. I must do something about it.'

'Why don't you talk to Father and tell him what Aculf is doing?'

21

Oswald laughed rather bitterly. 'I don't think Father wants to hear anything I have to say. But today when I was with Brother Wilfred, I thought of something. If Brinin were free, then Aculf could do nothing to him.'

'But, Oswald, he's Father's slave. Surely only Father can free him. He would have to be *your* slave for you to do it.'

'It can't wait until then! And who knows if I'll live that long, with the Danes almost at our door?'

'And, Oswald, if he were free, how would he live? He has no land. Where would he go? What would he do? And what about his brother? If his brother were still a slave, would Brinin even want his freedom? Would he want it alone?'

'I don't know, but I have to do something! He's my friend, and you know what he did for me. I can't overlook what is happening.'

'I know you can't but I still think if you would talk to Father—'

'And I've told you why I can't! Father listens to Aculf, not to me, and he doesn't even know Brinin is my friend. I can't talk to him and I don't want you to either. It would only make everything worse.'

Edith opened her mouth to speak, but her brother shook his head in warning. He had seen their father come into the hall and knew they could say no more. This was not something for him to overhear.

'I spoke to Brother Wilfred, Oswald,' said Edrich, coming towards them as his son rose to meet him. 'He said you did well today. I was glad to hear it, but don't let me hear of you shirking it again, or I shall have to be very stern with you.'

'Yes, sir,' said Oswald meekly, and then on a whim and because throwing himself in might be better than creeping in, he suddenly found himself saying: 'Father, I think p... perhaps that Aculf may be mistaken in the slave Brinin.'

He was looking at his father, but out of the corner of his eye he caught sight of Edith's quick, sharp look. Edrich frowned. That was almost enough to make Oswald back down, but he took a deep breath and went on.

'When Aculf was speaking of Brinin at evening-meat and said that he is overproud and… and unbiddable, I think p… perhaps he was mistaken.'

Edrich looked at Oswald for what seemed like a long time before he answered.

'Were you there?' he asked.

What did his father mean? Was he where? At evening-meat?

'Were you with Aculf when he found the slave in the storehouse?'

'No, but—'

'So you did not see or hear what happened?'

'No, sir, but—' Oswald lowered his eyes. Why was he doing this? He had known he was right when he had told Edith that their father wouldn't want to listen to him.

'Then, Oswald, I don't see how you could know if Aculf is mistaken.' Edrich turned to leave, as though showing his son that he had nothing further to say.

'I think p… perhaps that Aculf dislikes him.' Edith touched her brother's arm to embolden him, but Oswald could feel himself shrink under his father's eyes.

'Why do you think that? Are we to let a slave—a young slave, barely even a man—pay no heed to the word of those over him? Would I let *you* do that, although you're not a slave?'

All that Oswald could have said melted before his father, and he felt it, an unspoken chiding that smarted like punishment, and was a small boy again.

'No, sir,' he sighed.

'Punishment is hardly a token of dislike. Or perhaps there is something else that makes you think that Aculf dislikes the slave?'

Although he knew that Aculf hated Brinin, although he could have named many times when he was sure he had treated him harshly and unjustly, he could think of nothing at all to say. That drew another frown from Edrich, and although Oswald still kept his eyes down and did not see it, he heard and understood it when his father began to speak.

'Well then, Oswald, it hardly seems fitting that you, with fifteen winters, should find fault with a man who has been workreeve for so long, a man whom *I* made workreeve. You would do better to keep your mind on your bowmanship, your swordsmanship and your learning, and leave the overseeing of the slaves to those who know about such things. Now, if you have nothing further to say, I believe we both have other things to see to.'

Oswald watched as his father left the hall. Why had he listened to Edith? Now he was left feeling like a fool!

'I told you! I told you he wouldn't listen!'

'But, Oswald—'

'He listens to Aculf, not to me! And now I don't know what I'm going to do about Brinin!'

'But, Oswald, you didn't *tell* him anything! He asked you, and you didn't—'

'He doesn't want to listen to me! And you must say nothing either. Didn't I tell you it would only make things worse?'

And Oswald walked away, leaving his sister alone by the fire.

At the beginning of the harvest before their tenth winter, Oswald and Brinin had gone off to do great deeds together one morning. Oswald had woken up eager for something new and bold. He took some food from the hall when no one was watching and went off to find Brinin.

Brinin was working. Almost everyone was in the fields gathering in the grain. Some bent low with their sickles. Others piled the cut wheat into bundles. Everyone had work to do, and the fields were bustling with people.

'Must you stay here today?' asked Oswald, coming up beside Brinin, who was piling the wheat. 'Can't you come with me? I have food. We could go into the forest and play there for a while.'

Brinin shot a swift glance across to where the forest, dark and welcoming, thinned as it reached the edge of the fields. They both heard Aculf's barking voice nearby as he scolded someone for their slowness.

'I'm meant to be working,' Brinin frowned, but there was no heart in what he said.

'But there are so many people here. No one will even know you've gone.' And Oswald's words were as winning and welcoming as the trees. 'We could build a hut. I know a good place.'

A hut in the cool, green shade away from the heat and noise of harvest. Perhaps no one *would* see them if they slipped away.

'Perhaps for a little while,' said Brinin, and they crept away unseen.

Though Brinin knew more of work than play, once they had begun he seemed to have woodcraft in his fingers and an eye for how a hut should be. They were proud of it when they had finished and gone inside to eat. After their meal their hut became a stronghold, and they withstood the onslaught of their foes. They were a fyrd of two, one fiery-haired and the other as fair as hay in summer. A fearsome dragon came, but they saw him off with sticks and stones. With such daring deeds, the morning passed into afternoon and as they drove away the last of their foes they saw that the sun was getting low in the sky.

'I've stayed too long,' frowned Brinin suddenly.

'Perhaps we should go now,' said Oswald. 'Father doesn't like it if I am late to evening-meat.'

So they left their hut and the body of their dragon to make their way back to the village, full of what they might do the next time they went there. Sometimes danger does not come as a dragon or warrior foe, and as they reached the edge of the trees, they heard voices calling for Brinin and their hearts sank. Aculf and Row were already looking for them.

'Where have you been, you slacking young hound?' snapped Aculf, grabbing Brinin by his shirt and giving him a shake. 'Do you think you can shirk your work at harvest while we waste our time looking for you?'

Oswald hadn't spent all of his courage on the dragon and he stepped forward and put his hand on Aculf's arm.

'Please don't be angry with him. It was my fault. I asked him to come with me. He said he needed to work, but I made him come!'

Though Brinin thought that perhaps he had been much more willing than Oswald said, he saw that he was trying to save him from trouble and loved him for it.

'So you are to blame, are you, Oswald Child?' Aculf said, letting go of Brinin. 'What will your father say when I tell him that you've been taking his slaves away from their work?'

He reached up and twisted a strong but supple shoot from a nearby tree, then tore away the leaves and twigs that grew from it.

'You're all the father and mother the boy has now,' he said, handing the rod he had made to Row. 'I will leave you to deal with him, while I take this one to Edrich Thegn.'

Aculf marched the now somewhat downcast Oswald back to the hall, leaving Row and Brinin still by the edge of the forest. Row, who had no need for a rod, tossed it away as soon as they were out of sight. As he and Brinin walked to their hut, he told him that he wasn't free to play, even if it was the son of his lord who asked him to. And Brinin, knowing that he had missed trouble very narrowly, wished he hadn't gone.

Oswald fared rather less well. Aculf led him into the busy hall and stood him before his father.

'Why are you so late, boy? You know I have spoken to you about this before,' said Edrich sternly.

'P… please, Father, I—' began Oswald, looking at his feet.

'My lord,' said Aculf. 'Oswald Child took one of the slaves, Brinin, a boy like himself, away from his work to play. His brother and I spent a long time looking for him, my lord, when we could have been in the fields ourselves.'

Oswald heard the painful hush that suddenly fell on the room. Not daring to look up, he could feel his father's eyes upon him.

'Do you know that harvest is the busiest time of year?' Edrich's voice was soft and dreadful.

Oswald nodded.

'Answer me!'

'Yes, sir!' Oswald whispered.

'Do you think I keep slaves only to give you playfellows when you wish for them?'

'No, sir.' The whisper was little more than a breath now.

'It seemed, my lord,' said Aculf, 'that the slave did not want to leave his work, but that Oswald Child made him go with him.'

'Did the slave boy tell you that?'

'Oswald Child told me himself, my lord.'

'Then, Oswald, it seems to me that you knew what both you and the slave should have been doing but that you chose to forget. Why were you playing when there was work to be done? You should have been working as I was myself. Has the slave been punished?'

'Yes, my lord. I've already seen to that.'

'Then it would not be right for Oswald to be spared, not when he is much more to blame,' said Edrich, rising from his seat. 'Be so good as to give me your rod, Aculf.'

And Oswald settled in his mind that if he were to keep his friendship with Brinin, he must do his utmost to make sure that his father knew nothing about it.

DANES

The days lengthened, the ground softened and amid the lambing and lenten-fast, life came back to Oakdene. The greening of the forest and hills around the village called men to the plough and Edrich to the Witan. A little way up the hill was a beech tree, old and tall now. Long years and rain had washed away the earth to show its mossy roots, all twisted and gnarled like stretching fingers. Since boyhood, Brinin and Oswald had liked to go there to sit on the roots and talk in the dusk, the ground under their feet soft from fallen leaves and nutshells. Those meetings had become more seldom now that they were older, with fuller and at times harder days. But they still went when they could, and on one of those lenten evenings they sat there together.

'How has it been with Aculf?' asked Oswald.

'Aculf is Aculf.' Wasn't everything always the same? Never anything new, nor any hope of it either.

'The work will be harder now the ploughing has begun.'

'It makes the day go quicker.'

Oswald was short of speech that evening, with none of the village talk or booklore he sometimes came with. He was restless. He held a small stick, and Brinin watched as he turned it over and over in his hand and stared at it as though it might somehow teach him how to unburden himself of whatever was weighing him down.

'My father will ride to the Witan the day after tomorrow,' said Oswald at last. 'He says that this time I am to be in his place while he is away. He doesn't *mean* that I will be in his place, because if I were, the first thing I would do would be to find a new workreeve. But I am to listen to Aculf each day and ask him about the work, and seek his wisdom and Thurstan's if I need it. Does Aculf even *have* any wisdom?'

'He has cunning, but he calls it wisdom and loves to share it.'

'I wish I didn't have to listen to him at all. And I'm to be ready to welcome any wayfarers who may bring news or word of the Danes. And I am to know when to send a man to fetch my father back if need be.'

Oswald jabbed his stick into the ground, as though he could kill his worries that way.

'Do you think the Danes *are* coming? My father hardly talks about anything else, and that's what they'll talk about at the Witan. And if—when—we do have to go and fight them, it might be time for me to go too. I know my father doesn't think I'm good enough yet, but he might think I'm old enough. He wasn't much older himself when he first fought them.'

'It's what you've been raised to. There's no shirking it.'

'I don't want to shirk it but sometimes I wonder if he's right and I'm not good enough. If I can't even shoot straight or wield a sword when my father is watching, how will I do it when a crowd of Danes are charging at me with swords and axes?'

Oswald snapped his stick in two, then tossed the broken pieces away with a sigh.

'The word from East Anglia is dreadful, the talk of what the Danes have done there. Are they all as fearsome as everyone says?'

'Am I the one to tell you how bad the Danes are?' said Brinin, and a coolness crept into his voice to warn Oswald that it was better to tread softly past what Brinin stood over like a watchman. Better to handle the Danes carefully, if he handled them at all.

'I'm sorry,' said Oswald, meekly enough. More unthinking than unkind, Brinin thought. 'I forgot about your mother. But you're one of us. *She* was one of us. You never seem like one of them somehow. I need to go now, or I'll be late to evening-meat and I want to keep Father happy before he goes.'

After Oswald had gone, Brinin stayed in the gathering dusk for a while. One of us, one of them, one of neither, one of both. Here they were, all waiting for the Danes: murderous, fearsome, bloodthirsty. Brinin didn't know any more than Oswald did if the tales they had heard were true—more likely true than not—but he had known one Dane. He had known one Dane, wiser, kinder, better than all those he knew who called the Danes their foe.

Like Oswald, he hadn't forgotten the time the Danes had come to Wintanceaster. His mother had always told him the sagas she had learned as a child, but she had stopped for a time when the Danes came, and all the village talk of battles and raiders had seemed to unsettle her. He could still remember the tightness of her face. He hadn't understood it then, but he did now. He remembered how she had started to sit away from the other women, and how he had sometimes seen them whispering and watching her.

At the time, he hadn't fully understood her tears the day some other children had gathered round him and pelted him with clods of earth. He had kept telling her that it was only mud and had been rather frightened that his mother, always strong and steady, should suddenly be so upset. Now he saw that she was the one who had been frightened that day. Only now did he see how helpless she had been as a Danish woman, husband not long dead, alone with her children, while everything the Danes were doing could only make the men of Wessex hate them all the more. The only time he could remember his mother ever striking him was when he had spoken in her tongue outside their hut. It hadn't been a harsh blow—almost all the sting had been in the knowledge that it had come from her hand—but he hadn't understood it. Now he did. Perhaps that was why he still watched over her so carefully. Then she had been afraid, and he had been too small to help her. Now he was strong, and it was too late.

The firelight in their hut flickered with thoughts of their mother as Brinin sat there with Row that evening. He seemed to see her shape among the shadows, to catch the softness of her voice somewhere nearby. A mild foe. The gentlest of those bloodthirsty

Danes. He looked at the flames for a long time before he spoke to his brother.

'How many people here remember that our mother was a Dane?' he asked.

'No one has ever said anything about it. Not to me. Why?'

There was another long flickering silence as Brinin reached out and poked a stick into the fire. Oswald had said he had forgotten about it, but he was Oswald, all welcome and well-meant friendship. How many Oswalds were there in Oakdene? Not many. Not for two thralls with a Danish mother.

'The last time the Danes came to Wessex, it was hard for her. She was frightened, and others in the village didn't trust her any more.'

'You remember that? You couldn't have been more than four winters!'

'Five. I remember it well.'

'Why are you thinking about this now?'

'I've been talking to Oswald about the Danes. They'll likely come soon. Folk are scared, and when they're scared they could easily forget that our father was as much a Wessex man as any of them. They may begin to fear *us* when the Danes come—to hate us, perhaps—more so if they do in Wessex what they've done in East Anglia. We must be ready for that.'

'They may have forgotten.'

'Someone will remember.' Brinin leaned forward earnestly. 'Mother didn't like us to speak in her tongue outside the hut. I think she hoped that everyone would forget who she was. They didn't forget then. I'm glad we do still speak it together, even though she's gone—it reminds me that we haven't forgotten her. But we should be more careful now and only speak it in here as she wanted us to. Not because we're afraid—why be afraid before anything has happened—but because it's wise.'

'You're likely right, though we still don't know if the Danes will come. There's always so much talk. How can anyone be sure of anything?'

'They will come. We just don't know when.'

❧

Oswald lingered in the church on the day his father left for the Witan. It was strange how time was not always the same. Some days he longed to be outside, and the time spent on Latin felt sluggish and unending. On others, there wasn't enough of it to ask Brother Wilfred everything he wanted to know. But now with his father gone, he could linger and talk if he chose to, without being asked where he had been.

'The bookskins, sir,' said Oswald, still sitting on the bench long after he was free to leave. 'You told me once that you would tell me how you came by them, and I've been wondering.'

'I wrote them myself. You know that I am a Northumbrian and lived in a minster there before I came to Wessex. My father sent me to the minster as a young boy to become a monk and, he hoped, a learned man. I was taught to be skilled in bookcraft and was a scribe even before I became a priest. You have never seen one, but often when a book is made it is wonderfully brightened. If I had the ink and bookskin, I could make for you letters and patterns more beautiful than anything you have ever seen, more even than the best of sword hilts or arm rings. It was hard work, sitting all day in the cold—and, let me tell you, even the coldest day in Wessex is nothing to the east winds that chilled me in Northumbria! My back would ache from bending over the bookskin and my hand from holding the writing-feather. But a book is such a wonderful thing that all the work—and the aches—are well worth it. The little I have shown you is all there is left of everything I ever wrote. The rest is all lost. Burned.'

Now that Oswald had seen the bookskins and had handled and read them, he knew that a book was not like a waxboard, where the words could be quickly made and quickly lost when they were no longer needed. On the bookskins each word was carefully crafted, black and straight, none too big or too small. They were shaped to last long after the scribe had been forgotten. It was dreadful to think that the work of weeks, months and years could be suddenly lost, with no way of calling the words to mind again. It was more dreadful to think that, for all their worth, the books were likely not the worst of the loss. Oswald knew from the way Brother Wilfred had said it that there had been no mishap, no careless hand knocking over a candle. He had heard of what had happened in Northumbria.

'Did the Danes come?'

'In the night, when we least thought of them. Sometimes they take slaves when they come, but not that night, that I know of, unless they took some of the boys. They cut down all before them. We were monks. We had no weapons, but they didn't care about that. I saw many of my brothers fall before my eyes. That same morning I had been teaching the boys about the lives of some of the saints, how they faced death fearlessly. Then death came to me. Was I fearless? I ran for my life. And five winters later, I still see that night in my dreams.'

This was what they were waiting for in Wessex. This was why Oswald's father kept telling them all to be ready. But how could anyone be fearless, even with a sword in his hand?

'I hid in the woods all that night, shaking and weeping. And in the morning I crept back to see if they were gone. They *were* gone, and the gold and silver with them. The buildings were gone, still burning. The monks were gone, lying dead for me to bury. Some I never found. Only one monk still lived, Brother Ordgar who had taught me as a boy. He was very old by then and dreadfully wounded. He told me that he had seen them murder the abbot before the altar, a prayer still on his lips. Brother Ordgar was dead by midday, and I alone was left.'

It was little wonder that Brother Wilfred still saw it in his dreams, greater wonder that he slept at all and could sit and speak of it so steadily.

'To stay there alone, to be alive when all the others were dead… There seemed to be a shame in it. I feel it still. The abbot did not fear death. He knew the hope of heaven that lay beyond it. I know it and believe it, but I forgot it that night. It was… hard to stay where everything I saw called my fear to mind. Perhaps it would have been better if I had stayed to die with them. I waited for a while to see if any of the others had lived, but no one came. Those bookskins were among the little that was not burned, so I took them and came far away to Wessex. I met your father, who wanted to build a church and find a priest for it. He saw that I could also teach his son. So here I am, through his kindness, though even here I don't forget. And I still pray that when the Danes come to Wessex I will be ready for them.'

They were all to be ready: the King ready to gather the fyrd, Edrich Thegn ready to follow with his men, Oswald ready to go with his father. All ready, weapons in hand. But Brother Wilfred didn't mean that. He wanted to be ready to die.

'But doesn't everyone fear them? Everyone but the very bold, like my father or Thurstan—I don't know if they do. And, sir, if you don't flee when they come, they will likely kill you too.'

'Oswald, my boy, it is Lent! We ready ourselves for Easter. We look forward to the Ærist, the rising beyond death. So let us not fear death or even the Danes.'

ÆRIST

Brinin stood at the back of the church, by the door, with Row and the other slaves around him. He was always at the back, always by the door, so on this most holy day of Ærist, this day of great and sombre gladness that ended the long fast, he stood where he always did. And it was good enough to hear and understand what he could.

It was strange how the words Brother Wilfred said could be known from long hearing—some of them Brinin had heard so often he could almost have said them himself—yet so much without meaning. But there was meaning there if it could be found, meaning unheard in those words that only Brother Wilfred, and perhaps Oswald, could understand. He should ask Oswald about it sometime.

But that part—that meaningless, meaningful part—that was over now, and Brother Wilfred was stepping forward to talk to them in plain speech. This was what Brinin liked best, and he settled himself against the doorframe in readiness. When speech was needful there was nothing better than plain speech, and Brother Wilfred was good at it. He could always be heard, even by those at the back, and he spoke like a man who wanted to be understood.

'You all know of our Saviour's death, and we have in these days remembered it,' began Wilfred. 'And you all know that it was on this day that he rose from death. But it is good for me to speak again of these things so that they will not go from your minds.'

Brinin listened, frowning slightly, as Brother Wilfred spoke very plainly of the death of Christ. He had heard about it before. These things were not new to him, but as he listened, a thought, which had stayed only shadowy before, began to take shape in his mind. Surely it was a strange thing that Christ, a great King and God himself, should yield to such things. Edrich Thegn, though less than a king, would not yield to shame like that.

'Do these things seem strange to you?' Brother Wilfred went on, and Brinin stared at the monk in wonder—had he heard his thoughts? 'Think of it this way: we all know how the shepherd must save the sheep from foxes and wolves. The Gospeller John tells us that our Lord said, "I am the Good Shepherd who lays down his life for the sheep". Now the sheep are the people of God, who everywhere believe in his good word. The Lord, the Good Shepherd, saved them by laying down his own life.

'But what did he save them from? Think of it like this: does not a king go into battle to save his people from their foes? So Christ, the greatest King, went to the Cross as a brave warrior. He mounted it as a king goes into battle. And those who hated him thought that by his death they had defeated him. But it was not as they thought, and this day of his rising shows us the truth of that.

'Today is Easter Day. On this day, he broke death in pieces. And isn't death the great foe that our King has now defeated? He broke the Gates of Hell, and isn't Hell a greater foe still? And it *was* a great victory, for he freed his chosen from among the kin of Adam and shut for ever the Gates of Hell so that the righteous man who trusts in him need never see it.'

Now this was the strangest thing of all: a great victory that looked like shame and defeat. A victory won by death Brinin understood. In the tales, there were always great men who fell in battle, and their swordbrothers boasted of them. But this wasn't the same. It wasn't the kind of victory men spoke of round the fire and it wasn't won in the same way. But his thoughts were leading him away from Brother Wilfred. He could think of all that later.

'Now some of you will say that Christ is God, so well might he arise gladly from death. But think of this: he did not rise alone, because the Gospeller Matthew wrote in Christ's book that many holy men rose with him and walked abroad. Those men who rose with him were not God, but men and women as we are. Yet they rose with Christ, and so might we, so let none among us lose hope in his own rising. Death is all around us. We know it. It is our foe. But today we call to our minds that it is already defeated and we do not lose hope.'

And soon it was over and everyone left the church, but Brinin tarried by the door and did not heed Aculf's hiss for him to hurry. At last, he was the only one there but the monk and he turned slowly to leave, mindful suddenly that even on a holy day there were beasts to tend and Aculf would not like to be kept waiting. But as he left, Brother Wilfred called to him.

'I saw you thinking while I spoke, my boy,' he said, as he came towards Brinin.

Why should Brother Wilfred have seen *him* thinking as he stood by the door at the back? Why should he have seen him at all? Let Aculf wait. This was a time to gather words and say them.

'It seems, sir, that the ways of God are not the ways of men,' Brinin said at last. 'That this should be the way he chose to defeat death.'

Brother Wilfred did not answer at once. He thought, looked at Brinin keenly and took time over his words. Brinin liked him all the more for it.

'I had a master once, a long time ago in the minster when I was a boy. He was a most learned man. He said that the men of that time kept a death like that for those who were not their own kind.' Another keen look. 'And for slaves. Yet this is how our Lord chose to do his will. And now a slave may call God Father as boldly as the king.'

That was a new thought. Something seemed to be stirring, shifting in his mind, though Brinin could not have said what it was. Before he had time even to think more, he heard Aculf bellowing for him from outside. Brother Wilfred nodded to him by way of leave, and he left without another word.

'What do you think you are about?' Aculf met Brinin with a sharp blow to the back of the head and a shove once he was near enough to reach. 'Must work wait while you linger?'

But Brinin didn't care about Aculf or anything he did that day. Who could care for Aculf with such things stirring in his mind? Aculf could do as he liked and all those thoughts would still be there.

'What were you doing?' frowned Row, waiting for Brinin a little further along. 'Why make him angry when you know that's what he wants?'

They were already far from Aculf and pouring water into a trough before Brinin said a word.

'I was thinking.' His thoughts were still too shapeless to speak aloud, but one stood strong among the others. 'The God the Saxons worship is not as they are.'

TRUTH

Brinin laid down a heavy basket of firewood beside the woodpile outside the hall. He stretched his unburdened shoulders, which had left the weight of the plough only to take up another, then bent down to throw the wood onto the pile. At first he did not heed the slight scuffling nearby, likely a cat whose rest had been broken by the sound of the wood. But when he glanced down he saw that it was Ulf, Aculf's small son, hiding crouched behind the woodpile and gnawing hungrily at the flesh of a bone he clutched.

'Now what are you doing here?' smiled Brinin.

Ulf started and dropped the bone, his wide eyes darting fearfully towards the hall door.

'Oh, don't tell Father!' he gasped, lips trembling. 'I didn't mean to take it!'

Stooping, Brinin lifted the bone and reached it back to Ulf. How old was he? Four winters, five perhaps? Still young enough to think that he *could* take something without meaning to. Young enough to forget to be frightened when the flesh looked and smelt so good. But Ulf suddenly remembered to fear. His eyes grew wider still, and he dashed away without taking the bone. Brinin turned and saw Aculf walking out of the hall, an empty platter in one hand, his stick in the other.

'Who took this food?' shouted Aculf, looking around for someone to blame. His eye fell on Brinin almost at once.

Brinin looked down at the bone in his hand, then back at Aculf. It wasn't only anger he saw on Aculf's face. It was hunger, greed to fatten himself on another's shame. There was only one way this could end.

'You dare to steal my food!' spluttered Aculf. 'You dare to go into the hall unbidden and take what is not your own!'

Brinin had never seen war—and knew that he never would see it—but he had listened to the tales as keenly as any boy. And he was beginning to understand that Aculf was doing battle with him in much the same way as men did in the tales. First, they would eye each other like two war bands across the battlefield, and Aculf would hurl his insults. Hound, swine, slack, liar. They were always the same. He was no wordsmith. Then they would shake their weapons. Aculf had more: his anger, his words, his stick, his power. Brinin had only one: silence. It was as much a shield as it was a sword, but he knew how to wield it. Aculf was ready for the battle to begin now, strengthening his arm for blows. Brinin, tight-jawed, never hoped for victory, only that he might leave the battlefield with his weapon unbroken.

'What are you doing? Why are you shouting at him?'

It was Oswald, coming upon them seemingly from nowhere, with Edith quiet and quick-eyed at his side. He spoke breathlessly, flushed with anger, and made Brinin uneasy in a way that Aculf had not.

'This… this thieving young swine dared to go into the hall and steal my food!' Aculf pointed with his stick to the ground: the insults and the shaking of weapons. He turned back to Brinin. 'Kneel!'

'You will not kneel!' Oswald grabbed Brinin's arm. 'Aculf… no! This is… this is unjust! Why would you think that Brinin would do such a thing?'

'He has it in his hand, Oswald Child,' said Aculf, a growing sharpness in his voice.

Brinin heard the sharpness. He knew it well and he knew that the end of all this would be more painful now, thanks to Oswald. He tried to catch Oswald's eyes, to urge him away, but he was glaring at

Aculf and didn't see. Edith did see. She touched her brother's arm to make him understand, but he brushed her hand away.

'Did you ask him how he came to be holding it?' Oswald's words were growing louder and faster. 'Why don't you find out the truth instead of beating him before you know?'

Truth? If they were going to start looking for truth, he knew it. But if he chose to speak truth, neither Aculf nor Oswald would like what he would say. And even if he had wanted to use it to save himself, Brinin knew that truth was such a stranger to Aculf that he wouldn't know it if they met.

'He has it in his hand! And he has denied nothing.'

'He's *said* nothing! That isn't the same thing!' Oswald was shouting now.

'Oswald Child, your father left me to oversee the slaves while he was away.' Aculf's forbearance was fast waning. 'I am to see that everyone does their work and that any wrongdoing is punished. You are to obey your father and he did not bid you hinder me in my work. You can be about your own business now, and I will be about mine.'

'Please stop now and leave,' whispered Brinin in a voice so low that only Oswald could hear. Perhaps he might listen to words.

How would it be if he walked away and left them to do battle without him? But he wasn't Oswald. He couldn't taunt the foe, then leave the field unwounded. And the taunting and shaking of weapons had gone on long enough. Brinin took a step away from Oswald and knelt down on the ground. Strange how the kneeling could smart more than the stick sometimes, even though he had been kneeling all his life.

'I forbid you to strike him!' Nothing could make Oswald listen. Not words. Not friendship.

'Oh, so you forbid it, do you, Oswald Child? Well, your father will be back within the week. If you wish, this can wait until then. He can say what is to be done with this young hound, and I can ask him what to do when you hinder me.'

All at once, Oswald's boldness was gone. Anger and shame struggled with each other on his face, his eyes glistening with looming tears. This time, when Edith took his arm he let her lead him away, because fear had done what friendship could not. Brinin swayed slightly as the first blow fell and he saw Oswald wince as though it was his own back the stick was bruising. Another blow fell, and Brinin gripped his silence more tightly, like a man who swings his sword with both hands. Another fell. Oswald threw off Edith's hand from his arm and stormed into the hall. Others nearby stopped their work to watch. The clouds had grown heavy. It was going to rain. At the fourth blow, Brinin shut his eyes.

It did rain. The clouds wept great tears that poured down Brinin's face and soaked through his clothes until every part of him was wet as he worked, but the cold was welcome on his back now. The rain drove everyone to indoor work. Only the slaves shivered in the fields or with the beasts. He was thankful that Aculf was fool enough to put an axe into the hand of a slave he had just beaten. Or perhaps it was wisdom. Perhaps, whatever Aculf said, he knew that he could trust Brinin. Wisdom or folly, Brinin was thankful, because hewing wood was good work on an angry day. He could take his anger and make strength from it until it was gone. Or mostly gone.

'Brinin.' Oswald called to him as he came out of the hall. Had he come to listen—too late—now that the trouble was over?

Brinin reached down for another log, set it on the block and, with one mighty crash from the axe, split it in two.

'I asked you to stop, and you didn't listen,' he said without even looking at Oswald, and brought the axe down again.

'I was trying to help you!'

'I didn't ask you to help me. I asked you to stop. You would have done better to be about your own business, as Aculf said.' With another blow from the axe, another split log fell to the ground.

'You wanted me to stand aside and watch you be beaten?'

'No need to watch.'

Brinin could see Oswald's bewilderment as he stood watching him smash the axe through log after log. He didn't understand and he hadn't come to listen. He'd come to make himself feel better, to soothe his shame by talking about the good he had meant to do.

'But he didn't even try to find out the truth. You likely picked up the bone from the ground. Why didn't you tell him? I know you didn't do it. I know *you*. You're my friend.'

'So you say!' Brinin's words shot out like another swing of the axe, though he felt somewhat sorry for it when he saw Oswald feel the sting of them. He laid down the axe. If Oswald wanted truth, he could have it. 'We aren't children any more. You think you understand my life. But what do you know of it, with your reading and your Latinlore and your warcraft? You understand nothing. You will charge into battle and one day be the thegn, followed by all your men. I will work on the land till I die. Aculf is a fool. I'd rather be beaten than beg a fool for mercy and I'd rather be beaten than have you plead with him on my behalf. Did you want me to thank you for that? Do you think you can save me from my life? You can't change anything at all. And so much for friendship! Friendship wasn't enough to make you stop when I asked you to. You only stopped because you're scared of your father, and Aculf threatened to tell him.'

Oswald flinched as though Brinin had slapped him in the face. He opened his mouth to speak, found no words there, then turned and walked away through the rain.

Edith found her brother later, sitting in the gloom behind the thick curtain that hid his bed from the rest of the hall. He sat downcast and unhappy, staring at the floor with his head in his hands, and didn't speak or look at her as she sat down quietly beside him.

'Oswald,' she said in a low voice. 'Are you unwell? You didn't come to eat.'

He looked up at her then but didn't answer. Edith sat with him and waited.

'He's right,' Oswald sighed at last. 'I am too scared of Father to do anything.'

'I don't understand what you mean. No one said that. Do you mean Aculf?'

'No. Brinin. We talked afterwards. He's right. I *am* too scared. I want to help. I say I'm his friend but I'm too scared to do anything. He's right, Edith. Even the thought of doing anything Father wouldn't like… So much for friendship! That's what he said. He was angry with me.'

'You did make it very hard for him.'

'What do you mean? I wanted to help.'

'Didn't you see Ulf running away from Brinin as Aculf came out of the hall? I can't be sure, but it looked like Brinin was shielding him. You were pressing Aculf to find out the truth, and Brinin couldn't give it without shifting the blame onto a child not more than five winters. You made Aculf angrier than he already was, and he likely beat him all the harder because of it, and everyone else heard you shouting and stopped what they were doing to watch. You were too angry to see the way Brinin was looking at you. He wanted you to go, but you didn't.'

'I only wanted to help. I want to help so much. I can't stand it any more. But I'm too much of a blundering fool to see what's happening and too much of a coward to do anything about it anyway.'

When his sister had nothing to say to that, Oswald knew he was right. And he wished he wasn't, and that he could forget what Brinin had said and the way he had looked at him when he said it. It was heavy knowledge to bear, hard to think of, and it drove his head back into his hands again.

'Why don't you eat?' said Edith. 'I can bring you something here. You don't need to go out into the hall.'

But that made it worse. Wasn't she just trying to make him think of something else, like giving a child an apple to stop them from crying when they had hurt themselves?

'I couldn't eat anything. I'm going to bed.'

So Edith left him, and he did go to bed, but the night was well spent before he slept. Long after the nightgloom had fallen over the hall and the village, he lay awake in the darkness turning over in his mind everything that had happened that day. The truth seemed to hover ghostlike by his bed, whispering to him what he didn't want to hear. He was afraid, and Brinin knew it. He was afraid, and Aculf knew it and had wielded it as a weapon against him. He was afraid, and perhaps everyone knew it. He had always thought that Brinin was the weaker of the two of them, caught in his troubles like some small beast or bird in a snare. Yet Oswald had never seen whatever fear Brinin felt. It didn't grip him and it didn't stand in front of him and block his way.

The truth by his bed kept taunting him over and over: Aculf's threat, Brinin's anger. He couldn't shut the words out and the shame of them sickened him again. Restless, Oswald sat up in bed and leaned against the wall. He was the one in the snare, tangled up in it and not even trying to struggle out. And the snare was made up of the fear of small things: a frown, a stern word. Even at his most unsparing, his father had never beaten him as Aculf had beaten Brinin that day; stingingly enough, but never eagerly. But the small things were enough to trap him. He was afraid of even the least his father might do. He could see himself for what he was now. No friend, because he had left Aculf springing wolflike on Brinin and saved himself from small trouble.

There could be no more of that. Even if his father didn't like it, he had to do something now. Perhaps if he untangled his own snare, he could untangle Brinin's at the same time. And even if he couldn't get away from his fear altogether, he might learn to keep it as unseen as Brinin's was. But fearful or not, it was time to *do* something, and he couldn't rest that night until he knew what.

CABBAGE

T he next afternoon Brinin knelt among the cabbages, ridding them of all the weeds and leafworm he could find. Oswald came to him unheard and unseen. Brinin didn't even know he was there until he had knelt down and begun to pull up weeds beside him.

'I'm sorry,' said Oswald.

Brinin turned to look at Oswald, beside him on his knees. Perhaps he had been a little unkind to him the day before. Even if fear had been stronger than friendship, how could it be anything but friendship for a thegn's son to kneel in the dirt and beg forgiveness from a slave who had spoken to him as no slave should ever speak?

'You're right. I... I am scared of my father. There! I've said it now!' And Brinin could see on Oswald's face and hear in the way he drove the words out that it had been no easy thing to say, though perhaps that made it more worth the saying. 'That's not why I'm sorry, though. I'm sorry that I didn't see what was happening yesterday, and I'm sorry that I made everything worse, and didn't stop when you asked me to. Edith thought you were shielding Ulf, and if she's right then I understand now why you wouldn't speak. And likely you're right not to plead with Aculf and give him what he wants. So I'm sorry, though'—another quick breath to drive out the words—'though I still wish a little that I hadn't stopped and... and left you to him. He's such... such a wolf! I would love to break that stick of his over his head and... and make him eat it!'

There were times when Brinin was so tired, so bruised, when he heaved around with him such simmering anger that he meted out his smiles as sparingly as his words. But he couldn't help smiling at the thought of Aculf feasting on his own stick.

'We could serve it up to him with cabbage,' he grinned.

Brinin saw Oswald glance at him from time to time as they weeded together, saw him open his mouth to speak more than once. It seemed easier for him to pull out the weeds than it was to pull out whatever it was he wanted to say.

'Listen, Brinin,' Oswald said at last. 'I think you *were* shielding Ulf and I don't think it was the first time you've done something like that. Yes, yes, I know you won't tell me one way or the other, but I know I'm right. You don't walk away when someone needs your help, so can't you see why I have to do something about Aculf?'

'He hates you! And, what's worse, he has the ear of my father, so my father thinks badly of you too. While Aculf is workreeve, nothing will ever be better. All the other men who could be workreeve need to be ready for war. My father knows that Aculf can't fight, so he is left to oversee things. Aculf is going nowhere, but perhaps there is a way for *you* to go.'

'Go where?'

'There's a minster. I heard about it once from Brother Wilfred, though I didn't think about it much at the time. Brother Wilfred knows the prior there, and it seems he's a kind man, who would welcome you without asking too much. If we could find a way to get you there—it's in Wessex, but I'm not sure where—then you could stay there for a while. They would find work for you to do. They have land to work and beasts. Most minsters do, I think. Then if I live long enough—after the Danes come—to be thegn, I could fetch you back and give you your freedom. A slave *can* be freed, you know—I learned that from Brother Wilfred too—but I can't do it now. Only my father can.'

For a long time neither of them spoke. Brinin knew that nothing would change while Aculf was workreeve. To be rid of him, to have the hope of casting off slavery altogether, those were things he had seldom even let himself dream of. The trouble with dreams was that even the best of them were fleeting and didn't make the work any lighter in the morning. Why wish for what he could never have? Why make the day longer and the work more bitter by hoping that a dream might come true? Better to see his life for what it was and find ways to live it. Brinin had been very young when he learned that. Oswald was so earnest, so hopeful, but it was all as likely as fighting dragons, as they had played at as boys. He had liked the thought of fighting dragons then and he liked the thought of freedom from Aculf now. But there would be no freedom. Instead there would be swift capture, swift punishment and—here was the worst of it—swift blame falling upon Row.

It wasn't the same with Row. He worked almost unseen and Aculf's anger seldom reached him. Brinin could remember only one time, long ago, when Row had earned Aculf's stick, but he had never forgotten his helpless rage at seeing his brother beaten. Once had been enough to sear that into his mind. If he fled, Row would take the blame and most likely the punishment. With Brinin gone, Aculf would find someone new to wage war against, and it was sure to be Row. That was why he had to stay. Better to bear years of Aculf's harshness than to forsake his brother to even a day of it. And how could he walk away from a brother who had watched the rest of their kindred die one by one? He wouldn't spread sorrow to Row when he could keep it to himself.

'It can't be done,' said Brinin at last. Oswald didn't know, as he did, that too much hope was a dangerous thing.

'Why can't it be done? I'm sure we can do it if we think carefully and plan everything well.'

'If I flee, Row will be blamed. I'd be caught in a few days at most. And I'm all Row has now and I'm sticking to him. He's already lost everyone else. How can I go?'

'You won't even think about it? I've even thought of a way to make sure you won't be caught.'

'No. My life isn't bad enough to give up my brother. I think you worry about Aculf more than I do. Why would I let him make me do something I would never think of otherwise? I can wait until you're lord here.'

WISDOM

They looked for Edrich Thegn every day, and as each day passed and he didn't come, Aculf grew easier to anger. He strutted around finding fault where there was none and bidding the slaves to make ready things that were as ready as they would ever be. If Æthelred the King himself had been on his way, Aculf couldn't have been more fretful or harder to please. And although the ploughing was always the heaviest of all the work he did, Brinin was glad of it. It was better to lose himself in the furrows than to spend the day wondering when he would next be bruised by Aculf's tongue or stick.

He and Row had been at the plough for some time one morning, when they looked up and saw Eawig, Garulf's grandson, running down towards the fields. He kept looking behind him as he went and stumbled a little in his haste.

'Let's send Eawig back up to fetch water for the oxen,' said Row. 'It's time they stopped for a drink.'

Eawig was breathless when he reached them.

'Cynestan's come,' he panted. 'He says that Edrich Thegn will be back by midday, and Oswald Child has ridden out to meet him. Aculf is angry with everyone! I spilled a bucket of water, and he says he'll beat me if he sees me up there again today. And he slapped Ebba for dropping an egg. Only one egg! He's…'

Eawig didn't say what Aculf was, though Brinin understood him well enough. Wasn't it wisdom, after all, for a boy to keep such thoughts to himself, even about a man who had slapped his little sister? And it was wisdom for Row and Brinin to keep Eawig at the plough with them so that Aculf wouldn't see him again for a time.

'I'll fetch the water,' said Brinin. 'I won't be long.'

He heard Aculf long before he reached him, bellowing out his bidding to anyone lowly enough to be bound to heed it. Brinin saw Ebba first, her face red and stained with tears that all her wiping couldn't keep away. She looked up at him forlornly as he passed her, and Brinin felt the first little trickle of anger that morning. This was why it was better to be at the plough.

'We need more wood to be hewn for the hall,' Aculf snapped at Brinin as soon as he saw him. 'I left the axe here, and it's gone now. Did you take it?'

'I've been ploughing. I haven't seen it.' But Aculf must have known that. Hadn't everyone seen that Brinin had only now come up from the fields?

'You must have seen it! I saw you here earlier.'

Aculf had a plan for him that morning—that much was plain. Perhaps his stick had been too idle. Or perhaps little children hadn't been enough of a prey for him. If he was fool enough to think that a man could be in two places at the same time, then there was nothing Brinin could say to make him any wiser.

'You've taken it and are hiding it somewhere!' Aculf barked.

Ebba was weeping harder now. She hid behind her mother, who stood stiff and uneasy, as everyone did, waiting for the storm to burst. Their faces said everything: Brinin couldn't have taken the axe; likely it had never even been there at all. Perhaps this angered Aculf all the more. It was Ludan, the horseherd, who spoke up at last.

'I believe he has been in the fields all morning, sir. I don't think he could have taken it.'

'I did not ask you to speak!' yelled Aculf, turning on him. 'This boy is not to be trusted. If anyone were to hide a dangerous tool like an axe, he is the one who would do it. I have not been wise to let him work with that kind of tool. From now on, he won't. Where did you put it, boy?'

'I've been in the fields since dawn.' Like Eawig, he knew that it was wisdom to say little, to say enough and no more.

'You're lying! You give only trouble here. You're nothing but a dog of a Dane like your mother. It was a good day for Oakdene when she died!'

The trickle gushed out in a flood of anger, unlike anything Brinin had ever felt before. He knew how to hold his tongue. He could take a beating without a murmur. He had prided himself on keeping silent under the worst of Aculf's goading, but there were some things that no one should have to bear quietly.

'Better a Dane than a worthless fool!' He had said it now, heard them all gasp, thrown aside his wisdom and told Aculf what he most wanted him to know. 'I doubt there's a Dane alive who isn't a worthier man than you. Does it take much courage to beat those who are bound to take it? Without Edrich Thegn you would be nothing. In my eyes you're already less than nothing.'

And Brinin turned his back on Aculf and walked away, everyone watching him in stunned silence. Aculf, at first dumbstruck at what he was hearing, began to call after him in spluttering wrath.

'Stop! Stop, I tell you. Come here! You will not speak to me like that!'

But Brinin had flung himself so far into folly that it was too late for wisdom now. Let Aculf see his back. Let him learn what it was like to be unheeded.

'Quick, Thurstan! Help me catch him.'

Did Aculf need help to catch him when he wasn't running or going where he would not easily be found?

'You want me to help you beat a boy who has spoken truth to you?' Thurstan's voice was full of scorn that no one could have missed. 'Someone should have said all that to you long ago. I wish I'd said it myself. If you want to beat him for saying what everyone thinks, catch him yourself. I don't care that he's a slave. I'm having no part of it.'

Brinin kept walking. He knew he wouldn't be walking for long. He didn't go faster, or slower, or look behind him to see how near

Aculf was. He knew he was near. Brinin could somehow feel him coming up behind him like a looming cloud. He didn't know if it was Aculf's fist, or foot, or both that brought him down. It happened so quickly that he had no time to put out his hands to stop his face from hitting the ground. Then the storm broke.

BOLDNESS

Oswald loved the feel of the wind on his face, the cool brightness of the morning and the speed with which his horse bore him along. He'd always loved it since the first day he had sat on a horse. Now it was almost enough to help him forget the unease that had come on him when Cynestan had brought word of Edrich Thegn's homecoming. Why should he feel uneasy when all was well, he had asked himself, when there had been no trouble, and he had done his father's bidding? If only Aculf was a more forgiving kind of man... It was Edith who had thought of him riding out, because their father would like it and it was better than Oswald walking to and fro as he waited for him. So he went—Edith always seemed to know better than he did what would make their father happy—and now Oswald was glad that he had listened to her.

He had almost forgotten to worry when he looked up and saw his father and Saxulf ahead of him. All was well in Oakdene. He knew that. Why would there be any need to think otherwise? And now he would speak to his father first and give a good word before Aculf could give a bad one. Oswald drew a deep breath, then rode on more quickly to meet them.

He saw on his father's face as he reached them that his coming had not been foreseen. Surely Edith hadn't been wrong for once?

'Oswald! I didn't think to see you here,' frowned Edrich. 'Is something wrong?'

'Oh no, sir! I… I came to meet you to welcome you home.' What relief as his father's frown melted into a smile! Edith had been right. 'I hope you are well, Father.'

'I am well, my boy.' Edrich turned to Saxulf beside him. 'Your wife will be watching for you, Saxulf. Why don't you go ahead, and we'll follow?'

It was all very well to make his father happy, to ride out to him ready with a good word, but once they were alone Oswald's tongue seemed so stiff and slow. His father would have to do the talking. Wasn't it always that way?

'Now then, Oswald,' said Edrich, when the sound of Saxulf's horse had died away. 'How is it with Oakdene?'

'All is well, Father.'

'The ploughing?'

'Almost done, sir. The men have been working hard.'

'No trouble with anything?'

'No, sir.' Oswald felt himself faltering a little. His father needn't know about the trouble he'd had with Aculf. That wasn't the kind of trouble he meant. 'A wild boar got into the peas last week, but Thurstan killed it and we ate the flesh.'

'Any word of the Danes, or anything else?'

'No, sir. No one came to us, so we heard nothing.'

'Good. I'm glad to hear all this, Oswald, and Aculf will tell me more when I see him.'

'Yes, Father,' said Oswald, just holding back a wince at the thought of what Aculf might say. Why must he always do this to himself? Why must he always watch so warily for every frown or smile and try to see his father's mind? He had sworn to himself that there was to be no more of that, and now at the first sight of his father, fear was at his heels again ready to snare him. But there was to be no more of it.

'What of your learning, Oswald?'

'I have worked hard, sir, and Brother Wilfred will tell you if he thinks I have learned more.' Nothing to fear there, at least. Hadn't Brother Wilfred himself told him how happy his father would be?

'And Edith?'

'She is well, Father. She is always busy, and everyone loves and trusts her. She's making everything ready for you.'

'She's like her mother.'

And that was so unforeseen that it drove all Oswald's unease away at once. It had been four winters since they had buried his mother, by her side that little one who had opened his eyes only long enough to see the light of one morning. In all those four winters he had never known his father to speak of her, but he heard now in his voice that she wasn't forgotten, but too well remembered. Tears were suddenly hot in Oswald's eyes, and he lowered his head. He hadn't forgotten either.

'If Edith is waiting, we should go to her quickly,' said Edrich, and Oswald knew that for once he and his father had understood each other. 'I love a swift ride on a morning like this.'

'Edith has meat and drink for you now in the hall, Father,' said Oswald as he swung himself down from his horse. 'Shall I lead the horses to the horsehouse?'

'Yes, you take them,' said Edrich, handing Oswald his reins and looking about him. 'It seems that you have done well enough while I've been away.'

'Thank you, sir.' To be told by his father that he had done well enough came so near to praise that it was almost as good as it.

But for all this near praise, the unease stole back over him as his father strode away to the hall. Ludan, never carefree, took the horses with a glumness that was odd even for him. He looked back at Oswald as he left and opened his mouth to speak, then shook his head and muttered to himself before walking on. Oswald watched as Ludan stopped and whispered something to Wynith, Ebba's mother, and his heart sank a little. Surely he hadn't told his father that all was well, only for something to go wrong in the short time he had been away.

'Oswald Child, sir!' Row stepped out suddenly from the shadows beside the horsehouse, frowning and glancing all around as though looking for someone. 'Please, may I speak to you?'

'Yes, but what's wrong?'

'Please, sir, not here.'

Oswald, worried now, followed him back into the shadows, Row still watchful and unwilling to speak until he knew that they were alone with no one nearby to see or hear them. All was not well. All was far from well. It had to be Brinin. Why else would it be Row who had come to him?

'Something's happened, sir. I wasn't there myself but I've had it from Ludan,' began Row in a whisper, and the tale was told.

Oswald heard it with a kind of speechless horror, all the worse because thoughts of his own mother were still raw like a wound reopened. If Aculf—if anyone—had said such a thing of *his* mother… Oswald's anger seemed to swell hot in his head and tight in his chest.

'He's beaten him, badly I think, and locked him in the cowshed. Perhaps there's nothing you can do, sir, but I wanted you to know.'

'I *will* do something! I don't know what, but something. I swear it.'

Row slipped away to the fields before anyone could see him, and Oswald made his way to the cowshed door. He put his finger through the hole in the wooden lock but couldn't reach the pegs to slide the lock open. It wouldn't even heed him when he shook it and kicked the wall of the shed.

'Brinin,' he said in a low voice, his mouth against the door. 'It's me, Oswald. Can you hear me?'

There was stirring from within the shed and something like a stifled moan. Oswald shook the door again, harder this time. Wasn't a moan from Brinin like a cry of anguish from anyone else? Aculf would be sorry. He would *make* him sorry.

'Yes. I can hear you.'

'Listen, Brinin. I can't get you out now, but I'll think of something. My father's back and I have to go to him, but I'll come back later, whenever I can. Aculf will be sorry for this!'

'No need.'

'I *will* come.'

Oswald heard a sound behind him and turned to see Aculf walking towards the shed. But he didn't care. Not about Aculf, nor his father, nor about what trouble he would bring on himself if he tried to help Brinin. He felt such rage at the sight of Aculf, such loathing, that he couldn't care about any of that.

'Oswald Child,' snapped Aculf. 'No one is to go near the shed. I have told you before that your father would not like you to hinder me in my work. If I were to tell him…'

But Aculf could not quell him with that weapon. Not today. Oswald drew himself up and took a step towards Aculf.

'I will remember this,' he said.

'You know nothing of what he did. Had you been there to witness what—'

'The day is coming when you will answer to me, and you will find that I have not forgotten.'

The sight of the stick in Aculf's hand stirred in Oswald a reckless rage. Hadn't Row told him what Aculf had done? Hadn't he heard Brinin moan? He couldn't hurt Aculf, who had done this to his friend, but he could do the next best thing. He snatched the stick from Aculf, snapped it in two and flung the pieces at the workreeve's feet.

'Tell my father about that, if you wish!' Then he turned and strode away.

Still seething, but with a boldness that felt utterly new to him, Oswald went to the hall to find his father and Edith. Let Aculf threaten him! Let him do as he liked, then wish he hadn't when Oswald was his lord! Edith seemed to be watching him rather anxiously as he sat down. Likely she had heard what Aculf had done. Didn't she always hear everything? But she didn't know that her brother would make him wish this day had never dawned. Oswald would tell her as soon as he could.

'Ludan has taken the horses now, Father,' said Oswald, careful not to meet his sister's eye. 'Is there anything you want me to do before I go to Brother Wilfred?'

'No, Oswald, I have everything I need. I'll wait here until Aculf comes. Why don't you eat something now? I will tell you about the

Witan later when the men have gathered. Sad to say, everything with the Danes is as we thought.'

'Yes, Father. We will all be ready for them.'

Oswald knew Edith would follow him when he had eaten and taken his leave. He saw her get up from the bench when he went to fetch his waxboard and writing-seax. She came up behind him as he walked to the church and put her arm through his.

'You've heard about Brinin, haven't you?' she whispered.

'The time will come when Aculf will rue this day, and I have told him as much.' Why whisper? He didn't care who heard him. And Edith needn't look so shocked.

'You said that to him? Father won't like that.'

'So be it, but Aculf will be sorry, however long I have to wait.'

But fear followed Oswald into the church. He was still angry and bold when he sat down, too angry and bold to put his mind to learning. Brother Wilfred's voice seemed far away and hard to understand. Oswald sat, trying to listen, while fear crept nearer until it caught him and drove the boldness out. What kind of fool had he been? Warning Aculf was bold. Throwing his stick at him was madness! He might as well have thrown a stick at his father and saved Aculf the trouble of bearing the tale. The end of it would be the same. He knew how his father would see it. Hadn't his father warned him not to find fault with the man whom *he* had made workreeve? Oswald had forgotten that in his anger, but his father never forgot. And he had dared Aculf to tell him! Aculf was no doubt telling him even now, telling him in that way of his to make things look much worse than they had been. His father would be waiting for him when Brother Wilfred sent him away, and there would be anger to bear. What had he been thinking?

'Oswald, are you going to listen to me today? Or will you sit and wriggle like a small boy?' Surely it was a bad day indeed, if even Brother Wilfred was stern with him. 'I don't believe you have heard anything I have said, and you seem to have forgotten everything I taught you yesterday.'

And now he had thrown away his last hope of a good word. His father, freshly back, wouldn't even reach sunset still happy with him.

'I'm sorry, sir,' sighed Oswald. 'I can't seem to keep my mind on it today. I'm worried about something.'

'Wisdom is there for the asking, my boy,' said Brother Wilfred, less sternly but with a keen look. Could the monk read thoughts as well as books? Oswald had often wondered. 'I don't think we will go far with Latin today. You may go now.'

So Oswald went away from the church down-hearted, without so much as a shadow of his boldness left to go with him.

SHED

A long spear of light came through a hole high up where the cowshed roof met the wall. Brinin sat on the floor and watched the specks of dust that floated in and out of the light like so many little stars. House martins were nesting in the eaves on the outer side of the hole, and he could hear their twittering and scuffling as they came and went from their nest. They made flickers in the spear of light so that it seemed to quiver.

He was still feeling rather dazed by the ferocity with which Aculf's rage had fallen upon him. He had known what must follow as he had begun to speak—he was no stranger to Aculf's stick—but it had been unlike all the other times. The simmering warfare between them had boiled over and now he felt the burn of it. And he wouldn't stop feeling it for days. He moaned a little as he shifted in the darkness. He didn't mind moaning now that he was alone with the house martins and the spear of light. He could still taste blood in his mouth from where his face had hit the ground. Under the hailstorm of blows, he had come very near to crying out or groaning aloud and had only kept his silence by crawling into a kind of darkness inside his own head. He had kept it, but there was no need to now. No need to try. He didn't think he could do it now anyway.

There were no cows in the shed—they were all out to graze—but they had left their smell behind. How long would Aculf leave him there? It was likely for the best that he didn't have to work. Brinin hadn't even tried to move from where he had fallen when Aculf had shoved him in and slammed the door. It was easier to sit in the muck and straw and whatever else was strewn over the cowshed floor. But his lips were beginning to feel sticky as thirst dried them and the blood stiffened, and he would be hungry before long.

He couldn't blame Oswald for being angry, too angry even to be fearful. Brinin had heard him talking to Aculf. What had Oswald meant when he had told Aculf to tell his father? Tell him what? Whatever it was, Oswald would likely rue it when Aculf did. Though even Oswald, his boldness gone, would not need to rue Edrich Thegn's homecoming as much as Brinin himself would. Aculf would have the tale ready, his own part in it well cleaned and Brinin's blackened. Edrich Thegn would be angry, and then… That was too hard a thought when he was already so sore.

Another flutter from the house martins, another quiver in the spear of light. It was strange to sit and listen to the sounds of work outside, where all was daylight and fresh air. Voices were drawing nearer, as two speakers walked towards the shed. One of them was Ludan. Brinin knew the slow, deep way he spoke.

'He drove him too far,' he heard Ludan say. 'It's no wonder he lost his temper.'

That's what they all thought, that he had lost his temper. It had likely looked that way. Only a fool of a slave would speak as he had done in cold blood. He had spoken angrily—he had never been so angry in his life—but not hotly, not without thinking. He had chosen to speak knowing what must come of it. He had wanted to say it more than he wanted to stay unwounded. It had been no flight when he had turned and walked away. He had been speaking to Aculf with his back. Now, aching in the darkness, he still couldn't feel sorry for it, though it was better that Row had been in the fields and not there to see it all. Who wants to stand helpless and hear his mother called a dog, then watch his brother kicked and beaten like one? Row must have heard of it by now, but nothing could be done about that.

The thirst was so dogged that even his spit was beginning to forsake him now. He needed to go into his head, somewhere deep inside, away from the thirst, the throbbing soreness and the anger that kept flooding back when he thought of what Aculf had said.

There was such a place. It was one of those unseen parts of his mind where he could go to relive the unforgotten. It had been a day much like this one, clouded with anger and the smart of a beating, a little one but sore enough for a child. Then too he had sat in the darkness, but the light had come, not from a hole in the wall, but from the fire in his own hearth. He had not been alone. His mother and Row had been with him. And his mother's voice, soothing in the firelight, had borne him away from his troubles to a far-off land.

'Far away from here, much further than where the fields meet the forest and even further than the other side of the forest where you have never been, there lies a great mountain. The mountain is much higher than the hills behind our hut. It is covered with tall dark trees that never shed their leaves, even when the snow comes. It used to be that the top of the mountain was always hidden by cloud. Well, it looked like cloud, but it was smoke, for what do you think lived in a cave at the top of the mountain?'

'Was it a dragon?' Brinin had whispered.

'Yes, a dragon! A huge dragon, very fierce. With a swipe of its mighty tail, it could knock down ten men at once. In one breath from its mouth came fire enough to burn down the whole village. It had great eyes, which seemed to see all ways at once and were as yellow as the spearwort that grows along the riverbank. Everyone in that land lived in fear because they never knew when the dragon would come. Many brave warriors had climbed to the top of the mountain to kill the dragon, but none had ever come down again.'

'So no one could kill the dragon?' Brinin had said, with a thrill that seemed to be both glee and fright, all the smart and anger already forgotten.

'There was still one warrior left, and he was the bravest and cleverest of them all. He was very tall and strong. His hair was fiery like the flame in the hearth, and behind his eyes he kept hidden all the deep thoughts he never spoke.'

'Like my hair?'

'Yes, and like your eyes too. And this warrior even had the same name as you: Bruni.'

And Brinin had breathed a happy sigh and had known it would be a good tale. His mother had always kept the name 'Bruni' for the best tales, and the best always came on the worst of days.

'So Bruni took his sword and his spear and began the long, long climb up the mountain. And when he drew near the dragon's cave…'

Back in the cowshed, the firelight and the sound of his mother's voice in his head dwindled away. It didn't work any more. He was too thirsty, too sore and too old for tales to make it any better. The thoughts of his mother made what Aculf had said of her worse, and Brinin was glad to have spoken to him as he did. It was worth the pain that had followed. And now there was nothing to be done but suffer it and wait for Aculf to let him out.

OATH

It wasn't long before Oswald came upon his father, talking to Aculf outside the hall door. It was as he had feared. Aculf had wasted no time. Oswald couldn't hear what they were saying but he didn't need to. Aculf, somewhat red in the face, spoke warmly, waving his hands to strengthen his words, and pointed at the cowshed more than once. Hadn't it been at the cowshed where Oswald had thrown the stick? Edrich Thegn listened without a word. He stood with his arms folded across his chest, one hand raised to his beard, and with such a look of unmistakable anger that Oswald felt rather sick. He knew that look, that way of standing as though his father was holding the anger in until he had tamed it enough to let it out. Perhaps he should slip away somewhere to give his father time to cool a little, not that that would make it much better. But Oswald wavered too long. Aculf took his leave, and Edrich turned and caught sight of his son.

'Come here, Oswald,' called Edrich. What had happened to the frown? It softened into a smile as soon as he saw him. 'Brother Wilfred didn't keep you long today. From what I've been hearing it looks like we will make a thegn of you yet. Now I want to…'

What *had* Aculf been saying? To be ready for anger but meet unheard-of praise was so bewildering that Oswald barely heard what his father was telling him. Aculf mustn't have told his father what he had done. They must have been talking about Brinin, though that was worry enough. But *why* hadn't Aculf told his father about the broken stick?

'…so I will do that now, and we will talk about the rest later.'

Oswald was still staring after his father when a sudden hand on his arm startled him. He turned and saw that Edith had come upon him unseen.

'Oswald,' she whispered, leading him away from the hall. 'I need to tell you something. Please come with me somewhere where no one will hear.'

There were more ill tidings written on Edith's face than there was Latin on his waxboard. How could a day begin like any other, then gather so much unforeseen trouble? They found somewhere hidden, a little into the forest where the threeleaf and stitchwort were scattered white throughout the grass.

'It's Brinin, isn't it?' asked Oswald as they sat down. 'I saw Aculf talking to Father, and Father was angry.'

'I heard Aculf tell Father what Brinin did today.' Edith's eyes were very bright. One blink would be enough to make the tears overflow. 'Father is going to sell him, Oswald! It was Aculf who thought of it. He said that Brinin is bad for the village, and Father says he'll do it.'

Oswald's mouth suddenly felt too dry for speech and something hard seemed to be sitting in his throat. It wouldn't shift when he swallowed.

'When?'

'Soon. As soon as he can.'

Oswald shut his eyes and tried again to gulp away the hard lump. If his father had settled on it, then he would do it. He had never been a man to hop about from thought to thought. He always did what he said he would. Brinin would be torn from his brother and sent far away among strangers who would care nothing for him. There would be no coming back. It mustn't be done! But it would be. Oswald could do nothing about it, even if he had dared to try. He had sworn to Row that he would help. Had he bound himself with an oath he couldn't keep? He was no friend, no friend if his word was worth nothing.

'We can't do nothing, Oswald. This time one of us *must* speak to Father. Perhaps if we begged him not to—'

'When have you ever known Father to say one thing and do another? When has begging ever helped?'

'But this time, Oswald...'

This time. Time. Oswald suddenly brought his hand down hard on his waxboard, breaking the wax. He ran his finger along the crack.

'Time. I've thought of something! Perhaps it won't do any good, but it may be our only hope. Don't say anything to Father, Edith. Leave it to me.'

Oswald's mind was running faster than his feet as he rushed away. He didn't need to beg his father to do what he never did. He only needed him to wait. If his father were to be slow to keep his word—still with a mind to keep it, but lingering over it a little—then that would give Oswald time to get Brinin away to the minster. He could ask his father to wait. Aculf had said nothing of what he had done. His father was pleased with him. That was unlikely to last, so if there was ever a time to ask his father for anything, it was now.

For once Brinin would be the hard one to talk to. He was the one whom Oswald would likely have to beg. When Brinin set his mind on something it was no easy thing to shift him, and he had been so unwilling to even think about flight. But that was all because of Row. What if it was Row who asked him to go? What if Row were to go with him? He wouldn't be leaving Row to be blamed then. Brinin had to run away. What other way was there to keep them together?

Row was in the fields with Garulf, driving the oxen as they strained to pull the plough through the earth. His shoulders sagged as though he was feeling the weight more than the oxen did. He always seemed to see the good in any day, but he was working without a smile. Oswald felt a twinge of guilt when he saw him. Worry for his brother was a heavy burden for Row to bear, and here he had come to heap on something heavier.

'Row, can anyone else do this for a while?' asked Oswald as he ran up to the plough. 'I need to talk to you quickly before Aculf comes.'

'Go with Oswald Child, Row,' said Garulf, beckoning Eawig who was struggling towards them with a bucket of water for the oxen. 'It will be good for the boy to work more with the plough.'

'Everything's worse than I thought,' said Oswald, when he and Row were alone. 'But I think there is something we can do, so please don't lose hope.'

Row had never seemed more like Brinin than he did then. Oswald saw sorrow and fear in his eyes as he warned him of the likelihood of losing his last kinsman. But Row kept a tight hold on them, so they wouldn't overcome him.

'I spoke to Brinin about this not long ago,' Oswald went on. 'I knew things with Aculf wouldn't get any better, but I didn't think they would get worse so soon. I think he should leave, run away, and I will help him go. There's a minster I've heard of where they would likely welcome him. Then when I'm thegn, I'll call him back and give him his freedom. I told him all this before, but he wouldn't even think about it. He doesn't want to leave you behind. He told me that you would be blamed if he fled. He's likely right about that.

'But he *must* flee. If he's sold, you will never see each other again. He might be better off somewhere else, away from Aculf, but it could as easily be worse, and there would be nothing we could do about it. We wouldn't even know if he was dead or alive.'

'And if he were caught?'

'Then it would be bad. But listen. If we're careful, I think we could stop anyone from knowing where he had gone. Please don't tell Brinin this—you know how he won't let anyone help him—but I give you my word that I will do everything I can to make sure he isn't caught. But he does need to leave. We need to make him go. You know him better than anyone. Can you talk to him? More than that: would you even go with him?'

'For a slave to flee from his lord...' began Row slowly. He didn't need to say any more. They both knew what it meant. Fear suddenly seemed to crouch beside Oswald, ready to spring. What if his father—if anyone—should overhear them talking about this? 'I'd sooner flee than lose him, sir, and I'd sooner flee and be caught than do nothing. You're right. Brinin won't go without me, but I'm willing to go.'

'This evening I'll speak to my father and ask him to wait until after the harvest before he sells Brinin. Please, pray to God he listens to me. If he does, that will give us enough time to work out how to get you away without you being caught again at once. When everyone's asleep tonight, I'll get a key and take Brinin something to eat. Should I speak to him then?'

'No, sir. Let me talk to him when I can.'

'I know it won't be easy, Row, but I swear to you—'

'Oswald Child!' Row cut in as though to stop the oath in its tracks, as though to stop Oswald from speaking without wisdom. 'You do know that if anyone finds out you have helped us, it will go badly for you, thegn's son or not? Your father will be very angry.'

Fear put a hand on Oswald's shoulder. He could almost feel its breath by his ear. His father would be more than angry.

'I know,' he said quietly. 'But I *do* swear that I will do all I can. I have given you my word. Leave it all to me and be careful what you say to Brinin.'

TIME

The hall was busy. It was loud, hot and bustling, as a feast was made ready to welcome Edrich Thegn home. There was nothing easier than to lift a loaf of bread here, a chunk of cheese there, and to hide them under his cloak with a flask of ale that no one was likely to miss. Oswald could see that not even Edith knew what he had done as he slipped behind the curtain to his bed. The key would have to wait until later. Getting that would be harder.

The men of Oakdene came at last to eat, listen and talk. Only the greater men gathered, the strong and the worthy, not those too lowly to be heard or seen. Oswald sat among them, watching and listening and wishing the men away so that he and his father could be alone. He tried not to look at Aculf. Every time he caught sight of him, with his buttery smile, the anger simmered up again. Here was Aculf feasting while Brinin sat cold and sore and hungry in the dark. But he had to keep his wits about him that evening. Oswald saw Thurstan eyeing Aculf with such open scorn that it could only have been meant to goad the workreeve. Thurstan knew what Aculf was. Perhaps one day Oswald would see his father look at Aculf with scorn. It was something to hope for.

'Are we to ready ourselves for battle, my lord? I'm sure that every man among us—almost every man among us—' and Thurstan looked at Aculf as he said it, 'has the courage to stand against them.'

Edrich reached out to take more bread, seemingly unaware of Thurstan's sneer. Aculf heard it and reddened, and others heard it too.

'We must, but nothing has changed since I left.' Edrich leaned back in his seat and looked around at the men. 'As yet the Danes have drawn no nearer. When they do, we don't know which way they will come. They could come westwards from East Anglia, or they could go through Mercia and come on us from the north. We can only wait and be ready.'

'And the tidings we have heard of East Anglia, my lord, are they true?' asked Rædwald.

'As far as we know, yes, and worse too. The harrying of East Anglia must be a warning to us. This is what we in Wessex are facing if we do not withstand them. Northumbria has fallen to them. Mercia has fallen. East Anglia has fallen. Wessex alone is left. The King and Ælfred the Ætheling are ready to do battle with them when they come, and we too must be ready. Some among us here will no doubt fall, but we must stand against them or Wessex will be lost.'

It was all Danes and death, Witan and warcraft, the talk a little too heavy for a feast. Despite the mead and the ale, few were laughing as they left the hall. Oswald never took his eyes off his father, never let his ears stray far from Edrich's words. Tonight of all nights he must see his father's mind and choose his own words wisely. He had one chance, only one, to hit this target and he mustn't let the arrow fly wide.

'Surely, Father, there are no better men in all of Wessex,' said Oswald, when the last of the men had left for his own hearth. His gut tightened as stillness settled on the hall. The time had come.

'True. They are all brave men, and it is no light thing to lead them. It will fall to you one day. While I think of it, I want to see how your warcraft has come along while I was away.'

Oswald drew a deep breath and tried to crush the dread that such a thought always stirred in him. He would worry about that tomorrow. Now he had to draw another kind of bow. Fear seemed to be flitting about somewhere in the shadows, but he kept his eyes and mind on his father only.

'Father,' he said, as though it were the smallest of things he spoke of. 'Is it true that you are going to sell the slave Brinin?'

'I am. What of it?'

'I… I heard what he did earlier today, while I was riding out to meet you.'

'He's likely rueing it now. Aculf has seen to that. What the young fool was thinking, I don't know, but Aculf tells me he has become even worse than before, unbiddable, and has shown that he is not to be trusted.'

Beneath the table, Oswald was clenching his fists. Aculf was to blame for this, for all of it, and one day *he* would be the one rueing it.

'Yes, Father. I have heard Aculf speaking of it.' Better to turn the talk away from Aculf before he said what was in his mind. 'Brinin is a hard worker—I can say that for him. I saw it myself while you were away. He's very strong and works more quickly than anyone else. He's a good ploughman. But you must do what is best for Oakdene, as you always say. Will you wait until after the harvest before you sell him, so as not to lose his work at the busiest time of year? After that, there will be time enough to find a new slave before the next harvest comes round, or even before the ploughing.'

'I hadn't thought to, but there is wisdom in what you say!' Edrich looked rather pleased. 'Perhaps I will do that. What are another three or four months after all? Aculf can watch him carefully during that time, and I'll speak to him myself in the morning. I've often wondered how you will lead this place after I'm gone, but I can see you are learning how to think about things.'

'I will do my best to learn more from you, sir,' said Oswald meekly. 'Please, Father, may I go to bed now? I am tired this evening.'

'Yes, yes. Off you go then. Goodnight, my boy.'

Oswald's heart was racing as he walked to his bed. His father had listened and would wait for even longer than he had hoped. He had never shot a straighter arrow in his life! Three or four months would be long enough, more than long enough! He had time to breathe now, to think, to keep his word.

But there wasn't yet time to sleep. Sitting on his bed, Oswald turned his mind to the key. He only knew of two hinge keys that could open the cowshed door. One Aculf kept with him. The other was in a small chest beside his father's bed. Had it been hidden in a wolf's lair, Oswald could not have been less eager to fetch it. But he had told Brinin that he would come, and this was the only way to do it. He heard his father leave the table to go to bed. In the darkness Oswald felt beside his bed for a candle, wrapped up the bread, cheese and ale in his cloak and waited.

He waited for what felt like a long time—he dared not go too soon—then he picked up his bundle and began to feel his way through the hall to where his father slept. He stopped by his father's curtain and listened. Was his father asleep? Had he come too soon? He could hear his father's breathing, steady, slow. Was he daring to do such a thing? That same morning he wouldn't have believed it of himself. He laid his bundle on the floor, picked up his courage and slipped past his father's curtain.

Crouching down, Oswald felt for the chest. He rested his fingers on it, still listening to his father. With trembling hands, he carefully lifted the lid and reached inside. And his father stirred and Oswald froze. He would have darted away, but he was too scared to move. If his father should hear, should find him there in the darkness... Edrich snored, and to Oswald it was like such sweet song he could have wept for joy. His hand closed round the key, and he stole away as quickly as he could, stopping only to light his candle in the embers of the fire. Then he crept through the shadows to the cowshed door.

'Brinin,' he whispered as he went inside. 'Are you awake?'

'I told you you didn't need to come.'

'And I told you I would.' Oswald carefully closed the door behind him.

Brinin was lying on his side on the floor, propping himself up with his elbow. The candlelight fell on him, on his swollen lip, on the dark bruise on his cheek. Brinin's face had never been a loud one—it whispered now and then to those who knew him well—but it spoke his pain quite loudly as he sat up. Oswald saw it. He would remember it. He would not forget.

'Are you hungry?' asked Oswald, unwrapping the food from his cloak.

'Yes. Thirsty too.'

Oswald handed him the flask, and he took a long drink.

'How did you get a key?' Brinin asked.

'I took it from a chest beside my father's bed while he was sleeping.'

Brinin raised his eyebrows. There was nothing much to laugh about, but Oswald couldn't help it. He had taken a key from beside his father's bed. What a thought!

'At least, I think that's what I did,' he said. 'It might have been a dream—that seems more likely. Here's some bread and cheese. You should eat.'

Brinin ate so slowly and gingerly that Oswald couldn't bear to watch. No more laughing. It was hard to sit there knowing what he did yet saying nothing, to know that Brinin was so unaware of what was waiting for him. But Row was right. It was better that he told him. Likely there was already enough to keep Brinin awake that night.

'I thought he would let me out when the cows came in,' Brinin said at last. 'Where did they put them?'

'In the old storehouse.'

'It's small. They'll have a bad night.'

'Aculf doesn't care about that as long as you have a bad night.'

Not such a bad night now that he had eaten. His father had said he would speak to Brinin in the morning. Surely he would let him out then. Why keep him locked away any longer?

'I heard what you said to Aculf earlier,' said Brinin.

'And I heard about what you said to him too. Aculf has heard a lot today. Thurstan was goading him at evening-meat and as much as called him a coward to his face.'

'He won't be any the better for hearing it.'

'Listen, Brinin. Aculf told my father what you did earlier, and he was very angry. Who knows what Aculf told him? Not the truth. My father is going to speak to you about it himself tomorrow. I don't think he'll punish you again, though. That's not his way. With my father, it's always better to listen and to say as little as you can, but you're good at that.'

Oswald was growing a little restless. There was still one more dreaded thing to be done that night.

'Are you done with the flask?' he grimaced. 'I have to put the key back. I'd sooner go after one of those dragons we used to fight.'

'It was good of you to come.'

'I think my father will let you out of here in the morning. Whatever happens, I'll try to speak to you again soon. I'd better go.'

MORNING

T he sun was too low in the sky to make the spear of light,
but the house martins were scuffling and chirruping in
their nest. Brinin knew the morning had come at last from
the chinks of light coming through the gaps in the walls and round
the edge of the door. He could hear folk stirring around outside,
beginning the day's work, but no one came to let him out. He was
tired. He ached all over, and that and the cold and the hard floor
had plundered him of any sleep he might have had. He was
glad that Oswald had come. He didn't like to think about how
hungry and thirsty he'd be now if he hadn't. He was hungry again
as it was. And thirsty. And something was hammering in his head.
He sat, leaning against the wall, and waited.

'Shall I unlock the shed and let him out, my lord?' Brinin heard
Aculf on the other side of the door and Edrich Thegn with him, it
seemed. He drew in his breath in pain as he stood up to be ready for
them, one hand on the wall to steady himself.

'I will do so myself, Aculf. I'm sure you have other work to
see to.'

Brinin heard Edrich slide the lock across. The door was flung
open and the cowshed suddenly flooded with morning light. Brinin
blinked, the light stinging his eyes. And when the sting passed and he
could look through the doorway, he saw Edrich Thegn, unsmiling as
he stood and watched him.

'Come out, boy.'

Slowly and stiffly, Brinin walked out of the shed and stood before Edrich.

'You seem to have forgotten that you are a slave,' said Edrich sternly. 'You are not free to walk away, or to speak your mind, or to defy those who have been put over you. You need do only one thing: heed without a word unless one is asked of you.'

Had it not been for Edrich's eye upon him, Brinin could almost have laughed that he, of all people, was being told to heed without a word. Perhaps that was enough for Edrich Thegn, but Brinin had already learned that it wasn't enough for Aculf. He had defied Aculf once, only once, and now all the wordless heeding was forgotten.

'I am your lord. I may bid you as I see fit and punish you as I see fit. Do you think that you are free to withstand me?'

'No, my lord,' said Brinin. He could almost hear Aculf's cleaned-up tale, with little or nothing of the truth in it. Nothing about Aculf's thirst to find some misdeed to beat him for. Nothing about the axe that was never there. Nothing about the goading. Nothing about calling his mother a dog.

'I see. Why then do you think that you are free to withstand the bidding or punishment of the one I have put over you? What he does, he does in my name. You will listen to him, heed him, fear him as you would me. What made you proud enough to think you could do anything else? You're a slave, and I won't have a proud slave! Would you have spoken to me the way you spoke to Aculf yesterday?'

'No, my lord.' Edrich Thegn didn't seem to know that Aculf was not the same kind of man he was, and that he would be wise to keep his name away from him. If Edrich Thegn wanted Aculf to wield his name, then he ought to know him better. He ought to know him as Brinin knew him. Perhaps such thoughts were pride in a slave. Then he would have to be a bad slave.

'I thought not. If you flout my word, believe me, I will be very stern with you, and you will wish you had not. I am not even sure that there can be a place for you here at Oakdene. It is likely that I will not let you stay here, and lead others to do as you have done.

I will be watching you carefully, and if you displease me in any way, I will know what to do.'

Brinin drew a deep breath. Surely Edrich wasn't threatening to send him away? He had known that Oswald was too hopeful when he said that Edrich Thegn wouldn't punish him again. This was worse than punishment. How could he heed a warning against something he could do nothing about? How could he please him when it was Aculf he listened to?

'You have wasted enough of everyone's time. Go to the fields now and join in the ploughing. My son tells me that you know how to work hard. Let me hear of you doing it. And forget nothing I have said to you.'

'Yes, my lord.'

As steadily as he could and without looking at anyone, Brinin left Edrich and made his way down to the fields. Back throbbing, head pounding and feeling as though the ground he set his feet on wasn't always where it should be, he walked slowly. But he did walk. He would show Edrich Thegn that heeding without a word was something he knew and did every day, whatever Aculf had said.

Aculf had not been standing near enough to hear Edrich talk to Brinin, but he saw everything. He saw Edrich go back to the hall and Brinin as he walked away. He watched him carefully, then took a step to follow him. But he stopped suddenly when a hand fell heavily on his shoulder.

'Leave that boy alone,' said a soft voice. Aculf swung round and saw Thurstan standing behind him.

'What has this to do with you?' He thrust Thurstan's hand away from him. 'I oversee Edrich Thegn's slaves, not you!'

'Indeed, and I don't mind you beating a slave who's earned it, but that boy's had enough and you don't know when to stop. I think I rather like him. He seems to understand you.'

'Thurstan, I'm warning you. Edrich Thegn has left it to me to—'

'Warning me? Warning me of what? Are you thinking of running to Edrich Thegn with some tale about me? I wonder what he would say if I were to tell him how you goaded Brinin yesterday. Oh, you thought I didn't know about that? That I'd come too late to see it? Come now, Aculf. You've lived in Oakdene all your life. I *was* too late, but you know how folk talk. I wonder if Edrich Thegn would be pleased with you if he knew everything. He's a better man than you are. I know him well. Men come to know each other when they shed their blood side by side on the battlefield, but you wouldn't know anything about that. If there is to be any warning, I'll do it. I warn you to leave that boy alone. His only fault is having the wisdom to see you for what you are.'

Thurstan patted Aculf on the back in mock friendliness, then left without giving him time to say a word.

Brinin saw the glance that Row and Garulf shared as he came towards them. He saw Garulf's frown and the way Row's jaw and shoulders tightened. Perhaps he looked almost as bad he felt. He could do nothing about his face, but a stronger step might hide the rest if only his legs would heed him. He stumbled as he reached them and placed a hand upon the plough to steady himself.

'So Aculf let you out?' Row said slowly, too slowly.

Row wasn't asking—Brinin knew that. He was shielding him from what was truly in his mind. Why had he been such a fool as to stumble with Row there to see it? He hadn't meant to.

'Edrich Thegn did and sent me down here to work. I think I need to eat.' His words were steady at least.

Brinin watched as Garulf beckoned Eawig and sent him to fetch some food and drink from his mother. He kept his hand on the plough. He wouldn't make the same mistake twice.

'You can't work today,' said Row.

'I must. I'll be better when I've eaten.' And slept. And when enough days had gone by for his body to learn to stop aching. But Row and Garulf need not know that. Strange how even the field was shifting slightly under his feet. That wasn't helping his wayward legs. No doubt it would pass.

Row grabbed him by the arm as Brinin felt his legs suddenly give way. He steadied himself yet again and hated Aculf for bringing him so low that his body wouldn't do what his mind wanted.

'You *can't* work today,' said Row, looking much as their mother sometimes had on the bad days.

'I *must* work. You don't understand. I'm tired, that's all.' He couldn't leave Edrich Thegn and disobey him straightaway. Not with that threat hanging over him. Not when Aculf was bound to come soon. He had seen him watching when Edrich Thegn was speaking to him.

'You'll do as you're told!' said Row through shut teeth.

'Eat first, Brinin,' said Garulf firmly. He was looking at Brinin, but he reached out and put his hand on Row's arm. 'After that, we'll see if you can work. When Eawig comes back, I'll ask him to stand and watch out for Aculf. Stay near the plough and it will be easy for you to stand up and seem like you're at work if Aculf comes.'

Then he knew that he had to heed them because he saw in both their eyes that they would make him if he didn't choose to. And there were two of them and only one of him. The food did help a little, but it was the kind of day that was hard to remember well afterwards. He passed it foggily—sometimes standing, more often sitting—near the work without doing it.

Aculf didn't come. Brinin was ready for him—more ready the longer he waited—but he didn't see Aculf or even hear him. Only as the sun began to set, and Aculf blew his horn to bid them unyoke the oxen and rest from work, did Brinin see him far off. And he was gone long before they reached him.

Brinin was more than weary as he dropped himself onto the fleeces in the corner where he slept. It hurt, but he didn't care. He didn't care that he was hungry again. He drew his cloak around him. Row was kindling a fire and their nights together were slipping away. How could he tell Row that? Where were the words? All scattered in his head. He couldn't think them, couldn't say them, couldn't hear them over the crackle of the sticks. In the morning. He'd tell him in the morning. The fire felt warm on his face, so good, the smoke... In the morning.

FURROWS

Sleep was kind to Brinin. When he woke the earth was unstirring beneath him, and his legs would do his bidding again. With a steadier step he could meet Row's eye and say that he was better, and choose not to see his brother's look of disbelief. He knew how to set his teeth and drive the plough with aching back. It would pass. The wounds would dull like all the others and make way for new ones.

The coulter and the ploughshare cut through the earth, a deep furrow stretching behind them. The plough left scars that the land would never heal from. It drove one clod of earth away from its fellow, so they would never meet again. Brinin's thoughts were very straight in the cool light of morning. Now that he had slept and the first shock of Edrich Thegn's threat had passed, the coming wound stung more than the others, smarting before the blow had fallen. It was all the worse for not knowing when it might come. Today? Tomorrow? With the harvest? When winter darkened the sky? He could see himself shrinking from it each day, as he had never shrunk from Aculf's stick. Aculf had at last found the worst of weapons—he knew it was Aculf's weapon and not Edrich Thegn's—and there was no shield against it. Not for himself, not for Row. He couldn't shield Row from this. He could only warn him to strengthen himself and be ready.

'What did Edrich Thegn say to you yesterday?' asked Row, as they moved along the field. 'It was more than just sending you down to work, wasn't it?'

'I'm to fear Aculf as I would him. He said he will watch me and if I displease him, he will send me away—sell me, I think. I think he meant it for mercy, warning me to teach me to be better. But he won't *watch* me. He'll ask Aculf and hear whatever Aculf wants him to hear. Aculf will make sure he is displeased, whatever I do. I'll be gone from here. Soon. Who knows where? Even if I were to give Aculf what he wants and cringe before him like some of the others do, it might be too late now. And I don't know if I could. There's nothing we can do about this.'

He hadn't thought that Row would weep—they had both learned that it didn't help—though he knew that by telling him he was sharing the wound, stinging him with it too. He had thought there would be sorrow, the unspoken kind they both understood. But Brinin hadn't foreseen knowledge.

'I know.' And that was all Row said, then began to turn the oxen to plough back across the field again.

'You know? How do you know?'

'Oswald told me, while you were still in the cowshed. Edrich Thegn *was* going to sell you soon, straightaway, but Oswald went to his father and asked him to wait.'

It seemed that these days had been full of the unforeseen: he himself speaking truth and Oswald forgetting to be fearful. Was anything the way he knew it any more?

'Edrich Thegn *will* hear whatever Aculf wants him to. And when he does, you'll be sold. Aculf won't stop until you are. You can't cringe any more than you can fly, and it has already gone too far for that to help. But there may be something else we can do. Oswald thinks you should run away.'

'I told him before I wouldn't do it!' Brinin laughed bitterly. 'And what's the good of it now? I'm going to be sold! Either way, I'll still be gone!'

'I think he's right and I'm going with you.'

'No! I can't let you do that! If you're caught—'

'Let me? I'm not asking you to let me. Keep the plough straight. You're swerving off to the side. I've already settled it in my mind. You'll most likely have to leave whatever happens. Either we take the risk, I go with you and we stay together, or you leave on your own, and we never see each other again. And you could end up a thrall to a worse man than Aculf. There *are* worse men. You've never been anywhere else but here. You haven't seen what I've seen. This is not a hard choice, Bruni. And Oswald thinks we might not be caught.'

'No, Row. You wouldn't think of running away if it weren't for me. Your life isn't so bad here, even if you are a thrall. Aculf leaves you alone. And if we were caught… We would be caught, you know—Oswald's a fool if he thinks we wouldn't be—if we were caught, then I wouldn't so much mind what they would do to me, as what they would do to you.'

'I've already settled on it.' Row's voice had a stubborn edge to it, and that was the last proof that nothing was as Brinin knew it. 'You're the only one of my kinsmen left alive, and I'm not going to lose you too. Not without a fight. Oswald has thought of a way to stop us from being caught.'

'And if he was found helping us? Doesn't he know how angry his father would be? I can't let my brother and my friend do something like this. Don't you see that?'

'Things have changed since you last spoke to Oswald about it. He's coming to talk to you again, and you must listen to what he has to say.'

'I'll listen, but I won't go. I won't let either of you do this. It's madness!'

Oswald did come, as the evening called the men from field to fireside. He met them at the beech tree, dark and shadowy in the dimming light.

'I'm not going, Oswald,' said Brinin, as soon as his friend was near enough to hear him. 'I told you before.'

Oswald didn't answer, though Brinin knew he had heard him. He kept walking as though Brinin had not spoken and sat down on a root facing them.

'The minster I told you about is west of here and perhaps a little south,' began Oswald, leaning towards them in that earnest way of his.

Did Oswald think that Brinin had already yielded, that he could speak thegnlike without a thought that his words might go unheeded? He had a look of his father that evening, and it warned Brinin that this time his friend would not give way to him so readily.

'More than that, I can't tell you yet, but I'll find out. No one will think of you fleeing there. How would two slaves who never leave the village even know there was such a place? Everyone will think you have fled to somewhere you have heard of, like Wintanceaster, to hide among the townsfolk. Not to a small, far-off minster that almost no one knows about. They won't think of it, and I will help you by finding out where it is.'

'We'll leave tracks!' Couldn't Oswald see all the ways for this to go wrong, too many ways to name them all now? 'We'll be caught before a day is over.'

'Not if you're careful. There will be ways to go that will make it hard to follow you. We will think of them. *I* will think of them. Even if you were followed, there is enough forest that way for you to hide. But no one will think that you have gone that way.'

'If your father finds out that you have helped us—'

'Brinin, how will he even know? I can find out where the minster is from Brother Wilfred without my father knowing. And even if Brother Wilfred learned why I was asking, we can trust him.'

'I told you Oswald Child had thought of something, Bruni. You don't want me to be caught or Edrich Thegn to learn that Oswald Child has helped you. Now you can see that neither of those is likely.'

Brinin looked from his brother to his friend. It was beginning to get dark as the sun set, but not too dark for him to see that Row and Oswald sat as one man, a strong man who wouldn't shift until Brinin had weakened. And he did begin to feel weaker, he who had always been more unyielding than either of them.

'You should go back to the hall, Oswald,' said Brinin. 'Your father will be angry if you're late.'

'I'm not going until you've said you'll do it! There's more hope than danger. I've already told you that. Do you think we don't know you? We know you won't do it for yourself. Do it for Row, and for me.'

'Oswald Child is right.' Where Oswald stopped, Row began. One man, one voice. 'If we don't leave together, I lose my brother for good.'

'And I my friend,' said Oswald earnestly. 'But this way, when I am lord of this place I can come for you and give you both your freedom. If I am alive to see it done, I will do it. I swear it. Then you can come back here. Do it for Row. Do it for me. And let me hope for the day you will come back.'

Brinin sat for a long time with his head in his hands. Kinship, friendship, strong bonds that tethered him to them like a plough to the oxen. And they knew it. If they walked he would have to follow behind and cut the furrow the way the oxen went. The two of them were yoked together to pull him along, drag him along if need be. He was weakening, yielding. Kinship, friendship. They drove him to choose danger that came with a small hope, or else bring sure sorrow on the ones he most longed to keep it from.

'Very well then,' he said at last. 'But, Oswald, swear to me that you won't take any needless risks.'

Did Oswald waver then in the darkness, or was it only the moon making a shadow from the quivering leaves?

'There's no need to swear anything. More hope than danger. I'll go back to the hall now.'

FLIGHT

They reaped the hay when the days were heavy with the smells of summer and the air clouded with dust and chaff that caught the light. They spent long days in the meadow with their scythes. They heaped it into great ricks with their forks, and it grew more fallow with each day, more golden in the evening light as they went limb-weary to their hearths. They reaped the hay and Oswald reaped knowledge: where the minster was, the road that would lead there. He gathered it in blade by blade, not too quickly so that Brother Wilfred would not ask him why. He hid his knowledge away where no one would see it. Edith always seemed to be watching him, and this was something she mustn't know. If his father should learn what he was doing—and Oswald knew that he might—then his anger must be borne alone. For Edith to share it would be unthinkable.

Oswald's thoughts ripened with the wheat, filling his head with kernels ready for gathering. He knew at last what he would do, everything that Brinin and even Row must never learn. Oakdene harvested the crops in the long, dry days of late summer when the gold of the grain met the gold of the sky. Oswald harvested his plan and stored everything away like wheat for the winter. Not even a grain was to be left in the field.

Harvest was late starting that year, but when it came Oakdene spent weeks working under a bright sun, with little rain. Then the weather changed. It became sticky, a smell hanging in the air of rain that did not come. It grew so heavy that everyone could feel the weight of it. Then one morning Oswald woke to skies thick with dark clouds. He could feel the storm coming, and before long it was upon them.

He had wanted rain. He had built his plan on the hope of it. But there were still some weeks of the harvest left to run and his father said nothing more about selling Brinin. He'd said nothing about Brinin at all. If Aculf had brought his father a bad word of him then Oswald did not know it. He needed rain, but perhaps it was still too soon for flight. But what if there was no more rain until it was too late? It had begun to ease a little by the afternoon, but Oswald's mind had not. He stood in the doorway of the hall, still wrestling with himself, and stared at the little patch of blue sky that was growing far off to the south.

Then it happened, quickly and without warning, and Oswald knew what he would do. From the doorway, he saw Brinin carrying two large buckets of water. There didn't seem to be anyone else in sight. Aculf came striding towards Brinin, angry, though Oswald couldn't hear what he said. He shoved Brinin roughly and some of the water splashed to the ground. Aculf raised his stick and struck Brinin hard across the shoulders, once, twice, again. Oswald clenched his fists. He couldn't go this time. He must say nothing, do nothing as though he hadn't seen. To anger Aculf with his father near at hand to hear of it might be the deathwound to everything he had thought of. He mustn't let anything harm his plan now. Neither Brinin nor Aculf had seen him watching them, and he stepped back into the shadows to make sure they wouldn't.

Aculf left Brinin and walked towards the hall. He was near the doorway when he met his wife, Sægyth. Oswald, still unseen, could hear what Aculf said to her.

'I've had enough of him! Nothing can tame his pride, and I have borne with it long enough. Edrich Thegn will hear of it.'

Oswald watched them walk away through the rain. He clutched at the doorframe, his mind reeling at the knowledge that what he had thought of for so long was about to begin. There was no time to lose. He had the rain he had hoped for and he knew what it would mean when Aculf spoke to his father. His father had warned Brinin and he never warned without doing what he said. Oswald hadn't thought that they might flee at the height of harvest. He had hoped for another few weeks at least. But there was no time for that now. They must leave that same night, or it might be too late.

Almost at once, Oswald went down to the fields to find Row. Perhaps his face spoke his thoughts too loudly. On seeing him, Row quickly looked about him, then picked up a bundle of wheat and carried it away from the others.

'You must leave tonight,' whispered Oswald as soon as they were alone.

'So soon, sir? The harvest won't be in for some weeks.'

'I overheard Aculf talking. He's going to speak to my father about Brinin again. You know what that means. If you don't go now, it might be too late. And tonight's a good night. Don't ask me to tell you why.'

'I won't ask, sir. If Brinin isn't to know whatever it is you're going to do, then it's likely better that I don't.'

More hope than danger, he had told Brinin, to quell his misgivings and make him yield. And there was hope for Brinin and Row: hope that they would reach the minster, hope that Aculf had beaten Brinin for the last time. More hope for them than danger. As to the danger, Row was right. It was better that neither he nor Brinin knew too much.

'If you have food, take it with you, and I'll leave more in a hole under one of the roots of the beech tree—Brinin will know the one—and a knife. Can you shoot? I know you're forbidden to now, but I wondered if you'd learned before.'

'My father taught me a little when I was young. It was a long time ago, but I might remember with a bow in my hand.'

'I'll leave a bow and some arrows there too. I shouldn't, but you can't go so far with no weapons, and you won't look like slaves if you have them. I'll leave some money. It isn't much but it's all I've got, and you may need it.'

'Thank you, sir.'

'Go past the horsehouse and cowshed first, then back behind the church and the hall again. I know it's a strange way to go, when your hut is nearer the beech tree, but that way any tracks you leave will mingle with the others. Then get what I've left for you and go up into the hills. Leave as soon as you think everyone is sleeping. Don't stop tonight. It will be moonlit so you should see well enough. Keep going for as long as you can. Don't forget what I told you. Once you're over the hills go south until you find the western road, then after two or three days ask someone for Wielea. The minster is near the hills beyond it. You won't need to go so quickly after the first day or two, but keep away from farms and villages until you're well away from here. I know it's more dangerous to sleep outside, but if you stop to rest anywhere, they'll want to know who you are and who your lord is. You won't want to tell them, and they won't trust you unless you do. A fire at night should help keep wolves away if there are any.'

'This *is* the only way, isn't it, sir?'

Was Row wavering? It was hard to begin now that the time had come. But they were doing what should not be done to save Brinin from what must not be done.

'I can't think of any other way. You'd better get back to work before anyone sees you've gone. Tell Brinin, and I'll try to speak to him before tonight. Godspeed, Row. I'll do everything I can. And if I'm alive to do it, I will come for you both one day. I swear it.'

It was late in the afternoon before Brinin saw Oswald and later still before he could find any way to speak to him without being seen among the harvesters. Oswald understood him when he beckoned him with his eyes, and they slipped away unseen.

'Row told me it's tonight.' Tonight, stealing upon Brinin suddenly without saying why it had come.

'It has to be.'

'Why?'

'Tonight will be moonlit. It will be easier for you to see in the hills.'

'And easier for anyone else to see us go. The ground is soft from the rain. We'll leave tracks.'

'Not if you go past the horsehouse like I told Row. Any tracks you make will mingle with the others.'

Wasn't that a slight hope to hang so much on, scant when there was so much to be lost?

'If you want moonlight, the moon will shine on other, better nights when the earth will be harder. If we must do it, why not wait? Has your father said more about selling me?'

Oswald looked fearfully over his shoulder before he spoke. There was wisdom enough in a little careful fear. It wouldn't do to be seen or heard, and it wouldn't be long before Aculf learned that Brinin was gone from the fields. Better to speak quickly and be back there.

'Listen, Brinin, I saw Aculf beating you earlier—'

'It wasn't the first time since your father warned me and likely won't be the last.' The sun had risen that morning and would set that evening. Aculf had been angry, and Brinin had felt it. None of them great wonders that couldn't have been foreseen.

'Please, Brinin, *listen* to me! Afterwards, I heard him speaking to his wife. He said he'd had enough of you and that my father would hear of it. My father always does what he says he will. If you don't go tonight, it may be too late.'

Brinin had said that he would try to save them from sorrow by grasping at the small hope they offered him. And because he had said he would, then perhaps it would have to be tonight. He too knew that Edrich Thegn was a man of his word. He would have liked him for it if it had been another kind of word he had spoken.

'I've told Row everything you need to know to get there. Don't worry. More hope than danger. I said that before.' Another look behind him to watch for listening ears. 'I can't stay here any longer, and neither should you.'

'So this is goodbye, then,' said Brinin. Did he speak, or was it someone else? The voice didn't sound like his own somehow.

'Only for a time. I'll bring you home some day.'

A sudden strong grip of the hand, a token of the friendship that should never have been, and Oswald was gone. And Brinin went back to the fields to bend his back there perhaps for the last time.

Brinin had nothing to say by the fire in their hut that night. So much of the unforgotten had crowded in with them that it was almost easier to think of none of it. It was easier not to think of who had sat here or slept there, of who had eaten, spoken and died there. Whatever came of all this, something would be lost that night. If they were caught or not, if they reached the minster or not, nothing could ever be the same again. Would they ever come home as Oswald had said? Was this place even home, though it was the only one Brinin had ever known?

When all was dark and it was likely that the village slept, Row stamped out the fire in their hut, and they readied themselves to leave. They had little to take with them: the clothes they stood in, the old fleeces they lay on. But hanging from Row's belt was a leather pouch that had once been their father's, with their mother's comb inside it.

They met no one as they stole past the hall and other buildings and made their way to the beech tree. They quickly found all that Oswald had left for them and put it in their bundles, then started their slow climb through the darkness. They did not speak as they turned their backs on Oakdene. They must not let even a whisper creep back down to the village.

NIGHT

Oswald sat on his bed. He was restless and turned a wooden hammer over and over in his hands. His cloak lay beside him and his seax was tucked into his belt. Rope was wound over each shoulder where he could slip it off when he needed it. Everyone in the hall was most likely asleep now, but still he waited. If he were to go outside and find someone there, or if someone were to hear him at the horsehouse then all would be lost. He had waited for this night for so long, thought through everything so carefully. Now that it had come, he had to do it well.

Brinin and Row would be in the hills by now, making their way swiftly through the darkness. There had been no shouting or uproar to break the stillness of the night, so they must have got away unseen. It was strange to think of them leaving Oakdene behind them, and stranger still to think of Oakdene without them in the morning. That's when the uproar would come. When everyone went to the fields at dawn they wouldn't be there. Aculf, ready to spill out his wrath for their slowness, would send someone to find them. But their hut would be empty. No one would have seen them, and then everyone would know that they were gone. His father would be angry—very angry—but they would be gone. Let them go swiftly.

His heart was beating rather quickly, pounding like the ironsmith on a sword. Fear was no longer lurking nearby. It was clinging to him like his own skin. There was more hope than danger for Brinin and Row, if only they were quick. But there was more danger for himself; there were so many ways for everything to go wrong.

Oswald put his head in his hands and tried to shake off the fear, but it couldn't be done. It would have to come with him. He gathered up his cloak, his hammer and his daring and crept away from the bed.

He slipped warily through the dark hall, the last embers glowing red in the hearth. No candle tonight; only nighteyes and moonlight and care to steer his feet. He rested his hand on the long table to find his way more easily to the door. Every footstep as he went, every brush of his leg on the benches, every breath seemed loud enough to wake half the hall. He was near the door, almost there, when his finger caught something and sent it crashing thunderously to the floor.

Quick as a flash, he slipped his cloak and the hammer under the table and sat down, gripping the edge of the bench with quivering hands. Someone would hear. Someone would come, his father perhaps. He would say that he couldn't sleep and was sitting by the fire until he was tired. He mustn't linger. There was so much to do before dawn. Yet he mustn't go on, not while his ears strained for the footstep or voice calling out in the darkness. But no one came. Oswald gasped suddenly; he hadn't even known he had been holding his breath. Then, still trembling, he rose and crept to the door.

Once outside all Oswald could do was lean against the wall. He was out, unheard somehow. That had been the easy part. Time to gather his wits for what would be harder. He was alone with nothing to hear but the noises of night, nothing to worry him. It was easier to see in the moonlight as he glanced about him. The moon would be a friend to Brinin and Row in the hills, but to Oswald it was a foe. If anyone should be awake, they would see him at once. He must be unseen as he made his way to the horsehouse, hidden in the night. Stealthy in the shadows of the buildings, he tried to become no more than a shadow himself.

Oswald was almost at the horsehouse door when something brushed against his leg and made him start. He reached down and, with a sigh of relief, felt Wolf, one of his father's hounds, at his side. He had thought of this. Tucked into his belt was a large bone, still with plenty of flesh, that he had saved from evening-meat. He crouched down and rubbed the hound's head.

'Sorry, boy,' he whispered. 'You can't come this time, but look. I have something for you.'

He led the hound round to the back of the horsehouse and slipped one end of a rope over his neck, before giving him the bone. As Wolf was eating it with delight, Oswald tied the other end firmly to a fence post and crept back round to the horsehouse door.

There was more danger here, more to go wrong than anywhere else. The horsehouse door had a lock like the one on the cowshed, but there could be no key tonight. Oswald carefully folded his cloak and wrapped it round and round the handle of his seax. Running his fingers over the top of the lock, he felt for a little gap where the front was coming away a little. He had seen it when he had looked carefully at the door some weeks before. The gap was small, but the point of his seax fitted into it. He lifted his hammer and began to tap on the muffled end of the seax as hard as he dared, praying with pounding heart that he would not be heard. Slowly the gap grew, as he moved the seax from side to side to prise the front of the lock away a little. He tapped some more, and at last could slip his seax in far enough to reach the pegs and slide open the lock. In the morning they would see that it had been broken and that no key had been used.

He took his own horse and Edith's. They were further from the door and less likely to be missed so quickly, and perhaps there would be less anger when they were missed. He was fooling himself, wasn't he? His father would be too angry for less or more to matter. What would be worse? The loss of two horses or the loss of two slaves? It was hard to say. But the horses would only be gone for a time. Oswald led them to the doorway to see slightly better to saddle them up. Then he led them both outside. He shut the door behind him and swung himself onto his horse. There was no going back now, whatever happened.

Past the dark buildings he went, beyond the fence and down to the fields, the wet sound of the hooves soft on the sodden ground. The earth was still muddy from the rain. He needed tracks and he must be making them. The village still slept. He was still alone, but it was only when he was beyond the fields at the forest's edge that he felt the fear begin to slip away a little. No one would hear him now.

He had ridden this way before, going over and over it as much as he had dared, but it seemed unknown now. Nothing was the same as in the daylight: the damp woody smell of the trees after the rain; the twit of an owl somewhere nearby; the sudden scream of a fox that chilled his blood, even though he knew what it was. Slowly he made his way along the path, the sounds of night all around him, listening all the while for one sound—the sound of water. It felt like a long time before he heard it, but at last he came to the opening in the trees where he could leave the path and go down to the stream, where it bent a little to the east. The trees were not as thick there and the moonlight fell silvery on the shallow water as it tumbled over the stones beneath it. Without getting down, he led the horses to the stream until they stood in the water. Both horses stopped to drink and Oswald breathed more freely.

The tracks would lead anyone who followed them to the stream. No tracks would be seen under the water and everyone would think they had gone south-east, away from the village. No one fleeing with stolen horses would go back the way they had come. After the horses had drunk, he began to walk them north again.

It was easier to go quickly now that the light was better, and it didn't seem long before he reached the clearing where he and Brinin had fought their dragon so many years before. Not the best hiding place, but it was far enough from the village to make finding the horses unlikely. Everyone was busy with the harvest. Who would be wandering about among the trees? They didn't need to stay hidden for long, only until he could come back to free them. There was plenty of grass, a stream to drink from and a little shelter. He carefully laid the saddles under a large tree and tethered each horse fast, then started on his walk back to the village. It couldn't be long before dawn now, and he must be in his bed before then.

Back through the trees, back through the night, back through the darkness, back through the hall. A shadow again, he crept to his bed and lay sleepless and waited for morning.

THEFT

O swald was drifting into an uneasy sleep when the uproar began. The hall door burst open with a crash, the sound of heavy footsteps cutting through the stillness as someone ran across the floorboards. He sat up in bed. It hadn't taken long. The sun couldn't even be up yet. What had been found missing first? Horses or men?

'My lord, my lord!' It was Aculf, panting as he ran. 'Thieves, my lord!'

The horses, then. It was better that way. It gave Brinin and Row more time. Were they still going swiftly, not stopping to rest? Another heavy tread, his father most likely, freshly wakened. Everything was beginning now.

'What is it, Aculf?' His father's voice was still heavy with sleep.

'Thieves in the night, my lord! The horsehouse door has been broken open and two of the horses are gone.'

Oswald was on his feet now, standing stiffly as though waiting for a blow to fall. Had he ever angered his father so wilfully before? It was a little frightening, though no one knew it was him. They mustn't know. There were more voices now, folk rushing into the hall, everyone waking up.

'Did they leave tracks?' Oswald could hear it in his father's voice: the anger firmly held back. 'Do we know which way they went?'

'Past the fields and towards the forest, my lord.'

'Send for Thurstan and two or three others, all with weapons. No one will steal my horses!'

It was as he had hoped: tracks into the forest, men sent to follow them. It was all as he had hoped. More feet ran lightly across the floor.

'What is it, Father? What's happened?'

Edith. It was time he went out himself, but not too quickly, not too slowly.

'Horse thieves in the night.' Edrich's voice was grim and hard. 'But I'm sending men after them. Their tracks will be easy to follow after the rain.'

Oswald ran his hands through his hair, took a deep breath and stepped out into the hall, dimly lit by the light of Aculf's lamp. The first thing he saw was Ludan running through the doorway, his face all fear and sorrow blended, burdened with a word he didn't want to give. He whispered something to Aculf.

'We know the thieves, my lord!' Aculf turned to Edrich like a hunter proudly showing his prey. 'Row and Brinin are gone! Their hut is empty and the embers cold. There has been no fire there all night. Forgive me, my lord, but I did say we would have trouble with Brinin and, given the days we live in and what their mother was, I think we know where they may be going.'

Edith, finding her brother suddenly beside her, buried her face in his shoulder and wept. Oswald put his arm around her. At another time, he might have longed to strike Aculf for that last speech. He would have been unlikely to do it, not with his father standing by his side. But now he didn't care. This morning, he was the hunter and Aculf was stepping into his snare. They all were. Men would go after the horses, thinking to find the slaves, while Brinin and Row went safely the other way.

'You did say we would have trouble, and here it is. Who can say if they have gone to the Danes? They wouldn't go south for that, though east perhaps. But I can say this: they will rue it when they are caught.'

Oswald held his sister a little tighter. They wouldn't be caught. They mustn't be caught. Let them go swiftly. He watched as his father strode from the hall, Aculf by his side.

'Oswald, you're trembling,' whispered Edith. 'What if they find them? Is it wrong for me to wish them Godspeed when they stole our father's horses?'

'Is it wrong for me to wish the same? But don't let Father hear us say it. Don't cry, Edith, there's still hope. They haven't been caught yet.'

Now was the time to think—that would have been easier if he'd had more sleep. Why shouldn't the men go south-east at the stream, where the tracks stopped? After two or perhaps three days, he would go and free the horses. They would find their own way back and someone would be sent to fetch home the men. No one need ever know that he'd had anything to do with it. By the time the horses were found and the men were home, Brinin and Row would be so far away that no one would ever learn where they had gone. There was nothing to do now but wait.

'Oswald!' Oswald started as Edrich's voice sounded through the open door. Surely his father was too busy to want him now? He smiled wryly at Edith, then stepped outside.

'Yes, Father?'

'Fetch your cloak, weapons and something to eat. Go with Thurstan and the others on the hunt. Your horse is one of those stolen, but I have had Ludan saddle another for you.'

If that wasn't a deathwound it felt very near to one. Why hadn't he thought of this? How could he free the horses if he was with the men? He should have known his father might send him. Why hadn't he thought of it? What was he to do?

'Father, p… please don't send me! I beg you not to…'

'Do you dare to defy me? My own son as well as my slaves? You will heed me now!'

There could be no begging. Not with the warning he saw on his father's face, not when his father was already angry. He wasn't so reckless as that. He could only heed and go to fetch his cloak, breathing hard as he went. What was he to do? He had to go with the men and make the best of it. Perhaps he could even slow them down. Perhaps he could urge them to turn back after a day or two, then free the horses later. Anything to give Row and Brinin more time.

'Edith,' he whispered, stopping in the doorway before he left. 'I have to go. If you hear… anything, tell me when I get back.'

Brinin and Row were limb-weary by the time they saw the dawn that morning, but still they walked. A wide valley stretched out before them, dappled with many hues of green. Forest and field, golden with grain; the dark and distant thatch of scattered farms and villages. And a little to the south was the road—pale and oddly straight—reaching into the west. They found a fairly flat place to sit, well-hidden from the east, and stopped at last to rest and eat.

'They must know we're gone by now,' said Brinin, as he stared far west into the land that lay before them. 'I keep wanting to look over my shoulder to see if someone is coming.'

'Oswald was sure that no one would think we had come this way.'

'I hope he's right. It will be bad if they do come, Row.'

'We can worry about that when it happens.'

It was strange to Brinin to look out over that broad land. All his life he had been penned in by the well-known. He had gone from hut to field, from field to meadow; from cowshed to dung-heap; from dung-heap to beasts, to river, to trees, to stream. Every day he had walked where his feet had been before, by ways they would walk again tomorrow. Now their feet were taking them to unknown, hidden land, beyond even what they could see before them. New trees, new fields, new streams. As a small boy he had dreamed of going far away like men did in the tales. Then he had taught himself not to dream. If only Oswald was right, and they wouldn't be followed. If only their feet would bear them swiftly to a small hope.

FOREST

Had the missing horses been walking ahead of them, they couldn't have been any easier to follow. Oswald could see that he had chosen the right night. With the horses gone and such clear tracks, no one seemed to have asked if Row and Brinin might have left another way. And the ground was still so soft that any footprints they had left would soon be hidden by others. Everyone knew—or thought they knew—what had happened. They straightened up, sickles in hand, to watch as the riders went by the fields. What were they thinking? For Ludan, a slave, it had been a heavy blow; he wasn't to know that following the horses was a gift to Row and Brinin, not a danger. There was Garulf. Oswald had often seen Brinin working at his side, as a son might with his father. Oswald's eyes met Garulf's as he passed him, and there was sorrow in them too.

'The tracks go into the forest,' said Cynestan, pointing along the path between the trees. 'They went this way, without a doubt.'

'It was an unwise night for them to choose, with the ground so soft, but that helps us now,' Thurstan muttered. 'Two days earlier and the ground would have been too hard for tracks like these. Let's not waste time. I have a harvest to get back to, and so do the rest of you. They can't have gone fast in the darkness and neither of them is a rider. They would have been better to go on foot. We'll soon find them.'

Oswald hardly dared to open his mouth as they made their way along the path. It was harvest, and now that he thought of that he doubted himself. The fields had been so busy as they rode past them, and Thurstan wasn't happy to be away from his. None of them were, and it would only be worse when they found nothing. Perhaps three days would be too many before turning back. Two might be better. Was that long enough for Brinin and Row?

They were stealthy as hunters as they rode among the trees, the morning light fresh and green in the leaves. The cheek-cheek of a woodpecker sounded nearby, and the beating of his bill on some tree. It would have been all gladness if it hadn't felt so forbidden. The ground was leaf-soft beneath them until at last they came to the stream.

'Stop,' called Thurstan, drawing his horse up beside Oswald's. 'What do you make of that, Oswald?'

The grass by the side of the path was trampled, flattened a little. The horses' hooves had done their work well. Oswald looked down at it, though he knew how it would be before he saw it.

'It looks like they may have ridden off here to the left.' It somehow felt like a lie to speak the truth. 'The tracks don't keep going along the path.'

Thurstan patted him on the shoulder.

'Good. You need to have an eye for these things.' Thurstan beckoned to the others to join them. 'They left the path here and headed down towards the stream. Why, I wonder? Perhaps the horses were thirsty.'

'They weren't only watering the horses,' said Cynestan, leaping down from his horse and looking carefully at the ground. 'The tracks don't come back to the path and they don't keep going on the other side of the stream. They must have gone into the water and walked along it.'

'Without tracks, I don't see how we can follow them,' grumbled Saxulf. 'We should go to Edrich Thegn and tell him we lost them and then get back to our harvests.'

'Don't be a fool, Saxulf!' snapped Thurstan. 'Which way do you think they went? North and back to the village? We'll follow the stream south-east and watch out for tracks when they leave it again. I want to be back at my harvest as much as you do, but I'm at least going to try to do what we've been sent for first. You can go and tell Edrich Thegn that you've given up if you want to, but I wouldn't like to be you when you do.'

They were doing everything he wanted them to, and Thurstan wouldn't let them give up too quickly. It was all as he had hoped, though it was hard somehow to feel that it had been work well done. The men were irked now, though still going on, but the time would come when they would see that the horses they thought they were following had never left the stream. What then? Yet hadn't this been what he wanted?

The rest of the day was all slow riding. They rode deeper into the forest, and Oswald deeper into gloom as the men became ever more galled. Why hadn't he thought of this? He had thought so much about what his father would think. He had been ready for that, but it wouldn't only be his father who would be angry if they all knew what he had done. And how could he blame them for that? He liked these men and he had dragged them from their fields at the height of harvest to look for what they could never find. When he thought of it like that, he was almost angry himself. He hadn't meant to do it at harvest, but everything had happened so suddenly and quickly in the end. What else could he have done? Yet he didn't much like this plan, now that it was under way.

Oswald was almost asleep in the saddle when, towards evening, they stopped at a clearing to rest for the night. Cynestan built a fire, and they all sat round it to eat.

'In the saddle the whole day for nothing!' Saxulf tore at his bread as though he wished it was something else he was breaking. 'If we do find those two slaves—and I don't think we will—it will be all I can do not to thrash them myself. Couldn't they have had the wit to wait until the harvest was in? They've been on the land all their lives. They should have known better than to make off now.'

Oswald stared into the fire and said nothing. He couldn't bring himself to meet anyone's eyes and was glad of the growing darkness. Wasn't his guilt shouting out to them all from his face?

'Aculf says they've gone to join the Danes.' Rædwald always knew what everyone else had said. 'Their mother was a Dane, you know.'

'Aculf says a lot of things and most of them aren't worth listening to! Less worth telling the rest of us!' Thurstan exclaimed. 'Their father was as much a Wessex man as any of us. And what about you, Rædwald? Your father was a Mercian!'

Oswald was too tired to lie awake and worry. But he slept light, his rest often broken by the fear that someone would learn what he had done, or by the uneasy feeling that he didn't like himself much. It would have been better not to have done it during the harvest.

They were on their horses again shortly before dawn, and the men were of one mind: they would keep up the hunt for the morning only, then turn back if they had found nothing. Not even Thurstan wanted to go on longer than that. Their fields couldn't wait.

Rædwald was the one who heard it, near midday: a horseman far off. They stopped to listen. It was unmistakable, a horse ridden hard, breaking through the sounds of the forest and coming nearer.

'Unlikely to be the slaves. They couldn't ride like that,' said Saxulf. 'And it's coming from the north or north-west. Perhaps they've sent someone from Oakdene to call us back. About time too.'

Oswald gripped his horse's reins a little tighter, his breath quivering slightly as he drew it in. If the horseman was coming from Oakdene, had Brinin and Row been followed and caught? Or had someone found the horses? But if the horses had been found, unsaddled, tethered in the clearing, and not wandering as he had hoped, then his father would know, everyone in Oakdene would know, that there had been cunning.

Thurstan and the others started to ride back north towards the horseman, and Oswald had no choice but to follow them. They hadn't gone far when Swetrich came into sight, riding towards them, the water spraying before him and catching the light.

'You're to turn back!' he called, drawing up his horse beside them. 'They've found the horses! Someone had hidden them in a clearing in the forest.'

Fear drew round Oswald with the angry voices of the men. Brinin and Row were not found—he could be thankful for that—but now his father knew that someone had helped them. How long before he knew it was him?

'This was some wile to draw us away from where the slaves have gone!' Cynestan, never flustered, was angrier than Oswald had ever seen him. 'And we've been two days away from our fields for nothing!'

'Where were they hidden?' asked Rædwald. 'The tracks led to the stream.'

'In a clearing by the stream, not far from the village. You've spent the last two days going the wrong way.'

'So they went north at the stream!' Saxulf turned on Thurstan. 'And you called me a fool, Thurstan, and made us all go south!'

Thurstan glared at Saxulf but perhaps he thought that whatever was in his mind was better left unsaid.

'You only did what they wanted you to do,' said Swetrich. 'No one would have thought they had turned back to the village. I would have gone south too. Someone in Oakdene has helped the slaves. Edrich Thegn is already trying to find out who it was, and I believe Aculf thinks he knows.'

'When I find out who it was,' growled Thurstan, 'Edrich Thegn will be the least of his worries!'

Oswald rode behind the others with shaking hands. What should he do now? What *could* he do? His heart was pounding and his mind so full of fear that it was hard to think. His thoughts all seemed to be scattering to hide from trouble. Thurstan's last words were sounding over and over in his ears. If his father was as angry as the men were... Did his father and Aculf think he had done it? What if they blamed someone else? What then? That was a worse thought. He must be ready to tell his father what he had done if need be, but then how could he still shield Brinin and Row? Had they gone swiftly enough?

LIFE

Brinin and Row had almost reached the road by the second day. Strengthened by sleep, they went swiftly along, keeping away from farms and villages as much as they could. To walk freely by tree, track and hedgerow, to straighten their backs from bending with their sickles, to unburden their shoulders—there was a gladness to it all. Brinin felt it despite his unshakeable worry that there were horsemen at his heels. How long before they heard them behind them?

'Our tracks will have mingled with the others by the horsehouse,' he said, stopping to look behind him, not for the first time that day. 'But not after that. They'll have looked for tracks leading all ways out of the village, and it won't have been hard to find ours. It was the wrong night to leave, Row. They're bound to be after us by now.'

'It's been almost two days since we left.' Row took his brother by the arm and pulled him along. 'If they were coming, they'd already be here. Don't stop to think about it, Bruni. The quicker we get to the road, the better.'

'There'll be nowhere to hide on the road!'

They reached the road by evening and walked along it for a time before stopping for the night. It was like nothing Brinin had ever seen before, so straight, so strong underfoot. He knelt down to touch it and learn what it was like. Grass sprouted up between the smooth stones, and patches of nettles and yarrow lined the edge, while little moths and craneflies flitted about. When they had built their fire, they sat down to eat, backs against the trees, and watched the sun set far in the west. There was something almost dreamlike about these long work-free days far from home, if Oakdene was indeed home. Walking alone with Row seemed to open thoughts in Brinin that had seldom grown into words before.

'I hardly remember our father,' he said as they sat by their fire. He had often thought of him and wondered who it was that he had lost. 'I remember him once lifting me high above his head, so I could pick an apple from a tree, but I've forgotten his face.'

'You're very like him. Not to look at—you've always looked more like Mother—but your eyes are his.' Row laughed. 'I may have almost brought you up, but your eyes are so much like his that I've sometimes thought that if you looked at me and bade me do something, I'd heed you! You're like him in other ways too. He didn't always say much, but what he said was worth listening to. And when he thought someone was a fool, you knew from his eyes though he never said a word.'

'How did Father come to wed a Danish woman? No one ever told me. I've been thinking about it and it seems strange to me now. It didn't when I was a child because she was my mother.'

'Mother was taken from her kin and sold into thraldom sometime around her thirteenth or fourteenth winter, only a little younger than you are now. She didn't like to talk about it, so I don't know how it came about. Thorleif was her father and Fridgerd her mother. That's all I know. In time she came as a thrall to Cuthred, the lord of the place where Father was a freeman. It's less than a day's ride from Oakdene.'

'So Father was free when he met Mother?' He had known it, foggily, as a pain that no one spoke of, as a hard truth that he, the slave son of a freeborn father, didn't like to think about.

'Yes, and he somehow grew to love her. He wanted to buy her freedom and wed her. It's not often how a man finds himself a wife, but it's what Father did. He and Cuthred didn't like each other, and Cuthred set the price for Mother's freedom high and Father ended up losing almost half his land. He had set his mind on it and wouldn't shift from it, and if he was ever sorry afterwards I never heard him say so. But the loss of the land hit him hard.

'I think it was easier when we weren't so many. It was hard to grow enough to feed us, and the more we were the harder it became. He hunted a bit when he had time, though he seldom did. I was first, as you know, then Gytha. You would have loved her. She was so lively. She would make all of us laugh and by her fifth winter she could tell a tale almost as well as Mother. Then came Gyrich, who always thought he could do whatever anyone else could do, even though he was small.

'Even a good year was hard, but then the harvest failed, and we had very little to eat. It was hard for everyone in the village that year, but for us—well, sometimes we children cried because we were hungry, and Mother and Father would eat nothing so we could have more. Then before Yule came, Gyrich...' Row stopped suddenly and in the long silence that followed even the crackle of the fire sounded like pain, and when he spoke again it wounded Brinin to hear the quiver in his voice. 'Gyrich died before Yule came—it was only his third winter—and Gytha with the lambing.'

Row got up and walked back to the road. He stood looking away from Brinin, far along the stones to where the last sliver of the sun was slipping away, dying for the night. Many winters had chilled the earth since then. Many summers had softened it. There had been other tears since, and times to laugh. But even after so long, the pain could spring up fresh as a new shoot when Row thought of the little sister and brother he had lost. And Brinin ached for him.

'Soon after that Godwig Thegn came to see Cuthred. Godwig was Edrich Thegn's father, a kind man. Father went to him and asked, begged perhaps, that he take those of us who were left as his thralls so that we could live. If you had known Father, you would understand how hard it must have been for him to do. It would have been unthinkable to be Cuthred's thralls, but somehow he knew he could trust Godwig. That's how we came to Oakdene. I had just passed my ninth winter, and you were born with the harvest. I remember Godwig. He died about a year after we came to Oakdene. He was kind, as I say, but Father wasn't the kind of man who is made for thraldom. He must have lost all hope of keeping us alive another way. He gave up everything, and here we are. Thralls on the run, but we lived.'

SPEECH

Oswald was watching carefully as he rode into the village the next morning, watching out for even the smallest look that might warn him that his guilt was known. All he saw was that everyone was feeling the weight of the trouble. They worked half-heartedly, often stopping to stand in twos or threes to whisper before bending over the grain again. Where was Edith? She would know what was happening, and if he—or anyone—had been blamed. He didn't think he could bear it if it stretched on like this for days.

He had just handed his horse over to Eawig—he couldn't see Ludan anywhere—when he caught sight of Edith coming out of the hall. He ran to her, half-eager, half-dreading to hear what she might tell him.

'Oswald,' she said in a low voice. 'I'm so glad you're back! No one knows where they've gone, and you know that the horses were found. Brinin and Row didn't take them after all. Father says someone must have helped them, and Aculf has been trying to find out who it was. Also, Ealmund Thegn came to see Father about something else, but Father has asked him to stay to help.'

'I don't see what *he* could help with,' said Oswald, to make himself believe it as much as Edith. If his father wanted Ealmund, an older and wiser thegn than himself, then he wouldn't rest until he knew the truth, the truth he mustn't know.

'It's bad, Oswald. Father says someone hid the horses to outwit us all and make everyone think that Row and Brinin had gone into the forest. I don't want them to be found, but I hate to think of the men being sent from their fields for nothing! That's bad, isn't it? Father's very angry about it, and he's right to be, I think. Father says that whoever helped them is as guilty as Row and Brinin are. Aculf thinks it was Ludan and has already beaten him to make him tell what happened, but Ludan doesn't seem to know anything about it. I don't think it could have been him. I don't think he would do that. Father told Aculf to leave Ludan alone until they are sure.'

It was worse than he had feared. He wasn't steering any more. He was being borne along, helpless, on a horse he couldn't stop, rushing too quickly to where he didn't want to go. His father knowing wasn't the worst that could happen, though he had been so afraid of it. That Ludan had been blamed—and already beaten—was much worse. Ludan wouldn't be the last to suffer if he said nothing. There was no other way. He had to go to his father at once.

'Where's Father?' The words crept trembling from his mouth.

'In the hall with Ealmund Thegn. Oswald, what is it? You look so white.'

But there was no time for answers now. Edith would learn them soon enough. He was already halfway through the door before his sister had finished speaking.

Edrich stood with Aculf, Ealmund Thegn and others near the fire, deep in speech and frowning a little. He smiled grimly as he saw his son come in. Oswald wished he hadn't smiled. It made everything harder to be welcomed by a smile that would be gone so soon.

'Well, Oswald,' Edrich said. 'Back empty-handed from the hunt? There has been some cunning afoot, and I will not rest until we have sniffed it out. You may be sure of that! You should eat now. You must be hungry.'

'Father, I must speak to you.'

'Can it wait? Let me finish with Aculf first.'

'No, sir. I don't think it can wait.'

'Be quick then!'

Oswald had to be quick. It was the only way to do it. He had to speak swiftly, unthinkingly, before he was too scared to speak at all.

'Father, p… please forgive me.' Oswald's words tumbled over each other as he drove them out. 'I did it. Not Ludan.'

'You did what?' Edrich was staring at him without any understanding. Was it too dreadful a thing for him to understand that his son had done it?

'I hid the horses. It wasn't Ludan or anyone else. I—'

Oswald's words were cut off as Edrich snatched Aculf's stick from him and brought it down heavily across his son's shoulders. Oswald dropped his head, braced for more, longing for it to be over. He had known there would most likely be a beating, but not where he stood with his father still mid-speech among men and guests. Not without the waiting, the kneeling and the stern words to drive it home. His father must be even angrier than he had foreseen for his wrath to rush out so unbridled. But no more came. Oswald glanced up at the men wordless about him, at Edith standing frightened in the doorway, at his father. Edrich's arm was raised to strike again, but his face was all strength as he fought to bring himself to heel. He threw the stick to the floor with a clatter. Not over yet then. Not begun.

'You would dare do such a thing?' Edrich's voice shook with rage. 'Without you, we would have had them by now! And Thurstan and the others! Three days away from their fields during the harvest! What were you thinking?'

Oswald looked at the floor, wildly clutching for something, anything, to soften his father's anger. But there was nothing. He had known that once he had spoken there would be little he could do to help himself. The time for speech was over. Now was the time to hold his tongue and bear whatever came. This was only the first hot anger. Worse would be the cooler kind his father had thought about. He had known it would be this way.

'Take yourself away from here!' Edrich pointed to the door. 'I will see to you later.'

Still hanging his head, Oswald made his way not unwillingly to the door. It was better to be somewhere else, away from the hall and the watching eyes. Even behind his curtain he would still hear what they were saying about him. The talk had already begun. He heard Ealmund Thegn speaking softly to his father but he was too wretched to know or even care what he said.

'Speak to him? You may speak to him all you like!' Oswald had almost reached the threshold when his father's voice rose above the others. 'Perhaps you can learn why he has forgotten his duty to Oakdene and to me. Stop, Oswald!'

Oswald heard his father's heavy tread coming towards him. He didn't want Ealmund Thegn to speak to him. He didn't want anyone to speak to him. He only wanted to hide away somewhere to wait for his father to see to him, and for it all to be over. His father's shoes, the leather brown and shiny with wear, stopped in front of him.

'You have not heard the last I will have to say about this, Oswald!' said Edrich, then strode from the hall.

Ealmund Thegn beckoned Oswald back into the hall. Sighing slightly, Oswald followed him to a bench and sat down. What could he want with him? Why not leave his father to deal with him? Hadn't he seen that he would? Almost everyone had drifted from the hall now. Likely they all knew that it was better to busy themselves elsewhere, and no doubt they were keen to tell their neighbours what they had seen and heard.

'Oswald,' began Ealmund. 'You were right to tell your father what you had done, and he will see to you as he said. I think you know that you were wrong and that you already rue it. I can see it on your face. It can't be undone now, but you *can* show me how sorry you are by telling me the truth. And you must understand that if you don't tell me the truth, it will be much worse for you in the end.'

Perhaps there was hope here, after all. Ealmund was stern, but not angry like his father. He was ready to talk and keen to listen. It was now the third morning since Brinin and Row had fled; almost long enough, but another day or two would be better. The truth about what he had done couldn't harm him much more, but he must be careful about what he said about Brinin and Row.

'How did you know that the slaves had fled?' asked Ealmund.

If that was the kind of answer Ealmund wanted, then he couldn't have the truth. Could Oswald lie boldly to him? He couldn't have looked his father in the eye and done it. But how could anything but lies help Row and Brinin now?

'I couldn't sleep and went outside.' It was shocking how easily the lies came. 'I saw two men walking in the darkness and I followed them to see who they were. When I got near I saw that they were Row and Brinin.'

These last days had taught Oswald that he knew how to be cunning. It was an unwieldy knowledge, awkward to carry. He was learning more about himself than he wanted to.

'Did you speak to them or see which way they went?'

And so the tale bore fruit, one lie after another. Oswald bit his lip. He mustn't seem too ready to speak.

'I didn't speak to them, sir,' he said at last.

'Did you see which way they went?'

Oswald said nothing. A little more unwillingness, a little slowness of speech.

'Which way did they go, Oswald? Remember that you are answerable to your father and not to two runaway slaves.'

'North, sir. Towards Waneting.'

Ealmund beckoned to Aculf, who was still lurking nearby. He likely didn't want to miss anything.

'Have a few men ride north to Waneting. It seems the slaves may have gone that way. Have them ask about them in all the villages or farms they pass through. Someone will have seen them.'

Oswald's heart skipped a beat. That was the trouble with lies; they sometimes turned to strike a blow at their lord. He had forgotten that there were so many villages and farms on the way to Waneting, and now *more* men were being sent away from the harvest. But there was nothing he could do about it. It would give Row and Brinin the few more days they needed, and when his lies were known... Could it make things any worse than they already were?

'Then you made everyone think that they had gone into the forest so they wouldn't be followed. Why did you do that? Because you pitied them?'

'Yes, sir.' And more than that. He would have done almost anything to get them away. He was glad, so glad, that they hadn't been found, though he wished he'd thought of another way to do it.

'Did anyone help you with it?'

'No, sir. I did it alone and told no one.'

'Why did you come and tell your father?'

'I heard that Ludan had been blamed and that Aculf had already beaten him. I was afraid that, if I didn't speak, others might be blamed as well.'

They had strayed back into truth again, earnest truth that Oswald meant. Perhaps Ealmund could see that on his face.

'You did the right thing to tell me the truth, Oswald, and I shall tell your father everything you've said. Keep away from him now until he calls you. He is very angry with you, and rightly so.'

Late in the afternoon Oswald sat by the river, where Brinin had pulled him from the water so many years before. He felt drawn there somehow. He didn't see Edith coming until she was beside him but he had known that she would find him.

'Oswald.' Edith sat down on the bank next to him.

Oswald picked up a stone and threw it into the water. One stone and so many ripples spread from it. One deed and so much trouble came of it.

'Did you truly hide those horses? Or did you say you had done it to shield Ludan?'

'Both. I did it but I wouldn't have told Father if Ludan hadn't been blamed.'

'You *knew* Brinin and Row were going to run away, didn't you? You've known for a while. You've been worrying about something, but I didn't know what. Did you plan all this, Oswald? Why didn't you tell me?'

'Father said he would sell Brinin if he did anything wrong at all. I knew Aculf would give Father a bad word sooner or later, so I told Brinin and Row to flee. How could I let him be sold? I hid the horses to make everyone think they had gone into the forest, to give them time to get further away without being followed. It worked. Though not so well as I'd hoped.'

'But why didn't you tell me? You know you can trust me!'

'Then you would now be as much to blame as I am. Father isn't done with me yet. He hasn't even started. You saw how narrowly I missed a thrashing earlier. It's coming, though. I do trust you but I'd rather keep you out of it.'

'And now perhaps it will all be for nothing!' Edith's eyes were full of tears now. She wanted Brinin and Row to be safe as much as he did. 'I heard Father and Aculf sending men off to Waneting to find them. Did Ealmund Thegn make you tell him where they'd gone?'

Oswald threw another stone into the water. There were some things that Edith wasn't to know. He had done it alone, and she mustn't share the blame now.

'*Did* they go to Waneting? You didn't... you didn't lie to Ealmund Thegn, did you? Oswald, they've sent more men!'

'I don't want to bring you into this, Edith, and I've told you too much already.'

He saw it on her face. Neither of them had ever thought he would do something so bold, perhaps so foolish. And he saw on her face a little of the dread he himself was feeling: what would their father do when he learned he'd outwitted them not once, but twice?

'Edith, I won't come into the hall to eat this evening. I don't think I'll be very welcome.'

'Don't make Father any angrier than he already is.'

Oswald didn't meet his sister's eye. He stared dully at a leaf falling into the water, the river turning it, twisting it and bearing it far away.

'I don't think I *can* make him any angrier,' he sighed.

STARS

B rinin and Row lay stretched out on their backs on either side of the fire they had built. Brinin, his arms up so that he could rest his head on them, could feel the warmth of the fire—almost too hot, but not quite—down the side of his body. The crackle of the flames and the smell of the wood as it burned were so much like home that it was hard to believe that they were far away from Oakdene now. But there was no thatch above him in a smoky hut, no wall to reach out and touch. The darkness of the night was all around, very dark and black beyond the reach of the fire. And out here, far from any village and on such a clear night as this one, the stars were so uncountable, so beautiful, the sky so dusted with them, that he could think of almost nothing else he would rather be doing. To lie by the fire and look at the stars with his brother came near to full gladness, but... He rolled onto his side to look at Row through the flames.

'I hope no one in Oakdene has been blamed, Row,' he said.

'Why would anyone be blamed?' said Row, keeping his eyes on the stars.

'Because that's the way of things. Men always like to find someone to blame if they can, and men like Aculf more than most.'

'No one knew anything about our flight, Bruni.'

'Someone might have overheard.'

'We were too careful for that. No one heard. No one knows anything. If anyone had seen us go, they would have stopped us or they would have already caught us. Only Aculf and Edrich Thegn even knew why we might want to flee, and who would blame them?'

'Oswald knew.'

'Who would think of blaming Oswald? I don't think even Aculf would dare. Oswald will be careful—he won't want to give himself away.'

Nearby some small nightbeast was scuffling among the fallen leaves, and from above them came the long, haunting cry of an owl on the hunt. If those who hunted men cried out like that, they might be easier to hide from.

'Do you remember when Mother used to tell tales from the stars?' said Row. 'I always liked Ratatoskr the Squirrel best, rushing along with errands and insults. When I was a boy I loved watching squirrels. They were always so fast that it did seem that they were on an errand somewhere.'

'I always liked the Eagle because he was wise. There he is—do you see him? Ratatoskr talked too much, but I always thought it would be a fine thing to fly like an eagle or some other great bird and look down on everything below.'

'Mother always said that she thought you went far away in your own head.'

'Not so much now as I once did,' said Brinin and rolled onto his back again. There was a cry of another owl—or the same owl—further away this time.

Brinin turned his eyes to the sky once more. There was the long band like dust, where perhaps the stars gathered more thickly. His mother had said it was a great tree that rose into the heavens, and that all the beasts—Ratatoskr and the Eagle and the others—made their homes in it. But to Brinin it had always seemed like a river or stream, fast-flowing and bubbling.

It was a strange thing, he thought to himself rather sleepily, that they had walked many days from Oakdene yet the heavens and the stars had not changed. The sky looked just as it did when he and Row had watched the stars outside their hut. It changed only with the seasons, as everything did. But this harvest sky, far from the village, was just like a harvest sky at Oakdene. His mother had told them that there were men among her kin who could guide their ships by the stars, much as a man may guide his feet by the sunrise and sunset. His mother did not know how they did it, but Brinin, as he lay there, began to see how it might be done. The stars were so well known, the night sky so much like an old friend; and if the sky was the same everywhere, even far from home, then a man could follow the stars that pointed him to where he wanted to go.

'There are so many of them!' he said suddenly. 'No one could count them. Even if a man tried to count the stars in a small part of the sky, it couldn't be done!'

'It would be easier to count a handful of dust,' yawned Row.

It had been a long day of walking, good to walk along without work to be done, but long and tiring nonetheless. And the fire was warm, and the ground not too hard beneath them. They had chosen a good place to stop for the night, and all around them the little soft night noises were the ones they heard at home. Brinin yawned as though in answer to Row and seemed to be slowly losing himself in the stars and the darkness, the glow of the fire and the noises of the night. He started suddenly as Row began to talk again.

'When I was a boy,' Row was saying, 'I always thought the Eagle looked like an arrow in a drawn bow. Father was very good with a bow and arrow—better than anyone when he could spare the time—a good hunter. I wanted to be like him, and he had begun to teach me. But then we came to Oakdene, and after that neither of us could shoot.'

Brinin looked at the Eagle and saw how a bow and arrow could be seen in it. Maybe the stars could be made to look like anything.

'Once, just before that last winter before we came to Oakdene,' Row went on, 'I took Father's bow and arrows to go hunting on my own. I don't know what I was thinking—I hadn't even reached my ninth winter. The amazing thing is that I did shoot something at last—a hare, a big one too—though I couldn't even draw the bow fully. It was mostly luck, but I have sometimes wondered if I might have made a hunter too, had things not been the way they were.'

Who could say what would have been? Brinin had taught himself, since he was very young, to keep his mind away from such thoughts, but out here under the stars, playing at being free, it was harder to turn the thoughts away—for Row as well as for himself, it seemed.

'I went proudly home carrying my hare by the ears—my first kill—but on the way I met Father out looking for me and all my pride left me at once. I had never seen him so angry. He didn't say a word, only gave me one awful look and beckoned me to follow him. Then I knew that I'd been out far longer than I'd thought and that for a boy to take his father's bow and arrows unbidden was worse than foolish. Father took back his bow, and we walked without speaking all the rest of the way, I with heavy feet, because I knew what was coming to me as soon as we reached home.

'But when we got to the house, Mother said that she was glad of the meat for the pot and that we would eat well that night. She and Father looked at each other without saying anything, as they sometimes did, and each knew what the other meant. So I missed a beating, and Father took me outside to show me how to skin the hare, though while we were doing it he said some things to me that made me wonder if I had been spared after all. That was my first kill as a hunter and my last, as it turned out. I still remember how it tasted.'

Brinin looked up at the Eagle in the night sky, and it seemed to change into a bow and arrow stolen by a little boy. He would always see a bow and arrow there now. That was the way with the stars. They told tales. Not only the sagas men had told, father to son, over long years, but all the others that were woven in along the way.

DREAD

It seemed that Oswald and his father were of one mind: that it was better for him to keep away from evening-meat. Edrich said nothing to him about it. No one spoke to him or even looked at him when he went back to the hall to sleep. Someone had left a little food on his bed—Edith perhaps—but it was so dry and tasteless in his mouth that he could hardly swallow it.

In the morning he lingered, skulking behind his curtain, and did not dare to come out until he no longer heard his father's voice in the hall. He should have gone down to the fields, to show his sorrow by bending and sweating over the grain, but that was where his father would be. That was where they would all be. So he took his battle spear and went to the meadow instead. No one was likely to be there.

He couldn't throw his spear straight that morning. Something was gnawing at his gut—a foreboding that he couldn't shake off—and it wasn't long before he gave up and sat down on the grass to brood. Why hadn't his father seen to him as he had said he would? Why didn't he do it quickly and stop making him wait? He had been ready for that when he had gone to him but not for the dread of it.

First, he couldn't throw and then he couldn't even sit without shifting about. He got up and tramped across the meadow, kicking at any clumps of grass that grew above the others; to the trees and back, to the trees again. Brinin and Row were likely walking through grass somewhere as he was, free and far away. They should almost be at the minster by now if all had gone well. He had always known that he might be caught helping them. He had known what he was doing. But they would be free, and it would all be worthwhile.

He was sitting down again, pulling up handfuls of grass and tearing them into shreds, when he looked up and saw Thurstan coming round the side of the church and striding towards him. His heart sank. He hadn't forgotten how angry Thurstan had been in the forest the day before, and it seemed from the look on his face that his father might be the least of Oswald's worries after all. He stood to ready himself for the onslaught.

'Three days! Three wasted days!' Oswald couldn't bring himself to meet Thurstan's eye. 'Did you choose your time carefully to make as much trouble as you could? You didn't think to wait for a few weeks before dragging us through the forest on your games? Never in my life have I known anyone to be so utterly, utterly thoughtless! You heard us talking. You knew how keen we all were to get back to our fields, but you held your tongue and let us ride further and further from Oakdene.'

Oswald knew that Thurstan's tongue could be swordlike, but he had never felt it hacking at him. Now he was shieldless, and Thurstan was charging with all his weapons. Every word was a cut, a sting, too many arrows flying at him to hide from.

'How long were you going to let us go on? A week? Longer? It's a good thing that Swetrich came when he did. We couldn't have trusted you to put an end to it. If it had been down to you, we'd still be out there!'

'Please, Thurstan, I—'

'Most men who come upon some slaves on the run might think to stop them. Or if that was too much, at least leave them well alone to be caught in good time. But not you. Oh no! That wasn't enough for you! You couldn't be happy until your father's men had been sent off on a fool's errand!'

'I'm sorry. I thought—'

'No, you didn't think and it's a bit late to be sorry now! Did you think we all had no better way of busying ourselves? What were you going to do if the harvest was lost? I would have believed better of you, much better. I've always thought you had good sense, but now I'm wondering. This wasn't only thoughtless, it was downright mindless. You need a good thrashing, and if you were my son I'd see that you got one, and one you wouldn't quickly forget too!'

'Don't worry,' sighed Oswald, when Thurstan stopped for breath and the arrows stopped coming. 'My father will see to that!'

'Good! I hope he does! I would never have believed this of you. You know how hard we all work during the harvest. And now we're back, more men have been sent off! Are they going the wrong way too? It's almost unforgivable!'

Thurstan was right, and that was why his arrows stung. Wasn't that what he had learned in the forest? He had thought so much about Row and Brinin that he had forgotten to think about anyone else.

'I'm sorry. That's the truth, Thurstan. I wish now that I had done something else.'

Perhaps Thurstan could see that no more wounds were needed. He lowered his weapons.

'You're a young fool!' he said, still gruff but not so warlike. 'What on earth were you thinking?'

'Please don't ask me to tell you! I'll take a thrashing if I must and I won't mind. I won't say a word about it! There *was* a good reason for it, and I'll stand by that, but I can see that I shouldn't have done it the way I did. I didn't know what else to do. But please, don't ask me why. I can't tell you.'

What Thurstan would have said to this, Oswald never learned. Before he spoke, Eawig came running across the grass towards them.

'Please, Oswald Child, sir,' he panted. 'My lord your father asks you to go and see him now in the hall, sir.'

So there was to be no more waiting, and he minded more than he had said now that it was almost upon him. Oswald didn't move as Eawig left them. Rooted to the spot, he stood with his eyes shut, gripping his spear tightly, and tried to gather his last scattered scraps of boldness. They had mostly forsaken him now. He felt Thurstan's hand rest on his shoulder and looked up at him.

'Come now, Oswald. You knew it was coming. Best go quickly and get it over.'

Oswald nodded. Better for it to be over; better for it to be quick. Hadn't he been wishing for that a short while before? He handed Thurstan his spear and left him without another word.

Edith, restless and unsmiling, was waiting for him by the church.

'Alrich has come from Hildræd our uncle. Father wants you in the hall—did Eawig tell you—and he's sent everyone else out.'

Oswald grimaced and kept walking. It was Edith's warning for him to be ready. His father meant the thing to be hidden, away from watching eyes and listening ears. But it would be hidden from no one. Everyone knew what he had done. They all knew why they had been sent out. Anyone nearby would hear the hidden thing inside, and by dusk the whole village would know all about it. He had been a fool to think that he could do anything that would stay hidden. In Oakdene nothing was ever hidden; only what Aculf did. Nobody cared enough about that to look.

'Oswald!' called Alrich, cheerfully strolling towards him. His smile was gone before he reached Oswald. 'What's wrong with everyone today? When my father sent me, I came hoping for a warm welcome from my kinsmen, but all I've got has been sighs and worried looks. You look awful, Oswald. What's happened here?'

'I can't tell you now, Alrich. Edith is by the church. She'll give you your warm welcome.'

Some of those standing near the hall turned to watch Oswald as he went past, but he kept his eyes down and looked at no one. He stopped at the threshold and stood with his hand against the wall. Brinin and Row were not found. They were gone, no one knew where. They had not been followed. They were walking free somewhere, happier than he was. The door of the hall was open, and he stepped inside to find his father.

Edrich was at the far end, sitting wearily with his head in hands. He didn't seem to hear Oswald as he came in. Had Alrich brought bad tidings? The door creaked as Oswald shut it behind him, and his father heard it and glanced up. He stood and looked at his son for some time before he spoke.

'Come here, Oswald,' he said sternly.

FREEDOM

'**I**'m not sure that I even know what freedom means,' said Brinin, as he and Row walked along on the fourth day after their flight from Oakdene.

'I hardly know myself! All I remember from before we came to Oakdene was hard work and hunger. The work has never been any harder as a thrall, and I've always had enough to eat.'

Brinin glanced at his brother. That had always been how it was with Row, happy enough with food and a place to sleep. But was there no more to freedom than that? Everyone worked hard, but what was work for a thrall? It was never lingering a little by the fire on a cold morning; never daring to lean against the plough to drink in the brightness of the day or to watch a bird in flight; never gathering in the grain with the glad knowledge it was his own; never anything to hope for but evening shadows and the short rest they brought. There was a sure meal at the end of the day, perhaps, but plenty of bitterness to swallow before he tasted it. That was what made the work hard, not the strain nor the sweat. And Aculf had made it harder still.

'Perhaps it would be easier with a better lord,' he said.

'Is Edrich Thegn not a good lord? Others might be worse. And even Aculf wasn't always so bad, you know.'

'He didn't seem to dislike me so much when I was only a little child. He beat me sometimes, but not more than anyone else and only when I'd earned it.'

'You weren't so troublesome!' laughed Row. 'Come, Bruni! Everyone in Oakdene knows that you think Aculf is a fool, though you don't say a word about it. Aculf knows it and that's why he hates you. When you were too young to know your own mind, he treated you the same as everyone else. But that's not why he got worse.'

'Why was it then?'

'Oswald's mother died. She always knew everything that happened in Oakdene, and what she knew, Edrich Thegn knew. Now she's gone, there are some things that he knows nothing about. If Edrich Thegn knew what Aculf was like, I don't think he would still be workreeve. Edrich Thegn is stern, but he's never been like Aculf.'

Brinin remembered Oswald's mother, with her seeing eyes and listening ears. She had often come with food when his mother had been sick and lifted her head to help her eat it. That alone was enough to make Brinin like her. When his mother had died she had spoken kindly to him, though he was only a thrall; perhaps because he was young and so was her own son. But even the best of mothers die sometimes, first Brinin's, then Oswald's. A thrall and a thegn's son, they both learned that they could lose them. And Row was right. Everything *was* worse after that. First, any wrongdoing had earned him more and harder blows; then small misdeeds were enough; then had come the goading; then the blows for nothing at all. Before his thirteenth winter, he and Aculf were settled foes. If Edrich Thegn knew of it, he didn't seem to care. Why should he? Who would care about a thrall? But it was likely that he didn't know. He had always seemed like a man who knew what he ought to do and did it, and who thought that everyone else should do the same. He didn't know what Aculf did because he didn't think of it and he didn't have the kind of eyes and ears his wife had had.

'Edrich Thegn ought to know what happens in Oakdene!' Could a thrall even ask if his lord was a good one, or say what his lord ought to do? 'He's not a hard man to heed, seldom overharsh, but he trusts Aculf too much.'

They were near the hills now, which stretched far beyond them: wide land and woodland, rising and falling, trees yellow-green in the harvest sunlight. Hidden among them lay the minster. How long would it be their home? Would they ever leave it again? Would the prior be as welcoming as Oswald had said? Unfollowed, their feet had grown slower each day. There was more time to think and even to speak the thoughts aloud.

'I was wrong,' said Brinin, after they had stopped to rest and eat.

'Wrong about what?'

'When I said that a good lord made thraldom easier. A bad lord might make it worse, but a good lord can't make it better. A good lord doesn't make a man any less a thrall.'

'Come, Bruni! What man has no lord? Every freeman in Oakdene is bound to heed Edrich Thegn, and he must heed the king. You can't say everyone is a thrall just because they have a lord.'

'Everyone has a lord, but only freemen have worth! Don't you remember last year when Baldred lost his eye in that fight with Eadulf? Eadulf had to pay him for the loss of the eye. If it had been my eye, I wouldn't have got a penny, not any more than swine or sheep would be paid for the loss of an eye. It would have gone to Edrich Thegn. We're gone now, and what is the loss to him? No more than if two swine or sheep or cows were stolen. If he has the money he can buy a couple of new thralls, like he could go to market and buy some sheep. Well, I'm more than cows or sheep or swine. More than a horse too, though you wouldn't think it at market! If freedom is what it takes for me to be seen as a man and treated like one, then I'd rather be free and hungry than a thrall with no more worth than a beast!'

It was seldom that Brinin, who meted out his words so sparingly, made a speech like this; seldom that he let such thoughts be heard. He could see that Row was somewhat taken aback.

'You don't know what you're saying,' said Row at last. 'Edrich Thegn may not be as good a lord as he could be, but there are men who are much worse. Cuthred did things that Edrich Thegn would never think of. None of his women thralls were safe from him. Edrich Thegn has never been like that. I can only think of one flogging since I've been in Oakdene—Cymen, do you remember him—and at the time we all thought he had earned it. But for

Cuthred's thralls, there were often floggings—a man died once—brandings, other unspeakable things. All things you've never seen. What do you think I was afraid of when we thought you'd be sold? Losing you, yes, but more than that: I knew what you could be going to. Not all lords *are* the same. And besides, you don't know what it's like to be hungry.'

Brinin knew he had touched those wounds that, for Row, had never fully healed. Yet wasn't it true? Did any sorrow that his kindred had borne make it less true? Hunger had made Row happy to be a well-fed thrall, but shame had made Brinin unhappy. Was it not shame to be taller and stronger than Aculf, yet to kneel before him when bidden? Fear had not driven him to it, but pride had strengthened him to. He hadn't been driven by fear for a long time, not since he was very small. It was pride that drove him to take a beating without fear or to look Aculf in the eye and say nothing because he could choose to. What could he choose? Not to do this work before that, as most men could; not to reap here or sow there. There was almost nothing he could choose, but he could choose to show no fear and wordlessly say: 'See, I am stronger than you think I am.' He knew it was pride and that he clung greedily to every drop of it. Edrich Thegn had said he was proud and perhaps he was right. He had no worth, no choice, and until now no way out, but he had pride. Clinging to it was the only way he had known to bear the shame that Aculf had heaped upon him almost every day. But those were thoughts that belonged inside. He couldn't say them, not even to Row.

'It looks like Oswald was right, doesn't it?' said Brinin. If they spoke of other things they could forget all the unsaid thoughts.

'Right about what?'

'That no one would think of us coming this way. Surely no one will come now. Everyone will be busy with the harvest.'

'I told you that days ago! Is it only now that you believe me?' laughed Row.

'I can still hardly believe it!'

If no one would come, perhaps a kind of freedom was something he could hope for. Not true freedom—how could a runaway slave have that—but something that felt a little like it. Everyone worked hard, but perhaps at the minster the work would taste sweeter.

'Perhaps you're right about freedom being hard work just like thraldom,' said Brinin, 'but it would need to be very bad for me to kneel readily to a man like Aculf again. I hope for Oakdene's sake that Edrich Thegn does learn what he is.'

'It's strange to think how long it could be before we see Oakdene again,' said Row.

'It could be years,' said Brinin. 'Or perhaps never at all.'

WORMS

The walk from the door to the far end of the hall was a long one that morning, as Oswald made his way along the side of the table. The floorboards creaked as he went by the great hearth in the middle of the room—were they always so loud? A forsaken pot of broth hung simmering over the fire. There was leek in that pot; he could smell it. The walk was slow and his father was at the end of it, watching him.

'Sit down,' said Edrich, nodding to the bench next to him.

Oswald sat, but his father did not. There wasn't much between them now—another winter and Oswald might be the taller—but his father seemed very tall as he stood looking down at him. Oswald felt few of his fifteen winters.

'Since you were a small boy,' Edrich began, 'I have always tried to teach you that we who lead must think of the good of those who follow. You are a thegn's son. One day, we hope, you will be thegn yourself. We have land. We have men who follow us as we follow the king. We go with the king into battle and some of our men go with us. Our highest loyalty is to the king—more even than to our kinsmen—but is it only because he calls us that we fight? No! You know it isn't. I have taught you this many times. We also fight for those under us too weak to fight for themselves. I thought you understood all this, but now I learn that I was wrong.'

Edrich walked away, standing with his back to Oswald. Oswald gripped the edge of the bench and stared unhappily at the floor. By his feet he saw little holes, bored by worms in the wood. What would his father say if he told him everything? If it were thegnlike to lead for the good of the weak, to fight when they were threatened, wasn't that what he had done for Brinin? Hadn't he sent Brinin away for his own good? Or was a slave too small to be thought of? Could he tell his father all that, that he had done wrong meaning to do good?

'I thought you understood that not all men are the same.' Edrich turned and walked towards Oswald again. 'Each man has his own work—whether fighting or farming or praying—and if that work is not done all will feel the loss of it. The king does not say, "I will no longer be king. I choose to do something else." The thegn does not say, "I will not serve the king, or fight in the fyrd, or lead my men." Such things are not thought of. We must all do the work that is given to us, without shirking it. Now it seems that you, who should know better, have helped two slaves to forsake their work, and you have forsaken your own to do it. Are we all to do the same? Where will it end?'

Oswald could feel his father looking down at him but he was too scared and ashamed to look up. This was no loud anger, nothing for those outside to hear. The anger walked tame and biddable at his father's side, but sorrow walked with it. And it was hard for Oswald to hear them and to know that he was their maker.

'What you did—and I say "you" and not "they" because what you did was worse—what you did took good and trustworthy men from their fields for three days. Now more men have gone, when they could be harvesting. That brings me to what is hardest for me to understand, Oswald.' Edrich spoke slowly, weighing out each word. 'Have you forgotten that I am your father? I am your father, and those two slaves are mine. Yet when you knew they were fleeing, you did nothing, you said nothing, you helped them. Perhaps you did not think that you were stealing from me, your father, but that is what it was.'

Hot tears were pricking Oswald's eyes, ready to flow if he let them. Words like these smarted more than Thurstan's arrows: unthegnlike, a thief, the worst of sons. He knew how to withstand a flood of anger; how to toughen himself and hide beneath his shield until it was over. But these words, softly and sternly spoken, would creep wormlike into his mind and stay there. If only his father knew… If only he knew everything it might be better for both of them. But he had sworn to Row that he would help them. How could he forsake them now that he needed help himself?

'I cannot understand why you would do this, Oswald. I cannot understand it and I would like to. Have you anything at all to say?'

'No, sir.' Eyes still on the floor, still on the wormholes, still down so that his father wouldn't see the ready tears. If he looked at his father he might not be able to hold them back.

Edrich sighed deeply and once more walked away and turned his back, for longer this time. Oswald set his teeth. Wouldn't a thrashing be easier to bear than this?

'There is something I must know, Oswald,' Edrich said, turning around at last. 'Perhaps someone helped you. You are fond of your sister and often talk to her. I wondered if perhaps—'

'No, Father! Don't think that!' Oswald's head shot up, no longer caring what his father saw. 'Think of me what you wish, but not that! I did it alone, everything. I told no one, and no one helped me. Ludan too; he had nothing to do with it. Nor did anyone else.'

'Very well. I'm glad Edith knew nothing of it. That's better than I feared.' Oswald could hear his father's voice change with that fear swept away. If he wasn't a good son, perhaps he wasn't such a bad one as his father had thought. If only he knew… 'Oswald, how can I make you understand what you have done? One day, you must be lord here after me. These men need to know that you can lead them. Today they are doubting that, and I find myself asking how I failed to teach it to you.'

How long was it to go on: his father blaming him, his father blaming himself, Edith alone standing guiltless? He had wanted it to be over; soon done, for all the smart. Now it seemed that it would never stop. Once again he raised his eyes to meet his father's.

'If you're going to beat me, Father, p… please do it now. Don't make me wait any longer.'

'I had thought that my days of beating you were long over, but I don't know what choice you have left me with. I don't like it any more than you do, but what else can I do? I'm glad you seem to understand that. But there will be no beating today. Hildræd your uncle needs me to help him with something, and I am about to ride out to see him. I won't stay away long, not at a time like this. I hope to be back by tomorrow evening at the latest. Besides, if you are to learn anything from all this, you must take time to think about your wrongdoing first.'

Oswald dropped his head again, more wretched than before, with everything still to dread and now the wormlike words to brood over.

'I must go now, Oswald. Think about what I have said. Try to understand what you have done.'

And Edrich strode away, was gone, and Oswald was alone.

He was still sitting forlornly on the bench when Edith came and sat down beside him. He saw Alrich standing like a lost man in the doorway.

'Oswald,' said Edith gently. 'Father has gone to see Hildræd our uncle now. Did he beat you? Was it very bad?'

Oswald shook his head. He couldn't speak straightaway. If he did, more than words might flow from him.

'It was worse than that. He... he talked. And he's making me wait for the beating until he gets back!'

Folk were beginning to drift back into the hall now. He had to get away. He didn't want to see anyone. He walked away quickly and didn't look again at Edith, or Alrich as he passed him. He met Thurstan by the church, still with his spear, perhaps waiting to see him there when it was over.

'Still waiting!' said Oswald hoarsely and kept walking.

He passed the church but did not stop to speak to Brother Wilfred who was standing outside. He crossed the meadow, walking swiftly through the long grass. He reached the far end, near the trees and away from the village. There he threw himself on the ground to lie staring at the sunlight. It rippled through the leaves above him; the tears rippled in his eyes. And the worms began to crawl about in his head.

THEGN

'What are you going to do about it, Edrich?' said Ealmund, watching Edrich in the dim light of the hall when the lamps had burned low and most men slept.

Edrich had been quickly gone and quickly back. He had been with his wife's kin barely long enough for his horse to rest and was on the road again before dawn; swift greeting, swift business, swift riding to troubles at home.

'I was near the hall when you called Oswald yesterday,' Ealmund went on when Edrich didn't speak. 'I saw you both leave it afterwards. He looked rather wretched—you did too if I'm truthful—but it didn't seem to me that you had already punished him, not from what I heard and saw.'

'I haven't. Not yet,' Edrich sighed. 'It's hard to know what to do for the best as a father and as a thegn. What have I got? Runaway slaves, a wayward son, angry men. And I am the one who must find answers to all of it. I don't even know where to start!'

'There will be a way to think of everything, and I have some thoughts if you'll hear them.' There was a slight snore from one of the men asleep on the benches round the side of the hall; they were not alone. 'Why don't we walk outside where we can speak more freely?'

'I was still a boy when you became a thegn, and your sons are already grown men. If you have any wisdom for me I would welcome it.'

'Come then, and we will talk.'

'I don't understand him, Ealmund!' exclaimed Edrich, as they walked through the night. 'He hasn't been a bad son. Fearful at times—that's worried me—and I've often had to speak to him about forgetting to be where he ought to. But not bad—better than I was myself, not overly wilful or unbiddable. And now this, without any warning, and all the village talking about it! Let's stop here. The roots of this tree make good seats. I often came here as a boy.'

They had come to the beech tree on the hill where Oswald often met with Brinin. Edrich and Ealmund sat down in the darkness, Edrich with another heavy sigh.

'You're talking as a father, and if that was all you had to think about, I'd tell you to give him a sound thrashing and be done with it. He's young, and we all did foolish things when we were young. I once set fire to the cowshed because I wanted to try lighting a fire and thought that was a good place to hide. I didn't do it twice, I can tell you!'

'I will most likely beat him for it. I must, I think. Isn't that the worst of being a father, that and burying a child? I would have beaten him yesterday had it not been for Hildræd; that and... He sat so dumb before me! I *think* I saw sorrow on his face. He was near to tears the whole time, likely would have wept if I'd talked for much longer. I almost felt like weeping myself! But he would barely speak. I asked him why he did it, and I've not often done that because knowing why seldom makes wrongdoing less wrong. I hated being asked why I'd done something as a boy—half the time I hardly knew. But I did ask, and he wouldn't tell me; and if he was as sorry as he looked, he didn't say so. He wanted nothing more than to have the beating over and be gone from me. He would have been happy to bear that so long as he didn't have to say anything.'

'Didn't we all want it to be over and be gone when we were boys? Put all that from your mind for now and think of it as a thegn. Have you talked to the men you sent out?'

'They've talked to me! Thurstan was so angry that if Oswald had been near at hand he'd have likely done my work as a father for me. I do feel answerable to them as I sent them out.'

'That's why you must think about all this as a thegn. The men are angry, and rightly so. In the fields, you are two slaves short at the busiest time of year. Everyone is talking about it, as you said. I overheard a lot while you were with Hildræd. "What is Edrich Thegn going to do about it?" they are asking. I even heard someone say that it's easy enough for a slave to flee as long as he has the right friends. There is not even a child in Oakdene who does not know that Oswald did this. And he will one day be their thegn!'

'That's what worries me, Ealmund. He *will* one day be their thegn and, given the times we live in, he could be their thegn sooner than we think.'

'So then Oakdene needs to see that he knows how wrong he was and rues it; and that you, their thegn, have not overlooked it.'

'Overlooked it! I didn't say I was going to overlook it. He'll be beaten for it—in the morning most likely. I don't like it, but I won't shirk it.'

'Come now, Edrich. If it were anyone else, you wouldn't be talking to him behind shut doors. You would have him before the Moot and deal with him there.'

'The Moot! I know he's done wrong, but bringing it before the Moot is too much. I am his father and I can deal with him in my own way!'

'You are not any father, and he is not any son. Don't fool yourself, Edrich. You can't deal with him like he's a wilful boy of ten winters: a few sharp blows and a stern word, tears shed and it's all over. Likely he is still young enough to learn from that, but the law says he is a man.'

'That may well be so, but even a thegn may punish his children without speaking to the whole village first!'

'Yes, he may. But when the law has been broken—here, by two slaves fleeing their lord; when someone is known to have helped break it—here, Oswald; then the Moot must be gathered. You are their thegn. It is for you to uphold the law here. Yet you are thinking as a father only when you ought to think as a thegn first and foremost.'

'But, Ealmund, I *am* his father and I was before I was thegn. He's ready to be beaten; he almost told me as much. But I said nothing to him about the Moot. Such a thought never came into my mind, and I won't think of it now!'

'Edrich, if anyone other than your own son had done this, you wouldn't waver. You can see all the trouble that's come of it. At such a time you must gather the Moot. You know that.'

'I'm not wavering because he is my son! I've never held back earned punishment on those grounds. He needs to lead these men one day! Won't the shame of coming before the Moot make it harder for him to be thegn when his time comes? Oakdene would not forget that quickly.'

'Oakdene won't forget what he has done either! That's where the shame lies and it's too late to do anything about that. But they know he's young. If they feel it was well dealt with then they may choose to overlook it. If it seems that he went unpunished, you can have no hope of that.'

'I have told you time and again that I *will* deal with him!'

'Unless you are thinking of taking him outside and beating him for all to see—and I know you aren't—then it will seem that he has gone unpunished. When the law has been broken, everyone always wants something to be done. With Oswald, more than with anyone else, they must see that it has been, or you will be wounding him before he has even become thegn.'

Edrich did not speak for a long time. He got up and walked away from the tree as though he might find wisdom hidden in the darkness.

'If I were to gather the Moot—and I am not saying that I will—how would it be done?' he said, sitting down again at last. 'I am his father, so it hardly seems right that I oversee it. And it is so unlike anything I have ever met with before that I don't know how I would begin.'

'When you think about it you may find that it is not wholly unlike other things you have met with, but leave that for now. First tell me what you would do if the slaves were found.'

'The slaves won't be found, Ealmund. I told the men to turn back by midday today at the latest if they had learned nothing. They'll already be on their way. I will bear the loss and that will be the end of it.'

'What do you mean? How can you know that they won't be found?'

'I've been thinking about it. Oswald took time over what he did, thought about it carefully. He must have done. Why then did you get the truth from him so easily, if it was the truth? It seemed that he spoke freely to you, but yesterday when I asked him why he did it, he had nothing to say.'

'He gave me to understand that he did it on a whim when he saw that the slaves were fleeing.'

'This was no whim.'

'You mean he lied to me?' Ealmund's voice grew somewhat harder.

'Yes. I wondered at the time and now I am almost sure of it. I think he lied to you but not to me. Perhaps, whatever else he had done, he couldn't bring himself to lie to his own father. I'm glad of that. It's the one good I can see in it all; that, and the way he won't let anyone else be blamed. He says he did it alone, and if that's a lie it's not a kind I mind so much. I won't ask him again if he knows where the slaves have gone. I think he does, but I'm not sending any more men to look for them.'

'We will see what the men say when they come back, but if you are right, then it must go before the Moot. Everyone must see that a man who helps a slave to flee—who helps any law to be broken—will answer for it. It's wise for you not to oversee it, though, so why don't I oversee it on your behalf? But let's come back to what I asked you before: if the slaves were found, what would you do?'

'I would have them soundly flogged; before the Moot, if you must know—you seem so keen on moots! I could put them to death, but I would see no need of that here and I would still lose two slaves that way. A flogging is fitting for a slave and would be enough, I think. One is young, and the other has always behaved well. But I don't see how that helps us, as they won't be found and I need to know what to do about Oswald.'

'We will come back to Oswald, but first let me ask you something else. Let us say that there was some wrongdoing here in Oakdene, a theft or perhaps a man burning his neighbour's crops. Now let's say that the man's kinsman or neighbour was aware of this, but said nothing and did nothing to stop him. If the man himself could not be brought before the Moot, who would answer for it?'

'Then the kinsman or neighbour would answer for it. If the man himself could not pay the fine, or if he were to flee, then the kinsman or neighbour must pay or bear the punishment.' Edrich stopped suddenly, and there was unease in his voice when he spoke again. 'Surely you don't think we should do something like that here?'

'What other way is there? You have already said that you don't believe the slaves will be found, but that if they were you would have them flogged. You have said that a man should answer for what another has done if he does not stop him or warn anyone. What has happened here? Two slaves have fled their lord. They cannot now be brought before the Moot as you would wish. Not only did Oswald fail to warn anyone or stop them, he even helped them. He is as much to blame as they are and must answer for what they have done. That's still true whether they are found or not, as his guilt is as great as theirs. It would be wholly fitting to have Oswald flogged, as they cannot be.'

'Flogged! He's not yet reached his sixteenth winter!'

'The law says he's a man and old enough to fight in the fyrd. If he can stand before the Danes, he can stand before the Moot. Isn't one of the slaves also young, yet you said a flogging was fitting for him? With him, you thought it was merciful!'

'He's a slave! My son is not, and a flogging can never be fitting for him!'

'He is young, though, as you say, so it wouldn't need to be overly harsh. But we *do* want to make sure that he never does anything like it again, and that others are warned off trying the same thing.'

'But, Ealmund, a flogging? He's a freeman and a thegn's son. The shame of such a thing! It's… it's unheard of!'

'What about a thegn's son helping his own father's slaves to flee? Now that is unheard of! But making a man answer for what another has done is not. Deal with this as it is, Edrich. It is unheard of and unfitting for a thegn's son to do what he did. Meet it with a punishment that is unheard of and unfitting for a thegn's son. What else can you do? You can't make him pay you for the loss of the slaves. He has no money. You would end up having to pay yourself! You want to make him a thegn who never forgets what he ought to do. This will be the way to teach him that. It's the best way and easy to make lighter or harsher as we see fit. Oakdene will see that it has been dealt with and when he is thegn they will overlook it. Besides, we could offer him mercy if he shows us that he understands his guilt and begs for forgiveness. That's how we can make him say what he must say for his own good. Only a very stubborn and wilful boy—or man when it comes to it—would turn down a lighter flogging, and you said he wasn't stubborn or wilful.'

'Almost never, but—'

'But what? He'll be frightened, Edrich, and he'll do what we need him to do.'

'He was frightened yesterday, but still more ready to be beaten than to speak. And he told me himself that he did it rather than let Ludan be blamed. I don't understand why Aculf was so sure it was Ludan. He overstepped himself there. I shall have to speak to him about it.' Edrich sat with his head in his hands for a long time, and there was something unthegnlike in his voice when he spoke again. 'I can see that there is wisdom in what you are saying, Ealmund, for Oakdene, perhaps even for Oswald, but… but if there were another way…'

'There is no other way, Edrich. Remember, Oakdene will be more ready to follow a thegn who knows he was wrong and has been punished for it, than one who seemed to go unpunished.'

'Yes, I can see that. But… but for a father to think of such a thing…'

'You are a father, but don't forget that you are also a thegn.'

MEADOW

On the third day after they had gone, the men came back from Waneting. They had found nothing but the anger they wore on their faces. Their voices were loud in the hall as they told Edrich Thegn: there had been no slaves; no one had seen them; they couldn't have gone that way. Alrich heard it all and slipped away to find Edith.

'They didn't find them,' he said, meeting her as she came up from the fields.

'And my father knows now?'

'I was there when the men told him. They're all very angry. They say Oswald lied. I can't say I fully understand everything that has been happening. I thought he had told Ealmund Thegn where they had gone.'

'He told him they had gone north. Now they know that wasn't true.'

'Oswald lied to Ealmund? Why? Is he mad?'

'Not mad. Loyal,' said Edith and ran to the hall, leaving Alrich staring after her in bewilderment.

The men were leaving the hall when she reached it, still talking angrily amongst themselves. Her father was inside, standing by the fire with Ealmund Thegn, both of them with their backs to her. They were too deep in speech to see her creep nearer to them.

'It seems that you were right, Edrich,' Ealmund was saying. 'He did lie to me and outwitted everyone not once, but twice. Can you see now why it must go before the Moot? You saw how angry the men are. This isn't only about Oswald any more.'

'Perhaps there is no other way.' Edrich sighed deeply. 'But I won't oversee it. How can I oversee the Moot when my own son is before it? I won't even speak. And… and if he is to be flogged, it would be better done by one of the men you came with, rather than an Oakdene man.'

'Very well then, I will see to that. But if I am overseeing, you must leave me to deal with it in my own way. You're wise not to speak. Let me do the talking and say what is to be done. Otherwise, I won't oversee it. You will find that I can bring it all to a much better end than you might have foreseen. Meanwhile, call the Moot to gather here in the hall this afternoon.'

Oswald sat at the far end of the meadow, his head in his hands. He was still waiting for his father to call him again; still being chewed at by dread; still hiding from everyone; still waiting for the men to come back from Waneting and make it all worse. But this was the sixth morning. Brinin and Row must be at the minster by now. He looked up and saw Edith running across the grass towards him, flushed and tearful.

'Edith! What is it?'

'The men are back!' she gasped. 'Father knows you lied. I heard him talking to Ealmund Thegn. They're gathering the Moot, Oswald, and they said you may be flogged!'

'What?' Oswald sprang to his feet. How could that be true? It sounded too much like a nightmare to be true, like some needless worry a man frets about when he can't sleep.

'They said you may be flogged,' said Edith again, her tears now flowing freely.

'It must be a mistake!'

'I heard them!'

Turning his back to her, Oswald walked away a little. It must be a mistake. He drew a deep breath and looked back at her to speak. She believed it. She thought it was the truth. Oswald turned away again without speaking, walked further and stood with his face in his hand. Edith was wrong. She must be. He went back to her and grasped her arm.

'B… but that can't be right! Father said he would b… beat me. He said nothing about the Moot. He wouldn't do that. Not to me!'

'Oswald, I heard them! Oh, what shall we do?'

Oswald shut his eyes, breathing hard. If she had heard; if there was no mistake…

'Brinin and Row are far away by now.' Who was he soothing, Edith or himself? 'No one knows where they went. I haven't even told you. They should be safe now, so I have done what I meant to.'

'But what about you? Can't you understand what I'm telling you?' wept Edith.

'Of course I understand! But… but don't think about it. Brinin and Row are safe.'

But this made Edith sob all the harder and Oswald put his arm around her. The thought of it was bad enough; she mustn't see it or hear it.

'Edith,' he said, steadying his voice and bearing it along like a wounded man. 'The Moot will likely gather in the hall. Don't stay there, or anywhere nearby. Go somewhere far away where you won't hear or see anything—take one of the women if you like—and ask Alrich to come and tell you when it's over. Don't come back before then. I think… I think I will find it easier if I know you aren't nearby to… to hear it. Go and tell Father where I am. I won't leave the meadow. He'll send someone to fetch me when they're ready.'

So Edith left him, unwillingly enough, but she seemed to know that he was right. Perhaps she was as fearful of hearing it as he was of being heard. Oswald watched her walk across the meadow and behind the church. Fear was no longer clinging to him or standing at his side; it was right inside him, twisting his gut. He rushed behind a small shrub, retching and spewing onto the grass, then stood leaning with his hands against a tree. He had known for days that he could not hide from what must come to him; but he had thought his father would give him a beating that would smart and be over, where he could set his teeth and bear it, then walk away and try to forget. But a flogging didn't simply smart: it was tearing and wounding and shame for all to see. He had never seen one, but he had heard one meted out on a slave once, long ago when he was a small boy; he had heard the screams, had seen them carry him away afterwards. It was the best Brinin and Row could have hoped for had they been caught, but they were slaves. How could *he* be flogged, a freeman and a thegn's son? It was worse, much worse, than anything he had feared.

'Come now, Oswald.' Let him speak to himself, man to man, like swordbrothers getting ready to stand against their foes. 'There is nothing to be done. Bear it and it will be over. Brinin and Row are safe.'

Then he sat back down on the grass to wait.

MIST

I t had been a long road, but an easy one with one wet day only, the others all bright and dry and good for the harvest they had left behind them. After a time they stopped hurrying along. It seemed that no one *would* follow them, not now that they had gone so far and so many days had passed. They walked at their ease and looked at the land about them; they talked more and stopped for longer. They spoke to a man on the road who told them that the shortest way to the minster was over the nearby hills. And they took that way, not only because it would be quicker, but because it would be a change from the old stones under their feet.

And it was a change. These hills were not like the little hills round Oakdene. They stretched out unevenly before them, sometimes rolling gently, sometimes barren and rocky. The day they climbed into the hills was the best of days. They were safe now and even the wind seemed to taste of freedom and gladness. Standing aloft on one of the pale rocks that jutted out everywhere from the rough grass, Brinin looked across the rocks, across the hills, down over the land below and far, far away to where the land met the sky in a dark blue mist. The wind was in his face, and he felt like shouting out, or leaping or waving his arms, or doing a score of things he never did. And it seemed that he was flying, eaglelike, as he had dreamed of doing as a boy.

But the blue skies were gone in the morning. A mist so thick had fallen in the night that they could see nothing beyond the few feet in front of them. The hills were gone; the far-off land was gone; the sun was gone. There was nothing but the mist which clung to them, cold and damp like soft rain, but white and smokelike.

'We can't walk in this,' said Brinin. 'Much better to stay where we are.'

'It may lift,' said Row. 'It's still early. There's no harm in waiting for a time.'

They stayed where they were, and the mist stayed with them. It hung thick and wet about them and chilled them to the bone. It drowned any hope of a fire and stole the heat of the sun. They sat huddled in their cloaks for warmth; they stood and stamped their feet and struck themselves on the arms, but it didn't lift and Row grew restless again.

'Why sit here and freeze?' He kicked at a clump of grass. 'We'd be much better to walk and keep warm.'

'How would we even know which way to go? We can't see the sun. We can't see anything!'

'The sun set last night beyond that rock. That's west. We want to go south. We can start from the rock and walk slowly.'

'It will be too easy to stray,' said Brinin doggedly. 'Once we leave here we'll lose our way. Why hurry? Why not stay here until it lifts?'

'Because it isn't lifting, and we've already waited! It's too cold and wet to sit here. It may be better further along, and we won't know unless we keep going.'

'It may not be any better.'

'It's too cold and wet to stay here, Bruni. We can walk slowly.'

And Brinin did yield at last, because he *was* cold and because it was easier to yield to a brother who had been so fatherlike to him over the years. His qualms hung about him like the mist did. Yet hadn't Row been right that no one would follow them? Hadn't Brinin's misgivings about that proved groundless?

They picked their way along. The hills were still and dim, without so much as a breath of wind to drive the mist away. They walked in a dreamlike, ghostly world, where everything they saw was ashen and deathbearing. The rocks, boulders and little shrubs scattered along their path glided out at them noiselessly, taking shape suddenly before them. They looked shadowy and bodyless, though hard enough to touch. Even their voices did not sound the same any more. The mist wanted to drown their voices, to choke their words.

It didn't lift, and after what felt like a long time they stopped to sit and eat. How could they know how long it had been without a sight of the sun to tell them? How could they know whether they were nearer the minster or not? How could they know where they were as they wandered in an unknown land without even their eyes to help them? Some would have said they were fools to flee from Oakdene, but surely they needn't be so unwise as this.

'I'm warmer now that we've been walking. Aren't you, Bruni?' Row was all cheer, all ready to see the best when there was little of it to see.

'I'd rather be cold and know where I was!'

'We're not as lost as all that! I don't think we've strayed far at all.'

'When the mist clears, we'll see that we have.'

Row sighed. Brinin knew that Row's mind was not his as they sat there: two men, two minds, two wishes. They hadn't often been two-minded over the years. He ought to be the one to bend, as biddable as he was younger, but Brinin had yielded once that day and they were no better for it. And he would rather they sat wise and two-minded than walk unwise as one.

'Why not stay here for a while then?' said Row, choosing to bend this time. 'We don't need to hurry, as you said, and if the mist lifts we can go on.'

'That would be wiser.'

They sat, wise and one-minded, and grew cold again together; but they talked and remembered and even laughed a little so that they did not mind the cold so much. They sat close together and kept a little warmer that way, while the mist hovered white and wraithlike around them. But after a time, Row grew restless once more.

'We can't go much further today,' he said. 'We would have been better not coming this way, though the man on the road did say it was quicker. But this is no place to spend the night—it's too open and we're unlikely to get much of a fire tonight. Why don't we go a

little further and see if we can find somewhere more sheltered?
Then we can stop until morning.'

So they set off again, creeping towards the hidden things that
crept back at them; creeping slowly, very slowly, through the mist,
which stretched beyond them without fading.

MOOT

Oswald was never sure afterwards how long he waited that day—perhaps it wasn't as long as it seemed—but at last he looked up to see Thurstan, grim-faced, walking towards him across the grass, and he knew it was time.

'Has the Moot already gathered?' Oswald asked as he stood up.

'It has been gathered for some time now, and we have been talking about what is to be done with you, should you be found guilty, that is. I've been sent to take you there now.'

'It's not going to go well for me, is it?'

The look Thurstan gave him, before he even spoke, was a loud answer: the answer Oswald had foreseen and feared.

'Did you think it would? You *are* guilty, after all,' Thurstan sighed. 'I can't say that dragging you before the Moot is how I would have handled this, but you've brought it upon yourself, Oswald.'

'I know.'

'Let's not keep them waiting, then,' said Thurstan gruffly.

Oswald stared straight ahead as they walked to the hall but he saw almost nothing. He breathed slowly to strengthen himself and tame the sudden urge he had to run the other way. Thurstan was unlikely to let him run if he'd tried, and where would he go? They had almost reached the hall when Thurstan stopped him, a hand on his arm.

'Listen, Oswald,' he said earnestly. 'Most of the men in there are angry with you, and who could blame them? They want sorrow from you and to know that you rue what you did. If you are wise

146

you will give it to them. This is no time to be stubborn. Answer them as meekly as you can and perhaps then they may pity you.'

Could such counsel come from Thurstan, so bold and unshakeable, whom Oswald had never known to utter a meek word? If this was what Thurstan thought was wisdom, then couldn't he be all meekness without shame?

'Is that what you would do, Thurstan?'

'Well, perhaps not,' he said wryly. 'But it's what you should do.'

Ealmund sat on a great seat—Oswald's father's seat—at the top of the hall. Edrich, heavy about the eyes as though he hadn't slept, sat next to him; and on benches on either side of them were almost a score of freemen. He saw Saxulf, Rædwald and Cynestan among them, and the men who had ridden to Waneting. Thurstan was right: they were all angry. Aculf was there; he wouldn't look at him. Worse than being called before the men his father's age was seeing the young—Leofwine, Beorn, Sigelm, all a little older than himself. They had played together as boys and now they had come to see his shame. He saw Alrich, troubled and unhappy, but Brother Wilfred was not there and for that Oswald was glad. Thurstan led him before the men.

'Don't forget what I said to you,' Thurstan whispered, his hand again on Oswald's arm in a last token of friendship before it began.

Thurstan went to sit on a bench with the men, throwing Ealmund a look that couldn't have been less friendly if Ealmund had been a Dane. Oswald was left to stand alone, facing the Moot.

'Oswald,' began Ealmund, sternly though not unkindly. 'You are accused of helping two of your father's slaves to flee. It seems that when you learned that they had gone, you did all you could to stop them from being followed. You wilfully misled those who were looking for the slaves, so that six days were wasted. Not only were many of the men here sent from their fields at the height of harvest, but now the slaves cannot be found. Before I call the witnesses, do you have anything to say?'

'Everything you said is true,' said Oswald. What else was he to say? They only knew he had done it because he had told them.

Wasn't it shame enough to be standing before them without having witnesses speak aloud his wrongdoings one by one?

'Very well. You should know that your father would rather bear the loss himself than send out any more men.' At this there was a murmur from the benches; this was the kind of lord they liked. 'What you did has brought your own father loss. Can you tell us why you did such a thing?'

Perhaps he should tell them. If his father would send no more men, why not tell them everything? Mightn't they understand then? Mightn't they see that he was not so bad, not so unsonlike as they thought? He almost spoke but before he opened his mouth, his eyes met his father's and what he saw there stopped his tongue. It wasn't anger. It was sorrow. There was nothing he could say that would not somehow blame his father and bring him more sorrow. Could he tell them all that his father did not know his own workreeve, who had been so wolflike that flight had seemed the only way? Could he say that he had been trying to save Brinin and Row from unjust sorrow without seeming to lay the blame for it at his father's feet? How could he say any of that here? How could he shame his father before all his men? If there had been a time to speak, it was already gone. It was better to say nothing and let them think of him what they liked.

'No, sir,' he said.

There was another murmur from the benches, and Oswald caught the words, 'So we were all sent off for days for nothing at all!'

'You have all heard what he has to say,' said Ealmund. 'Let us now hear from the witnesses.'

Saxulf rose to speak, but Thurstan sprung to his feet before he could say a word.

'He told us he did it! He hasn't asked any of us to swear to his good name, though I for one would say that it *is* good. Why listen to witnesses?'

'Sit down, Thurstan! We will do this as it is always done,' said Ealmund sharply. He turned to Saxulf. 'Please go on.'

'We rode into the forest for a day and a half before we heard that the horses had been found. All the while, Oswald Child listened to us speaking about getting back to our harvests but said nothing. He let us ride further from Oakdene knowing that we were wasting our time.'

'Ealmund Thegn,' said Cynestan, rising to join Saxulf. 'You said that Oswald Child did it when he learned that the slaves had fled. Forgive me, sir, but that cannot be so. The tracks we followed had been carefully laid.'

'That's true enough!' said Saxulf. 'Thurstan here called me a fool when I said that we couldn't be sure which way to go at the stream, but I was right!'

Thurstan scowled at him and had the look been words Saxulf would likely have been called a choicer name than 'fool'.

'I could forgive a whim,' went on Cynestan. 'Weren't we all at times unthinking when we were young? But he knew that they were going to flee and thought of a way to outwit us. Thurstan *was* right. No horse thieves or fleeing slaves would have turned back to the village on reaching the stream. Oswald Child meant us to go south, and we did. I've always been fond of you, Oswald Child, but you knew it was harvest and that we needed to be in our fields. It is much harder to forgive that than a whim.'

Ealmund turned to Oswald again. 'Is it true that you knew beforehand that the slaves were going to flee and wilfully thought of a way to mislead us?'

'Yes, sir.' Oswald kept his head down as a hum of anger rose from the men. He dared not look at any of them, least of all his father. He *had* been right to help Brinin and Row—he knew he had—but somehow it was hard to stand before all these angry men and not think of himself as they did.

'Let me also say,' said Ealmund, 'that I asked Oswald to tell me the truth, and he told me that he had seen the two slaves going north. It seems now that this was untrue. You lied to me, didn't you, Oswald?'

Oswald wished now that he hadn't lied. Wouldn't it have been better to have said nothing? He hadn't known what else to do. How could something that had begun as the best thing he had ever wished for be ending now like this?

'Yes, sir,' he said, and shame pushed his head down a little further.

Rædwald had risen to his feet. 'I heard that the slaves may have gone to join the Danes. Their mother was one. I wouldn't like to think that Oswald Child was helping them with that, but someone needs to ask it.'

How could anyone even think such a thing? Oswald did look up then and saw his father half-rise to his feet, but Thurstan had already leapt up before Edrich could speak.

'We're not judging him on hearsay! There is nothing to make us think that the slaves have gone to the Danes.'

'There's nothing to make us think that they haven't either!' Rædwald snapped.

Thurstan turned to look down scornfully at Aculf before he answered.

'There may be men fool enough to start some tale, Rædwald. That doesn't mean you should be a bigger fool and believe it.'

Thurstan was growing sharper-tongued every time he spoke, more men feeling the edge of it. It wasn't only Oswald they were angry with now, and Ealmund seemed keen to push things along before the anger boiled over.

'I think we have all heard enough now unless anyone else has something to say.'

Oswald bit his lip as Aculf stood. It was hard to hear about his misdeeds from the lips of worthy men. To hear about them from Aculf would be unbearable.

'Blame fell on another because of what Oswald Child did,' said Aculf smoothly. 'Whether he meant it to be that way or not, I cannot say.'

'That had nothing to do with Oswald!' It was his father, speaking for the first time since the whole dreadful thing had begun! 'That was wholly your doing, Aculf. He came to me as soon as he heard Ludan had been beaten and if he hadn't, who knows if we would ever have learned that he had done it? Now sit down and hold your tongue!'

Oswald had hardly looked at his father, but now he tried to catch his eye in bewildered thanks. Even if his father was so angry and ashamed that he was doing this to him, at least he wouldn't let Aculf fling about his near lies. But Edrich was glaring at Aculf and did not see his son's look.

'We have heard enough,' said Ealmund. 'He helped two slaves to flee; he lied and misled us; many men were sent away from their harvests because of him. We can only be thankful that the harvest was not lost. He ought to have stopped the slaves' flight when he knew of it, or raise the alarm. Instead, he helped them. He is as much to blame as they are. Are we all of one mind on this?'

And the voices from the benches were one voice; the men who sat there were one man, sharing one mind as Ealmund had said. There seemed to be no one to stand beside Oswald and speak for him; nothing they could have said had they wanted to. How could there be? Ealmund had told no lies. Ealmund turned to Oswald once more.

'Had the slaves been caught, this Moot would most likely have had them flogged. They cannot be caught now. But you are also to blame and you *can* be flogged.'

It was coming now, as Edith had said. She hadn't been mistaken. It had been too unbelievable to be true; now it was too true to be disbelieved. Given how hard his heart was pounding, it was a wonder that he could stand so still, though he clenched his fists to steady his quivering hands. He saw Thurstan stand again to speak.

'You all already know what I think about this, but as some of you seem to be a little slow, I'm happy to say it again. He did wrong, and I've already told him so myself. I was as angry as any of you, but this is a needless show. Let his father deal with him. That should be more than enough.'

'Sit down, Thurstan! You already know what we think about it and why it must come before the Moot.' Ealmund turned to Oswald again. 'You are young, though already a man under the law, and I understand that with youth comes much foolishness. But everyone needs to learn that the man who knows of lawbreaking and does nothing is as guilty as the man who does it. You understand that you must be punished?'

'Yes, sir,' said Oswald. It was striding towards him, too quickly to flee from, too all-seeing to hide from.

'I thought you did. We all know that you are young and because of that and because of your father, who has long been my friend, I would like to be merciful to you. None of us here wish to be overly harsh. You must be punished, but perhaps it is just as needful for you to show us, here before the Moot, before the men whose time you have wasted, that you understand how wrongly you have behaved and for you to ask for forgiveness. Then we might find a way to soften it—a lighter flogging, so to speak—four or five lashes at the most. What do you say?'

Oswald stared at Ealmund. Was he handing him an easier way out? Perhaps Thurstan had known and that was why he had told him to be meek. It would be bad enough but quickly done. He had never been too proud to ask for forgiveness and he had known since that first morning in the forest that so much of what he had done had been wrong. He would never be sorry that Brinin and Row were gone, but almost everything he had done to help them he had done badly. Let him ask forgiveness for the men's trouble and for the lying. Then he could bear the shame and be done with it, and this worst of all days could be over.

'I thank you for your kindness, sir,' he said, and the words came out so steadily that it was a wonder even to himself. He looked from Thurstan and Rædwald to Saxulf and Cynestan and to the others who had ridden to Waneting. 'I *am* sorry that I took you away from your harvests. You are right to be angry with me, and I ask your forgiveness. I have learned that it isn't enough to think of the outcome. I should have thought of everyone. I won't forget that easily. And I am sorry that I lied to you, sir. I do feel ashamed of myself for that.'

He knew that he meant it, that every word was as true as the lies had not been. Once again he saw Thurstan stand. Oswald felt very warm towards Thurstan. He was more than a friend—perhaps his only friend now—however angry he had been.

'I think we can be happy with that, Ealmund,' he said. 'He's done what you asked, and now you can keep your side of it.'

But Ealmund was still stern. There was no nod to show that Thurstan had said what was in his own mind; not even the beginning of a smile. Surely it had been enough? What else was he meant to say? Did Ealmund want him to beg on his knees?

'I'm not sure that we can be happy with it,' said Ealmund. 'You still haven't shown me that you are sorry for forsaking your duty to your father and to Oakdene. You said nothing about—'

'I know my duty to my father!' It all burst out in a sudden flood of words. 'It might not have looked like it, but I do! And I did what you asked. Why isn't that enough? What do you want me to say? I'm sorry. Please forgive me!'

'Let me make this easier for you, Oswald.' Ealmund was slow and soft and cold as ice. 'I asked you to *show* us how sorry you are. You know what you ought to have done. Show us that you are as sorry as you say by doing it: tell us where the slaves have gone.'

So that was what Ealmund wanted. It was all a trap. What he had mistaken for kindness was only a way to make him say what they wanted, and his hope of mercy crumbled before his eyes. Meekness had been wisdom. But Ealmund hadn't been handing him a gift. He wanted to sell him a lighter flogging at the price of two slaves. Oswald didn't love his own skin enough for that.

'I am waiting for your answer, Oswald,' said Ealmund.

'It was enough, Ealmund.' Thurstan was unshifting, someone to stand with Oswald after all. 'Let's forget the rest of it.'

'Thurstan, would you hold your tongue? I am waiting, Oswald.'

Wasn't it enough without this? Oswald looked at his father, wordlessly begging him to do something, anything to help him. He saw Edrich lean over to Ealmund and whisper something to him. Ealmund frowned and shook his head before answering in a low voice that Oswald couldn't hear.

'What do you have to say, Oswald?' he said sternly.

'I can't!' said Oswald. Mercy was out of his reach now. The price for it was too high.

'Don't be foolish, Oswald!' Ealmund was angry now. He was a man whose word almost never went unheeded. 'They are two slaves. You owe them nothing. You are answerable only to your father and not to two slaves. Stubbornness won't help you here. Why would you throw mercy away?'

The room seemed to swim before Oswald's eyes and his back was awake, already shying from looming pain. Why did Ealmund keep speaking as though he had a choice? This was no choice. Foolish pain was the only thing he could ask for. He hadn't come to the Moot hoping for mercy and now he wouldn't get it. Perhaps he wasn't any worse off than at the beginning, when harshness was all he had foreseen.

'I can't!' he said again, this time with a firmness that belied how sick with fear he was beginning to feel. 'I was more to blame than they were and I can't give them up.'

The noise grew in the hall as all the men began to talk at once. Edrich, staring at his son in disbelief, half-rose from his seat again. Ealmund raised a hand to still the men and looked at Oswald sternly.

'I think you mean that you won't!' he said. 'You must understand that I cannot give you—'

'Ealmund! What he said was enough!' Thurstan was as angry as Ealmund now, speaking mercy that no one would listen to, trying to hold back something that wouldn't stop.

'Nothing more from you, Thurstan! You must understand, Oswald, that I cannot give you mercy if you won't do what I ask. Now for the last time: where did they go?'

'I have nothing more to say, sir,' said Oswald. That was it. Ealmund would not get another word from him.

'You won't do what I ask?' said Ealmund.

Oswald looked at Ealmund—at Ealmund only, not at his father nor anyone else—then bowed his head.

After that everything was dreamlike, all dread and the drumming of his own heart. He saw Ealmund and his father in swift speech, but it was Thurstan's voice he heard: 'Ealmund, this is too much!' Ealmund beckoning one of his own men. His father leaning forward with his head in his hands. A dreadful, sickening thrill as he caught sight of the whip, dark and stranded, in the man's hand. Ealmund's voice, angry, hard: 'Lay them on well. I'll tell you when to stop.'

154

Thurstan again: 'For pity's sake, Ealmund!' His hands were shaking more now, despite his clenched fists. But in the quiet of his own head, he took hold of himself: 'It will be over soon. Brinin and Row are not found. Breathe. Breathe. It will all be over soon.' Ealmund's man was walking towards him, but what relief, what thankful relief, that he was a stranger and not a man he had to live alongside afterwards.

'Very well then.' Ealmund nodded to his man. 'Get him ready.'

AFTER

I t was Alrich who found Edith afterwards, alone under a tree beyond the fields and far from the hall. She looked very small as she sat there, resting her chin on her knees, pale and tight-lipped and wretched as she waited. She had gone far from any sight or sound as Oswald had wished, but there was nowhere to hide from the knowledge of it.

'Is it over?' Edith's voice quivered like the leaves above her.

'Over now,' said Alrich, sitting down on the grass beside her. 'I've come to fetch you back.'

'Tell me what happened. You don't need to spare me, Alrich. You can't make me more unhappy than I am already. And... and even if I don't know, I will see it in my mind all the same.'

'He acknowledged what he had done quite openly, so we didn't need to listen to witnesses for long. Ealmund offered him a lighter flogging if Oswald would beg for forgiveness and show that he knew how wrong he had been.'

'*Did* he beg for forgiveness?' asked Edith, whispering now.

'Yes, for wasting the men's time and for lying, but Ealmund said that wasn't enough. He asked him to show that he was sorry by telling him where the slaves had gone.'

'But... but... Oswald would never do that!'

'He didn't. I don't think Ealmund wanted so much to be merciful as to frighten him into doing what he wanted. He *was* afraid, I think—anyone would be—but not enough for that. Ealmund asked him three or four times, but he wouldn't. Ealmund was angry about that.'

'So they… they did it?'

Alrich's first answer was wordless, as it had to be when an unwilling speaker was being driven by an eager listener. Edith seemed to understand the answer before the words came. She stiffened a little and looked away from Alrich, keeping her eyes on the grass.

'I've seen it before, and this wasn't as bad as it could have been but it was harsh enough. He didn't fight it at all, didn't even struggle when they bound him. He was fairly quiet, but his face—' Alrich stopped sharply and let the wind in the trees speak and stop him from saying too much. 'He fainted before the end, and Thurstan told Ealmund that it was time to stop, but the man—it was one of Ealmund's men—struck him again before any word was given. Then your father shouted, "It's enough!" And they untied Oswald and carried him out.'

Edith hid her face in her knees. She sat very still for a long time, while the sound of far-off voices drifted down to them from the fields. The leaves rustled a little as the wind passed through them, and all was as it should be on a harvest afternoon. Yet nothing was as it should be.

'And my father? Is he very angry with Oswald?' she said at last.

'I saw more sorrow than anger. He barely spoke. He couldn't stay seated after the first lash and walked up and down behind where we were sitting. When it was over, it was your father and Thurstan who carried Oswald away to his bed. I know you've been thinking of Oswald, Edith, but think of your father too and be kind to him.'

'Have you seen Oswald since… did you see him afterwards?'

'No, only Brother Wilfred, who was tending to him. He asked me to come and find you and to tell you not to worry, but that you shouldn't come to see him yet. He will call for you when he's ready. It was right for you to stay away, Edith. Oswald wouldn't have wanted you even to hear it. It's a shameful thing to be flogged before the Moot. It's for slaves, unheard of for someone like Oswald. Yet when he wouldn't say where they had gone, I couldn't help thinking he was rather brave. I don't understand why he did it, though. Why would he want to help two runaway slaves?'

'Brinin saved his life once, years ago when they were small boys, and Father was going to sell him and send him away from here and from his brother. I think Oswald would have done almost anything to save Brinin from that.'

'So that's why you said he was loyal? Your father ought to know that, don't you think?'

'Oswald won't tell him—he never tells Father anything—and he made me swear that I wouldn't. Perhaps I can find a way to tell him even a little, now that it's all over.'

Alrich stood up and held out his hand to Edith.

'Come, Edith,' he said. 'Let's go back to the hall.'

The hall was almost empty when they reached it. A few women were cooking by the hearth, and Brother Wilfred was stirring something in a copper bowl. Edrich sat at the table, his head leaning on one hand, his other hand resting on some crumpled cloth that lay on the table. He seemed so weary and heavy-hearted that Alrich left and let Edith go to him alone. She sat down beside him but did not speak.

'My lord,' said Brother Wilfred. 'I have made a salve of wine, garlic, leek and honey. It will help the wounds to heal.'

Edrich nodded, and Edith watched as Brother Wilfred stepped behind Oswald's curtain. She reached out and laid her hand on her father's arm. Edrich put his own hand on Edith's, and she suddenly saw that it was Oswald's shirt he had been resting his hand on. Just then they heard a cry from behind the curtain, and Edith buried her face in her father's arm to weep.

All that night, Oswald seemed to be drowning in a river of darkness and pain. He would sink into feverish, frightening dreams: Brinin and Row were followed by horsemen that Oswald couldn't stop, and when he called out to warn them nothing came from his mouth; he stepped outside the hall to see Brinin dragged across the grass, caught and facing death, but when he tried to run to help him his legs seemed fastened to the ground; he was under the lash again, hearing the crack, his whole back ablaze with its cuts.

When the dawn, cold and grey, crept in at last, Oswald was weary and sick with pain but he wasn't afraid. It was over, all the stiff waiting and fretting; the sleepless nights and wary days; the months with little else in his mind. It was over. Nothing could be worse now and there seemed to be little to worry about.

Throughout the day he drifted in and out of sleep, a broken sleep, but a dreamless one. He was aware of Brother Wilfred giving him sips of some drink; it had a bitterness to it, and he didn't know what it was. He heard his own voice, strange and far away, cry out in pain as the good monk tended his wounds with hands as gentle as a mother's.

On the second day, or perhaps it was the third, he woke early when all was still dark before dawn. When had he last eaten? He couldn't remember and he was hungry. Perhaps if he crept out of bed he could find some bread or something left from the night before. But it was long work to ease himself up, so slow to turn from his chest to his side and draw his feet to the floor. Every inch he shifted was all the sorer. He went no further than the edge of his bed, where he sat in the darkness. There could be no creeping. Better to be still and wait for Brother Wilfred to come. Folk were beginning to wake now. He could hear voices outside.

'My dear boy!' said Brother Wilfred, coming to him some time later. 'I didn't think I would find you awake. Is it wise for you to get up so soon?'

'I'm hungry,' said Oswald.

'That's good! You must be mending if you want to eat. Now, lie down while I fetch you some food.'

'Please let me sit. It hurts more if I move, but I can bear it if I sit still like this. I'll lie down again when I've eaten.'

It was no feast that Brother Wilfred brought—bread and butter, apples and ale—but every bite was strengthening, and the burning of his back seemed a little more bearable with a full belly.

'Where's Edith?' asked Oswald at last. He hadn't seen her since he had sent her away weeping from the meadow; he had barely thought of her. She must be worrying by now.

'Prowling around like a cat after a mouse.'

'Should I ask her to come now? Or is it better if she doesn't see me yet?'

'Is it kind to keep her away? Your sister is stronger than you think she is.'

Not kind, and perhaps she was stronger than he was. But if she came she would see him, and he would have to watch her seeing him; and she would see the shame that would be written over his back until he died. Wouldn't it make it more shameful for her eyes to fall on it, even though it was nothing she didn't already know? Yet he would be unkind to keep her away.

'Would you please help me put a shirt on and then ask her to come?'

'A shirt! I don't think that is wise.'

'I don't want her to see my back.' It was better to hide what they both knew.

'A cloak, then, but not a shirt.'

Oswald could never have believed that the soft, woollen folds of his cloak could have felt so heavy and knifelike as they did when Brother Wilfred carefully draped them over his shoulders. He drew in his breath sharply as the cloak touched his back and it might as well have been made of nettles or thorns from the smart. Brother Wilfred went to find Edith, leaving Oswald sitting stiffly, afraid that the cloak would tear his back with the smallest start or twitch. It wasn't long before he heard her running across the floor with swift steps. She burst past the curtain ready to fling her arms around him, but Oswald flinched as Edith reached him and she drew back just in time.

'I'm sorry, Oswald. I won't hug you yet.' And she bent down and kissed him gently on his head.

'Are you in much pain now?' she asked, pulling up a stool and sitting down near him.

Edith was so full of care and wary hope that a truthful answer would not do. Was he to tell her that he was so raw that he didn't know where one wound ended and the next began? That the slightest stirring sent arrows of fire shooting across his back, searing as they went? And that keeping still was only a little better?

'Not as much now as at the beginning,' he said. That would have to be truth enough for Edith. Hadn't he eaten? Wasn't he sitting up? And the pain perhaps wasn't as great as it had been when the lash was still falling.

'Oswald,' said Edith at last. 'Alrich told me that Ealmund offered you mercy and that you wouldn't take it.'

'It wasn't mercy. He wanted me to sell Brinin and Row to him: tell him where they'd gone and get only a few lashes; hold my tongue and get more. What else was I to do? There would have been no mercy offered to Brinin and Row if they'd found them.'

'Alrich said you were very brave.'

Brave? On that sickening, fearful, shameful day? When all had been trembling and dread? He knew what courage was. He'd heard men talk of it since he was a small boy, and there had been none at the Moot.

'No, he's wrong. I was... I was very scared. I felt sick, and my hands wouldn't stop shaking.'

'And even then you wouldn't do what Ealmund asked,' said his sister. 'I think that was a kind of courage.'

SHAME

Oswald's curtain was thick and heavy and hid him away from any eyes or light that might otherwise fall on him. It was dim as he lay face down on his bed some days later; he didn't know how many days later. The days crept along with weary feet, so painfully slowly that there were times when he could almost have wept. That would at least have given him something to do. Sometimes he could hear what they were saying in the hall. Now someone was being scolded for spilling something, the hard words rising above the other voices and the sounds of work and cooking. Why hadn't they been more careful? Hadn't they been warned about it before? Oswald didn't know who was being scolded or what they had spilled, but it was something to listen to. Better that than the still darkness with nothing but the little scuffling mousethieves who came scratching to gather the crumbs he had dropped. Once he had lit a candle and sat with his waxboard in hand, but his mind had been so brooding that the Latin wouldn't stick there. He had tossed his waxboard aside and blown out the candle. Why waste the light when the gloom matched his thoughts better?

The food for evening-meat was almost ready, and the smell made his belly feel empty. Outside the sun was drawing nearer to the earth, the fields all golden with the stubble left by the gathered wheat. He could see it all in his mind, could feel the freshness of the evening, cooler now that summer had ended. And he longed for it all, longed to be outside so much that it was like a kind of ache to sit with the other, worse one. Likely he *could* go out now. His back still hurt, but not with the same burning, not with the same breathtaking pain as before. He could bear it well enough now. He had to bear it, so he did. He was not so sore now that he couldn't walk about or leave his bed to eat. But here in the dark he was alone. Out in the longed-for light there would be eyes everywhere: eyes that had not been at the Moot but had been waiting to see him, eyes that had watched everything done to him there, his father's eyes to look away from so his own did not meet them. It was no longer a torn back that kept him to his bed. That smart grew a little less each day. The other grew keener. He reached out his hand and touched the curtain. He lay in such a small dark place. The outside was so near, and so far away.

He had learned the sound of Edith's feet as he spent long days on his bed. She always walked quickly, and he could hear her steps above the others. She was coming towards the curtain now. Oswald eased himself up—that still hurt more than lying still—and drew his cloak around his shoulders.

'Oswald, are you awake?'

'Yes. You can come in.'

Edith held a candle, and its light shone on her face and on the one stray lock, golden as the wheat, that had slipped out from under her headcloth and hung long and twisted down the side of her cheek. She was frowning a little.

'Evening-meat is almost ready,' she said. 'None of the men will be here tonight. You should come out to eat when it will only be Father and me there.'

Couldn't Edith understand that that would be worst of all—to sit with their father without his men to keep him talking and draw his thoughts away from his son? She couldn't understand that, though she often seemed to learn things without him knowing how.

'You aren't ill, Oswald! You aren't so weak that you can't come out. I can see that. You can't stay in here for ever and if you don't come out tonight it will be harder to do it tomorrow and worse the day after that.'

He hadn't meant to share his thoughts. He had meant to keep them to himself and tell no one, not even Edith. But if she was going to drive him like this, if she was going to say things he didn't want to hear, then he might say what she wouldn't like either.

'Who out there do you think even wants to eat with me?'

'Oswald!' She didn't like that. He had known she wouldn't, but he didn't much care. 'No one has said anything like that to me. Perhaps they wouldn't say it to me, but I haven't even overheard anyone talking like that. Some have asked me how you are, if you're getting stronger, and they are wondering when—'

'I knew they'd be wondering. They all want something to talk about now that the Moot is old news!'

Edith looked down at him, a sharp look for her, but she kept talking as if he hadn't spoken. Perhaps she thought that if something shouldn't have been said it was best to speak as though it hadn't been.

'Father will be pleased if you come out now. I know that's what he wants. Why not do it before he bids you to? Then everyone can forget about the Moot and—'

'No one will ever forget about it, Edith, Father least of all.' That was the trouble with Edith. She so often thought that everyone else was just like her. 'You always think the best of everyone, but some don't find it so easy to overlook others' faults. I'm glad that Brinin and Row are safely away. If I didn't have that to be glad about… I've been thinking while I've been lying here. It's very shameful, isn't it? A thegn's son flogged before the Moot like a slave! Who ever heard of such a thing? They'll hear of it now. Ealmund Thegn will have talked about it when he got home, and Alrich will have told his father. The word will spread. And the shame doesn't only fall on me. It falls on Father too. I'm sure he is very unhappy with me for bringing it on him.'

'I don't think he is still angry with you, Oswald.'

Angry? Hadn't all the anger, and more, been meted out on him already?

'No need to be angry now, is there? Not after that. But no one could blame him for being ashamed. I can't even blame him myself. I understand it, but it's hard. And do you know what the hardest part is? I was ready to be beaten for it. I was dreading it, but I was ready. I knew it was the price I had to pay for getting them away.

Father had no choice. And—think of this, Edith—I even asked him to do it, to get it over, but he made me wait and wait, and then—'

He broke off. If his father's anger was gone now, perhaps he had given it all to him. Oswald could hear it creeping into his voice.

'But, Oswald, you do that all the time. You say, "I'll do it, I'll do it." But you wait because you don't want to do whatever it is. Perhaps Father made you wait because he hated the thought of doing it.'

'Hated the thought of it? If he hated the thought of it so much why did he do something much worse? He told me that he would beat me himself—he told me he would, Edith—and then he called me before the Moot instead!'

'He did hate it. I was with him when it was over. If you had seen the way he looked, you would know. I've never seen him like that before, not since… since Mother died. He must have thought there was nothing else he could do. You know he always thinks about everything carefully.'

'How does telling me he thought about it make it better? It would be easier if he had done it without thinking, then wished he hadn't later. But if he thought about it carefully, and then did something that should never be done…'

That was too hard a thought to say aloud. Edith sat down on a stool by his feet. She had come to bid him from his bed, then swiftly leave, but perhaps she saw that now his words were gushing out they wouldn't stop soon.

'I know I was guilty. I did everything they said I did. There had to be some kind of punishment, and I got what Brinin and Row would have had—no, no, they would have had worse. I know all that, but…'

He could feel the anger straining and snarling like an angry hound held back by the collar. He had seen the hound on his father's face when he had told him what he had done. His father was stronger than he was, more skilled at taming it. Oswald didn't want to tame it. He wanted to set it loose.

'Why did I have to go before the Moot at all and be flogged for all to see?' The words burst from him, houndlike. 'Nothing ever happens in Oakdene without everyone hearing of it. If Father had beaten me, all the men would have learned of it and it would have been enough for them. I know it was Ealmund who oversaw it all, but Father rules this village. Ealmund could have done nothing that Father didn't want him to, and I don't understand why he wanted him to do that.'

Edith reached out to put her hand on his, haltingly as if she didn't know if he was safe to touch. If she had been anyone else he would likely have thrust her hand away.

'It was so shameful, Edith, so… I can't even say what it was like! They were all there to watch, all sitting there looking on! At the time, I hardly thought about that—it hurt so much I couldn't think about anything at all—but now when I remember it I… I blush to think of it. It shouldn't even have been done to me. They don't flog freemen, only slaves. To think of walking out among those men after that, or of sitting and eating with them, when they were all there, it's… it's very hard. Father knows I have to lead them one day. He never lets me forget it. Why did he have to shame me before them all?'

'Oswald, I don't understand it either, but the men who were at the Moot didn't like it. They weren't happy about it. And even though it was shameful, Alrich thought you were brave—do you remember me telling you that? I'm sure he wasn't the only one.'

'Alrich is like you. He thinks the best of everyone; and besides, I hadn't put him to any trouble, so he wasn't angry with me to begin with. There was no courage at all in it. I had no choice. What must they all think of me now? And Father must think worse of me than any of them.'

'Not as badly as you think, Oswald, but no one understands it. Think of Father, how he must be feeling. Don't you see that it's hard for him too, for you to have done what you did without him knowing why? Now that it's all over can't you talk to him? If you are worried that he thinks badly of you, why don't you tell him the truth?'

'I've thought about that. At the Moot Ealmund asked why I'd done it and when he said that Father wouldn't send any more men, I almost did tell them all.'

'Then why don't you? Even if Father still thinks you were wrong to do it, won't it be easier for both of you if he knows everything?'

'I can't, Edith. I swore to Row I would do everything I could for them. And Father made Aculf workreeve and listens to him, and everything that happened and everything I did was because Aculf isn't the kind of man Father thinks he is. I can't say why I did it without seeming to blame Father for not knowing Aculf. I wish he did know him, but I won't blame Father for what Aculf has done. It's bad enough for him to have me for a son.'

'Oswald, what do you even mean by that?'

It was a hard, hidden truth that he'd known for a long time. Sometimes he had felt it sharp as a new wound. Sometimes he had buried it away where he didn't have to think about it. Sometimes he had struggled to make it a lie. But it was too late for any of that now. It was true, sharp and couldn't be buried. Only Edith was too kind to see what everyone else knew. Why let her stay blind?

'Even before all this, I was never good enough. He must think even worse of me now. How would I even begin to tell him? It's strange. I was always too scared to talk to him before. I don't feel scared of anything now, but I don't know how to talk to him. I don't even want to. Not now. Not after what he did. Why tell him? Even if he knew, it can't change anything. There's no going back.'

The food was ready now. Oswald heard his father speaking to the cook and sighed deeply. Even if Edith was right, it was too late.

'Please, Oswald,' whispered Edith. 'I know it's hard, but you are going to have to go out there sometime.'

'Not this evening, Edith. Would you bring me something to eat?'

Edith stood up, one hand on the curtain, ready to leave. But she turned back to her brother before she went.

'I know I'm only your sister, no one you must listen to. Oh, you think you listen, but you don't. You only talk! Whatever you say, you don't think that I could ever know anything better than you do. Perhaps if you had listened to me before… You *will* listen now. I'll bring you food this evening, but not after that. You'll have to come out, or you won't eat.'

Then she slipped past the curtain and was gone.

TEARS

Edith felt the first small chill of coming winter as she walked on the hillside the next day. She loved the hills, loved to sit alone there and watch the valley below. She would look down over the hall and the village, the fields and beyond the trees as far as she could see. And the land was always new, always changing by season, sunlight and shadow. That morning the yellowing leaves were somewhat shocking against the blue of the sky. Edith drank in the bright coolness, and if her father and brother had not both been so wretched she would have been happy.

She had watched the way her father walked about like a man bearing a heavy load; had seen how his eyes strayed often to Oswald's curtain; had seen him go and stand by the curtain, wavering, before walking away again. More than once in the night, when her father thought she was asleep, she had seen him sitting on a stool with his head in his hands near where Oswald lay hidden from them, moaning as he slept. Oswald often moaned in his sleep now. Edith heard it, and her father heard it too. And she didn't know whether to be angry with both of them or to weep.

Oswald hadn't believed her when she had warned him of what she would do—she had seen the disbelief on his face—but she hadn't gone to him that morning and she hadn't gone at midday. He would be hungry by now. She couldn't bid her father or push him into where Oswald was and make him stay there until they had made everything better. But she could starve Oswald into wisdom, whether he wanted to be wise or not. She would drive him from his bed, but she didn't mind coaxing him too. The brambles were heavy with sweet blackberries, late blackberries but still good. Picking and eating as she went, she loaded her basket with the biggest and ripest as a gift for Oswald. Oswald loved blackberries, and the hope of their sharp sweetness on his tongue might be enough to draw him out.

She had almost reached the foot of the hill, near the village, when she was startled by the sudden snap of a twig behind her. She turned to look, half thinking she would see one of the village children following her for a game. But there was no stifled laugh, no sudden scurrying away. Perhaps her own foot had snapped it after all.

'My lady Edith!' whispered a voice behind her.

Shocking, chilling, the most unwelcome of well-known voices, the last voice she wanted to hear so near the village. Edith spun round and saw Brinin staring at her through the shrubs.

'Brinin!' she gasped. 'What are you doing here?'

He didn't speak, only looked at her. That wasn't how she knew something was wrong. Brinin had always given more looks than words. But there was a darkness in his eyes she hadn't seen there before, a deadness, and he was alone. He hadn't left Oakdene alone.

'Where's Row?' She cast swift glances all around, to the trees, to the shrubs. Surely he hadn't gone into the village and been taken?

Brinin opened his mouth to speak then. Edith could see him reaching for the words, grasping but catching none of them.

'Where is he?' She was still looking everywhere, fearful now. His eyes were shouting at her, and she didn't want to hear what they were saying. 'No, Brinin, not…'

'Fallen, my lady Edith.' She had known. She had seen the answer in his eyes.

'No, Brinin…' Could she bid it not to be true? Would calling it a lie make it one?

'We were nearly there, but then a mist came so thick we could hardly see.' Brinin was finding words now, but it was like a kind of pain to hear the heaviness in his voice as he spoke aloud what should never be said. 'We strayed too near the edge. We didn't know how steep it was. We couldn't see. He was ahead of me, and it crumbled away, the path. I climbed down after him, but…'

Edith didn't feel the tears come. She didn't know she was weeping until she felt them suddenly wet on her cheeks as she listened to him. A tear dropped onto her hand, still clutching the basket. She saw Brinin's eyes follow it as it fell, and his voice faltered. His face twisted a little and the darkness in his eyes lightened, and they sat down on the hillside and wept together.

'There was nothing I could do. He was already dead when I found him. He…' The words slipped from Brinin's grasp again and when he caught them, they flooded from him as his tears did. 'I didn't want to go! Why did we even go? It would have been better for me to be sold and know he was safe, even if I never did see him again! I only went because he'd already lost everyone else. I didn't think I would end up losing him!'

No one had thought it. 'Brinin and Row are safe.' Oswald had told her that in the meadow to make her believe, to make himself believe that not everything was as bad as it seemed. How many times had she said it to herself as she sat by the trees, far from the hall and all the dreadful sounds that Oswald didn't want her to hear? They hadn't known if they were strengthening themselves with truth or lies, if they were clinging to a rock or a shadow. It had been something to hold fast to so they wouldn't sink under the weight of the rest. But Brinin and Row hadn't been safe. Brinin had been bearing much worse than Oswald, and it was too late to help him. There was nothing she could do or say to make anything any better.

'I was halfway back here before I knew what I was doing. I don't even remember starting out. I don't care. I only went for Row. I don't care if I'm caught now.' Brinin stood up, wiping his eyes with his sleeve. 'I was on my way to the village when I met you. I'll go now. I don't care what they do to me.'

Edith could see how it would be. In her mind she could see him walking into the village, hear the shouts of someone catching sight of him. Brinin unstruggling as strong hands grab him, the word spreading from mouth to mouth as they drag him roughly to the hall. She could see her father there, angry, Brinin wordless before him, Aculf all gloating glee, Oswald hearing it from his bed and stumbling out ashen-faced into a kind of nightmare. She could see it all: the Moot, the whip, no mercy, no pity, everything worse than it had been for Oswald, and Brinin too sorrowful and strengthless to bear any of it. What was she doing? This was no time to sit and weep!

'No!' Edith sprang up and gripped him by the arm. 'Don't go now, not yet. Oswald will want to see you first. There's a cave nearby—well, almost a cave—where you can hide. It's well hidden and no one knows about it but me. When did you last eat or sleep?'

'I haven't eaten for a day or two, and since… I've not slept much, only a little here and there.'

'Come with me, Brinin.' She had known that would be his answer—he looked so hollow and worn. 'Come to the cave and rest. You *must* eat and sleep before you do anything else.'

Brinin, no will left to withstand her, let her pull him away by the arm like he was a small child. Further up the hillside, further from the village, further from everyone who must not see him, she led him to a little hollowed cleft in the hillside. It was small but dry inside, and so much gorse grew around it, and so many brambles, that a man could walk very near it without even knowing it was there.

'Eat these,' said Edith, thrusting her basket into his hands. 'I'll go and get you some more food. I'll be back soon.'

'If anyone finds out that you are helping me, my lady Edith…' Brinin began.

'You'll be safe in the cave.' That had always been the way with Brinin, more ready to help than to be helped. But this was no time to weep and it was no time to worry about who might learn what she was doing. 'Don't go anywhere until you've seen Oswald. He's been… he's been busy but I'll talk to him as soon as I can. I think I'll bring you another cloak. It will be cold here when night comes and you shouldn't light a fire. Now, swear to me that you'll stay in the cave.'

Brinin looked at her wearily. His tears had already gone and his eyes were dark again.

'Swear to me, Brinin!'

'Very well, my lady Edith,' he sighed. 'I'll stay in the cave.'

There was a spring that gushed cool and clear from the side of the hill, and Edith stopped by it when she had left him. Kneeling down, she splashed the water over her face to wash away whatever the tears had left there. The coldness made her mind sit up ready to work. No one could be wise without food and sleep. Let Brinin eat and rest and weep. If she could make him do that for a few days then he might not be so ready to fling himself into harm. Then they could think and learn what would be wise. She was walking swiftly now, a woman with work to do, every step taking her nearer to the hall. Bread, meat, ale, cheese, cloak. She wanted to be back with Brinin quickly. She couldn't leave him long alone, alone in every way he could be, after what she had seen in his eyes. At the thought of that her tears threatened to flow again, but this was no time to weep. Weeping could wait until she had time for it. How was she to tell Oswald that it had all been for nothing and the worst had happened? She didn't know how to say it. How could she speak to him alone if he wouldn't leave his bed? There could be no coaxing now. She would *make* him heed her. But not yet. She would deal with Oswald later. Brinin first.

KNOWLEDGE

'**M**y lord!'

Edrich, standing alone in the meadow, looked up and saw Thurstan striding with strong steps towards him.

'It may not be my place to say anything, my lord, but I must speak!'

'Has that ever stopped you before?' asked Edrich wearily.

'Seldom, my lord, and it won't stop me now either. You already know my mind on the Moot, but there is something I haven't said. Can't you see that there is more to all this than Oswald Child is telling us?'

'I asked him why he did it and he wouldn't tell me.'

'He told me there was a good reason for it, but begged me not to ask him anything more.'

'He said more to you than to me, then,' said Edrich, turning as though to walk away.

'Why didn't you make him tell you, my lord? I would have done had he not been called away by you first. He didn't think he could do what he did and never be found out. Perhaps he hoped he wouldn't be, but he must have known it was only a small hope. He's no fool. He may have been thoughtless, but it didn't come from nowhere. He must have had some grounds for doing it. A man could see that in the dark with his eyes shut, so why didn't you find out why?'

'I have already told you that I did ask him why! What do you think I should have done? Beaten it out of him?'

'What you did, or let Ealmund do, came very near that, my lord, and it was too much.'

'Be careful how you speak to me, Thurstan! I am your lord now. We aren't boys any more.' There was anger in Edrich Thegn's voice now, enough to make most men back down.

'You're right, my lord. We're men now, which is why we, you most of all, must understand it. I would be the first to say he had to be punished for it, and I told him so. But you could have beaten him yourself. Better still, you could have made him work for those of us who were sent out to pay us for our lost time. You could have had him beg our forgiveness on his knees! You could have done any of those things and it would have been enough. But instead, you made him wait for days then shamed him before the whole village. And that without—'

'Stop there! I am not bound to tell you anything or to speak with you about this, but don't you see that if I had felt that I had any other choice, I would have taken it?'

'I know it was harrowing for you, my lord. That much was plain, and I can see that you feel it still. It will be a long time before I forget it myself, and I'm not his father. But we were too quick, all of us at the Moot. We should have made him tell us, and I am now ashamed of myself that I didn't. We should have waited until he had, even if that meant sitting there all night. Yes, he had to be punished somehow, but we didn't need to rush to that before we knew the whole truth.'

'What makes you think that we *could* have made him tell us? You were there. You saw how... how frightened he was, yet he wouldn't say a word—and, believe me, he knows where they went. Do you think that sitting there all night would have shifted him when not even—'

'We were too quick, my lord.'

'What do you think I could have done? I couldn't think only of Oswald. I had to think of Oakdene. He helped two slaves flee! My men were angry at being sent from their fields for nothing!'

'I was angry too, my lord, but—'

'If there had been anything else I could have done, don't you think I would have done it? I would have done almost anything else if I had thought I could. Do you think I wanted to sit there and see such a thing done to my own son?'

'It didn't need to be done, my lord. You are the lord here. If you didn't want it, your word was enough to stop it. You didn't need to let another man lead.'

'You have said enough!'

'And it would not be right for me to tell my thegn what I think of him for letting Ealmund offer mercy he didn't mean to give! He was angry because a boy had shown him to be a fool, and you didn't stop him, my lord.'

'Thurstan, you will—'

'How many boys do you know who would have done for anyone what he did for those two slaves? If he had done it for his lord, the bards would have made a song of it. But because it was for two slaves it is madness. But wrong or not, madness or not, he showed courage, my lord, and you will not find a man in Oakdene who does not see that.'

'Don't you think I know that?' shouted Edrich, his voice shaking. 'He showed so much courage he made me proud to be his father, however wrong he'd been!'

'Then tell him!' yelled back Thurstan.

That seemed to break the rising tide of anger between them.

'Tell him, my lord,' said Thurstan again, more quietly. 'You don't understand why he wouldn't talk to you. Here's your answer: you have made it so hard for him to please you that you have left him unable to tell you anything.'

'You have forgotten who you are speaking to, Thurstan! You have now gone far beyond what it is right for you to say!'

'I know who I'm speaking to, my lord! I am speaking to the boy who was my friend for as long as I can remember, to the man I have shed my blood with on the battlefield. I am speaking to my lord and if it was anyone else I would leave them to their troubles and wouldn't bother. But because I have not forgotten who you are, I will speak! As I have already angered you, I can't make things much worse by saying more! There is much that neither of us knows. But I know him and I know you. And I knew you, better than most, when you were not so very unlike him. Oswald is one of the best bowmen I have ever known, but when you are watching he can barely hit the target. He has knocked the sword from my hand more than once—and *I'm* the best swordsman in the village—yet for you he cannot fight. It isn't courage he lacks! We've seen that now. As to what he does need, you're the only one who can give it to him. Hearten him a little, and you may find that there is a lot more to your son than you ever thought!'

'Are you done?'

'For now, my lord, yes. But hear this: whatever you do, I'm not going to rest until I know *everything* he isn't telling us!'

SUNLIGHT

Well into the afternoon, Oswald sat restlessly and waited for Edith. He had thought she would give in before now. Didn't Edith almost always do what he wanted? He hadn't thought she had meant what she said, though he had kept back a little bread for the morning nonetheless. Now the bread was long gone, midday long past and still there was no Edith. He was beginning to wonder if he had been wrong about her. And he was hungry. He had even put on a shirt ready to slip out and find something if the hall seemed quiet, but when was it ever quiet?

Then suddenly he heard what could only be Edith, her footsteps swifter than ever, coming towards him. She didn't even stop to call his name, but threw his curtain aside and stood, slightly flushed, looking down at him.

'Where have you been?' said Oswald, reaching out for the bread she held in her hand, not much for one who had waited all day for it. 'Why didn't you come before?'

'You know why I didn't come. I told you I wouldn't.' Edith stepped away from him a little and put the bread behind her back. 'You can have it, but only outside. I'll wait for you there.'

Then she turned and walked away to the door, where the brightness of the day was streaming in. The curtain fell back into place as she left, to shield him from the hall and the sunlight. Oswald had more than half a mind to be stubborn. Was he to let Edith, younger than he was, a sister, bid him like this? But his belly was not ready to be cheated of that small loaf, and the hall was busy and would be until after nightfall. He sighed and fastened his belt round his shirt—not too tightly—then slipped on his shoes. He hadn't thought she had meant it.

The sun was so bright when Oswald stepped outside, so overwhelmingly bright after the long days of darkness that it pricked his eyes like needles, and he had to hide them. And when he took his hand away and could see again, what he saw was that everyone was looking at him. They were watching him and they all knew everything. They didn't need to have been at the Moot to know all about it. Perhaps someone had listened outside, had run down to the fields to tell of what he had heard. They had all talked about it over the sheaves and by their hearths when darkness fell. Those who had been there had had more to say about it, and now there was not a man nor a woman, not a child, not a slave who didn't know everything. Could he walk out and meet their eyes when they knew his shame?

'Edith,' he whispered, the bread forgotten now. 'Let's go back inside. They're all looking at me.'

'No!' Edith took his arm and led him away from the door. 'You're not going back inside now I've got you out at last. Look at the sky, Oswald. See how blue it is today. There won't be many more days like this before winter comes.'

He hardly knew why he went with her. Perhaps it was because she had so suddenly become like a mother or father who would make him heed. He went with her without a word, but she led him by ways where he would be most seen, where most people would be. As they walked near the fields, Oswald began to eat the bread that she had given him, breaking it slowly, bit by bit, looking at that rather than the men and women watching him. He could see them stop their work to stare, could often see one whisper to his fellow. But no one spoke to him. It was only when they had turned to walk back to the hall that Garulf came still straightening his back, stiff with work.

'God bless you, Oswald Child, sir,' he whispered. He took Oswald's hand tightly in both his own and Oswald, slightly bewildered, thought he saw tears gleaming in his eyes. 'May God bless you.'

Garulf didn't wait for an answer before going back to his work, but Oswald saw the old man wipe his hand across his eyes as he left and knew that the gleam *had* been tears.

'He... he was weeping!' It hardly seemed believable.

'Don't you know why?' said Edith, as they walked on. 'You didn't listen when I told you before, Oswald. I don't think anyone here hates you.'

'One man doesn't, perhaps. And he's a slave like Brinin and Row, so that's most likely why.'

'The men at the Moot thought you showed courage.'

'You don't know what you're talking about!'

'I heard one of them say it!' This new sister was stout-hearted and not ready to give way to him. Had she always been like this without him knowing?

'Who?'

'Thurstan! I heard him tell Swetrich.'

'Oh, Thurstan! Thurstan hardly speaks for everyone. He didn't even think I should have come before the Moot at all.'

'But, Oswald—'

'You weren't there, Edith. I can better say how the men of Oakdene see me now.'

They met Cynestan next, coming from work, his hair wet with sweat. His flail rested on his shoulder, the swingle swaying to and fro behind him as he walked. He was coming straight towards them, and there was no way to turn aside. Oswald met him stiffly, ready for a cold greeting of knowledge but not of friendship. Hadn't it been Cynestan who had said that what he had done was hard to forgive?

'Well now, Oswald Child, it's good to see you!' said Cynestan, his face warm with the old, unlooked-for smile. He drew his hand across his brow. 'Threshing does make a man hot. That's most of my harvest in now. The beans have been good this year.'

'Oh! I'm... I'm glad,' stammered Oswald. This was Cynestan as he had always been. 'I *am* sorry for...'

'Say no more about it! You have already begged forgiveness well enough.' Cynestan walked on a little, before turning back to them. 'It *is* good to see you!'

'I told you,' whispered Edith, as Cynestan left them.

'That's only two men, and Thurstan, but—'

'Stop, Oswald! What good is this doing you? You'll have to see these men every day. It's over! Stop wondering all the time what they are thinking of you. You are thinking about it more than any of them are, and it will never get better unless you try to forget about it. I have to go inside and make sure everything is ready for evening-meat. You've never liked staying indoors and it will do you good to be outside. Walk about and speak to those you meet. You'll see that I'm right.'

Edith didn't wait for him to speak, to tell her that she was wrong and that he knew more about it all than she did. He watched her as she left, with an uneasy feeling that perhaps she was right; not about what the village thought of him—he knew she was wrong about that—but about it being better to be outside. It was a cool, clear evening, a slight breeze rustling in the trees and tugging at the dying leaves. With the low sun warming everything around him with light as friendly as hearthfire, it was hard to feel so wretched as before. His heart could not lie so low as it did in the darkness. But he would not seek anyone out, whatever Edith said.

'Oswald, my dear boy!' Brother Wilfred came up beside him unseen, as he was staring after his sister. 'How good to see you out of your bed! I have written something for you to learn on a waxboard. Come with me to the church and let me give it to you. It wouldn't be good to forget your Latin by laying it aside for too long.'

'I did try to learn some more Latin,' said Oswald, as they walked along, 'but I couldn't keep it in my mind.'

'Perhaps then it is time to be sterner with your mind.' They went into the church, already a little dark in the gathering dusk. Brother Wilfred handed Oswald the waxboard, filled with his small, careful writing. 'See how much of this you can learn before tomorrow, and we will talk more about it then. Give your mind work to do and don't let your thoughts wander away until they have done your bidding.'

Wouldn't it be easier to bid the wind not to wander through the trees? Perhaps Brother Wilfred, old now and with less to worry him, could bid his thoughts and have them heed him. Perhaps he did not have so many dark thoughts pushing in on him. Yet the old life, with only work and warcraft and waxboards to think about, was very welcoming. It called to him, and he would have gone there if only he knew the way.

'Can anything ever be as it was before, sir?' he asked suddenly.

'Sit down, Oswald,' said Brother Wilfred, with one of those keen looks that always made Oswald feel that the monk saw inside him. 'If you mean what I think you do, then I don't think it can be. Now, don't look so downcast, my boy! I have more to say. What you did was shocking—you know that, don't you? No one will forget it, but in time they will stop talking and thinking about it—once they have something new to talk about.'

'I told Edith that no one would forget it,' Oswald sighed. 'No one will ever think well of me again. Edith doesn't believe me, but I know they won't.'

'Now, I didn't say that, Oswald,' said Wilfred gently. 'They won't forget it, and neither will you, but no one will think about it as much as you do yourself. You feel it keenly, don't you? As the thegn's son, shame like that is new to you. The slaves whom you helped have known more shame than you have and could never hide away from it. Yes, my boy, I *do* understand why you have been slow to come outside, which is why I am so glad to see you now.'

'Edith made me!' Oswald couldn't help smiling suddenly. 'She said that if I wanted to eat I had to come out. What could I do?'

'You did well to heed her. Listen, it has seemed to me that all of this has come about, not because you wanted to do wrong, but because you didn't know how to be wise. I have been watching and listening and thinking, and I'm going to tell you what I know. Perhaps in time you will want to tell me what I don't know. You have been friends with Brinin for some time now, I think. I have seen you look at each other as only friends do. And on the days when his troubles were greater, you seemed to feel the burden of them. That much I saw soon after I came to Oakdene. I remember how keen you were to know about the freeing of slaves when we learned about Aidan the Bishop. It has been long in your mind to help Brinin, and I think I know where you sent him.'

Oswald looked up sharply, his heart suddenly beating a little faster. Were all his thoughts to be laid bare? Was nothing hidden? Would Brother Wilfred tell someone?

'Don't worry. I have said nothing about this to anyone. And I have heard that your father does not want to send more men to look for the slaves, so I don't see why I should tell anyone now. You were clever, Oswald, but I seldom forget what someone says to me, or what I say to them.' Brother Wilfred, who had been standing until now, sat down beside Oswald on the bench. 'I have been listening, as I told you, and there are two things I have heard that have stayed very much in my mind. The first is this: you went to your father and told him what you had done to save another from blame. However wrong you had been, you were right when you did that, and it took courage.'

'No, I was scared!' How could it be that when he had felt more fear than he had ever done in his life, no one had seen it? Not Alrich nor Edith, not Brother Wilfred, not even Thurstan, who should have known better? How could they all be so blind to it? Had he hidden it so well? He hadn't tried to.

'It took courage, even if you did feel afraid. You knew that you would be punished once you had spoken, but you chose to speak so the guiltless would not be blamed. I was proud of you when I heard that, my boy. The other thing is this: you were offered mercy that you would not take because taking it would have meant giving the slaves up for punishment. If you did not know how to be wise, Oswald, you knew how to be a friend, and a friend to those more helpless than yourself. You chose pain to spare those whom few would ever think of, and if I was proud of you before, I was prouder of you for that.'

'It wasn't a choice. There was nothing else that I could have done.'

'It *was* a choice, and you made it so firmly that you didn't think of doing anything else—perhaps that was why it didn't feel like one—but it was a choice that few would have made. Do many care whether slaves are flogged or not? Those are the two things that have been in my mind, and it may be that I am not the only one who has thought of them. But try not to dwell too much on what others think of you, Oswald. It would be better if you tried to think about yourself as little as you can.'

'It is hard, though,' sighed Oswald. 'Much harder than I thought it would be. And worst of all is knowing that my father is so ashamed of me.'

'It will be hard for a time, but not for ever,' said Brother Wilfred, very gentle now. 'And I doubt that anyone thinks as badly of you as you say. As for your father, he hasn't spoken to me about it, so I can't say if he is ashamed of you or not. I do know that when he called me to tend to you, he was very distressed.'

'Because I had brought shame on him.'

'Perhaps. Or perhaps because he is your father, and you were in pain. He didn't sleep at all that first night but walked up and down beside your curtain, near where you were lying. I know, because I was there. He did the same for much of the next day too and asked me to show him everything that I was doing.'

That was so unlike everything Oswald thought he knew of his father that he felt himself soften a little. But then one thing he did know that he couldn't hide from: his father was thegn and without his bidding, none of the awful shame of the Moot could ever have happened. If his father had not wished it… And something hardened within him again.

Oswald rose to leave, knowing that evening-meat would soon begin, but before he left he turned once more to Wilfred.

'What shall I do, sir?' he asked.

'What you have always done. Work, obey your father, learn how to fight and lead. There is nothing new to be done now, though nothing will be quite the same as before. Whatever wrong you did, you have already been punished for it and there's nothing to be gained by thinking about it too much. It's over now. As for the shame of the thing, remember that you thought it was worth bearing when you chose to shield the others. If it was worth bearing then, it's worth bearing now. But don't be *too* ashamed and remember why you chose to do what you did. I also think that you should speak to your father about it all. You owe him that, don't you think? Go and eat now.'

SHADOWS

The sun was already lost behind the hills when Oswald left the church. Firelight glowed in the doorways and the village was full of dark corners as the shadows of twilight stole over it. He was half-heartened, half-weary as he trudged back to the hall. Brother Wilfred had seen a little good in him, but there was still evening-meat with his father to sit through, and again tomorrow and the day after, anger and shame to swallow with every bite. Whatever Brother Wilfred had said, speaking to his father was the last thing he was going to do. Sitting with him would be hard enough.

'Oswald Child, sir.'

Oswald turned and saw Ludan looking at him from among the shadows, standing in the dark under the eaves of the hall.

'May I speak with you, sir?' he said haltingly.

'Yes,' said Oswald, a little puzzled. What could Ludan want?

'Thank you for speaking up for me, sir.' There was warmth in Ludan's voice, as there had been strength in Garulf's grip.

'I'm sorry you were beaten.' It seemed so long ago now, that dreadful morning when Edith had told Oswald what had happened. 'I didn't think you would be blamed. I would have stopped it had I been here.'

'My lord your father stopped it, sir, as soon as he knew. I think Aculf did it without his leave.' Ludan seemed to be gathering words he wasn't at all sure he should say. 'You could have held your tongue. No one had thought of you, sir.'

'I couldn't do that when you'd been blamed.'

'Well, not everyone would have done what you did, sir. There's been a lot of talk—among the slaves, sir—and folk are saying that you don't mind who a man is, that you'll see he's treated right all the same. Not everyone would have spoken up for a slave and not everyone would have done what you did for Row and Brinin. Folk will remember that, sir.' Then, suddenly shrinking from saying any more, Ludan stopped. 'Let me be about my work now, sir.'

Ludan melted away into the shadows as swiftly as he had come, leaving Oswald to make his way to the hall alone. What was he left with? Only a priest and some slaves in all the village to think well of him. Cynestan had forgiven him. Thurstan had upbraided him like a father, had called him a fool like a brother, then stuck to him like both. He had the friendship of those few, and he would have to settle for that and hope that one day things might be better. Oswald's heart sank a little as he reached the door and heard the voices inside. Had Edith known that their father was gathering his men that night? She must have known. Edith always knew, but she might have warned him. Keeping his head down, he slipped into his place without a word.

'I don't know about the rest of you,' said Thurstan, and though he seemed to speak to all the men when Oswald glanced up he saw that he was looking at him only, 'but I gathered in the last of my harvest today. I am ready to feast now and ready for winter.'

It was a kind of forgiveness, and Thurstan was giving him a token of it. Harvest in, trouble forgotten. And he was handing him his forgiveness aloud so that everyone else would hear it.

'Mine will be in tomorrow,' said Cynestan, and one by one the other men joined him. All their harvests were either in, or almost in. They followed Thurstan's lead and offered forgiveness in the same way he had done. These men had been angry with him, but if they were still angry they were willing to lay their anger aside. Perhaps they understood that if they were all to live side by side, then it was better to overlook it, better to forget, even if Oswald himself couldn't.

'Now that the harvesting is over, shall we feast, my lord?' asked Swetrich.

'Eh?' Edrich looked up like a man suddenly wakened. 'What did you say, Swetrich?'

'Shall we feast now that the harvest is safely in, my lord?'

'Oh, yes, yes. We will feast before the week is out.'

This was not his father's way, to be dreaming among his men. Oswald had been keeping his eyes away from his father, looking anywhere else but where he sat. But he glanced up at him now, then quickly looked away when he saw that he was watching him. Oswald kept his eyes on his food after that, only half hearing what the men were saying. His father's speechlessness seemed very loud now.

'Not all of the harvest is in.' It was Aculf, leaning towards Oswald and speaking softly to be heard by him and missed by all the others. 'With two slaves gone, we have been slow to gather Edrich Thegn's harvest this year. I can only hope—'

Aculf stopped suddenly with a gasp as a large jug of ale emptied itself onto his lap. He leapt to his feet and stood dripping and glaring round the table as the other men began to laugh. Oswald, who had felt himself reddening with anger and shame as Aculf was speaking, struggled not to laugh himself. He had not seen how the jug had fallen but Thurstan was smiling wryly. Not wholly by chance then.

'Forgive me, Aculf,' said Thurstan coolly. 'Clumsy of me.'

'What a waste of ale!' laughed Rædwald. 'Couldn't you at least have tried to catch some of it, Aculf? I have more need of it than your breeches do!'

'My lord!' spluttered Aculf, shaking off his clothes. 'Please, my lord, have I your leave to go?'

'Very well, Aculf!' Edrich frowned at Thurstan. 'You ought to be more careful, Thurstan!'

Thurstan grinned at Oswald as Aculf scuttled out of the hall. Forgiveness and friendship; Thurstan led the way in all of it. Perhaps he could learn to live among these men again. Despite Aculf, nothing had been so bad as he had feared—not nearly so bad thanks to Thurstan—but he had no heart to linger and took his leave as quickly as he could.

Later, Oswald sat sleepless on his bed, listening as the last of the men left for his own hearth. In the stillness he heard footsteps coming across the floor, drawing nearer to his curtain.

'Oswald, are you awake?'

Oswald stiffened slightly as he heard his father speak. Had he already been lying down he would have shut his eyes and lain as though asleep until his father left. But he couldn't lie down without his father hearing him, and if he sat where he was without answering his father might lift the curtain and see him there.

'Yes, sir.' Oswald stood and waited unsmilingly.

Edrich drew aside the curtain and stepped past it, a candle in his hand. Its light flickered on the wall and the curtain, the bed and the stool beside it, on the father and on the son. Flickering light, shadowed faces. For a long time he didn't speak. He stood looking at his son, while Oswald looked back at his father's hair or ear or shoulder—anywhere but his eyes.

'You went out today,' said Edrich at last. 'Your back is healing, then?'

'As well as can be hoped, sir.'

The shadow spread on Edrich's face and Oswald grew stiffer. Why had his father come asking about his back which without him wouldn't have needed to heal?

'You ought to go back to Brother Wilfred before you forget what you have learned. It's not good for you to be without work.'

'Yes, sir. I will go to Brother Wilfred tomorrow.' Oswald was very stiff now in the shadows, without a flicker of softening to be seen in the candlelight. 'It may be longer before I shoot or wield a sword.'

Months later, Oswald wished that he had waited to hear his father speak. In the candlelight he saw speech begin to grow on his father's face, but that night he didn't want to hear it and stopped it before the words came.

'May I go to bed now, sir? I am rather tired. I haven't been sleeping well.'

Another shadow on Edrich's face, darker this time. He stood, wavering, flickering, until Oswald began to wonder if his father was going to make him listen.

'Yes. Good night,' said Edrich at last and walked away with the candle and the shadows and left only darkness.

CAVE

The path broke away, crumbling underfoot. He stumbled and was gone, hidden by the mist that shrouded everything. One cry, one sickening thud, then nothing. In the darkness of the cave, Brinin sat up suddenly gasping for breath. He leaned against the cold wall, breathing heavily. He always woke the same way now, his own half-shout, half-scream of his brother's name dragging him from sleep. But that was better than being stuck in the nightmare.

The dreams weren't all the same. Sometimes he was scrambling down to find him, calling out again and again, but knowing in his heart that all hope was already gone. Sometimes he knelt shaking at Row's side, not seeing the mist lift or the darkness of night creep over him. But always there was the same bitter sickness in his throat that stopped his breath. He had never thought he would see such a day. He hadn't known to dread it. And now he had to live it again many times every night. He was so weary, so painfully weary. He longed for sleep, and feared it and fought against it more than anything on earth. How could he ever sleep willingly again?

Brinin shut his eyes and tried to bring his thoughts to heel, to think of his brother's face, not the last time he had seen it, but before. He drove himself to see it again—the smile, the laugh, the eyes, even the frown—to see it as it had been when neither of them had known how suddenly he would be gone. He was struck with a worse fear then, worse even than the fear of sleep: perhaps he would forget Row's face as he had forgotten their father's. A sob broke from his lips, but no tears came with it. They had come only once for a little while when he had wept with Edith, then left him again, an ache in their place. The tears had been better.

He reached out for the other cloak and wrapped it round him, glad of it now the nights were growing colder, but he wished he could light a fire. He couldn't hide here for much longer. Why *was* he hiding? He couldn't remember why he had listened to Edith. It had been two days since he had first seen her and still Oswald hadn't come—perhaps she hadn't told him yet—but it was time now to go down to the village whether Oswald came or not. They could do as they liked to him. He would tell Edith that when she came.

Brinin stood in the mouth of the cave and looked out at the stars—Ratatoskr, the Eagle, a bow and arrow stolen by a small boy. It was the best of nights for stars: clear, crisp, cloudless. It would not be many weeks—perhaps not many days—until the first frost came. But the stars held no wonder for him now. They taunted him with the thoughts of better days and twisted the ache within him into a more bitter one. Brinin dropped his head and turned away. If he had to watch the stars alone he couldn't bear to look at them at all.

It hadn't been like this when his mother died. He had known death was coming to her. Although so young, he had understood. First she had been tired, then weak, then too sick to get up from where she lay. The other women had brought her food, but she had eaten less and less. Brinin had been ready for the end when it came. They had all been ready. Death had come in kindness like a friend, and he had known the women were right when they had said it was better. Better to be a small boy without her and to know she had no pain. But death had been no friend to Row. It had come as a raider, unlooked-for and unmerciful. No time to be ready, no way to see it coming. It was over before he even knew it had happened.

'I wasn't ready,' he whispered into the darkness. 'I wasn't ready.'

Edith came again in the morning. She came with meat and drink and unspoken friendship. Even more than he was for the meat, Brinin was thankful for the way she sat as he ate it. She didn't ask him anything or try to make him talk. She only sat and it was good to have someone near who knew.

'My lady Edith,' he said at last when he had eaten. 'Oswald hasn't come, and I will go down to the village now. You have been good to me, but it's time.'

'No, Brinin!' Edith looked up with a swift, unforeseen fierceness. 'You mustn't! I won't let you!'

It was hard to go against her wishes when she had been so kind, so kind even now in wanting to shield him from what must come. It must come. He couldn't stay in the cave for ever.

'If you go down there, they will flog you for running away. There will be no mercy.'

'I know,' he said. And there was no fear in it, no dread at the thought of this painful, shameful thing. It was odd how far off it all felt, as though Edith spoke of it falling on some stranger he had never met.

'Then why would you go down? No! You must stay here until we know what to do!'

'I don't care what they do.'

He was ready to go, ready to get to his feet and go quickly, rather than stay and watch her growing distress as she pleaded with him. She seemed to be struggling with herself, staring at him with her lips pressed tightly together. Surely she was being kinder to him than she needed to be. He wouldn't forget that now that nothing more could be done.

'But... but... Oswald was flogged!' Tears and words burst out together, the words all well known but with little meaning.

Brinin stared at her in utter bewilderment as she sat sobbing. How could Oswald be flogged? Someone like Oswald was never flogged.

'They called him before the Moot,' said Edith when she could speak again. 'Because they hadn't caught you, they flogged him instead.'

'I don't understand. Why Oswald?' The more she told him, the less he could grasp. There was some riddle in all this to baffle him.

'Because he helped you,' sobbed Edith. 'They said you would have been caught if it hadn't been for him so... so they did it to him because they couldn't do it to you. They offered him mercy if he would tell them where you'd gone, but he wouldn't. He could hardly get out of bed for days afterwards. That's why he hasn't come. I haven't told him yet. He thought he'd saved you both. How can I tell him he didn't? How can I?'

Wasn't this what he had feared? That someone was bound to be blamed? Hadn't he told Row that? Oswald had known. He had helped him and someone, somehow had learned of it. Suddenly the horror at such a thing was not so far off any more. He couldn't feel it before because it had seemed a slighter wound than the mist had dealt him. But he felt it now.

'Why did they blame him, my lady Edith?' he said at last. 'Did someone hear him speaking to us about it?'

'Because of the horses.'

Perhaps Edith could see on his face that she had slipped back into meaningless riddles again, that he knew much less than she thought he did.

'Don't you know?' she said. 'I thought you knew. He took some horses and led them into the forest to make everyone think that's where you'd gone. They wasted six days going the wrong way—first south, then north—until it was too late to find you. But they found the horses and Oswald told Father it was him. Aculf was blaming Ludan.'

Oswald? Could Oswald—so fearful, always so ready to yield—have done such a thing? Brinin found himself beset with so many bewildering feelings that he could hardly untangle them all in his head. No wonder Oswald had been so sure that they wouldn't be followed. It had seemed like such a small hope to Brinin, too brittle to put much weight on. But Oswald had known from the beginning that he meant to outwit them all.

'Brinin, don't you see why you can't go back?' said Edith, wiping her eyes again and looking at him steadily. She had a look of her brother then, Oswald at his most earnest. 'Not now. Not after that. If you do, it will all be for nothing.'

All for nothing. That would be the end of it. It had been strong bonds that had pulled him from Oakdene—kinship, friendship—and he felt them fast on him still. They were stronger now, stronger than he had ever known they could be. They had dragged him away and they must keep him away. Brinin sat wordless for a long time and shuddered to think of what would have happened if he hadn't met Edith when he did.

'I understand, Lady Edith,' he said at last. 'I will do as you wish.'

Edith clutched his arm.

'Thank you!' she whispered. 'I will come back tomorrow. And I'll tell Oswald. I have to. I think he'll come soon.'

SORROW

'Now my harvest is in, it's time for some warcraft,' said Thurstan, striding towards Oswald as soon as he came out from behind his curtain that morning. 'No good forgetting how to fight when the Danes may be upon us any day.'

'I am healing, Thurstan,' said Oswald, eyeing the weapons in Thurstan's hand with no great longing. 'But I don't think I'm ready to—'

'Your back still hurts?'

'Yes, unless I move carefully.'

'So much the better!' Thurstan handed Oswald a wooden sword. Then he rolled up the sleeve of his shield arm and showed him a long scar. 'I was wounded early in the battle where I got this, but I fought to the end. In battle, a man can't stop to rest. The only way he learns to keep fighting when he is wounded is by doing it, so let's go! It will likely hurt, but not to worry. I won't kill you if you weaken! Come. We'll go to the meadow and meet swords.'

Surely Thurstan wasn't in earnest. Oswald could feel the sting even at the thought of such a thing. A man might well fight wounded if it was a choice between that and death but... He winced suddenly as Thurstan patted him cheerfully on the shoulder.

'Come, Oswald! No time to lose! It may rain later, or the Danes may come!'

'Very well then,' sighed Oswald. Thurstan often had a way of getting what he wanted.

Thurstan drove him hard, coming at him again and again and not letting him stop until the stiff tightness of his back was burning, and he was hot and breathless. But they did stop at last, and Oswald threw aside his weapons and flung himself down to catch his breath.

'Now, don't you feel better for that?' The sweat glistened on Thurstan's brow, but he was smiling broadly.

'No! I feel worse!' laughed Oswald. It was hard not to laugh with Thurstan sometimes. 'But I'm glad I did it.'

'I thought you would be. Nothing like sitting idle to make a man brood.' Thurstan sat down on the grass beside him. 'Now that you're out of your bed, you can tell me what on earth you were thinking when you helped those two slaves. You were about to that day when your father called you away.'

'I wasn't. I told you not to ask me anything.'

'Well, yes, but you didn't think I would heed you, did you? Come now. I knew there was something you weren't telling us. Why else would you have been so stubborn when Ealmund offered you mercy? As to whether *that* was courage or folly, I'm of two minds about it. I've always thought that courage and folly stand shoulder to shoulder. Sometimes it can be hard to tell one from the other.'

It had never been hard to talk to Thurstan, and he was so friendly as he sat there, so fatherlike, that Oswald half wanted to speak. But he knew that once he had begun he would say much more than he should. Angry though he was with his father, there were still things he must not say. If Thurstan didn't like what he told him, he would think nothing of going to Aculf or even to his father to speak his mind. And others would hear of it and soon it would be no better than if it had all been said at the Moot. He wasn't angry enough for that. Nothing would make anyone forget now, and talking couldn't help.

'You were at the Moot, Thurstan,' he said at last. 'I said everything there that I'm going to say.'

It seemed from the look in Thurstan's eye that he might drive him to speak as he had driven him to fight. Thurstan had never been a man to back down easily, and Oswald readied himself to stand his ground. He knew he could now. That was one thing the

Moot had taught him. But Thurstan only looked at him for a while, then stood up.

'Perhaps it's too soon, after all,' he said. 'We'll talk about it another day. You'll have the wisdom to tell me in time.'

Oswald sat there, aching, long after Thurstan had left him, half wondering if he should have spoken, half wishing that Thurstan had never asked. There was a chill in the air that morning, good when he had been hot from fighting, but not to sit in now. He had just got to his feet when he caught sight of Edith coming into the meadow, coming the wrong way into the meadow, not from the village but from the hillside. She drew nearer and he saw her face.

'Edith!' Oswald ran to her and took her arm. 'What's wrong?'

Aching back forgotten, he pulled his sister down to sit beside him, near the trees where they might not be easily seen from the village. He watched her helplessly, not knowing what to say. Edith wept sometimes, but never like this; never without speech, almost without breath. She opened her mouth to speak, but nothing came.

'What is it, Edith?'

'I've wanted to tell you for days.'

'Tell me what?'

Something dreadful, worse than dreadful. But what could it be that he wouldn't already have heard about? His eyes followed Edith's glance as she looked swiftly back towards the hillside. What dreadful thing could come from the hills? Not Danes, or wolves, or everyone would already know. There would be screaming and running in fear.

'Tell me, Edith!'

'Brinin came back! He's hiding in a cave in the hillside.'

'What?' Her words hit him fistlike in the gut. 'They can't come back! Are they fools? Which cave? Where is it? I'm going up there to make them leave!'

'Wait! Row fell and… and…' But her sobs took her then, choked her, swallowed her words.

'What happened?' Oswald's chest grew tight, a cold swelling stealing his breath and making it quick and shallow. 'Did he die, Edith?'

But she wept, and the tightness grew.

'Is he dead?' shouted Oswald.

Edith nodded. Oswald stumbled to his feet, his head throbbing. He staggered away unseeing, blindly, not knowing where he went. He felt someone grasp him strongly, and Brother Wilfred was beside him. He led him into the church, far in, away from the door, and sat with him on a bench.

'Oswald,' said Brother Wilfred. 'What's happened?'

But the choking tears had spread to Oswald from his sister, swallowing his words too. He buried his face in his hands and wept as he hadn't wept for a long time, not for years, not since his mother had died. He wept and Wilfred sat with him, his hand never leaving his arm, steady somehow when everything else was crumbling.

'Row died on the way,' he gasped when the words struggled out from among the tears at last. 'Brinin has come back. And it's all my fault!'

'Oh, my dear boy!' Brother Wilfred pulled Oswald towards him.

'I told them to go!' Oswald wept on Wilfred's shoulder now, as a boy might weep on his father's. 'They would never have gone without me. I thought of it. It's all my fault. Row was all he had. Now he has no one. I'll never forgive myself. And now he'll be taken. I can't bear it. It's all my fault!'

'Come with me, Oswald,' said Wilfred and led him to the little cell at the back of the church where he slept. He sat Oswald down on a stool, poured a cup of ale and thrust it into his hands. 'Has Brinin come into the village?'

'Edith said he's hiding in a cave on the hillside.'

'Listen, Oswald,' said Wilfred, crouching in front of him. 'Stay here until I come back. Weep as much as you wish. Pray. Sleep if you will, but don't leave the cell. If anyone sees you as you are now, they may ask more than would be wise for you to answer. Do you understand me?'

Oswald nodded, wiping his eyes with the back of his hand. He watched as Wilfred walked to the door of the cell, unable even to care where he was going. Wilfred turned to him once more before he left.

'Don't leave the cell,' he said.

Oswald sat in the gloom, clutching the cup of ale but not trying to drink it, hardly knowing that he held it. He had done this thing, this worst of things as surely as if he had killed Row himself. He had done it. To his best friend, to the nearest thing he had ever had to a brother. He had urged Brinin to go against his will, and now he was alone, without his brother and in danger. He had done it. How would Brinin ever forgive him? How could he even ask him to? He would never forgive himself. And there was nothing that he could do, nothing that he could even think of doing to help Brinin now.

He was still sitting, the ale undrunk in his hands, when he heard Brother Wilfred's feet in the church some time later. He stared ahead of him, dry-eyed but unseeing, and did not even look up as the monk came in.

'Oswald,' said Brother Wilfred. 'On the morrow, Oakdene will feast to mark the harvest. The day after, you and I will ride to the minster where my friend, Sygbald, is the prior.'

Through the wretchedness he was wrapped in, Oswald was aware of slight bewilderment. Why was Brother Wilfred speaking to him of harvest and minsters? What did those have to do with anything?

'I have spoken to your father, Oswald, and he has given me leave to take you to the minster for a short time to see the books. We will ride a little south to join the road west. On the way, we may meet someone to ride with us.'

'Someone?'

'Yes. Don't you think that we may meet someone who will ride to the minster with us? Do you understand me, Oswald?'

Suddenly he did understand and almost began to weep again. He didn't need to think or do anything to help Brinin. Brother Wilfred had already done all the thinking and he was going to get them both away from this place.

'Thank you,' he said, clutching Wilfred's arm. 'I didn't know what to do.'

'Ready yourself for the road, my boy,' smiled Wilfred. 'If anyone is to meet us, he should set off at once. Someone should tell him that.'

TOGETHER

There was a sudden flurry of startled birds outside. Someone was coming. Brinin could hear them among the trees and shrubs, two walking together, talking in low voices as they drew nearer. There had been enough time now for Oswald to be told, and Edith had said she would do it. Brinin heard Oswald's voice and knew it, knew the swift way his words so often rushed out. And he went to stand in the opening of the cave to wait.

And there was Oswald standing looking back at him, the white of Edith's headcloth slipping into the trees as she left them. So much for friendship. He'd said that to Oswald once—angry with him, with Aculf, with everything that made his life bitter. So much for friendship. If he had doubted Oswald's friendship then, he couldn't doubt it now. Not only because of what Edith had told him—that would have been enough—but because of Oswald's face. There was sorrow on it.

Oswald stood wordless, looking. They both did. What were the right words for what needed to be said between them now? But suddenly Oswald darted forward, stumbling through the shrubs, and flung his arms around him, weeping on his shoulder. Brinin felt the tears wet on his shirt. So much for friendship. He wished he hadn't said that now.

'I'm sorry,' Oswald wept. 'I'm so sorry.'

They were together in it, not only in the cave where they sat, but in sorrow. It was Brinin's but Oswald had taken it up and it seemed more bearable shared than sorrow carried alone. It cut more smoothly, like a plough driven by two men instead of one; still cutting deep furrows inside, but more cleanly, not so roughly. Oswald's tears were wet enough for both of them. Brinin wept dry, silent tears, hidden and hurting. But perhaps that too was a kind of weeping and it was not so bitter as when he had been alone.

'It was quick,' said Brinin, as words came to him. Oswald wanted to know and it was right that he should. 'There was nothing I could do. It was too rocky even to bury him where he fell. I had to move him somewhere better and I only had the knife and stones and my own hands to make the hole. It... it wasn't right to bury him like that with no priest to speak over him.'

For a long time after that neither of them spoke. Oswald couldn't, and Brinin, as so often, thought it better not to. It was strange to hear the sounds of life outside as though nothing had changed. The wind still rustled the leaves. The birds still sat in the trees. They lived and knew nothing of death, nor of how soon it came.

'Can you ever forgive me?' said Oswald at last, and Brinin heard in his voice the threads of guilt that were woven through the sorrow. 'This was my fault. You would never have gone if it hadn't been for me.'

'Forgive you for what? Giving me friendship? I went because Row wanted me to. And we should never have kept walking on that last day. How could any of us have known what was going to happen?'

Was Oswald, full of thoughts and tears for him and the brother he had lost, going to say nothing at all about what he had done after they had left Oakdene? How could Oswald have come to do such a thing? Where had courage like that even come from? And he was still feeling it. The pain was still there. Brinin could see it in the tightness of Oswald's face, in the stiffness when he moved. He sat with him, saying nothing about it, with a back not fully healed. There were many things that didn't need to be said, but some that mustn't be left unsaid. And if Oswald wouldn't say them, Brinin would.

'I understand now why no one followed us,' he said at last.

Oswald looked up at him with a frown. 'Did Edith tell you? I wish I'd told her not to.'

'If she hadn't, I would have given myself up. I was on my way down to the village when I met her.' Brinin stopped to strengthen his voice. It was beginning to stumble a bit, like a man with unsteady feet. And though he waited for his words to find their footing, when he spoke again they were still not wholly steady. 'She told me… she told me they flogged you for it. Worse because you wouldn't tell them where we'd gone.'

'She *has* told you everything! We don't need to talk about it. I don't like to remember it.'

Who would like to remember it? And who could ever forget it?

'I'll never speak of it again if you don't want me to, but I will speak now.' Another pause for his words to be footsure. 'It was a shock to me that such a thing could be done to a thegn's son, that you were willing to risk it for me.'

'I didn't know that's what I was risking.'

Oswald was set on making little of it. Brinin understood that—he would have done the same—but he wouldn't let him cast it aside like something small.

'Oswald, I…' His voice stumbled then and the words were lost, and he hardly knew what they were to find them again. Oswald would have to understand without them.

'It's over now,' said Oswald. 'We should forget all about it.'

Perhaps Oswald would never understand. How could he, a thegn's son? Brinin found his voice, strengthened it, steadied it.

'I will *never* forget it,' he said.

'You can't stay here, not with winter coming,' said Oswald, and Brinin knew that the rest was to stay unsaid from now on. 'Brother Wilfred has told me what to do.'

'Brother Wilfred! Does *he* know I'm here?'

'He does now. I saw him after Edith told me. He knew something was wrong, and I told him. He went and asked my father for leave to take me to the minster to see their books. He says you are to meet us on the road.'

'And you're sure that he won't tell anyone? If anyone knew that you were *still* helping me, or that Edith had—'

'We can trust him, Brinin! He told me that he thought you had gone to the minster, but he said nothing to anyone. He and I will ride out the day after tomorrow and meet you as soon as we can.'

'The same way as before?' Brinin hardly knew why he asked. What other way would there be? But to go that way alone, so lately gone with Row... He must strengthen his mind to it.

'Yes, the same way. Edith is bringing you food for the road. As soon as you have it, you must go. Don't wait for dark, but take good care not to be seen. We'll soon get you away from here and to safety.'

CHILL

They were ready to leave before dawn, when the village was still and lifeless, more like night than like morning. It was better that way; better to go while folk still slept, than to ride out with all Oakdene watching and wondering. Oswald had made up his bundle the night before, so there was no need to linger. He slipped past Edith's curtain to say his farewells—and made her stay where she was, out of the cold—then crept through the hall and out into the chill air.

He likely should have taken leave of his father, who had after all freed him to go. It was what he ought to have done, but he told himself that there was no need to rouse his father so early, that it was a kindness to let him sleep. That was why he left the hall without stopping by his father's bedside as he had done by his sister's. But when he reached the horsehouse and found his father, lantern in hand, there with Brother Wilfred and Ludan, the horses already saddled, he felt a kind of stiffening within and knew that he had been lying to himself.

'There's still a good while before dawn, Ludan,' he heard his father say. 'Go back inside and rest until it is time to begin work. No need to stay here.'

'Thank you, my lord,' said Ludan, then turned to Oswald warmly. 'A good road to you, Oswald Child, sir.'

Oswald, fastening his bundle to the back of his horse, listened to Ludan's steps as he blended into the darkness. And he listened to the stillness of the morning and the louder stillness that stood between him and his father, made all the louder because Brother Wilfred was beside them to hear it.

'It's good for you to go to the minster and learn what you can, Oswald,' said Edrich at last. 'With the days as they are, who knows what further time you will have for learning after this?'

'Yes, sir. I thank you,' said Oswald, and the words came coldly from his mouth, borne on his smoky breath into the bitter air of the morning. The warm light of his father's lantern fell on Oswald's breath, but it did not melt the words.

The silence grew loud again until Edrich Thegn began to speak a little to Brother Wilfred. Oswald did not hear them. He stood, hand on his horse, and looked into the darkness, away from his father's lantern, away from his father's face. Somewhere, deep enough within to smother it, he had an unsettling feeling that he was being unkind; that he held something in his hand that he knew was small and easily broken, but that he was choosing to crush.

Then suddenly it was time for them to mount their horses and leave the village. Edrich raised his lantern higher and looked up at his son, and Oswald, unwilling though he was to look at anything, did see his father.

'It may also be good for you, Oswald, to be away from here for a time,' Edrich said, the lantern casting strange shadows on his face. 'Not only to learn, as I said before, but for you—for both of us—to think about what has been, to forget and to see what can be made fresh when you come back.'

'Yes, sir,' said Oswald, still all cold, hard meekness, and then before he could stop himself, heard himself say: 'If such a thing can ever be done.'

He could hardly believe he had said it, a bolder answer than any he had ever given his father. His words hung in the air as an icicle hangs from the eaves in winter, glistening, ice-cold and almost sharp enough to draw blood. They were so sharp that he felt them stab him somewhere in his chest, and in the lanternlight he saw that they had stabbed his father too. He could have wept then, he could have blurted out something—anything—to dull, to melt, to soften that icicle of words. But once he spoke so much hurt might come gushing out that it would be hard to stop the flow. Better to leave the words hanging. Better to let his father feel the pain of their sharpness. Oswald set his teeth as though to keep further speech inside, and lowered his eyes. He himself had borne enough pain already, after all.

'Goodbye, sir,' he said, and though he meant them to be warmer, the air between them was already so cold that the words came out frosty nonetheless.

Leave was taken, and they rode south out of the village to where they would later join the western road. Oswald looked back once, only once, and saw a far-off glow where his father still stood where they had left him, the lantern low now, hanging by his side; and as Oswald watched he saw the light move, as his father went back to the hall alone.

The morning was bright, though still young, before they stopped to eat. They had ridden mostly without speech, keen to make good time; and though they hadn't driven the horses hard, both man and beast were glad to stop.

'The road can be good for many things, for all its dangers,' said Brother Wilfred, sitting on the stump of some long-felled tree. 'I have always liked to see how the land changes as I go; and to go with a friend is much better because then there can be time for speech that might otherwise be lost. Would you like some cheese, my boy?'

He reached out and handed Oswald a piece of cheese, then cut another for himself.

'I have sometimes before told you of my time in the minster when I was a boy. One of my masters there, Brother Ordgar, was harsher than the others and frightened us boys very much. He would never overlook even the smallest mistake or fault, and there was seldom a day when one or other of us did not feel the weight of his rod. In time I almost came to hate him. One boy, some winters younger than myself, was so scared of him that as soon as he saw Brother Ordgar he would forget everything he had learned. That boy was beaten more than anyone.

'I was quick to learn, and the abbot wished me to help teach the others, so I was more with Brother Ordgar than before. Sometimes I heard him speak to the other monks with such care or worry for the boys that it seemed he didn't loathe us all as much as we thought. I began to wonder if I even knew the man! One day, I was with him when he overheard that hapless boy telling a friend what he had learned. I will never forget Brother Ordgar's amazement. And when a little later, the boy could barely stammer out even a few words, Brother Ordgar did not even scold him. He had suddenly seen what any of us could have told him but what he himself had missed, and knew why the boy had always seemed so dull. Brother Ordgar was still harsh after that—that is, after all, how boys are taught—but never again with that boy. Now, what do you think I learned from all of that, Oswald?'

'That it is better to be kind than to be harsh?' said Oswald, wondering why Brother Wilfred was suddenly sharing this long tale from his youth. 'You have never been harsh with me, sir, and I know I've learned from you.'

'Yes, I believe you have learned, my boy, and though at the beginning I thought of being sterner, I think that with you it would be more of a hindrance than a help, and that words seem to go far enough. However, that is not what I learned from Brother Ordgar. I learned that a man can be wrong, however well meaning he is, and that he can learn that he has been wrong and try to put it right.'

Oswald looked down, with a growing uneasy feeling that all this talk might be about to become much less about the monk's youth and more about himself.

'You have done what you now rue, haven't you, Oswald?' went on Brother Wilfred. 'I wonder if you think that you are the only one who is to be left to learn from his mistakes without being endlessly reminded of them. Is that what you think?'

'No, sir,' mumbled Oswald, now sure that Wilfred was taking him where he didn't want to go, and that they would go there whether he dragged his heels or not.

'Do you think you were kind to your father this morning, that you spoke to him as a son ought to speak? It is clear, to me at least, that he is still much wounded by all that has happened and that he wanted you to leave him happier than either of you have been. It may even be that he also has some things he is sorry about—it seemed so to me, though I can't be sure. Yet while you want others to forget what you have done, you are not ready to do the same with your own father.'

Couldn't Brother Wilfred see why it had all been so hard; why what he had done and what his father had done were not the same? But before he had a chance to speak Brother Wilfred raised a hand to stop him.

'Wait, my boy!' he said firmly. 'You should say nothing now, I think, until you have thought about this a little more. What you have once said, you cannot unsay. You would have done better to remember that this morning. I have no wish to chide you when these past weeks have been so hard, nor when you are feeling the loss of Row—we will talk more of that later, Oswald, as I have much to say to you that you couldn't have heard before—but it would not be right for me to say nothing after what passed this morning.

'I don't understand any more than you do why your father handled it all as he did—he didn't do what I thought he might. But as you were not guiltless, what your father did worries me less than you not letting him mend things between you now. I know it's been hard for you. It's been hard for him too. And remember that we always do better to ask where we ourselves are at fault than to look for fault in others.'

Brother Wilfred packed the rest of the food into his bundle, then made his way to his horse. Oswald, feeling rather small now, followed him without a word.

'The road is also a good time for thought, and you have much thinking to do, haven't you, my boy?' said Wilfred, less stern now. 'Let's not stop again until at least midday. It would be good if we could meet Brinin before nightfall.'

WHISPERS

T he road stretched out before him into the west as Brinin walked slowly along it. No need to hurry; the sooner Oswald and Brother Wilfred reached him the better, and it wouldn't do to be too far ahead of them. The cold grey stones had taken on a warmer hue in the evening light, dappled with long rippling shadows as the breeze moved the trees that shaped them. It was a strange thing, this stone road, worn smooth now by many feet. How long since men had made it? It must have been heavy slow work to build a road so straight, where the rain would roll off without even leaving mud. They had known what they were about, those road-builders, though it was strange that they had felt the need of it.

Brinin turned to look behind him. Surely it wouldn't be long before they reached him. Then it would be easier than walking alone with shadowy thoughts of his brother at his side; where snatches of recalled speech were whispered to him from where they had passed together. Easier to think about the smoothness of the stones and the straightness of the road, than to let himself listen to the whispers. Perhaps Oswald and Brother Wilfred would drown the whispers out.

It was almost dusk when he heard it, the unmistakable sound of horses drawing near—slowly, at no more than a trot—and his heart lifted a little in hope. He had hoped twice already that day and twice it had come to nothing, but this time he sat down on a boulder to wait. It wasn't long before his straining eyes made out the shadow of two riders, and his heart lifted further. Then Brother Wilfred's well-known voice reached his ear.

'So you see, my boy, what you must learn from all this is that wisdom is there for the asking,' Brother Wilfred was saying. 'There are always men around who are ready to help—I myself, or even your father—so you need not wholly lean on your own thoughts. And perhaps most of all remember that, as a king deals out rings to his followers, so Heaven's King can give wisdom to those who ask.'

They had not yet seen him in the shade of the trees, but Brinin could see them plainly now. Brother Wilfred looked very earnest as he spoke, and Oswald's face—which almost always shared his thoughts—and the droop of his shoulders told Brinin that there had been hard things to say and to hear on the road. Brinin stepped out of the shadows and they saw him.

'Brinin!' Oswald was down from his horse almost at once. 'I didn't see you there!'

'My dear boy!' said Brother Wilfred. 'How weary you must be. You have been so much on the road and known so much sorrow since I last saw you.'

And he said it with such unforeseen warmth and kindness that something hard grew in Brinin's throat, and he could say nothing at all.

'I know you've never ridden,' said Oswald, 'but I think we can ride with two on one horse. You'll have to sit straight and hold on well. Let's see if we can get you up.'

It was already dark when, road-weary, they stopped for the night. Brinin, a little sore from his first ride, was glad to have his feet on the ground again and gladder still to think of a night under thatch after so long without.

It was barely a village, only a few houses huddled together, the biggest of them barely a hall; but Brother Wilfred had stayed there before, and they remembered and welcomed him. Guest oaths were taken and a mead cup shared, and Oswald gave the house-lord a seax with a skilfully carved bone handle, a gift from his father in thanks for their welcome.

Brinin, as a slave, was not welcomed to the table. He ate in a corner of the hall with two other men, slaves too, most likely. They said little to him, but he didn't mind that with warm food in his belly. It meant that he didn't need to say much to them, and that was all the better.

When the meal was over and it was time for men to sleep, there were fleece-covered benches for Oswald and Brother Wilfred and a place on the floor for Brinin. But it was a warm place, safe from bad weather and wild beasts, and under the thatch he need not look at the stars and remember. The whispers might be harder to hear.

It was easy to lie down, easy to grow warm, hard to dare to shut his eyes. Sleep meant dreams. Would he groan or shout out in the night, waking all around him? Sleep would take him—he was tired and he knew it would come—but it was hard to yield to it willingly when he knew what it held. When everyone else around him seemed to be asleep, Brinin sat up again. He would sit and watch the embers for a while until he lost the fight.

'Are you not tired, my boy?' said a voice behind him, soft in the darkness, and Brinin looked up to see Brother Wilfred standing beside him. 'You seemed to be when we met you on the road.'

'I thought I might watch the fire for a while, sir.'

Brinin thought the monk would leave him then to go back to his own rest—surely he too was tired—but he didn't. He said nothing more, but sat down on the floor beside him; and for a time they watched the embers together, a warm, welcoming glow in the darkness of the house.

'There are times when sleep can be most unwelcome, even when we are most in need of it,' said Brother Wilfred at last, his words almost a whisper so as not to wake the others. Brinin looked at him in mild wonder. How had the monk heard what he had not told him? 'I have had such times myself. You may know that, before I came to Oakdene, I lived in a minster in Northumbria. I went there as a small boy, and there was another boy about my age, Dunstan, who came soon after I did. He became like a brother to me, and not only in the way that all monks are to one another. We were always together: worked and learned together; played together when we could; ate and slept together; were beaten together when we angered our masters. We were children together and became men together. We were together until six winters ago and could not have been dearer to one another if we had been born of the same mother. I almost felt we had been.'

Brother Wilfred said nothing more for a time and when he spoke again the words were slower, softer, guided very carefully. Brinin heard the care and saw it for what it was, so he almost felt that he had known what was coming when the monk began to speak.

'One night raiders came to the minster and he, Dunstan—I haven't spoken his name since that night, you know—he was slain before my eyes. They were all slain. I was the only one who lived. And after that, when I slept I would see it all again in my dreams. For a long time, I was most unwilling to sleep.'

'And did the dreams stop in time, sir?' Brinin asked and he too spoke carefully, guiding his voice.

'It is seldom now that they come—not so often as before—but sometimes they do, even now.' The fire seemed to breathe like those who slept around them, the embers sometimes brighter, sometimes dim. Someone snored, and Brinin heard the creak of the boards and rustle of the straw as another turned in their sleep. 'It's very painful, isn't it?'

Brinin kept his head down then. He couldn't have spoken if he had tried. How did Brother Wilfred understand so well? He seemed to *know*. How had he even seen, or cared, that he wasn't sleeping? He felt the monk's hand rest on his shoulder; a strengthening hand that Brinin thought a father might give, if he had only known what a father was. Together in the darkness, they both knew sorrow.

'Could you find the place again?' Brother Wilfred said. 'Where you buried him?'

Brinin nodded, then somehow found his voice and kept a tight hold of it.

'I can't forget the place, sir, and I marked it with stones.'

'We will go there together, I think. We will go to the minster first and rest for a time. Then we will find the place together before I go back to Oakdene. We will have time to talk, you and I. I'm going to sleep now, my boy, and I will pray that tonight at least, your own sleep will be empty.'

WONDER

They reached the minster late in the afternoon of the third day. It was hidden, lying back from the road, the hills rising behind it. Brinin and Row had known they were near safety on that last day. Only now did Brinin see how near they had been. Had the day been clear, perhaps they could have seen the minster before them; but by the time the mist had lifted, Row was already gone and Brinin hadn't even tried to look.

The buildings were like any other, wood and thatch; they were fewer than in Oakdene, though otherwise much the same. There were stalls for beasts, fields to till, and all was shut in by a tall wooden fence to keep out thieves and wild beasts.

Two monks met them as they came through the gate and bowed most meekly to them—to all three of them—by way of greeting. That was the first wonder. Laughing seemed too bold, though Brinin almost reached out a hand to stop them; but he glanced at Brother Wilfred and saw that he did not seem to think that anything was wrong. Perhaps this was the way with monks. Likely there would be less of the bowing once these brothers knew that only two were worthy among their guests. One of them said a prayer, and the younger of the two left to tell the prior of their coming.

They were led to a building where there was a fire burning in the hearth, and benches where they could sit and rest. Oswald was walking very stiffly. He didn't sit down; he stood wordless by the fire and Brinin knew that he was feeling the wounds they must never speak of. The younger monk came back: the prior was on his way, and he himself would ready the water for their feet.

'Hadn't we better tell them, sir?' whispered Brinin. It was all becoming too much. 'They don't know… what I am. Let me wait outside until they are done with you and Oswald.'

'My dear boy,' smiled Brother Wilfred. 'Sygbald the Prior here is an old friend of mine, and I have never known a man who did his work with more care. There are few, anywhere, who lead their minsters as he does his. As prior, he must welcome all guests as though he welcomed our Lord himself. Whatever you may be, you are his guest and welcome you he must.'

What passed then Brinin watched as though it were happening to someone else. He watched as the prior himself came and washed his feet as he washed Oswald's and Brother Wilfred's—the second wonder. He watched as Sygbald beckoned all of them to eat with him, and as he served out the food himself—the third. Oswald had told Brinin all those months ago in Oakdene that he had heard that the prior here was likely to welcome them. But Brinin had thought that that had meant he wouldn't turn them away. He had thought that he might give them some corner to sleep in and leave to work for their bread. Perhaps he might even have welcomed them by not asking too much about who they were or where they had come from. But all of this went beyond welcome, and it was almost dreamlike.

'How glad I am to welcome you here, my brother—to welcome all of you,' said Sygbald to Wilfred as they ate together. 'Guests are not unknown to us—not many out here, but they do come. I can't tell you how I felt upon reaching the guest house to learn that one of them is an old friend.'

'The gladness is as much mine!' Brother Wilfred's smile was warm in the candlelight. 'And I hope you can stretch your welcome for some months—not to me, for I must leave before the new moon—but to the boys here. Oswald's father, my lord the thegn, is a most worthy man. He built a church in his village and found a priest for it. Not only that, but when he heard of how the Ætheling loves knowledge, and that I could bestow it, he asked me to teach his son, although he himself is wholly without learning. Oswald has been quick to learn, but we have reached the end of what we can do without books. His father gave me leave to bring him here to read further.'

'His father must indeed be a worthy man. I can't think of even a score of men in the kingdom who have any time for learning, and most of those are in the church. But are you telling me that you have taught the boy without books?'

'We had a little of the writings of Bede, but it is amazing what can be done with a waxboard and a memory. I have found myself thankful for what Brother Ordgar drove into my mind, though I didn't always love him for it at the time.'

'Ah, Brother Ordgar!' smiled Sygbald. 'Which of us did love him for it at the time? Even now I do not dare to forget anything he taught us. So, the boy can read and write in Latin? Yes? You have done well then, Wilfred. These days, even in minsters, learning in Latin seems to stop with saying paternosters and psalms without any understanding. Most monks and even some abbots hardly know the rule they follow. You would have to look long and hard to find a handful of men south of the Humber who could even write a short letter in Latin.'

'Who knows if you would find many more north of the Humber either, since the Danes came?'

'True, true. We live in evil days.' Sygbald looked at Oswald with a smile. 'A boy who can read Latin! Does his father mean to put him in the church, Wilfred?'

'He is the only son of his father and is to be thegn after him.'

'A shame,' sighed Sygbald, 'when there is so little learning. Still, he must learn what he can, and perhaps one day he will have a son he puts in the church. We have the Latin psalter, with some English in the text, and one or two smaller scrolls. He need not be idle while he is here.'

'Indeed not. I want neither of them to be idle. If you will let them, it would be good for them to follow the life of the minster as much as they can, praying when the brothers do, eating, sleeping and working at the same times.'

'I don't mind that if they are willing to heed our rule here. It isn't an easy life, for all it is worthwhile.' Sygbald looked at Brinin now, before turning back to Brother Wilfred. 'I have heard about Oswald, but what of Brinin here? Has he also come for the books?'

'He has come with us as a friend to Oswald. Brinin cannot read or write but he knows how to work hard. I have seen it myself. I know he will be willing to do any work or learn any skill you ask of him. He must likely stay here longer than Oswald, so it would be good if you can give him work to do. He is not free to become a monk, though. It is in my mind that he will be called back to Oakdene, perhaps sooner than we think, but let him work here while he can.'

'Well, my boy,' said Sygbald, turning back to Brinin. 'What skills do you have?'

'I can work as I am bidden, sir,' said Brinin.

'Obedience is something we all must seek, so I am glad you have learned it. We have a brother here, Cwichelm, who is a woodsmith, very skilled in his craft. He is old now and I have been wanting him to teach his craft to one of the younger brothers. It is no harder to teach two than to teach one, so perhaps Brinin too can learn from Brother Cwichelm. You should also understand, my boy, that I make all the brothers here learn to read and write, at the very least in English—these days it mostly goes no further than that. There is no harm in you also learning while you are here. A little woodcraft and a little wordcraft, so to speak, and whatever other work I can find for you to do. What do you say, my boy?'

'I will do whatever you ask of me, sir,' said Brinin. Sygbald liked this answer, but neither he nor the others seemed to hear the wonder hidden by the words. Surely it was all only the best of dreams.

'Now,' said Wilfred. 'We have had days on the road and though, no doubt, these two would say they are men now—in many ways they are—they are both young and both have seen many troubles these last weeks. So with your leave, my brother, I will bid them to bed, although it is still early.'

Brinin and Oswald were taken to where some beds stood in readiness for guests, and Brother Wilfred and Sygbald the Prior left them to have more speech alone.

'You will be safe here until you can go back to Oakdene. The Prior will be kind to you. I wonder what Brother Wilfred meant when he said that he thought you would be called back,' said Oswald, easing himself down, still stiff, onto one of the beds. 'Isn't it good to lie down and to know that we don't have to mount our horses again before dawn?'

'He washed my feet himself!' said Brinin, and that was all he could say.

He didn't say that he had never slept on a bed before, nor eaten seated at a table. There were so many things he didn't say. How could he begin to speak of the welcome they had been given, or of what the Prior wanted him to learn? He could only lie and wonder at it all. He could do more with the woodcraft—that was a good skill to have—but the wordcraft was of more worth. Even if he never read or wrote another word after he had learned, the knowledge that he *could* do this thing that so few could do, that knowledge would stay buried hoardlike in his breast and give him gladness. If only Row could have known what had awaited them in this place. They had been so near.

WORDCRAFT

The bewilderment passed. One day flowed from another, all so alike that it did not take long to learn the way of things. Lauds, Prime, Terce. Words without meaning came to have meaning because they grew to rule Brinin's days. Every day there was Latin to be heard: Latin in prayer and song, haunting song unlike any other Brinin had ever known. He heard it so much and so often that many of the words were sown in his mind, and he knew their sounds as a man knows his own field. Brother Wilfred taught him some of the words most often said—Brinin had heard the Paternoster so often in Oakdene that he could almost say it already—and he taught him the meaning in plain speech. That was another wonder. He had lost count of them now.

When they weren't at prayer, there was work to be done, hard work of the kind that must be done anywhere, in villages, in minsters, or on farms that stood alone. And because Brinin was young and strong and ready to do anything asked of him, he soon found work to turn his hand to. The woodcraft he did each day with Brother Cwichelm and Brother Leofa was a joy. Sygbald the Prior had been right about Cwichelm—he was very skilled in his craft—and Brinin and Leofa learned quickly from him. Leofa was only a little older than himself and Brinin liked him. The day their first stools were ready was a proud one for both of them.

Brinin had from time to time seen Oswald's waxboard in Oakdene. It had seemed then almost like witchcraft for a man to look at the strange markings Oswald held on it and make speech from them, even if he himself had not made the markings. Now, as bidden by the prior, he went every day to learn his wordcraft from Brother Deor, who was old and somewhat forbidding—and from what Leofa had said Brinin was glad not to be one of the boys that Deor had taught over the years. And he found that making speech from markings in wax was no more witchcraft than knowing a tree or plant from the shape of its leaf. Perhaps the greatest wonder of all was that he was quick to know the shapes and make speech from them. Brother Deor praised him for that, though praise sat awkwardly on Brinin, it was so unknown to him. Making the markings was harder. His hands were too big and rough for that kind of work, and the writing-seax too small to hold. Brother Deor would make him do it again and again before it was good enough. Not much was good enough for Brother Deor.

'You have made four mistakes while reading to me, and I won't listen to any more,' he said sternly one morning. 'Had you been one of the boys I have taught to be monks, I would likely have beaten you for it. As it is, you are a guest and too big for me to beat'—Brinin thought somewhat wryly that someone should have told Aculf that—'but I don't see why I should listen to poor reading when we both know that you are quick to learn. Go away and don't let me see you again until you can do it better.'

And Brinin left with his waxboard, not at all unhappy to be chided, and read the words over and over to himself until he could almost say them with his eyes shut. He didn't mind Brother Deor's sternness in the slightest. He would have borne much worse quite happily because, wonder of wonders, he could read.

The days slipped by, each following swiftly on the other, and the time drew near for Brother Wilfred to leave them; but before that there was one last thing to be done. One morning Brinin left early with Brother Wilfred and Oswald to find that place he couldn't forget, where he had left Row buried in the earth.

He remembered the whiteness of the mist and the shape of the hills as it had lifted. They were for ever in his head. He had seen it all many, many times in his sleep, and when he saw those hills draw near he knew them again with a knowledge that sat heavy in his gut like sickness. They were so near—they were there before midday—and he found the heap of stones where he had left it.

Brother Wilfred said those words a priest says, which it had seemed so wrong to bury Row without; and he prayed and said other things that were strengthening somehow. Oswald wept, and Brinin wished he could because weeping might hurt less than the ache he felt instead, but his weeping had almost always been deep inside and hidden. So he listened, aching, to Brother Wilfred and looked at the stones, but saw his brother's face instead. And he remembered how fearful he had been that he would forget his face. He knew now that he would never forget.

When it was almost time to go back to the minster, Brother Wilfred beckoned to Oswald, and they walked away a little. But Brinin lingered and stood there alone. It had been good to come—bitter, aching, but good—because he knew now that he had done everything he could, and somehow it was over. Still hurting, like a knife twisting inside him, but done. He reached down and picked up one of the stones, only a small one, then left the place and followed the others.

The next day Brother Wilfred came to Brother Deor and asked his leave for Brinin to sit with Oswald that morning. What could this be about? What could Oswald be learning that he would even begin to understand, he with his little reading and ill-scratched words?

'I can see you are both wondering why I have brought Brinin here,' smiled Brother Wilfred, when they reached Oswald. 'Sit down here, my boy. All I ask you to do is to sit and listen. Oswald, you won't need your waxboard this morning. I have with me a Latin prayer—let me spread the scroll here, like this. Read the Latin first, then draw out the English. I will help you with any words you do not know.'

'*Deus pater omnipotens domine caeli ac terrae,*' began Oswald strongly, it seemed to Brinin, with no fear of reading it awry. 'God and Father Almighty, Lord of Heaven and Earth. *Deduc me obsecro te per misericordiam pietatis tuae.* Lead me in your kind mercy, I pray… to where throngs of saints are glad, singing to the Lord with strong peace in the land of the living.'

Brinin knew then what Oswald was reading and why Brother Wilfred had wanted him to hear it. Surely this prayer was about the Ærist, the Rising of the Dead, and the things there would be after it.

'Where there is happiness… where there is safety… where there is always health…' went on Oswald, and Brinin saw that he too was beginning to understand. 'Where there is no ache.'

No ache. Whatever else there would be, today that alone seemed worth waiting for. Oswald read on, but for some time Brinin hardly heard him.

'Where no one… no one p… perishes.' Oswald was beginning to sound a little choked. 'Where the poor man does not weep… where there is gladness… where there is no trouble… where there is life and truth… where there… where there is no…'

Oswald faltered then, bowing his head, but Brother Wilfred nodded for him to go on. It seemed that he was as keen for Oswald to say it as he was for Brinin to hear it. Brinin saw Oswald set his teeth, bracing himself to drive out the words.

'Where there is no… b… bitter death.'

Then he stopped, and Brother Wilfred did not make him keep going. They sat without speaking—those last words growing tall in Brinin's mind—until Oswald was ready.

'*Ubi caritas firma.* Where there is strong love… where things are right… where there is the God of gods… where there is the Lord of lords… *Ubi nox nulla tetra.* Where there is no dark night. *Ubi regnum regnorum saeculorum in saecula. Amen.* Where the King of kings rules for ever and ever. Amen.'

Perhaps there could be gladness side by side with the ache, gladness to think of what would come. That's how it would be for the living: gladness and ache, sometimes more of one than the other. But if what Brother Wilfred said were true—why should he doubt him—then another day was coming. If Brinin strained his eyes he could see it, like a friend far off and long looked for. When that time came, the ache would be gone and only the gladness left.

STEERING

T he days grew short and the nights long and everyone was glad of fire in the hearths and cloaks to warm them as they slept. Almost all Oswald's work was that of the mind: reading a psalm; learning to say it in Latin to the prior without mistakes; writing the English on his waxboard and showing that to the prior too; starting again with a new psalm. The prior gave him other work each day; some he had never done before, like drawing water or hewing wood. But he mostly sat alone with the psalter and his waxboard, whispering the words to himself as he worked. And as the darkness of winter stole in around them, he sometimes longed for the heavier work that Brinin had, because that was warmer.

Brother Wilfred had told him that there were books more beautiful than anything he had ever seen, and now that he had seen the psalter, he knew he had been right. It was so startling to see, huebright with reds, blues, golds. Sometimes it was hard to keep his mind on his work when there was so much else to see. There was one likeness of David the King and his singers that Oswald loved to look at. They all held horns and harps, and he wondered if their songs were like monks' songs, or the village songs, or like something else. They sang psalms like the monks, but some were dancing and clapping their hands and the monks never did that. To think that the minster, wood and thatch, held a book like that! Even the shape of the letters was to be wondered at, and the prior was letting him read it.

At first there was so much to fill his mind and so much to learn, that he thought little of Oakdene and all that had happened there.

But as the darkening days bore him nearer to Yule, and nearer to the road home, he began to remember and to think. And when he thought about it all, nothing looked the same any more. He wasn't the same any more. He didn't know how it had happened. Perhaps it was what Brother Wilfred had said to him on the road; or the daily psalms and prayers that made him think beyond himself. Perhaps it was having time to live without everyone and everything seeming to shame him. However it had come about, he saw nothing as he had seen it before.

'The prior says it's good for us to talk about our wrongdoings,' he said to Brinin as they got ready to sleep one night. They were the only guests now, and the evenings were good for talking. 'And I have something to say to you and maybe even to him. Don't look like that; you'll understand when I say it. I always blamed Aculf for everything, you know. And he *was* to blame; but so was I, almost as much, because I said nothing about it to my father. If I hadn't been so fearful, if I'd done what was right, it might never have got so bad.'

'We were boys, Oswald. Can a boy tell his father what he should do? Why would I blame you for what Aculf did, or for what your father didn't know?'

'You once said yourself that I was too scared of my father to do anything.'

'I was angry when I said it. Forget it now.'

'But it was true. And I know things would have been better if I had said something; or at least if they weren't, I wouldn't have been to blame. But I *am* to blame because I did nothing about it, after all my talk of friendship; and that's what I want to ask your forgiveness for.'

'You think you did nothing? You think you need to ask my forgiveness after—yes, I know you don't want me to speak of it—after what you did?' Brinin's voice was full of disbelief. 'Even if there *was* anything to forgive, don't you think you did enough to make up for anything you didn't do?'

'I brought it on myself, by not doing what I ought to have done. I was very angry with my father, you know, because—well, I don't want to talk about that—because he didn't do what I thought he would. But I know now that I brought it on myself. I think I need to forget all of that—to try to at least—and only think about what I should have done and not what he should have done.'

'We were boys,' said Brinin doggedly. 'It's for the men—for your father—to lead the village, not for boys. And for the men to know what happens there.'

Oswald sighed. Even if Brinin did let his friendship dull his wisdom, he need not dull his own. He knew he was right and he knew what he needed to do about it.

'When I get back to Oakdene—it's not long before I go now—I'm going to tell my father everything. Not where you are until I know you'll be safe, but everything else. And I'll ask his forgiveness for doing nothing before. Even if I don't understand what he did, I can't do anything about that. It's for a son to ask forgiveness of his father, not the other way. I have to forget about everything else.'

They didn't speak of it again after that night, but Oswald was settled in his own mind. What would his father say? Would he hear him with anger or forgiveness? How could he know? But he wondered now if his father *had* wanted to speak and to listen. Oswald remembered that night when he had stopped his father's words and it felt shameful now. Whatever happened, nothing could ever be as bad again. If Oswald had learned one thing at the minster, it was how to steer his mind. He had learned to drive it as a man drives his beasts, to pen it in and choose his thoughts. The long slow days with the psalter had taught him that. Perhaps with a little steering, a little driving, he might begin to mend things; and the blame would be worth taking if he could go back to his father without the ice between them.

SEAX

Prime was over, and Brinin and Oswald went out from the church into the cold light of the morning. They came from psalm and song. *Deus, adiutorium meum intende;* God, come to my help. Brinin knew those words now. They said them every day, and he had learned the meaning. Often heard, well known.

They were just parting, each to his own work, when they were startled by the sound of a hard-driven horse thundering towards them beyond the fence. It was swiftly followed by the hammering of a fist on the gate, and one of the monks nearby ran to open it. And there, still on his horse, dusty and wind-swept from the road, was Thurstan.

'Thurstan?' exclaimed Oswald. 'Father must have sent him to fetch me back. I thought he said I was to go after Yule.'

But Brinin saw what it seemed Oswald did not. Thurstan's face was grim and set as he got off his horse. If Edrich Thegn had sent him, it was not with any good tidings. There was nothing glad on his face. Oswald saw Brinin's frown and misunderstood it.

'I don't care if he sees you,' said Oswald. 'Remember I'm going to tell my father everything. And we can trust Thurstan.'

He called out to him, and Thurstan turned to them at the sound of his name, starting slightly when he saw Brinin at Oswald's side.

'It's good to see you, Thurstan. How was the road? Has Father called me back now?' asked Oswald. 'He said I was to go back after Yuletide.'

'We must go straightaway,' said Thurstan. He turned to Brinin. 'I needn't ask what you're doing here. I think I know well enough, and there will be time for answers on the road.'

Thurstan had not yet smiled. Brinin glanced at Oswald and saw that he too was beginning to understand what Thurstan's face was telling them. Something was wrong, very wrong.

'There's no easy way to say this, Oswald, so I may as well tell you straight,' went on Thurstan. 'Your father was riding near Readingum with Swetrich and Cynestan when they were set upon by a band of Danes. Swetrich was killed outright, Cynestan was wounded and—'

'And my father?' Oswald's words were little more than a breath, a gasp.

'We don't know.' Thurstan reached out and laid a hand on Oswald's shoulder. 'Cynestan got back to Oakdene—that's wonder enough, given his wounds. He says he didn't see your father killed and didn't see his body anywhere nearby. He'll tell you everything himself when you get to Oakdene, but it looks like the Danes may have taken him. Who knows where? Cynestan spoke to two boys who saw four men ride past with a fifth man, bound and struggling.'

Oswald opened his mouth to speak, then shut it again without saying a word. But his face was louder than Brinin had ever seen it. Ashen, fearful, sorrowful, stricken, it shouted at them everything he couldn't say.

'We must find out where they have taken him!' Oswald's voice was shaking when at last he found words. 'We can't leave him to the Danes! Who knows what they might do to him?'

'You know I would be the first to go, Oswald.' There was to be no lying hope from Thurstan, only hard truth, kindly said. 'I would do everything I could to find him, even if I fell in the trying. But we don't know where they took him and we have no way of finding out. It's been five days now. There is little hope, almost none at all, that he's still alive. There is much we don't know, but we can be almost sure of that.'

Oswald clenched his fists, head bowed. Brinin saw his eyes glisten, saw the tears that Oswald was holding back.

'What's more,' said Thurstan, 'Æthelwulf Ealdorman has called us to join him. It's clear that the Danes may be upon us any day, and we must be ready to meet them. As far as we know, *you* are lord of Oakdene and you must leave here today—now—to go back there, then on to war.'

One look from Thurstan to Brinin, one sharp breath, and Oswald turned and walked away.

'I'll get ready to go,' he mumbled as he left them. Perhaps he needed to go quickly and strengthen himself somehow to be thegn.

'Is there anywhere here where a man can find water and fodder for his horse, and meat and ale for himself?' asked Thurstan, turning to Brinin.

Brinin nodded. He found someone to tend to the horse, then led Thurstan to the guest house. Oswald wasn't there. Perhaps he had already fetched all he needed and gone to the prior. The prior would have to be told. Brinin found food for Thurstan, then stood nearby as he ate it, but Thurstan beckoned him over and nodded for him to sit.

'I wonder if you know how much trouble came of your flight, not least to Oswald Child himself,' he said a little sternly.

'I know it,' said Brinin. Had he known then what he knew now, he would never have gone, would have stopped it all before it had begun. It's easy to be wise when it's too late. Well might Thurstan, though he knew less, speak sternly.

Thurstan broke off another piece of bread and ate it slowly. He took a long drink of ale and wiped his mouth with the back of his hand.

'You left Oakdene with your brother,' he said. 'Where is he?'

And there was the ache, coming on him swiftly and without warning, aching twice over this morning, for Oswald as well as himself. He had not much said it aloud, not since he had told Edith.

'Fallen,' he said at last. 'On the way here.'

'I'm sorry to hear it,' said Thurstan. 'The little I knew of your brother, I liked. He was good with the sheep.'

'Is there no hope that Edrich Thegn is still alive?' asked Brinin. Let them turn the speech from Row and the ache might lessen.

'If there is, it's such a small one that it won't do Oswald Child any good to have it.'

'You said they were near Readingum. Where's that?'

'East and a little north of Oakdene. But who knows where they went after that?'

'Why didn't they kill him where they fought?'

'I don't know. If they are about to do battle with us, perhaps they wanted to learn more about the land and thought they might make him tell them. Edrich Thegn is about the last man to tell them anything. More likely dead now.' Thurstan stopped, frowning, and took another drink. That was no easy thing to think of, even for a man who knew battle well. Little wonder he had said nothing of it to Oswald. 'If Edrich Thegn could bid us, he would bid us to battle and not after him. I would go. I would go now if I could. But Æthelwulf's call must be greater. That's the way of it. If only we knew…'

The ale cup was empty now, and Brinin watched as Thurstan, suddenly weary, laid it aside with a sigh. Nothing to know, nothing to be done, little to say.

'I'll go and find Oswald,' said Brinin and left Thurstan alone by the fire.

Oswald was ready to leave. His cloak hung from his shoulders, his quiver across his back, his sword at his side. Oswald's horse was already saddled, and he stood waiting for Thurstan, white and like he was freshly wakened and didn't know if he was still dreaming. He looked up as he saw Brinin coming towards him.

'Where's Thurstan?' he asked. 'I'm ready.'

'Eating. He'll be here soon. Do you have food for the road?'

Oswald nodded, then fell back to half dreaming again.

'What do you want me to do, Oswald?' asked Brinin at last. 'Shall I come with you now?'

There was no understanding on Oswald's face. He was too shocked, too sorrow-stricken to see that nothing was the same any more. They had left Prime friends, and Thurstan had come with word that had changed all that. If Oswald was thegn now, if he was lord, then Brinin was not only a friend. He was his slave.

'I know how it must be now,' he went on when Oswald didn't speak. 'I am ready to do your bidding. Tell me what you want.'

Sudden understanding flooded Oswald's face. He looked sharply at Brinin, then to Thurstan who was coming towards them with his horse.

'Are you ready? The sooner we're on the road the better,' said Thurstan. 'If we leave now and ride swiftly, we may reach Oakdene by nightfall tomorrow.'

'Yes,' said Oswald. 'There's only one thing left to be done.'

Oswald unfastened his belt and slid off his seax in its sheath. Holding it in both hands, he looked back to Thurstan again.

'Thurstan,' he said. 'I once swore to do all I could to give Brinin freedom. If I *am* lord of Oakdene, I can now and I want you to see me doing it.'

Oswald reached out and handed the seax to Brinin. Brinin took it quietly. He drew it from its sheath and turned it over in his hands. His eye followed the pattern rippling along the blade like water in a river. His finger ran along the carvings on the handle, twisting like a path of many turns. How strange that something so small as a knife passing from hand to hand could give back what his kin had lost and bestow what he himself had barely dreamed of.

'Thurstan, Brinin will *never* be a slave of mine!' Oswald was more earnest than he had ever been, fierce almost. 'If I fall to the Danes, you have seen that I gave him freedom today. If my father still lives—I pray he does—and it is not mine to give, I will ask him to give it himself. The seax is a token of my oath. If I fall, and my father lives, ask him for me, Thurstan.'

'Very well, my lord,' said Thurstan. 'I will do as you ask.'

Brinin had been staring down at the seax, but he looked up at Oswald now.

'What man has no lord?' He seemed to hear Row say it, as he had once done when they walked together, and his voice threatened to fail him. 'If Oakdene is my place then, free or not, *you* are my lord. What do you want me to do? Shall I come with you now?'

'No,' said Oswald as he got on his horse. 'Not yet. You've never been taught to go into battle. I'll send for you when I can. If you hear nothing by Easter, go to Oakdene then.'

Brinin stood for a long time after they had ridden out of sight. The seax had grown warm in his hand long before he fastened it to his belt. Freedom had a weight to it, as it hung at his side. He could touch it. Oswald had left him with no bidding beyond waiting, so Brinin knew what he would do. His first free deed would be to follow his own counsel.

SON

Throughout the morning and into the afternoon, Oswald and Thurstan rode as hard as their horses could bear, stopping little and slowing only when they had to. Everything was grey, the road and the sky. The clouds were so heavy that even the daylight had a darkness to it, and the grass seemed too dull to be called green. All grey, dark, dull. But it was better that way. If the sun had been bright it would have seemed like it was mocking him, and he might not have been able to hold back the tears. He was barely holding them back as it was. They were always too near for him to stop being wary of them and Oswald felt that he mustn't yield to them now. How could he lead men if he couldn't keep hold of himself? So he looked at the road and listened to the pounding of the hooves and tried to forget that his father was gone and that he, like a fool, had been too late to melt the ice.

They had to stop at last, for the horses more than themselves. There was a stream and a little grass, and Oswald and Thurstan ate their bread standing under a tree as a poor shelter from the mizzling rain.

'Where will we sleep tonight?' asked Oswald. He had been trying so hard not to think that he'd forgotten to think about that. 'The light won't last much longer.'

'There's a village I stopped at on the way. They know we're coming.' Thurstan cast a quick glance at Oswald but mostly kept his eyes on the horses. 'This isn't the best time to ask but if we wait for a

233

good one it will likely never come. How did Brinin come to be at the minster?'

'I sent him there to get him away from Aculf.'

'Then sent the horses the other way. So you did know where the slaves had gone. I thought you did.'

Oswald had settled on speaking of it and been thwarted, and now he didn't mind telling Thurstan what he would never have told him before.

'I can't tell you how harsh Aculf was to Brinin. He hated him and often beat him for nothing. It got so bad I had to do something, and at the time getting Brinin away was the only thing I could think of.'

Oswald told Thurstan everything then: more than he had told Brother Wilfred or Edith, more than Brinin would ever know, more even than he had meant to tell his father. Once he had started the tale kept coming.

'Surely,' said Thurstan, when Oswald had stopped at last, 'it would have been easier to tell your father all this?'

'I know that now!' said Oswald bitterly. He stopped to tell the threatening tears that he was their lord and not only Oakdene's. He would make them heed him. 'I was going to tell him everything when I got back. I know now that I was wrong not to tell him before, but it was hard to do, so I didn't. Brinin saved my life once—pulled me out of the river when we were small—but I never told my father. He'd forbidden me to play by the river and I thought he'd beat me if he learned that I hadn't heeded him. He didn't even know that Brinin and I were friends. Can you believe that? I can hardly believe it myself now. Perhaps if I had told him about the river—even if he had beaten me for it—everything else would have been easier. But I was scared and didn't think he would want to listen to me. I didn't think of my friendship with Brinin, or of what I ought to have done as a son. I only thought of myself.'

'You made up for that well enough in the end,' said Thurstan wryly. 'Talking to your father couldn't have been harder than going before the Moot.'

'No, but by then it was already too late. At first, I said nothing so they wouldn't be found. It was only at the Moot that I heard that my father wouldn't send any more men. But then I couldn't think of anything to say that didn't seem to blame him for being mistaken in Aculf. I thought it was better to say nothing and take what was coming to me.'

And then he had been so angry that he had wanted to make his father smart for it as much as he had. But he couldn't say that to Thurstan. Not today.

'I wish now that I'd never sent them away, but I was right not to tell Ealmund where they had gone. It's the one thing I'm not ashamed of. I would do it again! I was to blame, not them. And do you know the worst of it? Row died on the way.'

'So Brinin told me.'

'I'll never forgive myself for that. They need never have gone and Row might live, if I hadn't been so fearful and... and such a fool.'

Thurstan, already in the saddle again, looked down at Oswald with a sigh.

'You were a fool,' he said. 'But you were a brave fool in the end. I was a bigger fool than you were. I know what Aculf's like. I've never liked him and I saw some of what he did and warned him off. I even had half a mind to speak to your father about it, but Aculf seemed to leave Brinin alone and I forgot about it. It was months after that when they ran away and I didn't think of it then. Now you've told me all this, I wish I had. It must be the first time in my life I've wished I had said something instead of wishing I'd kept my mouth shut. I'm ashamed of myself now.'

There was so much to be ashamed of, so many mistakes, so much that had been left undone. It was hard not to stumble under the weight of it all.

'Your father didn't understand why you did it—none of us did,' said Thurstan. 'But he said something to me that perhaps he didn't say to you. He told me that, whatever you'd done, you showed so much courage at the Moot that you made him proud to be your father.'

'He… he said that?' Oswald's voice was quivering now.

'Those were his very words.'

Oswald dropped his head. He had never seen a thegn weep and he didn't want to be the first. He mustn't be the first. Thurstan, ever the friend, was swift to help him.

'On your horse! We've no time to lose.' He scowled up at the clouds. 'If this rain keeps up, we'll be soaked to the skin before we sleep tonight.'

Oswald was saddle-weary by the time they reached Oakdene a little after dusk the next evening. His feet had barely touched the ground when Edith ran through the darkness to fling herself sobbing into his arms.

'Oh, Oswald!' she wept. 'Oh, Oswald!'

But there was nothing to say, nothing he could say. He could only walk with her wordless to the hall, strengthening himself somehow to meet whomever he found there.

Rædwald was there, and a few of the other men. They stood by the fire, so welcoming after the road. Some of the fyrdmen had already gone to join Æthelwulf Ealdorman as Thurstan had told him they would, but others had waited for Oswald's homecoming as their lord. It was an easier homecoming with Thurstan at his side. Thurstan didn't even go back to his own house but followed Oswald and Edith into the hall.

They were barely in, barely met and greeted, sorrow barely shared, when Aculf came sidling forward from some shadowy place where Oswald hadn't seen him.

'Welcome… my lord,' he fawned. 'I trust you aren't too tired from the road.'

Oswald was ready for it. He had thought of it on the road and had known it would come. If Aculf wanted to win his friendship now, he was years too late.

'I haven't forgotten,' said Oswald.

'Forgotten, my lord? Forgotten what?' said Aculf, smiling as if he could fool him that way.

'You know what I'm talking about.' Oswald had never thought that the day for this would come so soon. But it was here now, and he had his word to keep. 'I told you that I wouldn't forget and I haven't. My father did not know what you are, but I do. If I had been wiser, I would have told him. You won't do in my name what you did in his. You aren't fit to be workreeve.'

Aculf's smile had gone now. He stared at Oswald like he was ready for battle. Long-held power didn't slip easily from his grip.

'Oswa... ah, my lord... the work won't be done if—'

'The work will be done without you. I will find a better man. Keep to your own field and eat by your own hearth. Go now. I have no further need of you.'

'You heard your new lord, Aculf,' said Thurstan, when Aculf didn't move. 'You do have a hearth, I think. Keep to it as he bids you.'

Aculf, red-faced now, threw one last look around the other men to see if he could find a friend among them. But there was none, and he slunk away.

'I'm glad I didn't go home,' whispered Thurstan to Oswald as they walked to the table. 'I've waited years for that. It was well done, my lord!'

Oswald ate where he had always eaten. He wasn't ready to sit in his father's seat. There was so much to talk about, battle to be ready for, but he could hardly think of any of it and left them all as soon as he could. Lying in the darkness on his bed, he listened as the voices died away and the hall fell into sleep and stillness. It was only then that he let himself weep, bitterly and unthegnlike, long into the night.

WEIGHT

The weight of Oakdene was a heavy one, too heavy for much sleep. It was still well before dawn when Oswald slipped from the hall the next morning. He had seldom felt so young. How could he lead a whole village, men old enough to be his own father or grandfather? How could he even know what wisdom was? Sometimes, as a boy, he had thought his father's mind was too full of such things: rights and wrongs, work and warcraft, field and fyrd. Now that his own shoulders felt the burden, he wondered how his father had ever thought of anything else.

He made his way to the church, all cold and still inside. It was too early even for the monk to be awake. Standing before the altar, he thought of Brother Wilfred and Thurstan. They should be leading, not him. He needed them. He needed them so much, with their many winters, with their eyes that had seen the world and minds that understood it. He wasn't too proud to ask for wisdom. He needed it and he had none. But they had it and they might help him. The altar stood dark before him, like the altar in the minster where, candle-bearing, the monks came by night to pray. Oswald dropped to his knees, and his prayer was more heartfelt than any he had ever prayed.

Brother Wilfred found him there some time later, still on his knees. Oswald heard his steps as he came towards him and rose to his feet.

'My dear boy!' Outside, the darkness was softening as the sun rose. Inside, Oswald couldn't see the monk's face but he heard the sorrow in his voice. 'Prayer is always what we need, even in our times of gladness. How much more in our times of hardship and mourning?'

'I can't do this! I'm not ready! I don't even know where to begin!'

'I'm glad then that I found you in prayer. That shows me that you do know where to begin. My dear Oswald, we live in evil days. We have a foe so godless that they don't even stop at cutting down the helpless as they pray before the altar.' Brother Wilfred knew better than any of them what it meant to live in evil days. Oswald hadn't forgotten that. 'What have we done to bring such harm upon ourselves? Our sins in this land have been many. Yet just as we should be begging Heaven's King for forgiveness and seeking his strength, all around us are men who love to boast. In our day, every man loves to speak of his own power in battle, of how it was his own sword who cut down the foe and how he won by his own strength and wisdom. I know you, Oswald. I know that you have looked at your own wisdom and seen where it falls short. You have felt more fear than courage.'

'That's why I can't lead!'

'It's why you can!' Brother Wilfred was all earnestness now. 'No one who trusts in himself will ever go to the only one who can give strength and wisdom. You've looked at yourself and seen where you are lacking, and so I find you on your knees. Keep going to your knees as you have today and the Father of heaven will give you the strength and wisdom you need.'

Oswald would ask for it. He would ask for all the wisdom anyone could give him—wisdom to be a leader, to be a man, to be a good son to a dead father.

'Swetrich has been buried,' he said, 'yet my father can't be. It seems wrong—faithless almost—to believe he's dead with no body. Thurstan says he's likely dead. But if he's alive, and I do nothing…'

Oswald walked away from Brother Wilfred and stood with his back to him. He needed time to find his words and teach them to be steady.

'I'm stuck!' He turned back suddenly to the monk again. 'There's nothing I can do that isn't wrong. I can't bury him as I should and I can't save his life. I know nothing and I can do nothing! Whatever I do, I fail him somehow!'

'And yet,' said Brother Wilfred gently, 'if he could see you now, if he could have seen you as I did, on your knees, praying as I often found him praying, then he would see you are not failing him. He would see that you are becoming the kind of man he raised you to be.'

'I wish we could bury him,' whispered Oswald, sitting down with his head in his hands. 'This is all wrong!'

'Yuletide is a time for prayer and fasting. You are right that we have no way of knowing if your father is dead or alive. But God knows, and we can pray. Call everyone together to pray and fast for him, either for his life or to remember him. It's not a burial, but it is fitting for one who was their lord.'

'Yes. Perhaps that's what I'll do. I'm going to call everyone together to speak to them before I go to battle. After that we'll come to the church.' Perhaps the weight would be lighter with the knowledge that he would do something, that he would try to be a good son. 'Will you help Edith when I'm gone? I'm leaving everything else to her. She can do it. She always sees more than I do. Let me go now. I need to speak to her and I need to see Cynestan.'

He stopped suddenly at the threshold and turned back again.

'Pray for me!' he said. 'I'm scared! I didn't know it would be like this.'

Edith was already at work, talking through the day's food with some of the women.

'Can they do this without you, Edith?' asked Oswald. 'I need to talk to you. Can we go to the church where it's not so busy?'

'Most of these women know better than I do what needs to be done,' she said. 'And I want to talk to you too.'

Oswald caught sight of Ebba as they left the hall and beckoned her over to him.

'Ebba, run and find Thurstan and tell him to come to talk to me in the church.'

'Yes, my lord!' said Ebba, dashing off to do his bidding.

'I talked to Father while you were away,' said Edith, slipping her arm through her brother's as they walked. 'I told him that you and Brinin were friends and that Brinin had once saved your life. Don't be angry with me! I know you didn't want me to, but I'm glad I did. I didn't tell him everything—only that you and Brinin were friends—and he said he would talk to you about it all when you came back. Don't be angry with me, Oswald. It's better that I did.'

'I'm… I'm not angry.'

She couldn't know that it was like a wound to hear that she had done what he wished he had. Perhaps the wound might heal in time with the knowledge that his father had at least known that. But it stung today. Edith seemed rather tearful, and he had been learning so much about tears.

'I've been thinking that our weeping needs to wait a little,' he said. 'Sometimes there's no time for weeping until after we've done what we need to.'

He didn't understand the look Edith gave him, one quick glance before she looked down again.

'I learned that a long time ago,' she said.

They had barely reached the church when Thurstan strode in. Ebba had not tarried. Brother Wilfred was still sitting where Oswald had left him.

'I wanted to talk to all of you,' Oswald began. 'If all the fighting men ride out to battle, how will Oakdene be defended? Must we go with *all* our men, Thurstan? Can't I leave a few here?'

'We defend Oakdene by meeting the Danes so they won't reach the village,' said Thurstan. 'But I see what you're thinking. If you must leave some, leave Rædwald. He's a fool in some ways—believes almost anything he's told—but he keeps his head when there's trouble and he's a good swordsman. And we can think of another man to stay with him.'

'Let it be Rædwald then,' said Oswald. 'The older boys, not yet old enough to fight in the fyrd, will be here. Some of them handle a sword well. And the other men and the slaves—'

'The slaves?' Thurstan frowned. 'No slave may bear a weapon.'

'No, but don't they bear spades and forks every day? If the Danes come, the only way to live will be to fight. And I wouldn't like it if someone were running at me with a shovel!'

'That's true enough,' said Thurstan.

'Edith,' said Oswald, turning now to his sister. 'If the Danes come, the women and children must hide. Don't wait. Find hiding places now and see to it that everyone knows how to get to them quickly. And have men and boys always watching, day and night. Everyone trusts you. If you ask them, they'll do it. Brother Wilfred will help you if you need it, and Rædwald. And we will trust to God that they won't come.'

Oswald stopped and looked from one to another. Perhaps the weight was easing a little, now that they knew how to be ready.

'I'm going to see Cynestan now and then Swetrich's wife. Thurstan, you talk to Rædwald and spread the word that I want to speak to everyone—everyone, mind, free and slave, and the women too. After that, we'll pray and fast for my father. I'm not riding to battle before that's done. We'll start with prayer and see to war later.'

HEARTH

'Cynestan first,' thought Oswald as he left the church. 'That will be easier.'

Cynestan's little daughter squatted outside the house, playing with some stones she was carefully laying out in a long row. She looked wide-eyed at Oswald as he came towards her.

'Run in, Leoflæd,' he called to her. 'Tell your father I am coming to see him.'

It was warm as Oswald stepped inside. A fire crackled in the hearth and the food for the day was already cooking. In the light streaming through the doorway Wynflæd, Cynestan's wife, sat at her loom, the loom-weights clinking softly as she worked. On a low bed in the corner, under the loft-shelf where they kept their food and tools, lay Cynestan, slowly pushing himself up so he didn't have to greet his new lord on his back.

'No, no, don't get up,' said Oswald. He pulled up a stool and sat down by the bed. 'Stay as you are.'

'Well now, Oswald Child! It's good to have you among us again,' said Cynestan warmly. Oswald was glad to be called by his old name. It was better than being called 'my lord' and feeling like a thief. 'I wish you could have come back at a happier time.'

'Are you in much pain, Cynestan?'

'Well now, what's pain, Oswald Child? It passes in time. I'm not one to speak of pain when I could be lying dead where I fell, and no one any the wiser as to what had become of us all.'

243

Oswald shuddered at the thought of that, at the thought of how it might have been if Cynestan hadn't lived. They would have been always waiting with no one coming, every far-off horseman raising hope only to crush it again. At least this way he knew to hold his hope lightly. He knew not to hold it at all.

Cynestan was in pain, though. Oswald could see that. There was a rough gash, half healing, on the side of his head, and his leg was wrapped up and strapped fast between two long pieces of wood.

'But you are healing?' said Oswald.

'Well enough. I can tell you this: they don't only teach prayer in those minsters. Brother Wilfred seems to know a good deal of leechcraft, says they had a book of it in the minster where he was before. Perhaps there is some good in booklore after all. He says the leg is broken, but that it should right itself with time. I'll walk again. Not perhaps quite straight, but well enough for my field.'

'Cynestan, can you tell me how it happened?' Oswald had been dreading this but he knew he had to ask. 'Thurstan told me some of it, but I'd like to hear it from you.'

'I don't know that there's much more to tell, Oswald Child. There were four of them and only three of us. We were on our way back home when they set upon us. It was all so quick. We fought as hard as we could, but Swetrich fell almost straightaway, so there were two against four. Last I remember, your father was fighting two of them at once, fighting hard. They must have thought I was dead to leave me alone. I fell off my horse in the fighting and took a bad knock to the head. When I opened my eyes again, they were gone and your father with them. I couldn't move much, because of the leg, but I couldn't see your father's body lying anywhere nearby. All the horses were gone. My sword was gone. I could see Swetrich's body. I called out to your father, but there was no answer. I tried to pull myself along a bit to see if I could find him, but when I moved my head seemed to spin.'

'How did you get back?' Thurstan had said it was a wonder that Cynestan had made it back, and now Oswald could see why.

'I lay there for a good while, shouting out from time to time. At last, two boys found me. I asked them to look around for your father, but they couldn't see him anywhere. They told me that earlier they had seen five men ride past, leading two other horses. One of the men was bound and was shouting and struggling. I think *that* was your father. I don't know where they went, and it's not likely he's still alive now. It was four against one, Oswald Child, four against one. I'm sorry. I would have fought to the death for him. He was a good man. A good man and a good thegn. There was none better.'

Oswald reached out and grasped Cynestan strongly by the hand. He did it on a whim because Cynestan was almost overcome and he was struggling himself. The grasp was easier than words were.

'You did what you could,' he said a little hoarsely, when he could speak. 'And, as you say, if you had fallen, how would we have known what had become of any of you?'

'The boys fetched their father, and he came with a cart. I'm for ever thankful to that man. He drove me all the way home and would take nothing for it. I lay in the cart the whole way, with… with Swetrich's body at my side.' Cynestan stopped short. Who would like to remember a long road at the side of a fallen swordbrother? 'Thurstan tells me that the Danes are almost upon us now and that Æthelwulf Ealdorman is gathering the fyrd. And I'm stuck on my back and can't even lift a sword against them!'

'Your son will go. Won't you, Leofwine?' said Oswald, looking up at Cynestan's son, who had come back to the house and stood by listening as they spoke. 'And to tell you the truth, Cynestan, I may need you more here.'

'What do you mean? How can I be of any good here or anywhere else?'

'I'm leaving my sister to see to things when I go to battle. Can she come and speak to you if she needs to? My father trusted you, and you could help her even from your bed. Would you do that for me?'

'Nothing would make me happier, Oswald Child!' Cynestan gripped Oswald's hand again, tighter this time. 'You're my lord now, and I'll follow you as I followed your father. Whatever you want from me, say the word and I'll do it!'

'Knowing that you are here to help is all I need,' said Oswald as he rose to leave.

When Oswald left Cynestan he made his way to Swetrich's house on the other side of the village. There was no one outside, and he stopped in the doorway to look in. Ælfwyn, Swetrich's widow, and her three daughters sat round the hearth, all with work in their hands and sorrow in their eyes. They didn't see Oswald at first, and he felt like an intruder to watch them. Ælfwyn, looking up suddenly, caught sight of him and sprung to her feet.

'Oh! You've come, my lord!' She gave her youngest daughter a little push. 'Run out, Bebbe, and fetch your brother. Come in, my lord! It's cold out this morning. Come here to the fire.'

She offered Oswald the stool her daughter had left, and he sat down among them.

'I have come from Cynestan,' he said. 'He told me how Swetrich fought and died bravely. It was such a sorrow to me to learn of it. Somehow the knowledge that a man died with courage doesn't much lessen the pain when it is a husband—or a father—who has fallen.'

Ælfwyn, tears in her eyes, reached out and took Oswald by the arm in such a motherly way that it felt like pain. Oswald was struck with a sudden hurting longing for his own mother that he hadn't felt in a long time. He caught his breath. He had come to strengthen this household and be kind, not to weep. He mustn't weep.

'So hard for you to lose your father so young,' said Ælfwyn. 'Swetrich was very fond of him. He always said he would rather fall suddenly in battle than die an old man who couldn't leave his bed. He would have been happy to know he had fallen fighting at your father's side. He would have followed him anywhere. It's not easy for you to take his place, but we know you have his courage and we'll pray God will give you his wisdom.'

A noise at the doorway saved Oswald just then when the danger was greatest. They looked up and saw Bebbe, back with her brother. Oswald knew Beorn well. Steady and hard-working, he was only a year or two older than Oswald himself.

'Good of you to come, my lord,' said Beorn as he came to the hearth. 'What sorrow the loss of your father has been to us.'

'And the loss of yours to me,' said Oswald. They were all bound in sorrow together, he and this household.

'Brother Wilfred has been very good to us,' Ælfwyn went on. 'Here every day. And your sister, too. What did I say, Beorn? Lady Hild will never be dead while that girl lives. Your sister is so kind, so like your mother!'

It seemed that Ælfwyn couldn't hold them back, all these stinging kindnesses. Oswald felt a kind of choking in his throat, but once more Beorn came unknowingly to help him.

'When will we ride out against the Danes, my lord?' he asked.

That was when Oswald saw it, the fear that sprung up swiftly to join the sorrow in Ælfwyn's eyes. He knew what she wasn't saying. Her husband had fallen. Was she now to lose her only son? That settled it for Oswald.

'Beorn,' he began. 'If you will forgive me for asking you, there's something you can help me with.'

'Anything, my lord!' said Beorn stoutly.

Perhaps they needed to speak away from the women at the hearth. Oswald foresaw strong urging. Beorn was unlikely to yield readily to what he was going to ask him—not without winning words. Oswald asked Beorn to follow him outside, and they stood a little way from the house.

'I've asked Rædwald to stay behind to watch over the village and I need another man to stay with him. If you are willing to stay, I would be more than thankful to you. If the Danes come when the fighting men are away—'

'The Danes have just killed my father, my lord,' Beorn said somewhat coldly. Perhaps his readiness to do 'anything' didn't stretch that far. 'I am ready, eager, to meet them with my sword. You can't ask me to sit at home like… like a woman, or boy not old enough to fight!'

'I've lost my father too. I wish I could go after them and find them, find my father if he's alive, those who killed him if he isn't. But Æthelwulf has called so I go to him. Lord before kin. Isn't that what they teach us all our lives? Isn't that what all the tales teach us?'

'Æthelwulf is also my lord, so I go too!'

'*I* am your lord and I'm asking you to stay here! I'm not asking you to sit at home. I'm asking you to defend Oakdene against the Danes and to defend it with fewer men, who know less of war. That's harder, not easier. What will become of your mother and sisters, of my sister, of all our women and children if the Danes come here while the fighting men are away? I need to know that there is someone here, someone I can trust, who is ready to fight them and fall if need be.'

When they were boys at play, Beorn had always been the one to do the great deed, the lone warrior who saved his swordbrothers. Perhaps there was some of that in him still, that longing for the lonelier but worthier battle. Or perhaps it was enough to think of his mother and sisters facing the Danes alone. Oswald could see the struggle as he yielded, yielded with no great eagerness. But it was always lord before kin. They both knew that.

'Very well, my lord,' said Beorn at last. 'I'll do it if you wish.'

Oswald turned and saw that Ælfwyn had come out of the house and was standing near the doorway. Had she heard them speak?

'Perhaps you have already been told that I've called the village together to speak to you all,' said Oswald, looking from Beorn to his mother. 'Forgive me that I can't stay with you longer.'

'Nothing to forgive, my lord,' said Beorn.

As Oswald walked away from the house, he suddenly felt a hand on his arm. Ælfwyn had followed him, and the tears he had seen in her eyes had brimmed over now.

'Thank you, my lord,' she whispered. She had heard then. She had likely listened to every word.

Oswald didn't know if it was fitting for a woman to embrace her thegn. Ælfwyn didn't stop to ask. Perhaps she saw that he was only a boy who had lost his father and had no mother to do what she could.

'Your father and mother would be proud if they could see you now,' she said.

After that Oswald had to go and be alone. He had to go and become lord of himself again before he could speak to Oakdene as theirs.

OAKDENE

Oakdene gathered, young and old, slave and free, and stood with their cloaks wrapped round them against the winter morning. Oswald watched them come from hearth and herd, from cow and cooking pot. They were men and women he had known all his life, men and women who had known his father as a boy, children Oswald could remember being born. They all came—sombre-faced, some fearful—and waited outside the hall to hear what Oswald Thegn would say to them.

Why should it be so hard to speak to those he knew so well? Oswald felt it, though he didn't understand it. He glanced at Edith, at Thurstan, at Brother Wilfred, then stepped up onto a stool so that everyone could see him. They all looked at him and he at them. His lips felt dry, but he wet them to be ready.

'I had hoped that I would not be your thegn for many years,' he said. His voice was louder than he thought it would be, his breath all misty and cloudlike in the cold. 'In truth, I wish I was not. We have lost Swetrich, fallen bravely fighting our foes. We thank God that Cynestan was spared. But my father? We don't know. He may live, but is likely dead.'

His father must have done this once, stood as thegn and wished he was only a thegn's son. Perhaps he too had wondered how he could do it. Oswald couldn't remember it. He had been too small to know anything beyond his mother's arms. But he wished he knew what his father might say at a time like this.

'You all know what kind of man he was, and I seek your prayers for me that I will be like him. As we cannot know what has become of him or bury him as we wish, I am calling us all to fasting and prayer for him. And I ask you to keep praying after I and the other men have gone.'

Brother Wilfred had been wise. He could see it in all their eyes. Even if they did not know, they must do something. A son must do something, and they would all follow him in it.

'I know I'm young—I feel it more than any of you—but there are men around me who are wise. And I know that I must lead and go into battle and…' Dare he say it? Dare he say what he had once said at the Moot? No one could have forgotten it, but dare he bring the Moot again to their minds? 'I have learned that I must think of everyone and not only the outcome. So we turn to plans.

'We don't know if we will keep the Danes away from Oakdene, but we do know that they are almost upon us in Wessex. If you have anything of worth, hide it. Find somewhere to hide some of our stored food. Some of our fyrdmen have already gone and later today, or perhaps tomorrow, I will ride out with the rest. I've asked Rædwald and Beorn to stay here to watch over the village. Every man still here, and every boy over twelve winters, should be ready to fight them if they come. If you have weapons, keep them always to hand. Those of you who don't—and you slaves too—fight them with what you have, with shovels and spades, with anything that comes to hand.

'My sister, the Lady Edith, will call on some of you to watch, day and night, so that if they do come the village can be warned. You women should find hiding places, so you can go there quickly with the children. Can you remember where you used to hide as a child? Among the trees, or on the hillside? If you have forgotten, your sons and daughters will tell you.' Oswald couldn't help grinning suddenly. 'You children all have places to hide when you want to keep out of trouble, don't you?'

'Yes!' exclaimed Ebba, then reddened to think that she had dared to speak before so many and hid in her mother's cloak.

'You see!' smiled Oswald. 'Ask Ebba. Ask all the children. They won't mind telling you if it will save Oakdene from the Danes. And perhaps you can thank them by not looking for them *too* hard the next time you are angry with them!'

Folk smiled at that. Many of the children drew themselves up, proud that they too could help to save Oakdene. But the smiles didn't last long. Oswald could feel the chill of their fear in the air that morning. They had all dreaded this time, dreaded it for long months, and now it had almost come.

'They are a fearsome foe and many. A great host, it is said. They don't fear men or God, but… but…' Oswald swallowed. 'But the Christian need not fear death. Let them come, and we will meet them not only with our swords. We will meet them in the strength of Christ, whether we ride to battle or stay in Oakdene, and he is stronger than a whole host of Danes.'

It was a cold fear, a cold morning. And it wasn't only the fear of the women and children, nor of the men who might not say they felt it. It was his own. He was speaking to himself more than to any of them.

'It's cold out here, so I won't keep you for much longer. Soon we will go to the church for prayer.'

Oswald caught sight of Aculf at the back of the crowd. He looked sullen and angry, his face too full of war for a man who couldn't swing a sword. Oswald sighed. He had forgotten about finding a new workreeve. He turned to his father's slaves—his slaves now—standing listening among the rest, and he remembered. Ludan's words had been warm, and Garulf's grip had been tight. Whatever anyone else thought about what he had done for Brinin, the slaves at least had loved him for it. And now they had a lord whose back had felt what only a slave need fear. Perhaps a new workreeve could wait.

'Let me speak to you slaves. Aculf will put his time into his own field and will no longer be workreeve.' From the glances that passed among them, it seemed that folk had already heard. Best not to look at Aculf now. 'You slaves know how to work. You know what needs to be done. You do it every day. Work, not because a workreeve is watching you, but because I have asked it of you. Where is Garulf?'

'I am here, my lord,' said Garulf, stepping out a little from the edge of the crowd.

'You are the oldest, Garulf, and know the land better than anyone. Let the slaves look to you, and take any trouble to my sister.' Back to everyone else now. 'My sister is here. Brother Wilfred, Rædwald, Beorn and Cynestan in his bed are here.'

That was enough. There was much that could be said, but no more that needed to be said.

'Come now. Let us go to prayer.'

ROAD

I t had been a long road, but Brinin had walked it swiftly. He
was near Readingum now, not up to a day away. He would ask
the first man he saw to point him there and then he might
learn if it was an empty hope he followed. The morning was clear,
better than the grey darkness he had started out in. The naked trees
stood stark against the sky, from bole to bough to twig, up and up,
stretching wide. His thoughts were like that, outstretched, with many
endings from one beginning: hope, life, death, loss.

He had left the minster on what seemed like whim. The thinking
had been done on the road. There had been plenty of time to turn
back. There was still time, but he didn't think he would. It was no
whim now, no reckless rushing ahead with no thought of the end.
Brinin knew what might come of it and he meant to do it all the
same.

He thought there must be a house ahead, hidden away where he
couldn't see it. Hearthsmoke rose into the sky, drifting a little on the
wind. As Brinin drew nearer he caught sight of a man walking by
the hedge around his field. This was the man he would ask.

'Is this the way to Readingum?' he said. 'Will I reach it today?'

'You haven't heard then?' The man was looking at him in some
bewilderment. 'It is the way, and you could reach it by dusk, but if
you have any wisdom, you'll turn back. The Danes came upon the
town yesterday, a great host of them. The townsfolk are dead or
fled. I am about to ride out to join Æthelwulf Ealdorman.'

Brinin stared at the man. They had come. Thurstan had said they would. The Danes were in Wessex. Everyone had waited for Danes for all those months, but all they had got was ploughing, seedtime and harvest. It had been a long slow year of waiting, and at last they had come. It would be easier to find them now.

'Thank you,' he said and set off again towards Readingum.

'Where are you going?' shouted the man after him. 'Didn't you hear what I said? The Danes have taken Readingum. Don't be a fool!'

Brinin quickened his step and didn't look back. Perhaps he was a fool, but he had settled on finding the Danes and the sooner he found them the better.

The Danish tongue of his mother felt sluggish on his lips now. He had tried to awaken it on the road, to hear it as though he spoke with her or Row. The seax whispered freedom as it hung from his belt, but he didn't know how to wield it. His tongue was his only weapon. He could ask a Saxon the way to Readingum, then greet the Danes when he got there. One mouth, two tongues. Once silence had been his sword, his shield too, but not now. Now speech was everything.

At midday he found somewhere to sit and eat, but not before more men on the road warned him that he was heading into danger. Sitting with his back against a tree, he ate the last of his bread. One last meal before the last walk.

Edrich Thegn was likely dead. It was such a small hope that had brought Brinin here. But he could find the Danes now. That was a start. And if he couldn't find Edrich, or if he learned that he *was* dead, then at least he would know that he'd tried. He couldn't forget Oswald's face, white and stricken and hopeless. He couldn't turn back, not while he thought of that.

He would walk in among the Danes, speaking their tongue as one of them. Perhaps he *was* one of them after all. A dog of a Dane like his mother. That's what Aculf had said. A Dane, just like his mother. He would walk in as one of them, and if they welcomed him he would learn what he could.

Brinin drew out his mother's comb from his father's pouch and turned both over in his hand. He had taken them from Row's belt before he buried him and they had not left him since that day. Wessex man. Dane. He would walk in among the Danes, and perhaps they wouldn't welcome him. They would likely kill him then. Or they might welcome him at first then kill him later. He had thought of all that. Death crept everywhere, but he wouldn't turn back for fear of it. He wasn't like Oswald, with a sister, a village, a battle and words unsaid. He had no kin to mourn him, no work that another couldn't do. He had left word for Oswald with the prior: 'Gone to Readingum to seek what is lost.' That would be enough if he didn't come back, and Oswald would know he had tried.

Death and loss. But what if Edrich Thegn lived? While he was dead, or thought to be dead, Brinin was free. It would be no easy thing to toss freedom away. But if Oswald was not thegn, then Brinin was still a slave, a runaway slave with a weapon. What if Edrich lived? What if he found him? What if, somehow, he got him away? That was an even smaller hope than the others. But what then? Oakdene would have its lord, Oswald his father and Brinin his slavery. He had told Row once that he would never willingly bow to it again, yet wasn't he doing just that? Edrich would likely be thankful but he might not bestow freedom to show it.

Death and life, loss and hope, slavery and freedom, up and up, stretching wide. But he had settled on it now. Wessex man. Dane. Brinin rose to his feet and began the last walk to meet his mother's people.

HALLVEIGSON

Dusk came early in this darkest of months, and shadow upon shadow dimmed tree and stone. Brinin was within a shout of Readingum now. He could see the lights of scattered fires and heard the sound of voices, borne to him on the breeze. That must be the Danish camp. If he had had a bow and had known how to draw one, he was near enough now to send an arrow among them. He stopped, not to waver, but to feel the gathering evening. It might be his last.

It was not a clear night, but patchy like his own shirt, many times mended. Amid the clouds was clearness, blacker and full of stars. The sight of the stars meant kith and kin, hut and household, nights sat side by side with a brother lost. He seldom looked at them now, seldom dared to raise his eyes to the sky. Starry nights made the ache so gnawing it was almost unbearable. But tonight, on perhaps this last night, he was willing to be wounded. Here, alone in the cold, alone in the darkness, he could look up. He didn't mind the ache tonight, as it told him what he'd had.

The sharp cold edge of a blade against his throat. Arms held behind him in a grip too strong to struggle with. Brinin had heard nothing, seen nothing in the darkness until it was too late. He tasted fear then, and it was bitter. Perhaps he had hoped for too much. It seemed now that all his hopes must die unborn along with him. Hadn't he known they might? Death and loss. At least the blade was sharp. It would be quick.

'See here, Herjolf!' said a voice, a Danish voice, at his ear. 'Here's a Saxon come to seek death!'

Footsteps came through the undergrowth, breaking the twigs. Why hadn't he heard them before?

'Is your sword so thirsty, Skorri, that it can't rest after a feast?' said the voice of another Dane.

Silence was not his friend here and wouldn't help him. And Brinin couldn't bring himself to bow to death without first trying to live.

'Will you slay me before I have spoken?' he asked.

Skorri started a little, but the blade stayed where it was.

'What's this?' said Skorri, at Brinin's ear.

'Bruni Hallveigson is my name,' he said, and the blade moved away ever so slightly. Perhaps death might wait a little longer. 'I have come to seek my mother's people.'

'Stay your sword, Skorri. There's something strange here!' said the other man. 'He doesn't sound like a Saxon and I don't think it's death he's seeking. Let's get him over to a fire and take a look at him.'

The man at Brinin's back let go of his arms and grabbed his shirt at the neck. The blade was taken from his throat, and he dared to swallow again, but he felt its point against his back.

'No harm in taking a look at him,' growled Skorri. 'But if my sword is too quick, Herjolf, isn't yours too slow? Is anyone to walk among us and get a hearing?'

'How many do you think will walk among us speaking our own tongue?' said Herjolf out of the darkness. 'Now stop talking and get going!'

Skorri gave Brinin a little shake.

'Walk then, Bruni Hallveigson, if that is indeed your name!' he said. 'But know this: my sword can run you through before you even feel it. Take care!'

So Brinin walked. He walked with the Danes in the darkness to the camp and the firelight and the voices on the breeze. He didn't speak again. There would be time enough for that. Time enough to die too, but he had hope now. Skorri didn't trust him, but Herjolf might learn to. He would talk to Herjolf as much as he could.

Four men were sitting round the fire they stopped at. They were roasting something on long sticks, and the smell was all meat and fat and burning wood. One of them laughed when he saw Brinin.

'What have you found yourself, Skorri?' he said. 'Are you going to keep him for a thrall?'

A thrall? Thurstan had said nothing of thraldom. Might they keep a man alive for that? Edrich Thegn wouldn't be a good thrall. He didn't know how to do it, and the learning would be hard.

'If it hadn't been for Herjolf, I'd have slit his throat!' Skorri shook Brinin again. 'Herjolf is too old now. He has no belly for blood any more!'

Suddenly the grip and sword point were gone as someone—Herjolf, most likely—shoved Skorri aside and landed a sharp cuff on the side of his head.

'If you were a winter or two younger, you'd feel my sword-belt across your back for that!' said Herjolf, still behind Brinin in the darkness. 'You did once, but it hasn't done you any good. You don't need to show us you can kill by doing it all the time. Your father was the same. Little wonder they called him Bloodaxe!'

Skorri turned and glared at Herjolf, and Brinin saw him at last. He was shorter than Brinin and not much older. His sword had made him seem bigger than that. The other men grinned as Skorri sheathed it and sat down. One of them said something that Brinin didn't understand. It was full of words he couldn't remember hearing before. But he saw the look on Skorri's face and heard how the other men laughed. Likely it was something his mother had never said.

Herjolf stepped forward to the fire, out of the darkness and into its flickering glow. He was old—as old as Garulf—and his grey hair reached his shoulders, blending into the fur of a grey wolfskin cloak that hung from them. He looked at Brinin for a long time before he spoke.

'I had thought you were older from your height,' he said at last. 'But you're young.'

'Sixteen winters,' said Brinin. Let all these men round the fire hear that he spoke their tongue. Let him wield this one sword of his.

'Who are you and why did you come here?' asked Herjolf.

Brinin was slow to answer. He meant to be slow, whatever they asked. They would think it was only his way, and he would always have time to think.

'I am Bruni Hallveigson and I came—'

'Yes, yes! I know! You came to seek your mother's people. But who is your mother? And how did you come to be here?'

'My mother was Hallveig Thorleifsdottir, and this is now the seventh winter since she died. If I have other kinsmen alive, I do not know of them.'

'That doesn't tell us how you, and she, came to be here among the Saxons.'

'I don't know how it came to be. I cannot remember it, and it was bitter to my mother. She would never speak of it.'

How could he remember what had happened long before he was born? They could have a little truth, these Danes, but they didn't need all of it.

'And your father?'

'He died before I could know him.' Foggy and bittersweet, a man with strong arms but no face. That wasn't true knowledge, but sharing it was a swift way to die. Tonight he was Bruni Hallveigson. Tonight Brinin, the son of Wulfstan, must be forgotten.

'How did you come to be walking this night towards our camp?' What a flood of thanks that Herjolf wasn't asking more about his father!

'I heard you were in Wessex and I came to find you.'

'Why?'

Herjolf was like a hound with a bone. He wouldn't drop it until he'd had all he wanted. Brinin looked at him steadily through the firelight. Truth, but not all of it.

'Do you think it is an easy thing for a boy to see his mother hated for being a Dane and to be too small to do anything about it?' he said. 'Or to hear her called a dog and be treated like one himself?'

It was a long time before Herjolf spoke again. Did he see that it hadn't been an answer?

'No easy thing, I should think,' Herjolf said at last. 'I had a son, my lastborn, much like you, until the fever took him four winters ago. You look like him. Come, Bruni Hallveigson. Sit here by the fire, and we will eat.'

And Brinin sat down among them, not dead after all. But he didn't like the way Skorri looked at him. There was dislike and distrust in his eyes. He would have to watch him.

HOERULANGR

B rinin didn't understand Herjolf's welcome, but he was thankful for it. He gave him meat to eat and brought him to sleep in his tent. Perhaps Skorri was right, and Herjolf was losing his taste for blood in his old age, or perhaps Brinin was somehow like his dead son. But for all the welcome, Brinin slept lightly, with one hand on the seax. Little good would it do him here among men like these.

He woke early—he always did—and sat outside the tent to watch the winter night become morning. As Readingum rose out of the shadows, Brinin looked on in amazement. Never before had he seen so many buildings. Some were far apart. Others had barely a child's breadth between them. Here they were huddled together. There they ran in a long row as furrows run in a field. They were large and small, houses for men and stalls for beasts. There were too many to see—two or three score at least—and everywhere he looked one seemed to hide behind another. Their wood and thatch were warm in the dawn, and from every house and many scattered tents, the great Danish host trickled out, roused from sleep.

The townsfolk hadn't been ready and where were they now? Dead or fled, the man on the road had told him. No more women at their looms or hearths, no children playing on the thresholds. Only a host of men with weapons ready for war. In Oakdene he had sometimes wondered if life with the Danes might be better—not often, only on the worst days. But thinking of the hearths and the thresholds he felt as much a stranger here. Perhaps it would always be that way, wherever he was.

There was a noise behind him and Brinin glanced up and saw Herjolf standing looking down at him.

'You rise early, Bruni Hallveigson,' he said, handing him a piece of roasted swine-flesh, left from the night before. 'I thought you had fled while I slept, or that perhaps I had only dreamed you.'

'I've been watching the dawn,' said Brinin. Strange to be called 'Bruni' again, without his mother or Row to say it. 'I have never seen anywhere like this before—so many houses, so many men.'

Herjolf sat beside him, easing himself down like a man who is indeed growing old and feels it, for all his anger at Skorri's slight. They didn't speak as they ate together. What kind of man was Herjolf? A warrior, an old warrior, a raider who had killed many times. And yet he had spared Brinin's life. He was alive among the Danes and must understand them if he were ever to learn anything. He must understand Herjolf, so he needed him to speak.

'Why didn't you let Skorri kill me?' asked Brinin at last.

'Skorri is too ready to kill without thought,' said Herjolf. 'He is sister's-son to me, the lastborn of his father, and has many older brothers and kinsmen, all warriors. He has spent so much of his life feeling small that now he makes himself big with his sword.'

'But why didn't you let him?'

'Ah, who can say? Perhaps because you sound like one of us and because you made me think of Bjarni, my son—even more now in the light than in the darkness. There is something in your eyes that was in his. And perhaps Skorri is right. I am old now. It is not for nothing that men call me Hœrulangr, the Long Grey Haired. I have spilled the blood of too many foes to have any taste for the blood of one who might be a friend. And are you not one of us, speaking as you do? Would a Saxon come here alone as you did and throw away his life?'

'The Saxons say that the Danish thirst for blood is never quenched, though my mother was such a mild woman that she only struck me once that I remember.' His tongue was his only weapon, but it wasn't enough. If Herjolf were to trust him, he needed to open his breasthoard, to dig it up and show what few had ever seen. 'But then, a woman is not a warrior, after all, and she likely saw that I would have enough blows from other hands.'

'It seems to me that your life among the Saxons has not been an easy one.'

Brinin glanced at Herjolf, tearing the last bits of flesh from the bone with his teeth. Who did have an easy life? Likely even the king shed tears. And there had been sagas to hear and dragons to slay, and friendship and kin and stars. It hadn't been all blows. But there had been more wounds than he liked to remember.

'Perhaps it was not only my mother who knew some things too bitter to speak of,' he said.

'But now you are here, with your own kind. Will you seek payment for all those blows?'

Payment. How far that was from what he had come to seek! Not payment for blows, only the one who could have stopped them but didn't. Herjolf wouldn't understand that. It sounded like folly.

'My mother told such sagas by our hearth that she made me long to do the kind of deeds she spoke of.' Not an answer, but something to say. His lips were not his own, speaking thoughts like these aloud. 'She put a sword in my heart, but couldn't put one in my hand. The only swords I have wielded were the sticks I played with as a boy. Wessex men do not readily put a sword into the hand of the likes of me.'

'It takes more than a sword to make a man a warrior. I, who have raised five sons to be fighters—and buried two of them—I could teach you how to wield one. I have lived too long in this world to be an ill judge of men. You are bold, I think, even if you have no sword.'

Brinin felt the pull then, a sudden little tug he hadn't foreseen. Did Herjolf know that he offered him what he had dreamed of as a boy, until he had been old enough to understand that it could never be and had starved the dreams to wither them? Fear had not made him waver, not even with a blade at his throat. But this was stronger than fear. It was the hope of something more than a life of thraldom. He saw Herjolf watching him keenly, perhaps seeing some of his thoughts or even a flicker of longing in his eyes.

'What *do* you know how to do?' asked Herjolf. 'You have hardly spent sixteen winters in idleness.'

'I know how to work when I am too tired to work,' said Brinin. There was much he had learned in sixteen winters by doing it day after day. 'How to watch and understand and how to bear pain without flinching.'

'A man needs all those things to be a warrior, and some never learn them. The wielding of swords and spears can come with time. And if you know how to work and how to wield a spade, if not yet a sword, there is work to be done in strengthening this place against the Saxons. Come, and let us be about it.'

As they walked westward through that bewildering hive of buildings, swarming with men, they passed what looked to have been a church. The townsfolk hadn't been ready. Had they been at their Yuletide fast? Had the women been at their looms and hearths, and the children on the thresholds? Perhaps he couldn't do it. Perhaps he could never be the kind of warrior Herjolf meant.

EYES

T here had been so little new in Brinin's life before his flight
to the minster. His days had been filled with well-known
work among folk he knew. But that morning was full of
half-caught snatches of speech between men whose names he didn't
know and whose faces he wouldn't remember. Herjolf kept him with
him all the time, pointing out things and people, as a father might to
his son. There were so many names that after a while Brinin couldn't
match them to the right man. Sigurd, Asfrith, Eirik, Gunnulf the
Short—he remembered him because he was so tall—and Toki. Toki
was Herjolf's son and looked much as his father must have done as a
younger man. Had he also been round the fire the night before?
Perhaps. It was hard to remember.

'Bruni is like Bjarni,' Herjolf said. 'There's something in the
eyes.'

Toki looked at Brinin, then said, 'No, my father, it's not only the
eyes. It's the hair—something between barley and sunset.'

Brinin touched his hair, his mother's hair. She had given him two
things that were helping him now: her tongue and her hair. But his
eyes were his father's, Saxon eyes. Row had told him that much.

Always watching, always listening, Brinin did begin to learn. He
learned that the camp was between two rivers, where they joined,
bending round like a drawn bow. He learned that some of the
Danes had come along the river in their ships—how he longed to
see them—and had left them further to the east. He listened as
Kjotvi, a jarl and great man among them, praised the scouts who

had gone ahead of the others, then urged them to come to Readingum.

So there had been scouts? That was the first true knowledge, and there was a thrill to it. Might not these scouts have been the band of Danes whom Edrich Thegn had met?

'This is a good place for a camp, between the two rivers,' Brinin whispered to Herjolf beside him.

'Yes,' said Herjolf, also in a low voice. 'We have often before made camp in places like this.'

'It was good that the scouts didn't meet any Saxons,' said Brinin. His whole body stiffened somehow. He could feel the strain in his back.

But Herjolf said nothing. Had he even heard Brinin speak? He was looking at Kjotvi, still listening to him. Brinin hardly heard a word the jarl said. If Herjolf said nothing, then his chance was gone. Brinin couldn't say it again—that would seem too eager. The small hope that had sprung up with the knowledge swiftly died. He had been a fool. He had let friendship make him a fool. There was no hope of learning anything here. Edrich Thegn was dead. How could he be alive among this great army, so fierce? And now Brinin was among them too, had put himself among them. And for what? To look for what couldn't be found. What was he to do? Go back to the minster? To Oakdene? Or stay, at least for a time, and let Herjolf teach him to fight? The tug was strong, although it was only small.

Brinin hadn't known that this was where the danger might lie, that he might want to stay when he got here. But Herjolf had talked to him and been kind, kinder than most Saxons had ever been. What did he owe the Saxons, after all? Was it not the Saxons who had kept his kin in thraldom? Was it not the Saxon, Aculf, who had rained so many blows upon him over the years that he had lost count of them long ago? Was it not the Saxon thegn, Edrich, who had been so blind to what happened in his own village that he had done nothing about it? Why should he? What did he owe a slave? Not justice, not kindness. Brinin was nothing to the Saxons. What did he owe them?

This foe, this Danish raider, had been kind to him. He had treated him like a man and offered to teach him to be one. Why shouldn't he stay with him? Could he not stay for a time to learn to wield a spear and sword and to draw a bow? Then he could leave them and go to some far place and find land to farm quietly. He didn't need to be a raider like they were.

'They did meet some Saxons,' Herjolf whispered, leaning towards him, eyes still on Kjotvi, 'but they were few and easily overcome.'

Sudden hope, soon dead. It wasn't enough. Herjolf had said nothing that could help him.

'Do you see that man with the silver arm ring?' Herjolf said, pointing to a man nearby. 'He was one of the scouts and Kjotvi gave him the ring as a gift.'

Strange how a few words could awaken a half-forgotten thought. Brinin saw them suddenly in his mind, their shadows long in the evening light, Brother Wilfred and Oswald on the road to the minster. As a king deals out rings, Brother Wilfred had said, so Heaven's King gives wisdom to those who ask. Wasn't that what he needed, here among the Danes? Wisdom, dealt out like a ring, a gift for the asking. He didn't know where to begin and didn't like where the tug was pulling him.

Thor and Odin, the gods of the Danes, were fierce and warlike as they were. He remembered what his mother had said of them. She had left them behind when she had wed his father, but she hadn't wholly forgotten them. But he also remembered what Brother Wilfred had told him. The God of the Saxons was not as they were. 'God, come to my help.' The monks had prayed it every day at the minster, and their God might listen to a freed slave who prayed. Free or not, Brinin had no worth to a Saxon, but their God, his father's God, his God, might listen if he prayed for wisdom, even here among this great heathen army. A slave could pray as boldly as the king.

After that he went back to watching and listening and tried to keep the tug from his mind. Kjotvi was so sure of the fall of Wessex. If Æthelred the King stood against them, Wessex would be as East Anglia and Æthelred would be as Edmund, the East Anglian king, taken and killed at their hands. On the morrow, he would lead some of them out to raid and forage—didn't this great army need to be fed? If the men of Wessex tried to withstand them, they would find themselves lying in their own blood.

Then the digging began. Herjolf told him that they were making a great earthen wall that stretched between the two rivers. It was to be wide and as tall as two men, with sides that sloped up as a hill does. There would be gates in the middle to go in and out, and the earthen wall would defend them in the west, as the rivers defended them in the north, south and east.

Digging was good for thought. Making sweat and straining his back had always sharpened his mind. Whatever he had borne from Saxon hands, the loyalty was somehow still there. He hardly knew why. Wasn't Wessex full of men like Garulf, children like Ebba? Weren't they the ones who would suffer when the Danish host went out from Readingum? He thought of Aculf dying at Danish hands and found that he couldn't wish it, even upon him. These were people he had known all his life.

And there was Oswald, who for so long had given him friendship where none could be asked for, who had taken upon his own back a slave's pain, a pain that no thegn's son should ever have to bear; who was waiting even now to fight the Danes and might fall when he did, whose sorrow had brought Brinin to Readingum to begin with.

Brinin stopped digging and leaned on his spade. All around him the Danish host were building their great earthen wall and speaking his mother's tongue. Herjolf was digging beside him. He had made old dreams sprout again, but loyalty to Oswald must make them wither. Brinin would stay here among the Danes for a few more days and if he found out nothing more, he would find a way to leave them. He must leave them. He knew that now.

Sometime after midday, Herjolf, eager to eat and rest, called Brinin from his digging to go with him. Many stopped then, though others kept on—the wall could not wait. As they walked along one of those long furrows of buildings, crowded with men, Brinin watched and listened and wondered what to do. Looking around him and feeling as bewildered as a village boy must feel in such a place, his eye fell on a shelter for swine, fenced all around. It was only a glance—he hadn't seen it that morning though he must have walked by it before—but there was something so homelike about swine that he found himself watching a large sow walk towards the fence.

And then he saw something more: filthy, bound, sitting among the swine, but unmistakably Edrich Thegn. Brinin caught his breath to stop himself from gasping aloud. Then Edrich Thegn saw him and their eyes met, and Brinin saw on his lord's face shock, bewilderment and sudden burning anger all at once. Brinin looked away quickly and kept walking. He mustn't look back, mustn't let anyone know that he had seen anything. Edrich Thegn might not have the wisdom to hold his tongue. How could he know how much was hanging on it?

As many men thronged between him and Edrich, Brinin's heart was pounding so hard that it almost hurt. He had prayed for wisdom to be dealt out giftlike, but he had been given more than that. He had been given eyes. It would have been so easy to have been looking the other way, so easy to have seen nothing. But he had seen. He had seen in a staggeringly unhoped-for way. He didn't know what to do, but surely if he had been given eyes, against all hope, then might not the wisdom he needed also be granted?

HEDGE

T he fyrd came together at Æthelwulf Ealdorman's call and made their camp west of Readingum. It was chilling—all wind, frost and mud—and Oswald longed for wall and thatch as he never had before. But they drew their cloaks about them, lit their fires and warmed themselves as best they could. Now they need only wait and ready their minds for battle.

Oakdene came together, fellows by the same fire; fellows to fight and even fall together. Saxulf was there with Sigulf and Sigelm, his sons; Leofwine and Baldred; Godræd, Dæglaf and Thurstan. Some, like Thurstan and Saxulf, were older, battlewise and battlescarred. Others, like Oswald and Leofwine, knew it only from tales and songs and the games they had played as boys.

The sight of a kinsman was hearthlike to Oswald at such a time, warm and welcoming in the cold. Alrich came with Hildræd, his father, and it was good to see them, strengthening to sit together in sorrow, not much spoken but still shared. Oswald had always found Hildræd less stern than his own father, more ready to laugh and with a look much like Oswald's mother. He was so full of unrushed, ready wisdom that by the time he left to see to other things, Oswald began to feel a little thegnlike for the first time since Thurstan had said he was one.

'You went away after... since I last saw you. To a minster,' said Alrich, when his father had left them alone.

There it was, that great unsaid, unsayable thing taking its seat between them by the fire. Oswald remembered Alrich's unhappy face at the Moot, before there had been too much fear and pain to see anything much. Likely Alrich's last sight of Oswald had been rather a worse one.

'Yes,' said Oswald. 'Brother Wilfred asked my father's leave to take me there to read and... and to be away. I didn't go back to Oakdene until... until Thurstan came to fetch me.'

'Father and I, and Aldred too, went to Oakdene while you were away. Aldred was sorry not to find you there. I was sorry too because I had hoped to talk to you about...' Alrich looked down, fidgeting with his seax. Oswald was thankful for the warning. It gave him time to ready himself for speech he likely didn't want to have. 'Oswald, I don't think that the Moot and everything that happened there was what your father wanted.'

'I don't like talking about all that now, Alrich, or thinking about it,' said Oswald, eyes on the fire. Why couldn't Alrich have left the thing unsaid?

'Neither do I. I've never seen anything I've more wished I could forget. But now your father... now that we've lost him, there is something you should know. Edith told me that you were angry with him for gathering the Moot.'

Angry. Alrich couldn't begin to know how angry he had been, nor how long the struggle to drive it from his mind. And if Alrich made him talk about it, he might be angry again and now he didn't want to be.

'The Moot wasn't unjust, given what I'd done. I know that. Though I'm a freeman so they shouldn't have... But my father as good as promised me a beating then gathered the Moot instead. I was ready to take the beating—I didn't see what else he could have done—and no one who knew anything about my father would have said that wasn't enough. But the Moot...' Oswald was speaking through shut teeth now, pushing the anger down, deep inside where it couldn't fill his mind again. 'I wasn't ready for that.'

'He likely meant it when he said it, but a promise, Oswald? You were only at the Moot for a little while that day. I was there for all of it, and that's what I want to tell you about. It was Ealmund who thought of it, not your father. I'm almost sure of that. Ealmund talked to everyone, before Thurstan was sent to fetch you, and much of what he said sounded like wisdom. He kept talking about upholding the law, teaching you and everyone else what must not be done. It wasn't long before he had everyone thinking that there could be nothing better than a flogging. Not too harsh, he kept saying, only a token to show you you'd been wrong. Ealmund is the kind of man who always gets what he wants, and everyone was angry and ready to be led. Everyone but Thurstan. He wouldn't listen to anything Ealmund said. He said it was enough to let your father deal with you, called Ealmund a fool more than once, said they were all fools. He even asked your father if he was going to sit there and let another man lead. He and Ealmund were shouting at each other by the end. It's a wonder you didn't hear them—perhaps you did. But everyone else thought Ealmund was speaking wisdom. It likely was wise to call a Moot—though perhaps not one that ended in a flogging—and no one could blame your father for letting Ealmund oversee it. But once he had done that, I think he felt bound not to speak. He barely said a word, but the longer they all talked, the more uneasy he looked.'

'So you're saying that my father didn't want it?'

'I think he hated it but didn't know what else to do. I overheard him say as much to Ealmund one night when they likely thought I was sleeping. They left the hall after that and I didn't hear any more. But I'm sure Ealmund thought of it and that it somehow sounded like wisdom. Afterwards, your father wished he had never asked for Ealmund's help. That's what he told my father.'

As he listened, Oswald grew a kind of hedge in his mind, thick and thorny, to keep Alrich's words from coming all the way in. He could stand behind the hedge and look out, listening to what Alrich said and thinking about it a little, but not too much. The words had to stay a little outside. If they broke through the hedge they might make him see and feel it all again.

'I do understand now that it can't have been easy for him to know what to do,' said Oswald. 'And that any of us can do something that afterwards we wish we hadn't.'

Neither of them spoke for a long time after that. The afternoon was well spent now. From behind the hedge, Oswald watched the fyrdmen milling to and fro and tried to keep his thoughts among them and not with what he wanted to forget.

'It was always harder for your father than it is for mine,' said Alrich at last. 'My father has three sons. If I fall, there's always Aldred or Aldulf—I've always thought that Aldred would make a better lord than I would anyway—but your father only had you.'

'I've been wondering what would happen to Oakdene if I fall, and Edith not yet wed. It would be hers but could she lead it on her own?'

'That's not what I meant,' said Alrich. 'More that he must have felt that he had to raise you to be almost faultless because you were the only one.'

That broke through the hedge a little, opened it up and began to creep in. Perhaps they had been the same, he and his father. He had always been afraid that he would never be good enough. And his father had been afraid too, that he wouldn't be a good enough father to raise a son who was wise and strong.

'It's strange that there was only ever Edith and me,' he said. 'Never any more but that one who was born and died when Mother died.'

'There were more,' said Alrich. 'Didn't you know?'

Then Oswald remembered all those times his mother had seemed ill, and how each illness had been followed by an unspoken sorrow. He had felt it as a child, but not understood it. And now that he suddenly saw what it had all meant, he could have forgiven his father anything.

Later in the twilight, Oswald was standing with Thurstan, Saxulf and some of the other Oakdene men, when he looked up and saw someone he knew coming towards him. He had known that he must be here among the fyrd, but he had thought that he might not see him among so many men. He came with three others, young and enough alike to be his sons. Ealmund Thegn.

Oswald saw a quick look, more of half-done battle than greeting, pass between Ealmund and Thurstan, and then Ealmund turned to Oswald.

'I can't tell you my sorrow upon hearing of the loss of your father,' he began and kept talking.

Likely there was nothing wrong with what he said. It was likely all kind words. Oswald knew that he answered him somehow, but he heard almost nothing of what was said. It was as though two other men were talking, and he himself was standing nearby only half aware of what they were saying.

The sight of Ealmund had been enough. The hedge was gone, withering away like some rot had struck it. Everything burst in for him to see, feel and live again. The long waiting in the meadow, the fear that shook his hands and twisted his gut, the mercy that was not mercy, the tearing pain that fell again and again, the slow aching days when shame had crept in on him like a hunter on its prey. And anger.

Oswald was suddenly aware that everyone was looking at him as though waiting for him to speak. He didn't know what he was meant to be saying, or what they wanted, but he did speak. He spoke then walked away.

'My father's workreeve mistreated one of the slaves, you know, a slave who had once saved my life,' he said. 'I was right not to tell you where they had gone, even though I was wrong about everything else.'

That night Oswald dreamt the Moot.

WALL

Brinin slept even less that night than he had the night before, but it was no uneasy watchfulness that stole his sleep. He needed to think. There could only be two endings now: he and Edrich Thegn would both walk free, or they would both die together. There must be no rushing and no blind groping in the dark. He must know every turning, every wrong turning, every path between the two. He must strain to see every unforeseen snare. He must think of everything.

He was half ready to go at once and do it in the nightgloom while the Danes slept. That would be the way to climb into the pen unseen. But there were bound to be men awake watching over the camp and they would wonder what he was about. What trustworthy man slinks thieflike through the night? Yet darkness might be his friend. If not in the dead of night, why not do the thing at dusk, when men might rightly be abroad? Many of the Danes would leave to raid in the morning, so the camp would not be so busy. Would they be back by dusk? Perhaps not if they met any Saxons to withstand them. But if they were back, and the danger seemed too great, he could bide his time until another day.

There was a time for thought and a time for sleep. Herjolf's soft snoring warned Brinin that he too should lie down. His wits would need to be sharp. He had the beginnings now. He had sown all the seeds. There would be more digging in the morning, more straining of the back. That would be the time for his thoughts to grow.

By dawn the raiders were ready to go out. Kjotvi wanted them at their work early. It was a sickening thought, frightful to think of them pouring out of Readingum, fearbearing and deathbearing. Perhaps the folk around the town had fled. Perhaps they had listened to the wisdom that he had shut his ears to. But where would they go? Where would they go in winter with raiders at their heels? They were dark thoughts, too dark for Brinin to see Herjolf coming up beside him.

'Work with Toki today, Bruni,' said Herjolf.

'Won't you be there?' asked Brinin, though he thought he knew the answer and wished he didn't.

'I'm going out with Kjotvi and the others.'

Herjolf was a raider—Brinin had almost forgotten that. He was as much of a raider as any of the others. But one night he had chosen to spare the life of a boy he found in the dark. He didn't know Herjolf. Such a short time did not give knowledge of a man, for all the welcome Herjolf had given him. And in all likelihood after that morning, they would never see each other again. By the time Herjolf came back to Readingum, Brinin might already be gone. Or dead.

'Very well. I will work with Toki.' Perhaps Brinin might have stayed if it hadn't been for Oswald, and Garulf and Ebba, and the townsfolk on the run. The tug might have been too strong. 'You've been kind to me, and I thank you for it.'

Herjolf placed a hand on his shoulder and Brinin saw the blood-red threads sewn, twisting and turning, along the sleeves and neck of his shirt.

'When I come back, Bruni Hallveigson, we will see about teaching you to wield a sword.'

And Herjolf walked away and was gone, hidden in the crowd. Brinin would remember him and his readiness to show mercy. The wolfskin cloak. The long grey hair. The way he listened, as few had ever done. Hœrulangr. He wouldn't forget him and he would try not to think about what he was following Kjotvi to do.

Brinin found Toki nearby and together they made their way to the wall to start back at the digging. He hadn't meant to look at

Edrich Thegn. He had meant to keep the throng between them so that their eyes wouldn't meet again. But he was struck with a sudden dreadful fear that Edrich Thegn might be gone, taken away or worse. A quick glance was enough—he was still there—but Brinin knew then how restless he himself had become. He prayed that Toki wouldn't see it.

They hadn't been digging long when Skorri joined them, and Brinin's heart sank. He had seen little of Skorri since they had sat by the fire, catching sight of him only once or twice. But he hadn't forgotten to be wary. Surely as much danger lay in Skorri as help had been found in Herjolf. He kept digging and didn't look up as Skorri sidled up to him.

'Why *are* you here?' said Skorri, but there was little of asking in his voice. Every word sounded like blame.

'You were the one who found me,' said Brinin in that steady voice he had kept for Aculf, if he had spoken to him at all. 'You were there when Herjolf, your mother's-brother, talked to me. You heard my answers.'

'I heard your answers and don't see why I should believe them,' growled Skorri. Brinin kept his eye on his work. There was no need to look at Skorri to see his mind. There was enough dislike in his voice for that. 'I don't see why a stranger should walk in and be welcomed because he speaks our tongue. It's foolery. We only know what you've told us.'

'Do you know all the men here in Readingum? Or are some of them also strangers to you?' asked Brinin, still not looking up from his digging.

'All we know about you is what you've told us!' said Skorri again, and Brinin could not help thinking that in many ways Skorri *was* wiser than Herjolf, who seemed to have been led mainly by thoughts of his lost son. 'If I had my way—'

'Leave him alone, Skorri!' snapped Toki, looking up from his spade. 'Must you stand there idle, talking when no one wants to listen? Get to work!'

'I'm only saying,' muttered Skorri doggedly, 'that it's foolery for Herjolf to welcome him so readily when—'

Toki shoved him aside roughly.

'Speak of my father like that again and I'll thrash you where you stand!' he exclaimed angrily. 'He's been as much a father to you since your own died, and you would do well to speak of him as one, as well as a kinsman and an old warrior who has more wisdom than you are ever likely to gain! Now, enough of your idleness! Do you think the Saxons will wait until we're done before they come?'

Perhaps Skorri knew well enough how likely Toki was to carry out his threat. He said nothing more and took up his spade, but Brinin was glad that he walked away a little before he began to dig.

ENGLAFELD

O ne of their jarls led them out, gushing from Readingum like blood from a wound to spatter with fear the fields and farms they passed through. They came westward and at the fifth mile, Æthelwulf Ealdorman met them, man upon man at his heel, each with a battle-spear in his hand and a sword at his side. Fresh from the brave speeches and battle oaths, he led the fyrd against the foe. While hearts stayed stout in Wessex and men true, no Dane would mar those fields unchecked.

As Oswald stood waiting for war, time became slow, and small things a man doesn't always see grew large in his eyes. The dull greens and browns and greys of winter stretched out to meet an almost white sky. A lone bird flew black against its emptiness. It was strange to see a bird at such a time. Soaring far above in the stillness, it could not know what was about to happen beneath it. In the cold air Oswald grew warm among so many men. He could smell their sweat. The earth, frozen when they had come, turned muddy under their feet.

Straining to see between the shoulders and above the heads of men taller than himself, he saw the Danes coming towards them. They were nearer than the broad, white sky and nearer even than the dark trees. And the fear of his childhood, long-dreaded, looked like men. They were men who could bleed as Wessex men could. Some of them would fall as Wessex men would. The Danes drew near and Oswald gripped his spear tighter. He might bleed and fall himself. And another bird, wings wide, soared high.

'This is it,' he said in a low voice to Thurstan, standing to his right.

'Almost.'

'When will we charge?'

'Wait for the word. Æthelwulf Ealdorman will give it.'

It was too late for fear now. What he felt was neither yearning nor dread. It was only a waiting for what must be, like the sure pain of landing after stumbling, or the sudden cold shock after plunging into a river.

'Look after Edith, Thurstan,' he said. 'If I fall.'

'And if I fall?'

Why did the death of Thurstan seem a harder thing to think of than his own?

'Then Alrich and Hildræd my uncle will. I asked them already.'

The Danes came no nearer. They stood eyeing them across the field. Then Æthelwulf Ealdorman, in the middle of the shield wall, raised his battle-spear high.

'Hear this, heathen army!' he thundered. And though his strong voice thinned as it drifted into the white of the sky, the words were heard by Dane and Wessex man alike. 'This is the land of Æthelred the King, and we are his sworn men. We bid you go back whence you came, for you will not come further without meeting our swords. You have come a long way only to shed your blood!'

And many of the men around Oswald banged on their shields, daring the Danes to come and die. Oswald found himself shouting with Thurstan and Saxulf at his side. Who, after all, were these Danes? Who were they to bring death to Wessex where men only wanted to work their land?

As the shouting died down, the leader of the Danes stood out. The bellow that reached them was in a strange tongue almost meaningless to Oswald, but enough of the words were like his own for him to understand their threat.

'No men...withstood...' the Dane shouted, fearless and sure of a win. 'You...fall...your king...Edmund the king. Now...pleasing... gold...blood...stand...your blood...today. After that...have gold... your land...daughters.'

'And if I have anything to do with it, it will be your blood spilled today, Dane,' muttered Thurstan, who had three daughters among his children. 'Not only for the king or Æthelwulf, but for all those daughters you speak of.'

The Dane's words could only be met with battle. The scorn hooted out by the rest of his men could only be met with swords. Æthelwulf raised his spear higher than before, and the fyrd behind him raised theirs.

'We withstand you!' he cried. 'The ends of our spears will be a sharp answer to you, and you will die here on our soil!'

Then he turned back to his men. There was a sudden stillness, swiftly gone. Oswald's heart skipped, but not only with fear or the end of the waiting. He was ready, ready for what he had been taught to do almost his whole life.

'Stand fast, all of you!' shouted Æthelwulf. 'Let no man among you fall back.'

The war-cry rose and it began.

At first it was noise and a great surge forward. A prayer rose unwrought in Oswald's breast, not for life but for courage. Arrows bore unheard death, fanged battle-adders biting where they fell. One sank into the shoulder of a man near Oswald, young and beardless like himself, and he dropped to his knees with a cry that Oswald heard above the shouts of battle.

And still the great surge, the roar, the eyes over-watchful both to dodge and give death. Foe drew near to foe, spears bringing men down all around. The shield wall opened and Oswald ran, almost without thought, his spear raised high for a throw. That skill had never faltered even under his father's eye. The spear flew true. A Dane fell under its deadly bite. A great shove from behind sent Oswald sprawling to the side. A Danish spear landed in the mud where he had been standing. He snatched it up as he scrambled to his feet, chilled suddenly: somehow the spear had been cheated of a kill. And the shield wall shut round him again.

The roar, the surge, the foe near enough to share breath. Time stretched and shrank so that it couldn't be felt, and the fall of one man became much like the fall of another. Swords sweated with blood. Shields shivered under blows. Oswald's world dwindled away, the sky and field forgotten. There was nothing beyond the few feet around him and the flint-grey eyes of a foe near enough to embrace.

Sword upon sword, sword upon shield. Thrust blocked, slash dodged, pain unfelt. Alone with his foe, a stranger old enough to be his father—perhaps he too had a son—the battle roar seemed far off like thunder. Winter sunlight flashed upon the fist-swung blade. A swift pouncing, a sudden piercing. The wounded fell to die on the field. And Oswald, breathless, saw that it was the Dane and not himself who had fallen.

The surge, the roar, time stopped and unpassing. And at last there was a change. The jarl fell in his pride among many of his men. The sun was low. The Danes fled, driven away. The battle shouts gave way to the moans of the dying, and the ravens circled black overhead.

It came as a shock to stand alive at the end, with death everywhere Oswald looked. The earth was spinning, rushing like he was hurtling down a hill. But it slowed, and he felt pain from wounds he didn't know he had. He saw Thurstan, Saxulf, Leofwine, and began to make his way to them, to share gladness at battle well-fought, but all around him Dane and Wessex man lay dead together. Here lay one, little more than a boy; there, an old Dane with a wolfskin cloak and red threads sewn into his shirt. It would be long before the sight of them left his mind.

Oswald bent down to lift a battle-spear that lay in the mud beneath him. His own was beyond finding and this one was sound. It wouldn't be long before he needed another. As he rose again, he caught sight of Ealmund's three sons kneeling by the body of a fallen warrior. He saw on their faces that it was their father who lay dead at their feet, and all the anger he had felt the day before fled at the sight of their sorrow. Old pain, old shame, old bitterness had no place here. Not now. And Oswald went to help them bear their father's body from the field.

TRUST

There were times that day when it seemed to Brinin that the sun had stopped. He always had his eye on the sky to watch out for the creeping darkness, was always listening, always looking to see the raiders come back. The winter days were short, rushing swiftly from gloom to gloom, but that day was summerlong to Brinin. If the raiders were back by the first glow of sunset, he would wait. Otherwise, he would do it.

He had thought he would have to wait, that Kjotvi would not keep the men out so long, but what did he know of such things? Then he looked up and saw the sun touch the earth, a tired sun with little fire to it. And still no raiders. No waiting then. It wasn't fear that he felt. It was nearer that settled grimness that had always fallen on him when trouble had loomed with Aculf, and he had readied his mind and strengthened his gut to bear what must be borne. There could be no backing out now.

The sun sank slowly, ever so slowly. Brinin glanced from side to side along the earthen wall. Most of the men who had stayed behind were at work, all but those keeping watch along the rivers. Halfdan, even greater among the Danes than Kjotvi, wanted the wall done, and his men knew better than to be idle. Let the sun sink a little lower and then it would be time.

At last the white of the sky grew dim. Brinin laid down his spade and turned to Toki.

'I left my flask back where we ate,' he said. It had been wilful forgetfulness and a thirsty afternoon. 'I am thirsty. Let me go now to fetch it and then come back here.'

'Go,' said Toki, 'but why come back? Soon it will be too dark to keep on at the wall, and you have barely stopped today.'

'I don't mind work,' said Brinin. It was better than fretful waiting.

And he left Toki and began to walk to the swine pen. He went swiftly once he was out of sight of the wall, his eyes turning everywhere on the watch for trouble. But he met almost no one, and those he saw through the gathering gloom did not seem to see him.

Brinin slipped between the huddled buildings, praying he would find his way. It was better to creep to the swine pen from behind than openly along the long furrow. It was darker here, still and shadowy in these narrow places where thatch almost touched thatch. The smell told him he had drawn near, just as he was fearing that he had lost his way. He knew the smell of swine too well to mistake it. He followed his nose then and came at last to the fence. Brinin stopped to listen, to glance about him one last time, to steel himself. Then he swung himself over the fence and landed softly in the mud on the other side.

Edrich Thegn was leaning against the fence, seemingly asleep. His hands and feet were bound, and a rope round his neck was fastened at the other end to the fence. Crouching low, Brinin inched towards him, but Edrich started and stared at him like a man who is not sure if he is awake. The only sounds were the snuffling and gentle grunting of the swine around them.

'I have come, my lord,' whispered Brinin at last.

'You!' gasped Edrich.

At least he had the wisdom to keep his voice low, though Brinin could see that Edrich had already settled in his mind why he was there.

'You dare to come here!' Edrich was all whispered outrage. 'You dare to *be* here! And my son! You had him help you. So you could come to these, these... My son...'

Edrich's words faded away in a simmering, helpless fury. Brinin understood it. Here he was, a runaway slave with a Danish mother, among the Danes in their camp. And given everything that had happened in Oakdene after he had fled, no wonder Edrich had been so angry when their eyes had met the day before. He had seen that on his face even then.

'Oswald Child knows nothing of me being here, my lord.'

'What lies did you tell him to make him help you?'

Brinin sighed slightly. This was not the time for lengthy speech, if indeed there ever was a time.

'My lord, if you will trust me and are willing to risk death in the trying, I think I can get you out of here.'

Brinin drew Oswald's seax from its sheath and chose not to see the sudden fear on Edrich Thegn's face at the sight of the blade. He cut through the rope that bound his lord's ankles. Edrich's anger seemed to fall away then. He held out his hands for the seax to free them, then sat rubbing his wrists where they had been burned by the rope. He did not flinch as Brinin cut the rope from his neck.

'Come, my lord,' said Brinin. 'It's darker on the other side of the fence, and they will be coming soon. If you listen, you can hear them on their way.'

The sound of the Danes, coming back to house and tent after long work, was borne on the evening air. Soon the long furrow would be full of them. Brinin and Edrich Thegn did not wait. They scrambled over the fence—Edrich a little stiffly—and squatted behind it while Brinin quickly told his lord what they must do.

'Wait!' said Edrich. 'We just walk out of this place?'

'Yes, my lord.'

'But… but it's madness! I know you asked me to risk death, but this means sure death for both of us!'

'My lord,' said Brinin, struggling to speak steadily while time slipped all too swiftly by. 'My mother was a Dane.'

'Yes. How does that help us now?'

'My tongue is their tongue, my lord. We won't creep out. We will walk boldly past their wall, and I will speak in their tongue the whole way. It's getting too dark for anyone to see us. They will only hear me speak and will likely not even ask themselves who we are.'

Edrich Thegn was still wavering but there was no time for wavering now.

'Please, my lord. It's our only hope. And besides, there's no going back now that I've already freed you.'

There was nothing else to be done. Edrich Thegn did follow him, the Danish voices drawing ever nearer. They did not walk boldly at first and Brinin did not speak. He crept slightly ahead of Edrich to find a way out, to find somewhere for their bold walk to begin.

Brinin left Edrich Thegn and slipped between two houses to see if the way was good. The scuffle that followed was sudden and soon over. Brinin was backed against a wall. Once again, Skorri's blade had come upon him swiftly—a knife this time, pointed at his heart—and how angry Brinin was with himself that he hadn't foreseen it. Edrich Thegn was waiting to be called, for a whisper to tell him to follow. He couldn't know of the danger or come to help and had no weapon if he did.

'I knew we shouldn't trust you!' Skorri hissed. 'I saw you creep away from the wall and now I find you skulking in the shadows, up to who knows what! There's no Herjolf or Toki to help you now!'

There was a little light left, enough to see Skorri's eyes, and Brinin met them with his own. No kin left to mourn him, no work that another couldn't do. But it was bitter to be so near to life then lose it, bitter that Edrich Thegn must now die too. His eyes never left Skorri's. He meant to die fearlessly. It was slow at the end, with time enough to think last thoughts. He seemed to see Brother Wilfred beside him on a bench, the scroll laid out before them. He heard Oswald's faltering voice: 'Where there is no bitter death. Where there is no ache.' A far-off friend. Would his father and mother and Row be there? Would he know them when he got there? Or would everyone and everything be changed?

WOUNDS

From among the dead and the dying they gathered their own, picking their way through the field as the daylight shrank from them. Some, too wounded for life, saw the sun set for the last time that day. Others would groan for a time, then fight again, if the fever did not come upon them. Still others were already gone before they reached them. Sigelm and Oswald had been boys together. They had often gathered their men and done battle against one another in the meadow. Sigelm, older and stronger, had almost always won their battles then. Now that they had at last done battle as men, side by side and not as foes, it was Oswald who still stood and Sigelm who had fallen. Oakdene had another warrior to mourn, and Saxulf only one son to bring back to his mother. They gathered their own. Battle won always comes with loss, always with wounds to bind and dead to bury. They all left the field at the end without some swordbrothers they had come with.

At dusk Oswald sat in the camp, stripped to the waist and shivering a little for all the heat of the fire, and while his wounds were tended he talked to Thurstan. It was better to talk. He had a cut to his shield arm and a long gash on his side and couldn't say how he had come by either. Speech kept his mind from the sting as salve was rubbed on and the wounds were wrapped.

'You'll mend,' said Thurstan, wiping his sword with a rag and turning it over in the firelight. 'I've seen men mend from worse.'

'Yes, likely I will,' said Oswald, grimacing a little as the salve stung. 'It could have been much worse.'

'It very nearly *was* much worse,' said Thurstan.

'What do you mean?'

'Next time you play the brave warrior,' Thurstan said wryly, standing up to sheathe his sword, 'do try to keep an eye on what spears are coming towards you and not only where yours is going. Standing still to watch it won't change its flight once it's left your hand.'

'Yes, you're right,' said Oswald and felt another kind of shiver at the thought of it. 'That one didn't miss by much, did it?'

'I am always ready to help, my lord!' said Thurstan with a grin.

'Oh! That was you! *You* pushed me away!' That sudden shove had cheated the spear, and at the time he couldn't think much about it. 'Thank you. You may have saved my life!'

'I did save it! As I have taught you warcraft more than anyone else, I ought to tell you how I think you've done. You are still alive and only slightly wounded. That says more than I could. Well done, my lord. You've made it through your first battle and you'll most likely live to fight another.'

His wounds bound, Oswald picked up his shirt and, a little gingerly, pulled it on again. The rushing, hurtling feeling had gone, and now he only ached, not so much bodily as somewhere inside. He and the boys he had played with hadn't known what they were playing: swordplay, battleplay. They had died, then gone home to eat, sleep and live to die again another day. But for Sigelm and Ealmund Thegn and so many more, there would be no other day. The play was over. It was how life was. It was how death came. He had known it before. But it was hard, bitter knowledge now that he saw it.

'It won't be long before we do have to fight them again, will it?' sighed Oswald wearily. 'One battle won't be enough to drive them out.'

'Unlikely to be,' said Thurstan. 'But now they know that we won't give way to them readily. That Dane who led them was too proud, and not so many of his men have lived.'

'So what do we do now?'

'We wait until we are led into battle again. That's the first thing you need to know. You don't get to choose what to do. You've sworn to follow Æthelwulf Ealdorman. You've sworn to follow the King. They do the leading. We do the following. But I believe the King and the Ætheling are gathering more men. It won't be long before we do battle again.'

'Northumbria, East Anglia and Mercia fell so easily, it seems. I wonder if we can withstand them for long.'

'Who knows? But isn't that why we should fight hard? And if you ever forget why we *are* fighting, think about what that Dane said before the battle.'

For all his weariness, it was a long time before Oswald slept that night. Seven nights had passed since he had slept in the minster, with little thought of the word that would come in the morning. Only seven nights. He had been a boy then, though he hadn't known it. He had thought he was a man, or near enough to one. But now he could never be a boy again, however much he wanted to be. His boyhood was a lost time, so long ago. It had died with his father. It had fallen on the battlefield and it could never come back again.

Even if they did defeat the Danes, even if they did drive them out of Wessex, even if he did live to see a time after it all, what would peace look like after war? Would the fields of Oakdene have more worth because blood had been spilled to keep the Danes out? Or would everything always seem a little broken—mended perhaps, patched up, but broken nonetheless? Thoughts of war would always creep nearby. Oakdene, free from threat, would always be haunted by the shadows of those who might still have been there if the Danes had never come.

Nothing would ever be the same again. How could it be? Wounds may heal in time, but there are always scars.

VOICE

As he waited for the knife to be thrust into his heart, Brinin saw nothing but Skorri's eyes. The walls round about him, the thatch in the twilight, the shadows on the ground all melted away. He waited for the sudden pain, the drowning darkness, or whatever death would be, but it was long in the coming. Skorri was slow for one so eager to kill. Did he hope to see Brinin's fear by lingering over it? Perhaps he was not yet so bloodthirsty as he liked to think. He was slow, and it dragged out to a lifetime.

They stood speechless, eye to eye. Neither spoke, neither stirred, neither looked away. The evening was still along with them, though the voices of the Danish host were all around them now, just out of their reach beyond the unseen place where they were standing. Eye to eye, breath to breath. Then a voice tore through the stillness, a whisper clear enough to be a shout above all those Danish voices.

'Brinin!' the whisper shouted.

Edrich Thegn. Hope and despair. Brinin did not dare to speak to warn him or call for help. He did not even dare to turn his eyes to Edrich's voice. But Skorri's eyes stirred. They flickered towards the voice and Brinin, whose eyes had stayed steady, saw them. Skorri's head jerked a little, ever so slightly, to follow his eyes. It was enough. The stillness between them was broken. Swifter than he knew he could be, Brinin wrenched away the knife and slammed his fist into Skorri's face with a strength that sent him sprawling into the other wall.

Skorri, dazed from the blow, had no time to struggle to his feet. Brinin was on him at once, sitting on his chest, knees pinning down his arms, with one hand over his mouth and the other holding Skorri's own knife to his throat. Death fled suddenly from Brinin, melting away like a snowflake caught on a child's hand. And once more he dared to hope.

Edrich Thegn, too battlewise to be much startled, came quickly to his side.

'What are you waiting for? Run him through and let us be away from here! Or at least give me the knife and I'll do it.'

Did Edrich Thegn see him waver, see that Brinin didn't know how to kill? Brinin could feel Skorri struggling under his weight. He could see the fear in his eyes. He had not forgotten how Herjolf had stayed Skorri's sword at such a time as this.

'My lord, on the night I came here, it was his kinsman who stopped them from killing me.' No need for Edrich to know that it had been Skorri's sword that had nearly slit his throat. 'Without his kinsman, I would have been dead before I even got into the camp, and you would still be with the swine.'

'If we spare him he will warn the others, and we'll both be lost!'

'His kinsman saved my life, my lord.'

He wouldn't kill Skorri and he wouldn't let Edrich Thegn do it either. Brinin hadn't tried disobeying him before, but it couldn't be helped. Besides, with his tongue and his knowledge of Readingum, he had all the power now. Strange how things can change.

'What else can we do with him then?' It seemed that Edrich Thegn wouldn't try to make him do it after all. Perhaps he understood that there were some things that shouldn't be done.

'Tear a strip from my cloak, my lord. We can bind it round his mouth, then tie him up and leave him here to be found.'

The work was soon done. Skorri lay gagged, his hands tied behind his back with his own belt and his feet trussed together with Edrich's. They dragged him to a darker, more hidden place and turned to leave. But Brinin stopped before he went and looked down at Skorri.

'You should remember this day, Skorri,' he said, slipping again into his mother's tongue. 'This is what mercy looks like. When you see Herjolf, tell him that it's because of his kindness to me that his sister's-son still lives. Tell him that I almost stayed with him, but that I had to go back to the men I knew.'

They left Skorri in the dark and walked out into the open. There were Danes everywhere. They stood talking on the thresholds. They lit fires and sat around them. They walked everywhere through the darkening evening, in ones and in twos and threes, and Brinin and Edrich Thegn walked among them. Slowly, not rushing, as though they were going nowhere at all, Brinin led the way back to the great earthen wall.

And all the way he talked. He talked as he had never talked before. He talked as he had never thought he could talk. He reached into his mind and, one by one, pulled out all the threads of speech he had thought of while digging that day. He wove the threads from his mouth like cloth from a loom. They poured out, tumbled out. He wrapped himself with them to muffle the sound of his pounding heart.

Edrich Thegn threw himself into it with as many speechlike sounds as he could muster. It was likely for the best that he could only understand a little of what Brinin was saying. Wasn't it a mild evening for the time of year? Might the dry weather hold until the wall was done? The work had been quick, though his back was starting to ache a little. Wessex would fall. It would surely fall with men like Halfdan and Bagsecg to lead them. Wessex would be like East Anglia, like Northumbria. Æthelred would be a fool to stand against them—it didn't seem fitting to call one's king a fool, but Brinin said it nonetheless. Kjotvi would have been proud of him as Brinin hurled his insults. And so he walked them unchallenged to the wall.

Some men were watching it and the stretch of land between the two rivers, but Brinin didn't look at them. He kept walking with Edrich Thegn, silent now, at his side. He felt drained, not so much of words but of the will to say them. His heart was much too swift. His breath felt light and shallow. He mustn't rush. He must keep walking slowly. Just as they were about to cross to the other side of the wall, he turned towards the men nearest to them.

'I left my knife out there earlier,' he lied cheerfully, though the words felt dry in his mouth. 'I need it this evening.'

But one of the men at the fire called after him.

'Wait!'

Brinin froze. He mustn't run, he mustn't run yet. Edrich Thegn, at his elbow, was breathing rather quickly. Not now. Not now with freedom so near.

'Won't it be easier to find it if you stop to light a torch?' called the man.

It was so friendly and well-meant that Brinin could have laughed. Or wept. A torch was the last thing they wanted.

'No need,' he called back. 'I know where it is and can easily find it.'

They walked on. Silent now. No one followed. No one called again. They came to the edge of the trees. The trees grew thicker. They stepped among them. It was darker with trees around them. No one could see them from the wall now.

'Run, my lord.'

DAWNING

S cratched by bramble and thorn, snatched and clawed at by bough and twig, scrambling, tripping, feeling their way, almost blindly they ran. Brinin could have been quicker. He could have run with all the fearful swiftness he had been holding back. But Edrich Thegn couldn't. He was older, wearier. Brinin heard it in his breath and tread and matched his steps as though his own weariness was as great. They ran, stumbled, walked, crept for a long time before they sank down among the trees. The earth was mossy and soft from leaves long fallen, damp and slippery. It was too dark to run now and—Brinin listened but heard no one following—perhaps there was no need to.

And all they could do then was to sit in breathless, wordless disbelief. They were away. They were gone. Edrich Thegn was not dead. Neither of them was dead. It had been such a small, dreamlike hope, so slight, but the only one to grasp at. Now that they were out Brinin wondered how they had dared.

'We walked out of the Danish camp. Walked!' Edrich's words were half-breath, half-laugh.

'Yes, my lord,' said Brinin. If the tale had been told in the firelight, men would not have believed it. Dragons seemed more likely, and there had been many long winters since any dragons had been seen in Wessex.

'Without even drawing their blood or shedding our own!' Edrich was still near to laughter.

'Skorri—that's the Dane we left bound, my lord—his nose was bleeding a good deal and...'

Brinin put a hand to his chest where his shirt was sticky with blood already drying. He had felt the sharpness of Skorri's knife as he'd wrenched it from his hand. It wasn't a deep cut, but enough to bleed. A wound had been too small a thing to speak of before they left the camp. No need to now that they were out.

'It seemed like madness! It *was* madness! I am thankful to you for thinking of it, more than thankful to you for getting me out, however you came to be there.'

Wessex man. Dane. Never quite one thing nor the other, mistrust might always be at his heels. He *had* been there, tugged, almost ready to stay. How could he blame Edrich Thegn for thinking what he did?

Then they heard it. Voices far off, cutting through the darkness and drawing near. Brinin stiffened. He hadn't thought they would come. He had thought they might stop them or kill them before they left, but not follow them once they had gone. Why hunt them down now, only two of them, when there was a wall to build and a camp to defend?

'Those voices are coming from the west, not the east,' whispered Edrich Thegn, as though he had heard Brinin's fears as he thought them. 'They are drawing nearer, but I don't think they are here among the trees as we are.'

Brinin didn't stop to ask what to do. He crept to the edge of the trees, not far from where they sat, then crouched behind one, hardly daring to breathe. Men, many of them, coming from the west as Edrich Thegn had said. They didn't try to hide their coming. There was no stealth or low voices. They called out to each other as they went, and Brinin heard snatches of their speech. Battle, loss, swordbrothers fallen; Saxons, bloodshed, Kjotvi dead. The raiders were back. They had been met in battle. And they had lost.

'The Danes who went out to raid this morning have come back, my lord,' Brinin whispered as he reached Edrich again. 'They have been put to flight.'

'The fyrd must have been gathered.'

'Thurstan said that Æthelwulf Ealdorman was gathering the fyrd, my lord.'

'Thurstan? I can see I'll have to ask you even more than I thought I would. There will be time enough for that. If Æthelwulf has gathered the fyrd, then it is to Æthelwulf we must go and not to Oakdene. Do you know where they might be?'

'No, my lord.'

'West of here somewhere, most likely. There will be ways to find them, but nothing can be done now. We will rest before we go further. Come. If we lean against this tree and stay close together, we may not be so cold. This is no time for a fire.'

So they sat, side by side, shoulder to shoulder, huddled together for warmth, their cloaks wrapped tightly about them. They did not speak again, and perhaps Edrich Thegn did sleep, but Brinin was still too shocked that they were alive even to shut his eyes at first. He stared into the darkness, raven-black and rife with nightnoise, and listened to the breathing of his lord at his side. The shock softened, the thrill dulled and the sudden jerking of his head told him that he had indeed slept, if not for long.

Edrich Thegn would have hard things to say and to ask in the morning. He had found, or rather been found by, his runaway slave among the Danes. Yet what was there to fear? Little, surely. Edrich Thegn was thankful. He had said so, and unless he was not the kind of man that Brinin had always thought he was, he was unlikely to meet the rest of it with any great harshness. But he was bound to have something to say. Then there was the seax. Brinin touched it rather fondly in the darkness. They could have one last night together, he and freedom, before they parted. It wasn't true freedom, now that Edrich Thegn lived. It was only a knife he wasn't meant to have.

They didn't make it until morning. They grew too cold, and it was long before sunrise when Edrich stood up and stretched with a groan.

'Enough of this,' he sighed wearily. 'We'll freeze unless we get going, and the sooner we start, the sooner we will find the fyrd.'

They picked their way through the trees, near the edge, the more easily to see the dawn. And at last, as the nightgloom grew a little grey, Edrich Thegn turned to look at him and Brinin knew the time for talking had come.

'You likely know that a runaway slave may be put to death, or flogged or whatever his lord sees fit,' Edrich began. 'However, you have saved my life, and I believe you once saved the life of my son. I am thankful to you twice over and have no heart to punish you. I have already seen more than enough punishment for what you did. You should know that your flight brought great trouble to Oakdene, and most of that trouble fell upon my son's shoulders. But you need not fear, and I give you my thanks.'

'Thank you, my lord,' said Brinin. No great harshness. He had thought it would be that way.

'And now,' said Edrich, as they walked along, 'answer me this. You left Oakdene with your brother. Is he still in Readingum among the Danes?'

'No, my lord.'

'Where is he, then?'

'Fallen, my lord. Not many days after we left Oakdene.'

The sounds around them were the sound of twigs that broke beneath their feet, the sound of the birds beginning to wake, the sound of the eager stillness waiting for more speech. No one would ever call him 'Bruni' again. Herjolf was the last. That was another achebearing thought to sit with the others.

'So, after he fell, did you go to the Danes?' went on Edrich. 'No, wait! That can't be right. You said you heard from Thurstan that Æthelwulf Ealdorman was gathering the fyrd. You can't have been so long among the Danes. How long *were* you among them?'

'I slept in their camp for two nights before we left, my lord.'

'Not long then. And before that, you somehow saw Thurstan. Did you go to Oakdene?'

Brinin knew he had to do it then, before he answered or Edrich asked anything more. Hope, life, slavery. But death had been near, and he had done more than he had hoped for. He stopped walking and drew the seax from his belt. Then with one last, longing look at it, he handed it to Edrich Thegn. His belt was light once more, and he felt the weight of freedom fly from his hand as Edrich took the seax from him.

Amber in the east, there was enough light now for Brinin to see all the unspoken asking on Edrich's face. Edrich looked down at the seax, then back up at Brinin. It was an older face since Brinin had seen it last, thinner and with a dark heaviness under the eyes. There had been more than one night of poor sleep, and other worse pain besides. It took no deep insight for Brinin to see that.

'Oswald Child gave it to me, my lord. He thought you were dead. He didn't know it wasn't his to give.' Brinin knew that it wasn't his to keep.

They were walking again now, but slowly. Edrich Thegn kept glancing at Brinin, frowning a little. Brinin could see his struggle: no knowledge of what to ask, hardly knowing what answers he was looking for.

'Let me understand this,' said Edrich at last. 'You left Oakdene and went to…?'

'The minster, my lord.'

'The same minster that my son went to? Yes.' Edrich broke off, muttering half to himself, 'I knew there was much I didn't know, but I begin to see that I knew even less than I thought I did. Where does Thurstan come into it?'

'Thurstan came to the minster with word that you had been taken by the Danes and were likely dead, my lord. Cynestan lived and was taken to Oakdene, much wounded. That's how Oakdene heard of it. Thurstan came to fetch Oswald Child back.'

'Cynestan lived! Thank God! I thought that he and Swetrich were both dead and that no one would ever know—' Edrich Thegn broke off, and Brinin saw him shut his lips tightly as Edith had done in the cave. 'So my son and Thurstan went back to Oakdene. When?'

'This is the seventh day since they left the minster, my lord.'

'And you? You said my son knew nothing of you being among the Danes, but you can't have left the minster long after him to have come to Readingum when you did.'

'The same day, my lord, as soon as Oswald Child and Thurstan had gone.'

This time it was Edrich who stopped walking. He turned to Brinin, frowning slightly again. But now understanding was growing on his face, dawning like the morning.

'Why?' said Edrich at last.

But that strayed too near the breasthoard. Brinin looked down. He had opened it for Herjolf, had shown him a little of what he hid there, but he didn't like another man to dig it up unbidden.

'I was told that sometimes you would not answer Aculf,' said Edrich Thegn. 'You will answer me. Why did you go to Readingum?'

'I thought you might not be dead, my lord,' said Brinin, looking up again. 'Thurstan said that Cynestan saw no body and that some boys had seen a bound man borne away by four others. And you were last seen near Readingum, my lord.'

'So you came to Readingum and...?'

'When I drew near I was told that a great host of Danes had taken the town, my lord.'

'Yet even then you did not turn back?'

'No, my lord.'

'Only because you thought I might be held by the Danes and not dead?'

'That is so, my lord.'

Edrich started to walk again and for a time they kept on without speaking.

'But death was more likely!' Edrich said suddenly. His voice had changed a little, as though his throat was too tight to get the words out. 'Death was much more likely. You must have known that!'

'Yes, my lord.'

Then for the first time Edrich saw that Brinin's shirt was dark with blood.

'You're wounded!'

'A small wound, my lord, from Skorri's knife. The bleeding has stopped.'

'A man might go after his lord or swordbrother.' Edrich still had his eyes on Brinin's shirt. 'But a boy, a slave, a runaway slave… Why did you do it?'

Oswald's face had been so white, his words so gasping. Sudden sorrow all the worse, Brinin knew, for what had been left unsaid.

'My lord, I was there when Oswald Child heard what had happened to you. I saw his face.'

And that was enough. There was no more asking. But Brinin, after a time, remembered that the fyrd had been gathered and Oswald, most likely, was among them.

'My lord, Oswald Child was going to lead the men to join Æthelwulf Ealdorman. Perhaps they have already done battle with the Danes.'

Edrich Thegn suddenly quickened his step, and Brinin could not have said what he saw on his face. There was too much there to untangle it all.

'We have been walking too slowly!' The tightness had come back. It seemed to be choking Edrich a little. 'There's a settlement up ahead. If any of them are still alive, maybe they can tell us where Æthelwulf and the fyrd are.'

GHOST

The morning was still young when they looked ahead and saw the Saxon camp before them. Edrich Thegn had driven them hard, never once letting them slacken their steps. He did not speak much to Brinin again. He only muttered to himself, often and with a burst of speed each time: they were walking too slowly; surely the fyrd must be somewhere nearby; they could be quicker than this, much quicker.

The fyrdmen were awake; eating, standing to talk together, sitting by the fires they had built. But everywhere Brinin looked he saw the wounded. Some seemed to be wounded only slightly, as he was; others so sickeningly that it was a wonder that they still lived, though likely they wouldn't for long. After a while Brinin kept his eyes down—the less he looked at, the less there would be to think of later—but not before he saw some men bearing away the body of one who had seen his last night. Edrich Thegn saw that too. His jaw tightened, and Brinin knew that they felt the same fear. Oswald might be here. He might be wounded, dreadfully wounded, already borne away. Edrich Thegn was turning everywhere as he walked, always watching for a well-known face. They were here now. They would know soon.

It wasn't long, though it felt like it, before Edrich Thegn broke into a run. Brinin looked up again then and saw Thurstan ahead of them. If Thurstan was here, then... Brinin began to run too, following after Edrich Thegn. The fear sat heavy in his gut now.

Thurstan stopped walking suddenly as he saw who was running towards him. Brinin had seldom seen more dumbstruck disbelief on a man's face. He stared, gaping, and Edrich Thegn was the first to speak.

'You didn't think to see *me* here, did you? I can see that,' he said. 'Answers will come in time, but now: where is my son?'

'Have you been raised from the dead, my lord, or do I see a ghost?' said Thurstan. Not dumbstruck for long, then.

'You can see I'm as alive as you are! Now answer me. Where is my son?'

Thurstan smiled warmly.

'Not cut to pieces after all, my lord!'

Everything changed then, as the air does on a summer day when long-threatened thunder and rain come at last. Edrich Thegn, still breathing heavily from the running, seemed to feel it too. His panting eased a little.

'Is he… is he at all wounded?'

'But slightly, my lord,' said Thurstan. He started, seeing Brinin now for the first time. 'What are you doing here? You seem to have a way of being where I least think I'll see you!'

'Where is my son, Thurstan?' said Edrich Thegn again. There was only one thing that needed to be asked now, and they hadn't had the answer yet.

'I'll take you to him now, my lord, if you will follow me. I left him a short time ago at his tent, about to have his wounds seen to. Slight wounds, as I say, my lord. Nothing to worry about.'

Thurstan led Edrich Thegn through the camp, with Brinin following a little behind, and as they walked Thurstan talked with an outstanding coolness for a man speaking to one he had thought was dead only a short while before.

'My lord, these seven days past Oswald Child has been a worthy lord to follow. I cannot tell you how well he has led for one so young.' And Thurstan spoke warmly of all Oswald had done since Brinin watched him ride ashen-faced into the grey morning: how he had thought of everything he could to defend the village; how he had led them in fasting and prayer. 'He went into battle at my side, my lord, and whatever fear he felt I did not see, though he did ask me to care for his sister should he fall. But he did not fall. He fought, my lord, and he did not turn back. He still stood at the end. Whatever startling noises the battlefield may have had, they did not seem to startle him.'

There was some heavy meaning in the way Thurstan looked at Edrich Thegn when he said this. Brinin saw it but couldn't unravel what it was. Perhaps Edrich Thegn understood it, but from behind Brinin couldn't tell.

'It may not be for me to say so, my lord, but—'

'You will never learn when you should speak and when you should not, Thurstan, so let us both stop fooling ourselves and speaking as though you do know!'

There was laughter in Edrich Thegn's voice. Laughter was like that sometimes, a ready friend to keep other feelings away. Like laughing with a brother in the mist—better than fretting then and better to remember afterwards. Thurstan smiled, grinned almost, but he was earnest when he spoke again.

'Oswald Child has done well, my lord, very well. Now that you have come back to us—almost as though you have come back from death itself—it will be good for him to hear you say it.'

They turned a corner between two tents and Thurstan nodded to where a few men were gathered not far ahead of them.

'There he is, my lord,' said Thurstan in a low voice. 'Your son.'

It was Oswald. It couldn't have been anyone else. He sat with his back to them while a wound on his side was tended. Brinin didn't see the wound. He saw the scars woven like a web across Oswald's back. And he wished he hadn't seen them, because what is seen cannot be unseen. That web would always stretch across Oswald's back, and Brinin knew that now it would always stretch across some corner of his own mind. He had been right to go to Readingum.

Before either Edrich Thegn or Thurstan could speak, Leofwine, who stood facing them, looked up and saw them coming. He stared at Edrich like a man who sees a ghost.

'My... my lord!' he stammered.

'Yes,' said Edrich Thegn and Oswald Thegn together as one man.

Brinin saw Oswald's shoulders stiffen and his head jerk up to look at Leofwine. Perhaps what he saw on Leofwine's face was enough. Scrambling to his feet, Oswald swung round and stared at his father, his face shifting between shock and bewilderment, gladness and disbelief.

'F… father!' he gasped. 'You…'

'I'm alive, as you see, Oswald,' said Edrich Thegn. His voice was all father, without much thegn.

'But… but I don't understand! If they didn't kill you, how did you flee from them?' Then Oswald saw Brinin, who had been hidden behind Thurstan. Brinin saw the bewilderment grow and fear spring up with it. 'Brinin!'

Thurstan gave Leofwine a little shove.

'Don't stand there like a dreamer!' he said. 'Go and find them something to eat!'

Leofwine rushed off, half-stumbling as he looked behind him as though to be sure that Edrich Thegn was still there. Little wonder. They stood by the fire with a tale to tell that couldn't be believed. Less likely than dragons.

'Sit down, Oswald,' said Edrich, taking a seat himself. 'Let them keep going with the wound.'

Oswald sat, still staring at Brinin, who stood back a little from the fire. He looked from Brinin to his father then back again, and more than once Brinin saw him open his mouth to speak. He did not even seem to feel the sting of the salve.

'But how…' he began, but his voice faltered.

'There will be time to hear it all,' said Edrich Thegn. 'But the short tale is that this boy, Brinin, went to Readingum and was welcomed because he speaks their tongue. Then he found me and we walked out.'

'Walked out!' And again that morning Brinin saw Thurstan gape.

'Walked slowly, at twilight, with Brinin speaking in the Danish tongue the whole way. No one stopped us because we seemed to be two Danes.'

Oswald, his lips shut tightly together, still stared from his father to Brinin. He didn't weep as Brinin was beginning to fear he might. He only gasped slightly. But Thurstan burst out laughing and slapped Brinin hard on the back.

'You walked out!' And everyone else laughed with him. 'That's one of the best things I've heard in years. I don't know when I last heard of anything so bold!'

'Now,' said Edrich Thegn, leaning towards Oswald with an earnestness new to Brinin yet so well-known. They were father and son; he could see it today. 'Oswald, you have been thegn in my place and, from what I have been told, a good one. You have done everything I ever taught you and much more besides.'

It seemed that Edrich Thegn wanted everyone to hear. Brinin saw Thurstan urging his thegn on with his eyes.

'It is strange for a father to see suddenly that his son is a man with…' Edrich was slow, meting out his words. 'With wisdom and courage. You have done very well, Oswald.'

It was better that no one spoke then. Better not to rush away. Better to let the words stay fresh, like a blackberry held in the mouth to keep the taste.

'Father,' said Oswald at last. 'Sigelm has fallen. Ealmund Thegn has fallen. Daglæf is wounded, but if wound fever does not come upon him, he will likely live. And, Father, should we send word to Oakdene? Edith is mourning and must be told.'

So Oswald Thegn stepped aside and once more was only the thegn's son, there to follow and not to lead. Leofwine came back with meat—and at the sight of it Brinin suddenly felt how hungry he was—and they ate. Edrich asked about Oakdene and the battle, then at last went to find his kinsmen, and Saxulf and Sigulf. The others followed, and Brinin was left alone with Oswald.

'You don't need to stand with me,' said Oswald. 'Come and sit by the fire.'

The fire was warm and Brinin was so tired, so achingly tired. It hit him with the heat of the flames as he sat down; and he wished he could lie down and sleep on the ground, curl up and shut his eyes and forget everything. It was so long until nightfall.

'You must have gone to look for my father as soon as Thurstan and I left,' said Oswald. 'The Danes could have killed you!'

'They didn't.'

Oswald saw Brinin's shirt then, frowning suddenly as his father had done.

'You're wounded!'

'Only slightly. Less than you are.'

'But it wasn't as easy to leave Readingum as my father said, was it?'

Easy? Near death twice, tugged so hard that he had almost forgotten friendship to follow a dream. But he was too weary to say that now and tomorrow he likely wouldn't want to. Best to leave it all behind in Readingum.

'I saw that my father had what looked like the seax I gave you tucked into his leg winding,' Oswald went on. 'And that there is none on your belt.'

'I gave it back to him. What else was to be done?'

'Nothing else,' sighed Oswald. 'I'm sorry. I'm so glad he's alive, but I wish you could still be free. I'll talk to him about it. He must be thankful.'

'He is. He said he was and that he won't punish me for running away.'

Oswald sighed again. Perhaps that would have to be good enough.

'It might be better now,' he said hopefully.

That had always been the way with Oswald, always thinking about how everything might be better. But perhaps there was some good in a little careful hope. If it hadn't been for hope Edrich Thegn would still be with the swine.

'Aculf isn't workreeve any more,' said Oswald. 'Telling him that was the first thing I did when I got back to Oakdene. When my father knows why, I don't think he'll make him workreeve again. I'm going to tell my father everything, what kind of man Aculf is, how he mistreated you—'

'He didn't, though, did he?'

'What do you mean? You know he did!'

'You *can't* mistreat a slave,' said Brinin wearily, too weary to speak or think of Aculf, but Oswald had never understood and it was time he did. 'The lord may do as he sees fit. *You* can speak of injustice because there are some things that should not be done to you, but there is no injustice for someone like me. Can a swine grumble if the lord says it is for the pot? Can a slave grumble? Not any more than the swine. Do I like it? No. But it's how it is. The lord does as he sees fit. If your father is happy with Aculf, then neither you nor I can do anything about it. So don't speak to me of injustice or mistreating or anything like that. Remember that you are free, and I am not; and almost anything can be done to me, so long as your father is happy with it.'

Before Oswald could speak, they heard a sudden cough. Edrich Thegn and Thurstan were standing behind them. Edrich Thegn had likely heard everything but he didn't seem angry, and Brinin was too tired now to care.

'Thurstan,' said Edrich Thegn. 'You see he is wounded. Be so good as to take him to have the wound seen to.'

'Be ready to set your teeth,' said Thurstan grimly. 'Your shirt is sticking to that wound, and seeing to it is going to hurt.'

So Brinin followed Thurstan to set his teeth. Perhaps after that they might let him find somewhere to sleep.

SPARKS

For a long time neither Oswald nor his father spoke. They sat together looking into the fire. The smoke was carried away to the east on the wind, full of little sparks, firebearing to anything ready to burn. They sprung out glowing, only to land already cold and black. If he and his father were ready, one spark might be enough to start their speech.

'Neither of us wants to talk about what we would both rather forget,' began Edrich, reaching out for some twigs beside him. He tossed them onto the fire and the flames leapt to lick them up. 'But we may go into battle again at any time and either or both of us may fall. It seems that I have not seen some of what happened in my own village. As my son, you can tell me. Let me start by asking how you came to help two runaway slaves—he won't be punished now so you needn't worry about that. Was it simply because he had saved your life that you felt you should help him when he asked?'

'I thought of it, not him,' said Oswald, keeping his eyes on the fire. Now that the time had come he felt that he would rather talk about almost anything else. But there could be no chill now, only warmth. If his father had thrown on the twigs, he must keep them burning. 'Brinin didn't want to go, and I wish I'd never sent him away. Row might still live if they had never left Oakdene. But... but I knew Aculf would make sure you heard a bad word about Brinin and that he would be sold. It seemed better for them to flee together, than for Brinin to be sold and sent away alone.'

One of the burning sticks fell, shifting all the others, and sending up a sudden flurry of sparks and smoke. Oswald glanced across at his father then, ready for sternness or the beginning of anger, but through the smoke he couldn't see it.

'Tell me about Aculf,' said Edrich. 'What did Brinin mean just now?'

So his father had heard that? Oswald hadn't been sure before, though perhaps it wasn't so bad that he had. It was another spark, another easy way to keep the fire burning.

'Aculf is no longer workreeve, Father. I told him to keep to his own field and hearth, as soon as I reached Oakdene. I see now that I was much to blame for saying nothing about it before—and I ask your forgiveness for that—but many times Aculf did in your name what I don't believe you would have done yourself. He is not fit to be workreeve.'

And because his father still did not seem to be angry with him, Oswald spoke, haltingly at first, but there were so many sparks now that the words warmed on his tongue. He told his father everything he could think of that showed what Aculf was.

'I did not think he should be your workreeve when he did not do as you do. You punish when you must, but you've never longed to punish, or to shame, or to be needlessly harsh. And even if a slave may hope for nothing, I thought it would not be your wish for a slave of yours to be treated as Brinin was by Aculf.'

At the end Oswald waited for the anger, even a flicker of it, but it did not come. He looked up again. Surely his father was much wearier, older than before. What had they done to him in Readingum? And as he looked at him, Oswald saw that he must answer what was not asked.

'I know I should have spoken about it before, Father. At first I...' But perhaps his father knew why—there was something on his face. It might not be kind to say too much. 'At first, I didn't. After they left I wanted to—I wanted to tell you everything, that's the truth—but I was afraid that if I did they would be caught and punished. And by the time of the Moot, it was too late. It didn't seem right to speak of Aculf then, because...'

'Because I, your father and thegn, should have been wiser in my choice of workreeve and should have been better at seeing.'

Had his father changed since he had come back from the Danes and death? He did seem to understand. Had Edith been right? Had he always been willing to listen? Perhaps he himself, not his father, was the one who had changed.

'I wasn't going to say *that*, Father,' said Oswald. 'You must do as you think best, but if Aculf is workreeve again, and if Brinin is still a slave—I know he gave you back the seax—then Aculf will make him suffer, more if you and I are much away at war, as it seems we must be.'

The fire was beginning to burn low again, and this time it was Oswald who threw on the wood to give it life. Through the smoke and heat, the tents nearby seemed dim and blurred.

'Father, there is much I have done that I now wish I hadn't,' he said, turning to look at his father with sudden earnestness. 'I know there is much I have been wrong about, but I don't think I'm wrong about Aculf. You must do as you see fit, sir, but please think about finding a better man to be workreeve instead.'

'Oswald, there is no one—no one at all—who has not sometimes done what he later rues,' said Edrich. And didn't that say all those hard unsaid things between them? 'Wisdom is when a man learns from his folly. I think you are right about Aculf. Given what you have told me—and Thurstan just now said much the same, and more about what arose from it all—given what you have told me, I think you were wise to do as you did. Yes, I am pleased that you did that, Oswald. I won't undo it.'

And if it were not freedom—not yet—it might at least be the beginning of something better. Oswald could not ask for more now, but a time for that would come. He could trust his father to be wiser now. They would both be wiser. There was a sudden beauty in the leaping glow of the fire, as he sat and watched it with his father. Something was burning deep inside him like the flames: pride, gladness—he didn't know the word for it. His father was alive and was pleased with him and had said so. And his father had made him understand even more than he had said. Perhaps that was better than saying it aloud, each making the other think of old pain. His father was pleased with him, and the cold morning seemed very bright.

'Now,' said Edrich Thegn, rising to his feet. 'I have altogether too much of the swine pen still on me for my liking. Let me go and find a stream or some other place to wash.'

WOLVES

The Danish wall was built, scarring the land from river to river. Æthelred the King and Ælfred the Ætheling gathered their men and Æthelwulf Ealdorman joined them with his. There was to be no waiting for the Danes to come out to them again. Hadn't Wessex already put them to flight? Let them heap defeat upon defeat on these Danes and drive them away. There would be no waiting. They would find the wolves in their lair and there slay and scatter them. They would drive the wolf pack far from Readingum, far from Wessex, back to where they had come from. Æthelred the King went out on the hunt, his men ready with their spears. Edrich Thegn, Oswald and Oakdene were among them.

They went early on the hunt, hoping to catch the wolves before they had uncurled themselves from sleep. East beyond the town, the sun rose red in a thin line before it flooded the sky with its blood. Oswald had watched many dawns—golden and burning, cool and grey—but he had never seen one like this and it chilled him for all its warmth. A red dawn, blood-red.

Some of the Danish pack walked unwary beyond their wall. Æthelred came with death upon them and the Saxon fyrd cut them down. The wall was built, but the Danes were not ready.

∾

Brinin, a slave, could not be among them and he watched the day dawn red from the camp, where he sat alone with the wounded. His belt felt even lighter as he saw them go after their king but not because he longed for bloodshed. The sight of the fyrdmen reminded him of what he was, of what he might always be.

He had heard talk in the camp: one win must swiftly follow another. The King and the Ætheling were coming with more men. Many of the Danes had fallen, they said, and it was time to strike again while they were weak. But had not many in Wessex fallen? Were not many wounded? It seemed so to Brinin, as he walked among the tents. And the wall was likely done now. It wouldn't be easy to storm, easier by far to defend.

Waiting without work is slow—waiting to learn who has fallen—and Brinin longed for some work to put his back to. Battle was a strange thing. Boys yearned for it, not truly knowing what it was. Men made it, even though they did know. Bards sang of it: glory, courage, blood and death. And here he sat feeling cheated because he was denied it. Denied what? Glory? Bloodshed? Death?

The Danes were ready. They burst like wolves through their gates, swords for claws and battle-axes for teeth, ready to spring and tear their prey. Snarling, snapping, the battle raged round Oswald like a wild beast. He had been proudly aware of his father's shoulder near his own, but now in the battlethrong he didn't even know where his father was.

There was no time for courage or great deeds of valour. It was only a fight to live, a gasping struggle not to die too soon. Swords everywhere, swung red all around. Spears flying, biting, lying broken underfoot. Shields bruised, beaten, battered, groaning under blows. And still the wolves poured from their lair. They tore. They swallowed. And though the King and his huntsmen came boldly in to slay, the Danish pack was strong and not ready to give up its lair or to turn tail.

They fell under the hungry swords. The Danes were ready for them and they fell. Æthelwulf Ealdorman saw darkness that day and breathed his last among many of his men. And they were driven back from Readingum, back from the wall, back from the blood that stained the ground as the sun had stained the sky, back to defeat, back to shame.

Death did not come to all who had been torn by the sword. Daglæf lived, though too wounded for war, his shield arm limp and helpless at his side. Brinin pitied him, for he saw on his face the shame of being left behind. So he fed Daglæf's fire and brought him meat and drink. He sat nearby while Daglæf ate and listened to him talk. Daglæf liked to talk, and Brinin didn't mind listening. Daglæf's words drowned out the sound of the waiting. For a long time he talked of battle and farming and the days when he was a boy, but at last he wanted to listen too.

'They tell me,' said Daglæf, between mouthfuls, 'that you went into the Danish camp to fetch Edrich Thegn out. What was it like? The fyrd has gone against it today, they say.'

'Defended by rivers on three sides, with a great earthen wall to defend it to the west. They were still building the wall when we left—it stretches between the rivers and is as tall as two men—but it's likely done by now.'

'The King may not find it an easy victory,' said Daglæf, and Brinin wondered if any kind of victory would be readily come by. 'And the Danes themselves, what were they like?'

'Like men,' said Brinin. Did Herjolf still live? Would he live after today? 'It was hard to believe that some of them were raiders. With others it was easy enough.'

The day was well spent when the first of the fyrdmen came back. Brinin saw defeat and shame on their faces before any of them said a word. And he and Daglæf waited, wordless now, for their own to come. A man walked by with a wound to the head. Little trickles of blood ran down his face. The wound was not a bad one, for he walked without help, but the blood ran down like claw marks, like he'd been torn by a wolf.

In shame and defeat they turned their backs on Readingum, and were driven to the sunset as that morning they had marched to the dawn. Many had fallen. Many were wounded, Alrich among them. Oswald tore his cloak into strips to bind his kinsman's wounds, doing anything they could to stop the blood.

At first Alrich stumbled along, his father and Oswald's bearing him up on either side. Oswald walked beside them, with Alrich's weapons and shield as well as his own. They crept towards the sunset, but even in the warmer light of evening, Alrich was white, and the strips that bound his wounds grew as red as the dawn had been that morning.

Then Alrich could stumble no further, and his father lifted him, and Oswald took his uncle's weapons too. And before they reached the camp they stopped, and Alrich lay in his father's arms and died there. It wasn't like the tales of war the bards told. There was no speech, no last words, only a shudder and he was gone. Oswald, kneeling beside him on the cold earth, felt pain. And he felt pain worse than battle-wounds when he saw his uncle's face.

SWORDBROTHER

Raw with wounds and raw with sorrow, they went out again to meet the Danes. Grown bolder, the Danish host had spilled out from Readingum in two great bands on the broad downs. So the fyrd split themselves to meet them—one band with the King, the other with the Ætheling—and readied themselves once more for the onslaught.

Raw with cold, Oswald left the camp—a new one, nearer to the foe—and followed with the others after the Ætheling. The morning was beautiful, bitterly beautiful, bitterly cold. All around them as they walked, the grass and scrub had been thickened and stiffened by frost. The sky was not bloodlike that morning but pale like the underbelly of a trout. Mist drifted over the fields like wafts of smoke on the breeze or steam from the pot. The sky hue spread through it so that even the frost was not wholly white, and the far-off trees not wholly black. Oswald saw it all as they walked to war and tasted it as he tasted the cold in his throat.

'We have been swordbrothers for a long time, my lord,' said Thurstan, as he and Edrich Thegn walked together. 'I still smile when I remember our first great victory together. I wonder if you remember it?'

'Aclea?' said Edrich. 'It was a great victory—I'll give you that—and I haven't forgotten it. But I don't think of it with a smile. I lost my two brothers there, and you your father.'

'Not Aclea, my lord. That great day when we hunted the hunters and came upon them as their bows were drawn to take their prey!'

Thurstan chuckled. 'Have you forgotten it? Our fathers wouldn't let us go with them on the hunt, so we followed them and took them unawares. I'll never forget their faces!'

'And I'll never forget the smart of my father's stick!' Edrich laughed, albeit a little ruefully. 'That was no victory! Unless you count them by the thrashing you had afterwards.'

'Even the greatest warrior may come home a little wounded, my lord. But was it not a great thing for two boys to creep up unseen on the men as we did? And let me remind you, my lord, that I was the one who thought of it, though now you do the leading and I the following.'

'You were always the one who thought of it when there was mischief to be made, and I too often was foolish enough to follow you into it!' laughed Edrich.

Oswald laughed too. Thurstan had likely been making mischief all his life. For his father to follow Thurstan into it: that was a new thought! But then in those days, his father had little thought of ever being thegn, not before the Battle of Aclea.

'Thank you, my lord,' said Thurstan. 'I'm glad you see that the glory was mine, though I was happy to share it with you.'

'I'm not sure I always liked your kind of glory! But you're right, Thurstan. We have been swordbrothers for a long time, you and I.'

Then suddenly they were there. The Danes in their two bands were waiting for them, the morning sun firelike on their spear tips and shield bosses. Oswald's heart sank a little when he saw them. It did not need much battlewisdom to know that the Danes had the better place: higher, looking down at them from the age-old pathway cut along the chalk.

They waited for the word to send them against the foe. They waited, but something was wrong. The Danes stood ready for them. They themselves were as ready as they would ever be. But the King was not there. Oswald raised himself up on his toes to look all around. He saw the edge of the camp far off, but not the King leading the fyrd towards them.

'Where is the King, Father?' he whispered.

'Not here yet,' said Edrich, glancing around with a frown. 'Perhaps the King and the Ætheling have some battle wile that we know nothing of.'

'This is no battle wile,' said Thurstan, who was taller than both of them and could see what they could not. 'The Ætheling keeps looking back to the camp and is tapping his hand against his sword. He doesn't know why the King isn't here either.'

So they waited and still the King did not come. Oswald could feel his mind grow tight among the restless stirring of the fyrdmen. The Danes above began to laugh and taunt, hurling down their scorn.

'Why doesn't the King come?' Edrich snapped suddenly like an overdrawn bow. 'We can't keep standing here! Either we go back or charge!'

It was almost as though the Ætheling had heard him. Perhaps he was near snapping himself. He turned back to the fyrdmen and called them to readiness, called them to fight for life, loved ones and land, called them to go forward in God's strength, trusting in his wisdom. Then he charged. Oswald saw him, wild and rushing headlong like a boar, running straight up at the Danes. He saw him with his sword aloft as he ran in that swift fleeting time before the fyrdmen hid him again.

The battle roar swelled across the downs, rolling as the land rolled, spreading out as the grass did. Men heard it far off, cracking the icy stillness of the morning. Brinin heard it, thunderlike, as he sat with set teeth in the camp. Oswald heard it, all around him, deafening him and filling his thoughts.

They remembered the shame of Readingum and fought to rid themselves of it. Oswald had not known that he could fight as he did that day. He felt wild and angry and could not drive the face of Alrich from his mind. When the King came at last Oswald did not know it, not until long afterwards. He was alone again in a small world: enemy eyes, enemy breath, enemy blows on quivering shield, always ready for death that did not come. And men fell all around him.

There was a thorn tree standing alone near where he fought. Sometimes, breathless between foes, he caught sight of its twisting boughs. Its thorns plunged everywhere, sharp and swordlike. And wherever he looked, swords were thrust thornlike to bring men down.

The men of Oakdene fought side by side, shoulder to shoulder, so that after a time no one knew to whom they owed their life or if they had already paid them back. They fought as hearthfellows, as swordbrothers, and faced the foe and bled together.

The sun had moved far through the sky when Oswald, bruised and weary, began to wonder if he could go on. But the noise in his head was no longer roaring but great glad shouting. The Danes were turning, running east and south across the downs, and Oswald saw that there were none near him but those already dead.

'Our foes will soon learn to flee when they see you and me coming, won't they, swordbrother?' said Thurstan from behind him. 'You see your father ahead of us there? After him now, and we'll drive those Danes back to where they came from!'

So Oswald followed his father, his thegn and now also his swordbrother. They flooded after the Danes until nightfall before going back to their camp, limb-weary but heart-glad. Some of the fyrdmen kept after them until dawn, and the shame of Readingum was almost forgotten.

There were wounds to bind and tales to tell as, one by one, the men of Oakdene drifted back to warm themselves round one fire. Daglæf was hungry to hear everything and yearning to share what he knew: the King had lingered at prayer in his tent and would not leave until the priest was done, nor forsake the worship of God to make war. And surely the Lord had blessed the King by giving him victory.

'Almost all back now—only Thurstan still to come,' said Oswald as he saw Saxulf come towards them through the twilight. 'And our wounds have not been—'

The firelight fell on Saxulf's face and Oswald saw dreadful truth in it. His breath seemed to leave him and took his words with it. Saxulf was going to speak but Oswald couldn't listen. He wouldn't hear him. He wouldn't know. He stumbled away from the fire to the little dark cluster of trees behind their tents and did not heed his father calling after him.

'We were too late. Three of them came upon him as—' he heard Saxulf say, but he stopped his ears and staggered further away. He would not listen and make it true. It couldn't be true.

But he knew it was true. He had known before Saxulf had said a word. How could such a thing be true? How could he still stand, little more than a boy, who knew almost nothing of battle? How could Thurstan—Thurstan of all men—so fearless, so strong, how could *he* fall when the battle was all but won? Already won! How could he believe such a thing? But sorrow spilled out of him in a kind of rage and made him believe it. He struck at the tree he stood beside, kicked it in the darkness and pounded it with his fists. The tree seemed to groan, half-strangled, under the blows. It was a while before he knew that it was his own groans he heard.

At last, worn out, he leaned against the tree, catching his breath with great heaving gasps. Someone came up behind him in the darkness and put a hand on his shoulder. Thurstan had often done that, but it wasn't Thurstan now.

'Oswald.'

It was his father, wounding sorrow in his voice too. He had lost his swordbrother. And Oswald pressed his head against the tree and wept like a child, and his father did not leave or take his hand away.

HOMECOMING

B ruised by victory and stung by defeat, the fyrdmen came back to Oakdene. The Danes had not taken Wessex, but neither were they driven out. The fyrdmen came back limb-weary, battle-weary, with little gladness. Sigulf was sent ahead with word of their homecoming, and by the time the clustered houses came into sight, folk were already trickling out to meet them. Edith ran to them, stumbling over her skirts. Her father was off his horse long before she reached him and caught her as she flung herself into his arms. And soon everyone was around them, tears of sorrow and relief all blending, and the fyrdmen were taken by their own kin back to their own hearths.

Brinin kept away from them all. When they saw him he knew they would ask what he did not feel like answering, and it was easy to slip unseen from among them. His hearth would be cold and there were no kin to sit with there, so he made his way down to the fields, empty now as everyone, slave and free, welcomed the fyrdmen home. He sat down on a tree root where he had sometimes sat to watch the ploughing when he had still been small enough to be left to sit and watch. The hills swept away to the west, the trees dark and naked against the sky. He was back and nothing had changed. It was Oakdene in winter, as in every winter he had ever known. He had come back, but he was changed, by loss, by knowledge, by danger. He was changed and yet he was only what he had been before. Perhaps that would make it all the harder.

It was Garulf who found him there, and the day seemed less cold at the sight of him. Perhaps Brinin *had* come home, changed though he was.

'I thought I had seen you, lad,' said Garulf. 'But before I was sure, you had gone. Come back with me. It's cold out here, and Wynith has something in the pot.'

The welcome in Garulf's hut was as warm as the fire in the hearth. Eawig was out with the swine, but when Ebba saw Brinin she gasped and flung her arms around his waist. Then he knew it was a homecoming. Wynith, Ebba's mother, gave him a stool by the fire and a bowl of steaming broth in his hands, with a chunk of bread to wipe it up with. But there couldn't be much gladness. They wanted to know where Row was, and sorrow was shared round the hearth.

'Give me some work to do, Garulf,' said Brinin, when his bowl was empty. 'I know it's too early for the ploughing, but there must be something. There's always something.'

'Come with me then, lad,' said Garulf, getting up from his stool. 'I was working on a broken fence. I have more to say to you, and you can help me with it.'

At first Garulf had little to say beyond speaking of the fence, but Brinin could see him watching his hands as he worked. Perhaps Garulf saw that he had come back with a skill he had not left with. There was a pride in telling him about the minster and Brother Cwichelm and the woodcraft. It was good to say it.

'The brother there taught me how to make stools and benches and so many other things,' he said, smiling to himself about that other hoardlike craft he need not speak of. 'I can help you more with the ploughs now and other things too if I have the tools.'

'Woodcraft! Now that is a craft worth having.' Garulf nodded with a little pride too, but when he spoke again it was with the beginning of a frown rather than a smile. 'Why did you go, Brinin? You must have known there would be trouble here and you were never one to leave trouble for another to bear. And Oswald Child bore it, you know. He took the blame. Almost all of it.'

'I do know and I wouldn't have gone had I known what he would do.'

'And now they've found you and brought you back, there'll be trouble for you too,' Garulf sighed, shaking his head sadly. 'I don't like to think of it, lad. I don't like to think of it.'

'Don't think of it,' said Brinin. He had no father, no mother, no brother to tell him he was wrong or to worry about what might come of it. But Garulf was all fatherlike, and that made Oakdene home. 'Edrich Thegn has spoken to me about it and has forgiven me.'

'Forgiven you! Now that's something I didn't think to see! It was bad here, you know, very bad. Perhaps that was more than enough for Edrich Thegn, and he has no wish for more.'

There was always work to be done, and Brinin found it. He worked as though he had never been away, making himself too busy to go back to his own hut. He found work in lonely places, but folk saw him nonetheless. Some only stared at him, others whispered among themselves. Many times that day he was asked where Row was, and the ache grew stronger with every telling, short tellings with few words. But he had nothing to say to those who wondered what likely punishment would be meted out on him now that he was found. They could find that out for themselves.

The sky darkened early that afternoon, yellow with coming snow. Brinin was back at work on the fence, alone now, when the first flakes began to fall. Scattered and wildly driven but few, they melted away as soon as they landed. Looking up to see if the flurry would ease or thicken, he caught sight of Aculf coming towards him, coming with the step and look of a man who knew what he wanted. He had heard that Brinin was back and had come to find him.

'Come here,' called Aculf. He stopped when he was still a little away, so that Brinin would have to walk that last part, to go as a hound called to heel.

And Brinin almost went. Long years had taught him that he must, and it wasn't so easy to forget that. But before he did, just in time, he remembered that Aculf was no longer workreeve. Oswald had said that he would never be workreeve again, that Edrich

Thegn himself had said as much. Why heed Aculf when he had work to do? The light wouldn't last much longer. So he turned away from Aculf back to the fence.

'Did you hear me?' called Aculf, this time a little louder, but still not coming any nearer.

Didn't Brinin have one lord, Edrich Thegn? He was slave to him, not to every man who wished to bid him. Edrich Thegn had not bidden him hear or heed this man who was no longer workreeve. But he was working on Edrich Thegn's fence. It was almost done now and would be soon if the snow fell no thicker. Why hear Aculf?

This time Aculf did take a few steps towards him. He was becoming angry now, reddening in that way Brinin knew only too well.

'You should know by now what it means not to heed me!' Aculf hissed.

'I heed my lord, his workreeve, or the one he bids me to heed,' said Brinin, still not looking up from the fence. One last gap to stop, and then he would be done. 'You are none of those.'

'Oh, you heard about that, did you? Oswald Child is young and the young are often foolish. Edrich Thegn was only ever happy with me, and now that he is back with us, I will be workreeve again.'

Brinin pitied Aculf then because he knew what Aculf did not, and because Aculf was clinging so tightly to such an empty hope. And he pitied him because Aculf was too much of a fool to know when he was being foolish, and because he was unlikely to have the wisdom to feel foolish when his hope was shown to be empty.

'Don't you know what will likely happen to you now that you've been caught?' Aculf went on. 'I would have thought that even you would have the wisdom not to bring more trouble on yourself. If I am not workreeve today, I will remember what you have done and when I am workreeve again, you will feel my stick. Now for the last time, come here!'

The last gap was stopped. Brinin gave the fence a little shake. It was strong now. It wouldn't break again easily. Then he looked at Aculf.

'I heed my lord, his workreeve, or the one he bids me to heed,' he said, this time more slowly. Aculf was finding it hard to understand.

That was too much for Aculf, even if he wasn't workreeve. He made a rush at Brinin, raising a hand to strike him, as he had done so many times before. But Brinin was too quick and caught his wrist before the blow fell.

'It wouldn't be right for me to let you strike another man's slave. You would have to pay Edrich Thegn if you wounded me. My lord may strike me, or his workreeve, or the one he bids to strike me. You are none of those.'

And he dropped Aculf's wrist and walked away. The flurry was already dying down. There would be no snow on the ground tonight. Likely Aculf would always be too much of a fool to know when he was being foolish.

The sun was setting as Brinin made his way back to Garulf's hut. Garulf had urged him to eat at his hearth and sleep under his thatch. It was better that way. Likely Garulf had known it would be. He wasn't ready to sleep in his own hut yet, or to see it. Perhaps tomorrow, or the day after…

Oswald seemed weary when Brinin met him, and not only from the road. His face was tightly set, and he was coming away from Thurstan's house slowly as though he bore a heavy load as he walked.

'I've been with my father to the houses of those who fell,' said Oswald hoarsely. 'We gave Thurstan's sword and seax to his son and… and it wasn't easy.'

Thurstan, fallen like those bold men the tales boast of, had left a wife and children without him at home, and the boasting of all the tales together wouldn't bring him back. He would lie, buried among the fallen, until the Day of Ærist. No homecoming.

'I looked for you after we came back,' said Oswald, 'but I couldn't see you. Where did you go?'

'To work.'

'So soon? Without even eating or resting from the road?'

'Garulf gave me something.'

'I wish it wasn't like this,' sighed Oswald. 'I spoke to my father twice about it, but he didn't say much. Nothing that gives me much hope other than that he won't make Aculf workreeve again. He's thinking of asking Cynestan to do it once he's strong enough.'

'It might be better, as you said before,' said Brinin. This was something new: him telling Oswald that everything might be better. 'Cynestan isn't like Aculf.'

Brinin knew that dreams were fleeting. He had learned young not to make the day longer by wishing they might come true. He knew that what he had was better than what it could be. He could forget what freedom tasted like, forget that he had touched it and held it for a time. He could even tell himself that he didn't mind. He had known what he was doing when he went to Readingum.

EARTH

Brinin left Garulf's hut a little before dawn the next morning, a cold, raw dawn when it is no easy thing to leave the hearth and step outside. Before he stopped to eat, he had already hewn wood and drawn water, tended beasts and shovelled dung. Then the word came that Edrich Thegn was calling everyone to speak to them. They were to stop their work and go. Brinin went with the others but kept to the back, behind them all. If Edrich Thegn was going to tell them all how he had come to stand alive before them, then it was better to be at the back. Better still not to be there at all, but that couldn't be helped.

'Often men come back glad from battle, with their foes put to flight,' began Edrich Thegn. 'But though we are glad that we fought as we could and that not all of us are fallen, there is no great boasting. We have not lost and we have not won: the Danes are still in Wessex. We are back only to wait for the next battle and to work our land for a little time. It won't be long—a week, perhaps two—before I lead the men out again. We have come back without our swordbrothers. We have lost Swetrich, Sigelm, Thurstan, the… the best of men. Death is not unknown to us, and yet it is hard to think of Oakdene without them. And if by God's help, we do drive the Danes away, more will fall in the doing of it. In these last weeks you have readied yourselves for them to come here. Stay ready at all times. We cannot know what tomorrow may bring.

'While I was in the hands of the Danes, I am told that you fasted and prayed for me. You all thought I was most likely dead. I thought

I was as good as dead myself. I can truly say that I did not think I would see any of you again. As to what passed in those days… it is better forgotten. Yet here I am, and it has almost been like coming back from death. I am thankful for your prayers and still more thankful to God for answering them. We sent you word that I was alive, but few of you know how it came about. Those who do know I asked not to speak of it because I wanted you all to hear it from my own mouth.'

It was coming now. Brinin was glad to be at the back, though he wished he wasn't so tall. It was a strange thing that thanking could feel so unwelcome. Though perhaps it wasn't the thanking. Perhaps it was all the eyes watching it.

'Where is Brinin?' asked Edrich Thegn. 'Let him come forward.'

Brinin saw all their bewildered looks and whispers to their neighbours. He saw them turn to watch him as he walked. None of them understood what was happening. They had thought he would be called before them for shame, a dreadful, painful shame like Garulf had feared for him and Oswald had already borne. Some of them had even told him as much. None of them understood why Edrich Thegn should call him now. Brinin was glad that he need not fear shame—thanks was so much better—though at least he knew what to do with shame. Perhaps a man more easily bears what he knows.

'Look at him well,' said Edrich, when Brinin was beside him. Brinin, so as not to see them all looking, kept his eyes on the earth, winterhard beneath his feet. 'He heard that I had been taken and set out to find me, though he knew that his death was much more likely. When he drew near Readingum, he heard that the Danes had come. But he went to their camp, and they welcomed him because he speaks their tongue. He saw me there, bound—and now I think it can only have been because of your prayers that he did see me. Then he came and freed me, and we walked out. Did you hear what I said? Walked out. At twilight when it was hard to see, and he spoke in their tongue all the way. They did not stop us because they thought we were two of their own.'

Some gasped. Others laughed as Thurstan had done. All were amazed, and Edrich Thegn had to raise his hand to still them before he could speak again. Must he speak again? Now he had told the tale, mightn't he let Brinin go instead of keeping him standing there? But it seemed that Edrich Thegn still had more to say.

'Look at him well,' Edrich went on. 'And now when you see him remember that it is thanks to him that I have my life, my children their father and you your lord. There were things you thought about him before. I know that. I thought them myself. But now we will not speak of them and from today we will forget them.

'When the Danes held me, you fasted and prayed. Let us not forget to give thanks for prayer answered. Come now, let us all go to the church for prayer.'

Brinin hoped then to slip away once more to the back, to stand by the church door where he always had. But somehow he was pushed along by the crowd—or perhaps it was Oswald who did the pushing—and he found himself further forward than he wanted to be.

It was a sorrowful thanksgiving. It was hard to be too glad for life spared while mourning life lost. And when all the prayers had been said, and it must now at last be time to leave, Edrich Thegn took Brinin by the arm but he didn't lead him to the door. He led him to the altar where Brother Wilfred stood smiling.

Three times Brother Wilfred led him round the altar while all the village watched. Three times Brinin went round the altar almost in a dream. Was this some way of thanking him? It was hard to understand. Why were they walking when the thanks had already been given? Three times Brother Wilfred and Brinin walked round together, and all the time Brother Wilfred said wonderful words, too wonderful for Brinin to think he had rightly heard them. Afterwards he could never remember what they were.

Then Edrich Thegn stepped forward and put a seax into Brinin's hands. It was so cold, so hard and sharp that he could not fail to understand. This was freedom. He had held it before, but this time it was weightier. And when he looked down, he saw that it was the same seax that Oswald had given him. Brinin had used it to free Edrich Thegn, and now Edrich Thegn was using it to free him.

Brinin stood there for a long time after everyone else had left the church. And after he had stood, he sat and turned the seax over in his hands as he had done at the minster. The ripples still flowed waterlike along the blade. It was a beautiful thing, all the more beautiful for what it meant. The carvings on the handle twisted round and round, just as he had walked round the altar.

'Brinin!'

Brinin looked up and saw Oswald striding towards him, his face full of all the wondering gladness that Brinin felt but could never begin to say. Oswald would likely say it. He'd always been better at that.

'I didn't know!' Oswald clutched Brinin's arm. 'I didn't know he was going to do it. He said nothing to me about it. I'm so glad I can hardly speak. I can't believe he didn't tell me. But come. My father is asking for you.'

So Brinin put his seax on his belt as he had done before and felt the weight of freedom hang there. Only a knife; such a small thing to do so much.

'I saw my father talking to Aculf, though I didn't hear what he said,' said Oswald, as Brinin walked with him to the hall. 'Aculf's face was very red—redder than I've ever seen it—and my father's wore the look that most frightened me as a child. I think that Aculf has heard now that he won't be workreeve again, and it looked like he was hearing a lot of other things as well.'

But Brinin cared nothing for Aculf. Why should thoughts of Aculf storm his mind on such a day? It was a day of unhoped-for wonder—greater than all the wonders of the minster—and Aculf didn't belong in it. It was hard to believe that he belonged in it himself.

Brinin had eaten in the hall before, in some far corner away from the fire, never near his lord and never seen, but today he was welcomed. Edith was very warm and Edrich Thegn was kind. Brinin never forgot the warmth of the fire and the welcome, though he forgot almost everything they said. The greatest wonders of that day drove everything else out.

When they had eaten, Edrich Thegn asked Brinin to follow him to the fields. Oswald and Edith went too. The winter sun in a pale sky did little to soften and heat the earth. The earth waited as though dead, waiting for the days to be warm enough and long enough to call life out from it again. Before them stretched that well-known land: fields, hills, trees. Brinin knew it so well. Perhaps it was home, after all.

'I have land enough to make me a thegn,' said Edrich. He held some short sticks and turned them over in his hands. 'A man without land is only a little better than a slave. I would not keep in bondage or want the one to whom I owe my life. From here…'

Edrich Thegn drove a stick into the earth and began to walk, Brinin and the others following a little behind.

'…to here.' He drove in another stick and walked again.

They walked until they came to where they had started, with Edrich Thegn driving sticks into the earth along the way. When they stopped, he turned again to Brinin.

'This land I have marked is now yours, and I am no less a thegn for the loss of it. With it, you need not fear hunger more than any other man does—who of us knows what tomorrow may bring? Come, Oswald, Edith. Let him be alone now to look at his field.'

They left him and Brinin looked at his field, his own field. Men buried their hoards in the earth, but perhaps the earth itself had more worth than the gold did. It gave food and life and freedom. Brinin knelt down and lifted a handful of soil, rubbing it between his fingers. Then he walked again around the edge of his field. He knew this land. He had ploughed it with Row, it seemed not so very long ago. He had bent his back on it with scythe and sickle. And now it was his. Tomorrow he would begin to make himself a plough.

Brinin went back to his hut then. It was time. The sun was already low. He had stayed longer than he thought in his field. The hut was cold and dark inside, with a smell of damp emptiness. Ashes lay in the hearth, the ashes of the fire that Row had stamped out the night they left. There was still a little wood in the pile and Brinin knelt to kindle a new fire. Perhaps that would drive out some of the cold and emptiness. He reached for the wood, but the earth from his field was still in his hand. He had forgotten he was holding it.

When the fire was burning, casting little flickering shadows on floor and walls, he sat on a stool beside it. His father, born free, had died a slave in this hut. His mother had died here, a slave. His brother had left it, a slave, to die a slave in a far-off place. He himself had been born a slave in this hut and now he sat by his own hearth, a free man.

The seax caught the light of the fire, and the ripples on the blade seemed to dance as the flames did. Tonight the ache and the gladness were so mingled that he did not know one from the other, or which hurt more. Ache and gladness. Always ache and gladness until that time when the ache would be gone and only the gladness left. And Brinin rose from the fire and took his stool outside to sit alone and look at the stars.

AFTERWORD

When I first had the idea for this novel, I said that I thought it would probably end up being 'historically-inspired fantasy'. With both my undergraduate and postgraduate degrees being in history, albeit with a focus on a later period, I was wary of writing something that would be *wrong*. But in the end, I couldn't help myself. The historical limitations that then arose turned out to be fundamental in developing the plot, while still allowing a certain degree of freedom, especially as very little written material has survived from the time.

With a few notable exceptions, I've never really enjoyed historical novels that attributed words and actions to people who were as real as we are. In *Kith*, the focus is on fictional characters in a fictional village, while the real events and people stay more on the periphery. The kings, ealdormen, battles and manuscripts mentioned are all real, as are some of the locations. Oakdene and its inhabitants are not.

Historical Events

The impact of the 'great host' of Danes that worked their way south throughout the 860s cannot be underestimated. The terror and uncertainty arising from this threat provides the backdrop to the novel and all the events relating to that threat are real, as are the battles at the end of the novel. The Battle of Englafeld (Englefield) was on 31 December 870, but contemporary accounts are very terse, so my account was inspired by Anglo-Saxon battle poetry, most notably *The Battle of Maldon*. This was also true for my accounts of the Battle of Reading on 4 January 871 (in 'Wolves') and the Battle of Ashdown on 8 January 871 (in 'Swordbrother'). However, these two battles were more fully described in *The Anglo-Saxon Chronicle* and Asser's *Life of Alfred* so much of the imagery also was inspired by those accounts.

Manuscripts

Brother Wilfred's few sheets of bookskin are taken from Bede's *Ecclesiastical History of the English People*. The Latin psalter that Oswald reads in the minster is based on *The Vespasian Psalter*. The prayer he translates is from *The Book of Cerne*. Both of these manuscripts are held in the British Library. The translations of all the Latin in the novel are my own. Brother Wilfred's sermon in 'Ærist' was based almost entirely on the writings of Ælfric of Eynsham.

Language and Culture

Details of historical events, people and places, and tangible features such as food, buildings and clothing are in many ways the easy part of researching a historical novel. More difficult is presenting something which reflects the culture of the time, especially when working from relatively sparse written material. Thurstan, as a self-confident, loyal and battle-hardened farmer, embodies many of the cultural values of the time. Society was highly stratified and I tried to reflect this by not having characters directly question ideas that now seem shocking, such as slavery. I have spent the last ten years living largely in a culture that is not individualistic. That certainly helped me to get into the mindset of a people living long before the rise of individualism.

In developing a linguistic style for the novel, I tried where possible to avoid using words that have come into English from Latin or French. I coined words by modernising some terms from Old English: workreeve, waxboard, writing-seax, evening-meat, summerlong. In other cases, I used an Old English style: wordcraft, warcraft, thegnlike. I used alliteration to reflect their poetic style and, especially in the battle chapters, made use of some of their metaphors.

This just touches on some of the background to the novel. If you are interested in finding out more, come to my website **julierowbory.com** where I'm adding more detailed information about some of the historical background and linguistic choices I made while writing it.

Julie Rowbory grew up in Northern Ireland and was educated at the University of Cambridge, where she obtained an MA and then an MPhil in history. She has worked as a Latin and history teacher, taught English in Asia and lived in East Africa. She is married to David, with whom she has four daughters. They divide their time between Scotland and West Africa.

Printed in Great Britain
by Amazon